THE LEGEND OF TYL ULENSPIEGEL

LAMME AND ULENSPIEGEL
AT THE MINNE-WATER

THE LEGEND OF THE
GLORIOUS ADVENTURES
of TYL ULENSPIEGEL IN THE
LAND OF FLANDERS & ELSEWHERE
By CHARLES DE COSTER

WITH TWENTY WOODCUTS BY
ALBERT DELSTANCHE

TRANSLATED FROM THE FRENCH
BY GEOFFREY WHITWORTH

THE JOURNEYMAN PRESS
LONDON & WEST NYACK

First published in Belgium, 1867
This illustrated translation published 1918
Reprinted 1978 by the Journeyman Press
97 Ferme Park Road, Crouch End, London N8 9SA
and 17 Old Mill Road, West Nyack, New York 10994

ISBN 0 904526 36 4

Printed in Great Britain by
Biddles Limited, Guildford

ILLUSTRATIONS

FOREWORD

THE book here offered in English to the English-speaking public has long been known and admired by students as the first and perhaps the most notable example of modern Belgian literature. Its author was born of obscure parentage in 1827, and, after a life passed in not much less obscurity, died in 1879. The ten years which were devoted to the composition of "The Legend of Tyl Ulenspiegel" were devoted to what proved, for de Coster, little more than a labour of love. Recognition came to him but from the few, and it was not till some thirty years after his death that an official monument was raised at Brussels to his memory, and an official oration delivered in his praise by Camille Lemonnier.

To the undiscerning among his contemporaries de Coster may have appeared little else than a rather eccentric journalist with archæological tastes. For a time, indeed, he held a post on the Royal Commission which was appointed in 1860 to investigate and publish old Flemish laws. And towards the end of his life he became a Professor of History and French Literature at the Military School in Brussels. Never, certainly, has a work of imagination, planned on an epic scale, been composed with a closer regard for historical detail than this Legend. But if our present age is less likely to be held by this than by those other qualities in the book of vitality and passion, it can only be that de Coster poured into his work not merely the knowledge and accuracy of an historian, but the love as well and the ardour of a poet and a patriot.

The objection—if it be an objection—that de Coster borrowed unblushingly from his predecessors need never be disputed. His style is frankly Rabelaisian. The stage whereon his actors play their parts is set, scene almost for scene, from the generally available documents that served such a writer as Thomas Motley for his "History of the Rise of the Dutch Republic." Even the name, the very lineaments of Ulenspiegel, are borrowed from that familiar figure of the sixteenth-century chap-books * whose jolly pranks and school-boy frolics have been crystallized in the French word *espièglerie*, and in our own day set to music in one of the symphonic poems of Richard Strauss.

Yet from such well-worn ingredients de Coster's genius has mixed a potion most individually his own. The style of Rabelais is tempered with a finish, a neatness, and a wit that are as truly the product of the modern spirit as was the flamboyant jollity of Rabelais the product of his own Renaissance age ; the sensible, historical foreground of a Motley becomes the coloured background to a romantic drama of human vice and virtue, linked in its turn to a conception of the cosmic process which has no other home, surely, than in the author's brain. While Ulenspiegel himself is now not simply the type of young high spirits and animal good humour, but a being as complex, as many-sided almost as humanity—all brightness of intellect, all warmth of heart, all honour, and all dream—the immortal Spirit of Flanders that knows not what it is to be beaten, whose last song must for ever remain unsung.

What shall we say of those other homely personages who fill the scene—symbols no less of Flemish character at its finest and of the enduringly domestic springs of Flemish national life ? Claes the trusty fatherhood, Soetkin the valiant motherhood of Flanders, Nele her true heart, Lamme Goedzak her great belly that hungers always for more and yet more good things to eat and is never satisfied ? Or what, again, of the tragic Katheline, half witch, half martyr, and the centre of that dark intrigue which seems to throb like a shuttle through the mazy pattern of the plot, threading it all into unity ?

---

* The Author's debt to such sources is especially noticeable in chapters xii, xxiv, xxvi, xxx, and xxxii of the First Book.

Foreword

From yet another standpoint: as an envisagement of the horrors of the Spanish Inquisition, de Coster's work is probably without parallel in an already well-tilled field. The sinister figure of the King of Spain broods over it all like a Kaiser, and the episodes of stake and torture are recorded with a realism which might appear exaggerated had not modern Belgium—though in terms of "scientific warfare"—an even more devilish tale to tell. The fact is that de Coster's trick of stating horror and leaving it to make its full effect without a touch of the rhetoric of indignation, proves the deadliest of all corrosive weapons; and it is hardly surprising that the book had been hailed in some quarters as a Protestant tract. But de Coster himself was in no sense a theological partisan, and his sympathy with the *Beggarmen* sprang from his enthusiasm for national liberty far more than from any bias towards the Protestant cause as such. That Catholicism has ever been identified with tyranny the best Catholic will most deplore, nor will de Coster's "traditional" irreverence blind such a reader's eyes to the spiritual generosity which permeates the whole work, and is, indeed, its most essential characteristic.

It remains to add that, in the interests of war-time publishing, the present version represents a curtailment of the Legend as it left the author's hands. Here and there also, to maintain the continuity of incident, the translator has permitted himself some slight modification of the original text. By this means it is hoped that the proportions of the whole have been fairly maintained, and that no vital aspect of plot or atmosphere has been altogether suppressed or allowed an undue prominence.

G. A. W.

HERE BEGINS THE FIRST BOOK OF
THE LEGEND OF THE GLORIOUS
JOYOUS AND HEROIC ADVENTURES
OF TYL ULENSPIEGEL AND LAMME
GOEDZAK IN THE LAND OF FLANDERS
AND ELSEWHERE

I

AT Damme, in Flanders, when the May hawthorn was coming into flower, Ulenspiegel was born, the son of Claes.

When she had wrapped him in warm swaddling-clothes, Katheline, the midwife, made a careful examination of the infant's head, and found a piece of skin hanging therefrom.

"Born with a caul!" she cried out joyfully. "Born under a lucky star!" But a moment later, noticing a small black mole on the baby's shoulder, she fell into lamentation.

"Alas!" she wept, "it is the black finger-print of the devil!"

"Monsieur Satan," said Claes, "must have risen early this morning, if already he has found time to set his sign upon my son!"

"Be sure, he never went to bed," answered Katheline. "Here is Chanticleer only just awakening the hens!"

And so saying she went out of the room, leaving the baby in the arms of Claes.

Then it was that the dawn came bursting through the clouds of night, and the swallows skimmed chirruping over the fields, while the sun began to show his dazzling face on the horizon. Claes opened the window and thus addressed himself to Ulenspiegel.

"O babe born with a caul, behold! Here is my Lord the Sun who comes to make his salutation to the land of Flanders. Gaze on Him whenever you can; and if ever in after years you come to be in any doubt or difficulty, not knowing what is right to do, ask counsel of Him. He is bright and He is warm. Be sincere as that brightness, and virtuous as that warmth."

"Claes, my good man," said Soetkin, "you are preaching to the deaf. Come, drink, son of mine."

AT DAMME WHEN THE
HAWTHORN WAS IN FLOWER

And so saying, the mother offered to her new-born babe a draught from the beautiful flasks nature had given her.

II

While Ulenspiegel nestled close and drank his fill, all the birds in the country-side began to waken.

Claes, who was tying up sticks, regarded his wife as she gave the breast to Ulenspiegel.

" Wife," he said, " hast made good provision of this fine milk ? "

" The pitchers are full," she said, " but that doth not suffice for my peace of mind."

" It seems that you are downhearted over your good fortune," said Claes.

" I was thinking," she said, " that there is not so much as a penny piece in that leather bag of ours hanging on the wall."

Claes took hold of the bag and shook it. But in vain. There was no sign of any money. He looked crestfallen. Nevertheless, hoping to comfort his good wife—

" What are you worrying about ? " says he. " Have we not in the bin that cake we offered Katheline yesterday ? And don't I see a great piece of meat over there that should make good milk for the child for three days at the least ? And this tub of butter, is it a ghost tub ? And are they spectres, those apples ranged like flags and banners all in battle order, row after row, in the storeroom ? And is there no promise of cool refreshment guarded safe in the paunch of our fine old cask of *cuyte de Bruges* ? "

Soetkin said : " When we take the child to be christened we shall have to give two *patards* to the priest, and a florin for the feasting."

But at this moment Katheline returned, with a great bundle of herbs in her arms.

" For the child that is born with a caul," she cried.

*

3

" *Angelica* that keeps men from luxury ; *fenel* that preserves them from Satan. . . ."

" Have you none of that herb," asked Claes, " which brings in *florins* ? "

" No," said she.

" Very well," he answered, " I shall go and see if I cannot find any growing in the canal."

And with that he went off, with his line and his fishing-net, knowing that he would not be likely to meet any one, since it was yet an hour before the *oosterzon*, which is, in the land of Flanders, six o'clock in the morning.

III

Claes came to the Bruges canal, not far from the sea. There, having baited his line, he cast it into the water and let down his net. On the opposite bank, a little boy was lying against a clump of earth, fast asleep. The boy, who was not dressed like a peasant, woke up at the noise that Claes was making, and began to run away, fearing no doubt that it was the village constable come to dislodge him from his bed and to hale him off as a vagabond to the *steen*. But he soon lost his fear when he recognized Claes, and when Claes called out to him :

" Would you like to earn a penny, my boy ? Well then, drive the fish over to my side ! "

At this proposal the little boy, who was somewhat stout for his years, jumped into the water, and arming himself with a plume of long reeds, he began to drive the fish towards Claes. When the fishing was over, Claes drew up his net, and came over by the lock gate towards where the youngster was standing.

" Your name," said Claes, " is Lamme by baptism, and *Goedzak* by nature, because you are of a gentle disposition, and you dwell in the rue Héron behind the Church of Our Lady. But tell me why it is that, young as you are, and

4

well dressed, you are yet obliged to sleep out here in the open ? "

" Woe is me, Mr. Charcoal-burner," answered the boy. " I have a sister at home, a year younger than I am, who fairly thrashes me at the least occasion of disagreement. But I dare not take my revenge upon her back for fear of doing her some injury, sir. Last night at supper I was very hungry, and I was clearing out with my fingers the bottom of a dish of beef and beans. She wanted to share it, but there was not enough for us both, sir. And when she saw me licking my lips because the sauce smelt good, she went mad with rage, and smote me with all her force, so hard indeed that I fled away from the house, beaten all black and blue."

Claes asked him what his father and mother were doing during this scene.

" My father hit me on one shoulder and my mother on the other, crying, ' Strike back at her, you coward ! ' but I, not wishing to strike a girl, made my escape."

All at once, Lamme went pale all over and began to tremble in every limb, and Claes saw a tall woman approaching, and by her side a young girl, very thin and fierce of aspect.

" Oh, oh ! " cried Lamme, holding on to Claes by his breeches, " here are my mother and my sister come to find me. Protect me, please, Mr. Charcoal-burner ! "

" Wait," said Claes. " First of all let me give you this penny-farthing as your wages, and now let us go and meet them without fear."

When the two women saw Lamme, they ran up and both began to belabour him—the mother because of the fright he had given her, the sister because it was her habit so to do. Lamme took refuge behind Claes, and cried out :

" I have earned a penny-farthing ! I have earned a penny-farthing ! Do not beat me ! "

By this time, however, his mother had begun to embrace

5

him, while the girl was trying to force open his hands and to get at the money. But Lamme shouted :

" The money belongs to me. You shall not have it."

And he kept his fingers tightly closed. But Claes shook the girl roughly by the ears, and said to her :

" If you go on picking quarrels like this with your brother, he that is as good and gentle as a lamb, I shall put you in a black charcoal-pit, and then it won't be I any longer that will be shaking you by the ears, but the red devil himself from hell, and he will pull you into pieces with his great claws and his teeth that are like forks."

At these words the girl averted her eyes from Claes, nor did she go near Lamme, but hid behind her mother's skirts, and when she got back into the town, she went about crying everywhere :

" The Charcoal-man has beaten me, and he keeps the devil in his cave."

Nevertheless she did not attack Lamme any more ; but being the bigger of the two, she made him work in her place, and the gentle simpleton obeyed her right willingly.

Now Claes, on his way home, sold his catch to a farmer that often used to buy fish from him. And when he was home again, he said to Soetkin :

" Behold ! Here's what I have found in the bellies of four pike, nine carp, and a basketful of eels." And he threw on the table a couple of florins and half a farthing.

" Why don't you go fishing every day, my man ? " asked Soetkin.

" For fear of becoming a fish myself, and being caught on the hook of the village constable," he told her.

IV

Claes, the father of Ulenspiegel, was known in Damme by the name of *Kooldraeger*, that is to say, the Charcoal-burner. Claes had a black head of hair, bright eyes, and a skin the

colour of his own merchandise—save only on Sundays and
Feast Days, when his cottage ran with soap and water. He
was a short, thick-set man, strong, and of a joyful countenance.

Towards the end of the day, when evening was coming on,
he would sometimes visit the tavern on the road to Bruges,
there to rinse his charcoal-blackened throat with a draught of
cuyte ; and then the women standing at their doorways to
sniff the evening dew would cry out to him in friendly greeting:

" A good night and a good drink to you, Charcoal-
burner."

" A good night to you, and a lively husband ! " Claes
would reply.

And sometimes the girls, trooping home together from
their work in the fields, would line up in front of him right
across the road, barring his way.

" What will you give us for the right of passage ? " they
would cry. " A scarlet ribbon, a buckle of gold, a pair of
velvet slippers, or a florin piece for alms ? "

But Claes, holding one of the girls fast by the waist,
would give her a hearty kiss on her fresh cheek or on her
neck, just whichever happened to be nearest, and then he
would say :

" You must ask the rest, my dears, of your sweethearts."

And off they would go amidst peals of laughter.

As for the children, they always recognized Claes by his
loud voice and by the noise his clogs made on the road, and
they would run up to him and cry:

" Good evening, Charcoal-burner."

" The same to you, my little angels," he would answer;
" but come no nearer, lest perchance I turn you into
blackamoors."

But the children were bold, and oftentimes would make
the venture. Then Claes would seize one of them by the
doublet, and rubbing his blackened hands up and down the

7

little fellow's nose, would send him off all sooty, but laughing just the same, to the huge delight of the others.

Soetkin, wife of Claes, was a good wife and mother. She was up with the dawn, and worked as diligently as any ant. She and Claes laboured together in the field, yoking themselves to the plough as though they had been oxen. It was hard work dragging it along, but even the plough was not so heavy as the harrow, that rustic implement whose task it was to tear up the hardened earth with teeth of wood. But Claes and his wife worked always with a gay heart, and enlivened themselves with singing. And in vain was the earth hard, in vain did the sun hurl down on them his hottest beams, in vain were their knees stiffened with bending and their loins tired with the cruel effort of dragging the harrow along, for they had only to stop a moment while Soetkin turned to Claes her gentle face, and while Claes kissed that mirror of a gentle heart, and straightway they forgot how tired they were.

V

Now the previous day, the town crier had given notice from before the Town Hall that Madame, the wife of the Emperor Charles, being near the time of her delivery, it behoved the people to say prayers on her behalf.

Katheline came to Claes in a great state of excitement.

" Whatever is the matter, my good woman ? " he asked.

" Alas ! " she cried, catching her breath, " behold ! This night the ghosts are mowing men down like grass. Little girls are being buried alive. The executioner is dancing on the body of the dead. And broken, this night, is that Stone which has been sweating blood these nine months past and more ! "

" Mercy on us ! " groaned Soetkin. " Mercy on us, O Lord ! This is a black omen indeed for the land of Flanders."

" Do you see these things with your own eyes wide awake, or perchance in a dream ? " Claes asked her.

CLAES AND SOETKIN

"With my own eyes," Katheline told him. And then all pale and tearful, she continued in these words:

"To-night two children are born: the one in Spain—the infant Philip—and the other in this land of Flanders—the son of Claes, he that later on shall be known by the name of Ulenspiegel. Philip will grow up to be a common hangman, being the child of the Emperor Charles the Fifth, the destroyer of our country. But Ulenspiegel will be a master of merry words and frolics of youth, yet good of heart withal, having for his father Claes, the brave working man that knows how to earn his own living with courage, honesty, and gentleness. Charles the Emperor and Philip the King will go riding their way through life, doing evil by battle, extortion, and other crimes. But Claes, working hard all the week, living according to right and according to law, and laughing at his laborious lot instead of being cast down thereby, will be the model of all the good workpeople of Flanders. Ulenspiegel, young and immortal, will ramble over the world and never settle in one place. And he will be peasant, nobleman, painter, sculptor, all in one. And he will continue his wanderings hither and thither, lauding things beautiful and good, and laughing stupidity to scorn. Claes, then, O noble people of Flanders, is your courage; Soetkin your valiant motherhood; Ulenspiegel your soul. A sweet and gentle maiden, lover of Ulenspiegel and immortal like him, shall be your heart; and Lamme Goedzak, with his pot-belly, shall be your stomach. And up aloft shall stand the devourers of the people; and beneath them their victims. On high the thieving hornets; and below the busy bees. While in heaven bleed for evermore the wounds of Christ."

And when she had thus spoken, Katheline, the kindly sorceress, went to sleep.

VI

One day Claes caught a large salmon, and on the Sunday he and Soetkin and Katheline and the little Ulenspiegel had it for their dinner. But Katheline only ate enough to satisfy a sparrow.

"How now, mother ? " said Claes. "What has happened to the air of Flanders ? Has it suddenly grown solid, so that to breathe it is as nourishing as a plate of beef ? Why, if such were the case, I suppose you will be telling me that the rain is as good as soup, and the hail like beans, and the snow some sort of celestial fricassee, fit cheer for a poor traveller ? "

But Katheline shook her head, and said not a word.

"Dear me," said Claes, "our mother is in the dumps it seems ! What can it be that grieves her so ? "

But Katheline spake as follows, in a voice that was like a breath of wind :

"The evil one . . ." she said. "The night falls blackly. He tells of his coming from afar, screaming like the sea-eagle. I tremble, and pray to Our Lady—all in vain. For the evil one knows neither walls, nor hedges, neither doors nor windows. Everywhere, like a spirit, he finds a way in. The ladder creaks. He has entered into the loft where I am sleeping. He seizes me in arms that are cold and hard as marble. His face is frozen, and his kisses damp as snow. The whole cottage seems to be tossed about over the earth, riding like a ship at sea. . . ."

Claes said : "I would counsel you to go every morning to Mass, that our Lord Christ may give you strength to chase away this phantom from hell."

"He is so beautiful ! " said Katheline.

VII

Ulenspiegel was weaned, and began to grow like a young poplar. And soon Claes gave up caressing him, but loved him in a roughish manner, fearing to make a milksop of him. And when Ulenspiegel came home complaining that he had got the worst of it in some boyish affray, Claes would give him a beating because, forsooth, he had not beaten the others. And with such an education Ulenspiegel grew up as valiant as a young lion.

When Claes was from home, Ulenspiegel would ask his mother to give him a *liard* with which he might go out and amuse himself. Soetkin would grow angry, and ask why he wanted to go out for amusement—he would do better to stay at home and tie up faggots. And when he saw that she was not going to give him anything, the boy would start yelling like an eagle, while Soetkin made a great clatter with the pots and pans that she was washing in the wooden tub, pretending that she did not hear his noise. Then Ulenspiegel would fall to weeping, and the gentle mother would stop her pretence at harshness, and would come and kiss him.

"Will a *denier* be enough for you?" she would say.

Now it should be noted that a *denier* is equal to six *liards*.

Thus did his mother dote on Ulenspiegel even to excess; and when Claes was not there, he was king in the house.

VIII

One morning Soetkin saw Claes pacing up and down the kitchen with head bent, like a man lost in thought.

"Whatever is the matter with you, my man?" she asked him. "You are pale, and you look angry and distracted."

Claes answered her in a low voice, like a dog growling.

"The Emperor is about to reissue those cursed placards. Death once again is hovering over the land of Flanders. The Informers are to have one half of the property of their victims, if so be that such property does not exceed the value of one hundred florins."

"We are poor," Soetkin said.

"Not poor enough," Claes answered. "Evil folk there are—crows and corpse-devouring vultures—who would as readily denounce us to the Emperor for half a sackful of coal as for half a sackful of florins. What had she, poor old

11

Widow Tanneken that was wife to Sis the tailor, she that was buried alive at Heyst? Nothing but a Latin Bible, three gold florins, and a few household utensils of English pewter. But they were coveted by a neighbour. Then there was Joanna Martens whom they burnt as a witch after she had been thrown into the water, for her body did not sink and they held it for a sign of sorcery. She had a few miserable pieces of furniture and seven gold pieces in a bag, and the Informer wanted his half of them. Alas! I could go on till to-morrow morning giving you instances of the same kind. But to cut a long story short, Mother, life's no longer worth living in Flanders, and all on account of these placards. Soon every night-time the death-cart will be passing through the town, and we shall hear the arid click of bones as the skeletons shake in the wind."

Soetkin said: "You ought not to try and frighten me, my man. The Emperor is the father of Flanders and Brabant, and as such he is endowed with long-suffering, gentleness, patience, and pity."

"He would be obliged to renounce too much if he were all that," Claes answered, "for he has inherited a great amount of confiscated property."

At that very moment the sound of a trumpet was heard, and the clash of the Heralds' cymbals. Claes and Soetkin, carrying Ulenspiegel in their arms by turns, rushed out towards where the sound came from, and with them went a great concourse of people. They came to the Town Hall, in front of which stood the Heralds on horseback, blowing their trumpets and sounding their cymbals, and the Provost with his staff of justice, and the Town Proctor, also on horseback and holding in his hands the Imperial Edict which he was preparing to read out to the assembled multitude.

Claes heard every word, how "that it was once again forbidden to all and sundry to print, read, to possess or to defend, the writings, books or doctrines of Martin Luther, of

12

John Wycliffe, John Hus, Marcilius de Padua, Æcolampadius, Ulricus Zwynglius, Philip Melanchton, Franciscus Lambertus, Joannes Pomeranus, Otto Brunselsius, Justus Jonas, Joannes Puperis, and Gorcianus ; as well as any copies of the New Testament printed by Adrien de Berghes, Christophe de Remonda, and Joannes Zel, which books were full of Lutheran and other kinds of heresy, and had been condemned and rejected by the Doctors of Theology at the University of Louvain.

" Likewise and in the same manner it was forbidden to paint, portray or cause to be painted or portrayed any opprobrious paintings or figures of God, or of the Blessed Virgin Mary, or of the saints ; or to break, destroy or deface the images or pictures made to the honour, remembrance or recollection of God, the Virgin Mary, or of the saints recognized by the Church.

" Furthermore," said the placard, " no one, whatever his position in life, should presume to discuss or dispute concerning Holy Writ, even in regard to matters admittedly doubtful, unless he were a theologian, well known and approved by some established university."

His Sacred Majesty decreed, among other penalties, that suspected persons should not be allowed to carry on any honourable occupation. And as for men who had fallen again into error, or who were obstinate in the same, they should be condemned to be burnt by fire, slow or fast, either in a covering of straw, or else bound to a stake, according to the discretion of the judge. Others, if they were men of noble or gentle birth, were to be executed by the sword, while common men were to be hung, and the women buried alive. Afterwards their heads were to be fixed on the top of poles for an example. The property of all the aforesaid, in so far as it was situate in places subject to confiscation, was to be made over to the benefit of the Emperor.

To the Informers His Sacred Majesty gave one half of

all the property of the dead, provided that such property did not exceed, on any one occasion, a hundred pounds gross in Flemish money. As for the half that went to the Emperor, he would reserve it for works of piety and mercy, as was done in the case of the confiscations at Rome.

And Claes went away sadly, with Soetkin and Ulenspiegel.

IX

Once again did Soetkin bear under her girdle the sign of approaching motherhood ; and Katheline also was in a like condition. But she was afraid, and never ventured out of her house.

When Soetkin went to see her, " Alas ! " said Katheline, " what shall I do ? Must I smother the ill-starred fruit of my womb ? I would rather die myself. And yet if the Sergeants summon me for having a child without being married, they will make me pay twenty florins like a girl of no reputation, and I shall be flogged in the Market Square."

Soetkin consoled and comforted her as sweetly as she could, then left her, and returned thoughtfully home.

One day she said to Claes :

" If I brought two children into the world instead of one, would you be angry ? Would you beat me, my man ? "

" That I cannot say," Claes answered.

" But if the second were not really mine, but turned out to be like this child of Katheline's, the offspring of some one unknown—the devil maybe ? "

" Devils beget fire, death, smoke," Claes replied, " but children—no. Yet will I take for my own the child of Katheline."

" You will ? " cried Soetkin. " You really will ? "

" I have said it," Claes replied.

Soetkin hurried off to tell Katheline the news, who when

she heard it could not contain her delight, but cried aloud
with joy.

" He has spoken, the good man, and his words are the
salvation of my body. He will be blessed by God—and
blessed by the devil as well, if really "—and she trembled as
she spoke the words—" if really it is the devil who is father to
the little one that begins to stir beneath my breast ! "

And in due time Soetkin and Katheline brought into the
world, the one a baby boy and the other a baby girl. Both
were brought to baptism as the children of Claes. Soetkin's
son was christened Hans, and did not live. But Katheline's
daughter, who was christened Nele, grew up finely.

She drank of the liquor of life from a fourfold flagon.
Two of the flagons belonged to Katheline, and two were
Soetkin's. And there was many a sweet dispute as to whose
turn it was to give the child to drink. But much against her
will, Katheline was obliged to let her milk dry up, lest questions should be asked as to where it came from, and she no
mother. . . .

But when the little Nele, that was her daughter, was
weaned, then Katheline took her home to live with her, nor
did she let her go back to Soetkin except when Nele called
for her " mother."

The neighbours said that it was a right and natural thing
to do for Katheline to look after the child of Claes and
Soetkin. For they were needy and poverty-stricken, whereas
Katheline was comparatively well off.

X

One day Soetkin said to Claes :

" Husband, I am heart-broken. This is now the third
day that Tyl has been away. Know you not where he is ? "

Claes answered her sadly :

" He is with all the others, roving vagabonds like himself,
on the high road. Verily, it was cruel of God to give us

such a son. When he was born I thought of him as the joy of our old age, and as another help in our house, for I hoped to make a good workman of him. But now some evil chance hath turned him into a thief and a good-for-nothing."

" You are too hard on him, my man," said Soetkin. " He is our son, and he is but nine years old, and filled with childish folly. It is needful that he also, like the trees of the field, should let fall his husks by the wayside ere he decks himself with the full foliage of virtue and honesty. He is mischievous ; I do not deny it. But later on this spirit of his will be turned to good account, if instead of driving him to tricks and frolics it is put to some useful purpose. He makes fun of the neighbours ; true. But one day you will find him take his rightful place in the midst of a circle of gay and happy friends. He is always laughing and frivolous ; yes, but a young face that is too serious bodes ill for the future. And if he is always running about, it is because his growing body needs to be exercised ; and if he is idle and does no work, it is because he is not yet old enough to feel the duty of labour. And if, now and then, he does stay away from us for half a week at a time, it is only because he fails to realize the grief he causes us ; for he has a good heart, husband, and at bottom he loves us."

Claes shook his head and said nothing, and went to sleep, leaving Soetkin to her lonely tears. And she, in the morning, afraid lest her son had fallen sick upon the road, went out and stood at the cottage doorstep to see if he were coming back. But there was no sign of him, and she came back into the cottage, and sat by the window, gazing out all the time into the street. And many a time did her heart dance within her bosom at the light footfall of some urchin that she thought might be her own ; but when the sound passed by, and she knew that it was not Ulenspiegel, then she wept, poor mother that she was.

Ulenspiegel, meanwhile, with the fellow-scamps that

bore him company, was away at Bruges, at the Saturday market.

There were to be seen the shoemakers and the cobblers, each in his separate stall, the tailors selling suits of clothes, the *miesevangers* from Antwerp (they that snare tom-tits by night with the aid of an owl) ; and the poulterers too, and the rascally dog-fanciers, and sellers of catskins that are made into gloves, and of breast-pads and doublets : buyers too of every kind, townsmen and townswomen, valets, servants, pantlers and butlers, and cooks, male and female, all together, buying and selling, each according to his quality shouting his wares, crying up or crying down, with every trick of the trade.

Now in one corner of the market-place stood a wonderful tent made of cloth, raised aloft on four piles. At the door of the tent was a peasant from the level land of Alost, and by his side two monks begged for alms. For the sum of one *patard* the peasant offered to show to the curious or devout a genuine piece of the shoulder-bone of St. Mary of Egypt. There he was, yelling out in his broken voice the merits of the saint, and not omitting from his song that tale which tells how she, being without money, paid the young ferryman in the beautiful coinage of Nature herself, lest by refusing a workman his due she might be guilty of sin. And all the while the two monks kept nodding their heads, as much as to say that it was Gospel truth that the peasant was speaking. And at their side was a fat, red-faced woman, as lewd-looking as Astarte, blowing a raucous bagpipe, while at her side a young girl sang in a voice sweet as a bird's, though no one heeded her. Now above the door of the tent, and swung between two poles by a cord fastened to either handle, was a tub of Holy Water which the fat woman affirmed had been brought from Rome ; and the two monks lolled their heads backwards and forwards in confirmation or what she said. Ulenspiegel, looking at thè tub, grew suddenly thoughtful.

For to one of the posts of the tent was tied a donkey—a donkey that to all appearance was wont to feed on hay rather than on oats. For its head was down, and it scanned the earth in futile hopes of seeing but a thistle growing there.

"Comrades," said Ulenspiegel, pointing to the fat old woman, the two monks, and the melancholy donkey, "since the masters play so well, let us also make the donkey dance."

And so saying he went to a stall close by and purchased six *liards*' worth of pepper. Then he lifted up the tail of the donkey, and placed the pepper underneath it.

When the donkey began to feel the sting of the pepper, he cast his eye backwards under his tail, endeavouring to discover the cause of the unaccustomed heat. Thinking that it must be at the least some fiery devil from hell, the donkey conceived the not unnatural desire to run away and escape him ; so he began to bray as loud as he could, and to kick up his heels, and to shake the post with all his strength. At the first shock, the tub hanging between the two poles tipped over, and the holy water ran about over the tent and over those that were inside. And soon the tent itself collapsed, covering with a dripping mantle all those who were listening to the wondrous tale of St. Mary of Egypt. And Ulenspiegel and his comrades could hear a mighty noise issuing from beneath the tent, a noise of moaning and lamentation. For the devout folk that were within began to accuse one another of having overturned the tub, and presently grew red with rage, and fell upon each other with many furious blows. The tent began to bulge here and there above the frantic efforts of the combatants. And each time that Ulenspiegel descried some rounded form outlined through the cloth of the tent, he went and gave it a prick with a pin. This was the signal for new and louder cries, and for fiercer and more general fisticuffs.

Ulenspiegel was delighted, and soon he was to become even more so, when he saw the donkey begin to run away, dragging behind him tent, tub, tent-posts and all, while the master of the tent, with his wife and daughter, hung on behind the baggage. At last the donkey, being able to go no farther, raised his nose in the air, and gave vent to bray after bray, a music that only ceased at those moments when he was looking back under his tail to see if the fire that still raged there would not soon go out.

All this time, the devout assembly in the tent were still a-fighting. But the two monks, without troubling at all about what was going on inside, began to gather up the money that had fallen from the collection-plate, and Ulenspiegel assisted them devotedly, but not without some profit to himself. . . .

XI

Now all this time that the vagabond son of the charcoal-burner was growing up in merriment and mischief, the moody scion of His Sacred Majesty the Emperor was vegetating like a weed in moody melancholy. The Lords and Ladies of the Court used to watch him as he mouched along the rooms and passages of the palace at Valladolid, a frail, pitiful specimen of humanity, with legs that shook and scarce seemed able to support the weight of the big head that was covered with stiff blond hair.

He loved to haunt dark corridors, and he would stay sitting there whole hours together, with his legs stretched out in front of him, hoping that some valet or other might trip over them by mistake ; then he would have the fellow flogged ; for he took pleasure in listening to his cries under the lash. But he never laughed.

Another day he would select some other corridor in which to lay a similar trap, and once again he would sit himself down with his legs stretched out in front of him. Then one of the Ladies of the Court, mayhap, or one of the Lords or pages, would stumble across him ; and if they fell down and hurt themselves, he took delight in their discomfiture.

But he never laughed. And if by chance any one knocked against him but did not fall down, he would cry out as if he had been struck. He liked to see the other's fright. But he never laughed.

His Sacred Majesty was informed of these goings-on, and he commanded that no notice should be taken of the child, saying that if his son did not want people to walk over his legs he should not place his legs in a position where they were liable to be walked over. Philip was angry at this, but he said nothing and was no more seen, till one fine summer day when he went out into the courtyard to warm his shivering body in the sun.

Charles, riding back from the war, saw his son thus brewing his melancholy.

" How now ? " cried the Emperor. " What a difference there is between us two, my son ! At your age I loved nothing better than to go climbing trees after squirrels. Or, with the aid of a rope, to clamber down some steep cliff to take young eagles out of their nests. I might easily have broken my bones at the game ; but they only grew the harder. And when I went out hunting, the deer fled into the thickets at sight of me, armed with my trusty arquebus."

" Ah, my Lord Father," sighed the child, " but you see, I have the stomach-ache."

" For that," said Charles, " good wine from Paxarete is a most certain remedy."

" I don't like wine. I have a headache, my Lord Father."

" Then you should run and jump and play about like other children of your age."

" I have stiff legs, my Lord Father."

" And how should it be otherwise," said Charles, " seeing that you make no more use of them than if they were of wood ? But you shall go riding on a high-mettled horse."

The child began to cry.

" Oh no, for mercy's sake ! I have a pain in my back ! "

"Come, come," said Charles, "are you ill everywhere then ? "

"I should not be ill at all," answered the child, "if only they would let me alone."

"Do you think to pass your royal life away in dreams like a scholar ? " the Emperor asked impatiently. "Such people as that, if indeed it be necessary for the inking of their parchments, may rightly seek out silence, solitude, retirement from the world. But for thee, son of the sword, I would desire warm blood, a lynx's eye, a fox's craft, and the strength of Hercules. Why do you cross yourself ? Blood of God ! What should a lion's cub be doing with this mimicry of women at their prayers ! "

"Hark ! It is the Angelus, my Lord Father," answered the child.

XII

May and June that year were in very truth the months of flowers. Never had Flanders known the hawthorn so fragrant, never the gardens so gay with roses, jasmine, and honeysuckle. And when the wind blew from England it carried eastwards with it the breath of all this flowery land, and the people, at Antwerp and elsewhere, sniffed the air joyfully and cried aloud,

"How good the scent of the wind that blows from Flanders ! "

Then it was that the bees were busy sucking honey from the flowers, making wax, and laying their eggs within the hives that were all too small to house the swarms. What workman's music they made, under that canopy of azure sky that was spread so dazzlingly over the rich earth !

Hives were made of rushes, straw, osiers or of wattled hay. The basket-makers, tub-makers, coopers, wore out their tools at the work. As for the bin-workers, this long time past their numbers were scarce sufficient for the work they had to do. In a single swarm there would be as many as three thousand

*

bees and two thousand seven hundred drones! The quality of the comb was so exquisite that the Dean of Damme dispatched eleven combs to the Emperor Charles out of gratitude for the new edicts that had revived in Flanders the earlier vigour of the Holy Inquisition. It was Philip, forsooth, that ate them all; but little good did they do him!

In Flanders, the rascals of the roads, the beggars and vagabonds and all that lazy good-for-nothing crowd who would risk hanging rather than a day's work, were soon enticed by the taste of the honey to come along and steal their share. And by night they prowled around the hives in gangs. Now Claes had made some hives for the purpose of attracting the wandering swarms of bees, and some of these hives were full already, but there were others that stood empty waiting for the bees. Claes kept watch all night to guard this sugary wealth of his; and when he was tired he asked Ulenspiegel to take his place, the which Ulenspiegel did right willingly.

It was a cold night, and Ulenspiegel to avoid the chill took refuge in one of the hives, curling himself up inside, and looking out from two openings that had been made in the roof.

Just as he was going off to sleep, he heard a rustle in the bushy hedge near by, and then the voices of two men. They were thieves, no doubt, and peering forth from the openings aforesaid, Ulenspiegel saw that they both had long hair and long beards, which was strange, for a long beard is usually the sign of a nobleman. However, the two men went peering from hive to hive, and coming at last to the one in which Ulenspiegel was hiding, they tried its weight, and then—

"Let us take this one," they said, "it is the heaviest."

Whereupon they slung it up between them, on a couple of poles, and carried it off. Ulenspiegel did not at all fancy being thus carted away in a hive. The night was clear,

The Adventure of the Hive

and the two thieves marched along with never a word. When they had gone about fifty paces they would stop to take breath, and then set off again. The man in front grumbled angrily all the time at the weight of his burden. And the man behind whined in a querulous fashion. Even so are there always to be found two sorts of idle fellows in this world, those who are angry at having to work, and those who merely whine at having to.

Ulenspiegel, since there seemed nothing else to do, took hold of the hair of the man in front and gave it a pull. And he did the same to the beard of the man at the rear; and to such purpose that the two men soon grew annoyed at what was happening, and Mr. Angry said to Mr. Whining:

"Hi there, stop pulling my hair, you, or else I'll give you such a whack on the head that it'll squash down into your chest, and then you'll be looking out of your two sides like a thief through the prison grille!"

"I should never think of doing such a thing as to pull your hair," said the whiner. "But what are you doing there, pulling at my beard?"

To which Mr. Angry made answer:

"It isn't I that would go hunting for fleas in the wool of a leper!"

"O sir," said the whiner, "for goodness' sake don't go shaking the hive about like this. My poor arms cannot support it any longer."

"I shall shake it out of your arms altogether," said the other. Then unloading himself, he placed the hive upon the ground and fell upon his companion. And so they fought together, the one cursing, and the other crying out for mercy.

Ulenspiegel, hearing the sound of blows, came out from the hive, dragged it behind him into the wood close by, and having placed it where he could find it again, returned to Claes.

And thus you may see what sort of a profit it is that thieves derive from their quarrels.

XIII

As he grew up, Ulenspiegel acquired the habit of wandering about among the fairs and markets of the country-side, and whenever he hit upon a man who played the oboe, the rebec, or the bagpipes, he would offer him a *patard* for a lesson in the art of making those instruments to sing.

He became especially accomplished in the art of playing the *rommelpot*, an instrument which is constructed out of a round pot, a bladder, and a straight piece of straw. And this is the way he played it. First of all he moistened the bladder and held it over the pot. Then he drew the centre of the bladder round the joint of a straw which itself was attached to the bottom of the pot. Finally he stretched the bladder as tightly as he dared over the sides of the pot. In the morning, when the bladder was dry, it sounded like a tambourine when struck, and if one rubbed the straw it gave forth a humming sound as fine in tone as that of any violin. And Ulenspiegel, with his musical pot that played music like the baying of a mastiff, went out with the other children on the day of Epiphany carrying a star made of luminous paper, and singing carols.

Sometimes an artist would come to Damme to paint the members of one of the Guilds, upon their knees. Ulenspiegel was always anxious to see how the artist worked, and he would beg to be allowed to grind the colours in return for nothing but a slice of bread, three *liards*, and a pint of ale. But while he worked away at the grinding he would carefully study the method of his master. When the artist went away Ulenspiegel would endeavour to paint pictures like him; and his favourite colour was scarlet. In this way he tried to paint the portraits of Claes, of Soetkin, and of Katheline and Nele, as well as those of the pots and pans in the kitchen. When Claes beheld these works of art he predicted that if only he worked hard enough Ulenspiegel would one day be able to earn florins by the dozen for painting the inscriptions on the festal cars, or *speel-wagen* as they are called in Zeeland and the land of Flanders.

Ulenspiegel also learnt to carve in wood and in stone, for once a master-mason came to Damme to carve a stall in the choir of Notre Dame. And this stall was made in such a way that the Dean—who was an old man—could sit down when he so desired, yet seem to all appearance as if he were still standing upright.

It was Ulenspiegel too who made the first carved knife-handle ever used by the people of Zeeland. He fashioned this handle in the form of a cage. Inside was a death's head that moved ; and above it a hound *couchant*. And this was the signification : " Soul true till death."

Thus it was that Ulenspiegel began to fulfil the prophecy that Katheline had made when she said that he would be painter, sculptor, workman, nobleman, all in one. For you must know that from father to son the family of Claes bore arms *three pint pots argent au naturel on a ground bruinbier*.

But Ulenspiegel would stick to no one profession, and Claes told him that if he went on in this good-for-nothing way he would chase him out of the house.

XIV

On his return from the wars, the Emperor wanted to know why his son Philip was not there to welcome him.

The Archbishop—the royal Governor—said that the child had refused to leave his solitude and the books which were the only things he loved.

The Emperor asked where he was to be found at the moment. The Governor did not know exactly, but said they had better go and look for him somewhere where it was dark. This they did.

When they had looked through a good number of rooms they came at last to a kind of closet, unpaved and lit only by a skylight. There they found a stake stuck into the ground, and a dear little monkey bound to the stake by a cord round the waist. (Now this monkey had been sent from the Indies as a present to His Highness to amuse him with its youthful gambols). . . . Round the bottom of the stake were some smoking sticks still glowing, and the closet was filled with a foul smell as of burning hair.

The poor animal had suffered so much pain while being burnt to death that its little body no longer looked the body of a living animal, but seemed rather like the fragment of some root, all wrinkled and distorted. And its mouth, still open with the death-cry, was filled with froth mixed with blood ; and the face was wet with tears.

" Who has done this ? " said the Emperor.

The Governor did not dare to answer, and the two men stood there silent, sad, and angry.

All at once, in the silence, there was heard a sound of feeble coughing that came from a corner in the shadow behind them. His Majesty turned and beheld Philip, his son, dressed all in black, sucking an orange.

" Don Philip," he said, " come and greet your father."

The child did not move, but gazed at his father with timid eyes that showed no spark of love.

" Is it you," asked the Emperor, " who have burnt alive in the fire this little animal ? "

The child bowed his head.

But the Emperor : " If you have been cruel enough to do such a deed, at least be brave enough to own up to it."

The child made no answer.

His Majesty seized the orange from the child's hands, threw it to the ground, and was about to beat his son, who was shaking with terror, when the Archbishop restrained him, whispering in his ear :

" The day will surely come when His Highness shall prove a mighty burner of heretics." The Emperor smiled,

PHILIP AND THE MONKEY

and the two of them went away, leaving Philip alone with the monkey.

But others there were, not monkeys, that were destined to meet their death in the flames. . . .

XV

November was come, the month of hail-storms, when sufferers from cold in the head abandon themselves freely to their concerts of coughing and spitting. This also is the month when the turnip-fields are filled with gangs of youths that there disport themselves and steal whatever they can, to the mighty wrath of the peasants, who try in vain to catch them, chasing after them with sticks and pitchforks.

Well, on an evening when Ulenspiegel was returning home from one of these raids, he heard close by, in a corner of the hedgerow, a sound as of groaning. He leant down, and beheld a dog lying stretched out on the stones.

"Hallo!" he cried. "Poor little beast! What are you doing out here so late at night?"

He patted the dog, and found that its back was all wet, as though some one had been trying to drown it. He took it in his arms to warm it, and when he had reached home he said:

"I have brought back a wounded animal. What shall we do with it?"

"Dress its wounds," said Claes.

Ulenspiegel laid the dog on the table; whereupon he and Claes and Soetkin saw that it was a little red-haired Luxemburg terrier, and that it was wounded in the back. Soetkin sponged the wounds, and anointed them with ointment, and bound them up with linen bandages. Then Ulenspiegel took the dog and put it in his bed; but Soetkin desired to have it in her own, saying she was afraid that Ulenspiegel would hurt the little red-haired thing. For in those days Ulenspiegel was wont to toss about in his sleep all night like a young devil in a stoup of holy water. Ulenspiegel, however, had his way, and he took such care of the dog that in the space of six days it was walking about like any other dog, and giving itself great airs.

And the village schoolmaster christened him Titus Bibulus Schnouffius : Titus after a certain good Emperor of the Romans who was fond of befriending lost dogs ; Bibulus because the dog loved beer with all the passion of a confirmed drunkard ; and Schnouffius because he would always run about sniffing and putting his nose into every rat-hole and mole-hole he could find.

XVI

The young prince of Spain was now fifteen years old, and his custom was to wander about the rooms and passages and stairways of the castle. But chiefly was he to be found prowling around the women's quarters, trying to pick a quarrel with one of the pages, who themselves were wont to lurk on the look out, like cats, in the corridors ; while others, again, out in the courtyard, would stand singing some tender ballad, nose in air. When the young prince heard one singing thus, he would show himself at one of the windows, and the heart of that poor page would be stricken with fear as he saw that white face there, instead of the gentle eyes of his beloved.

Now among the Ladies of the Court there was a gentle dame from Dudzeel near by Damme in Flanders. Fair-fleshed she was, like fine ripe fruit, and marvellously beautiful, for she had green eyes and reddish hair all wavy and gleaming gold. And of a gay humour was she, and of an ardent complexion, nor did she make any effort to conceal her taste for that fortunate lord to whom for the time being she was pleased to grant the freedom of the fair estate of her love. Such a one there was even now, handsome and proud, and she loved him well. Every day, at a certain hour, she went to find him—a thing which Philip was not long in finding out.

28

The Virtues of Woman

So, one day, sitting himself down on a bench that stood against a window, he lay in wait for her, and there she saw him as she passed by, with her bright eyes and her mouth half open, all meet for love and fresh from her bath, with the gear of her dress of yellow brocade swinging about her as she stepped along. Without rising from his seat, Philip accosted her.

"Madame," says he, "could you not spare a moment ?"

Restive as some eager mare, stayed in her course towards the gallant stallion that is neighing for her in the field, the lady made answer :

"All here must needs obey the royal will of your Highness."

"Then sit you down by my side," said the Prince. And gazing at her lewdly, harshly, cunningly, he spake again :

"I would have you recite to me the *Pater Noster* in Flemish. They taught it me once, but I no longer remember it."

The poor lady did as she was bid ; and then the Prince commanded her to say it all over again, but more slowly. And so on, and so on, until she had recited it ten times over. After that he began to speak flatteringly to her, praising her beautiful hair, her fresh complexion, and her bright eyes. But he dared not to say a word concerning her lovely shoulders or her rounded throat, or of aught else beside.

When at last she was beginning to hope that she might be able to get away, and was already scanning anxiously the courtyard where her lord was awaiting her, the Prince demanded of her if she could rightly tell him what were the several virtues of woman ? She answered nothing, fearing that she might say something to displease him. He then answered for her, setting the matter forth in this wise :

"The virtues of woman are these : chastity, regard for her own honour, and a modest manner of life." And he counselled her, therefore, that she should dress decently and should always be careful to hide those things which were

29

meet to be hidden. The lady nodded assent, saying that for His Hyperborean Highness she would certainly take care to cover herself with ten bear-skins rather than with a single length of muslin.

Having put him to shame by this answer, she made off gladly.

But in Philip's heart the fire of youth was alight—not the fiery glow that dares the souls of the brave to lofty deeds, but a dark fire from hell itself, the fire of Satan. And it flamed in his grey eyes like the beam of a winter's moon shining down upon a charnel-house. And it burned within him cruelly. . . .

XVII

Now this beautiful, gay-hearted lady left Valladolid one day for her Château of Dudzeel in Flanders.

Passing through Damme, with her fat attendant behind her, she noticed a lad of about fifteen years of age sitting against the wall of a cottage blowing a pair of bagpipes. In front of him was a dog with red hair howling dismally, because, as it seemed, he did not at all appreciate the music which his master was making. The sun shone brightly, and at the lad's side there stood a pretty young girl in fits of laughter at the pitiful howling of the dog.

This then was the sight that met the eye of the beautiful lady and her fat attendant as they passed in front of the cottage : none else but Ulenspiegel blowing his pipes, and Nele in fits of laughter, and Titus Bibulus Schnouffius howling with all his might.

"You naughty boy," said the dame to Ulenspiegel, " will you never stop making this poor red-hair howl like this ? "

But Ulenspiegel, staring back at her, blew his pipes more valiantly than ever, and Bibulus Schnouffius howled the more dismally, and Nele laughed all the louder.

The lady's attendant grew angry, and pointed at Ulenspiegel, saying :

Tyl and the Beautiful Lady

" An I beat this wretched little imp of a man with the scabbard of my sword he would give over his insolent row."

Ulenspiegel looked the attendant in the face and called him " Jan Papzak " because of his fat belly, and went on blowing his bagpipes. The attendant came up to him, and threatened him with his fist. But Bibulus Schnouffius went for him straightway and bit him in the leg, and the man fell down, crying for mercy :

" Help, help ! "

The dame only smiled, and said to Ulenspiegel :

" Tell me, my player of bagpipes, is the road still the same that leads from Damme to Dudzeel ? "

But Ulenspiegel went on playing, and only nodded his head and stared.

" Why do you look at me so fixedly ? " she asked him.

But he, still continuing to play, opened his eyes all the wider as though transported by an ecstasy of admiration.

" Are you not ashamed," she said, " young as you are, to stare at ladies so ? "

Ulenspiegel blushed faintly, but went on blowing his pipes, and staring more than ever.

" I have already asked you once," the lady insisted, " whether the road is still the same that leads from Damme to Dudzeel."

" It is green no longer since you deprived it of the honour of carrying you," Ulenspiegel answered.

" Will you show me the way ? " said the lady.

But Ulenspiegel still remained sitting where he was, and still went on staring at her. And she, seeing him so roguish, and knowing it all for the gamesomeness of youth, forgave him willingly.

He got up at last, and began to walk back into the cottage.

" Whither are you going ? " she asked him.

" To put on my best clothes," he replied.

" Very well," she said.

31

Then the lady sat herself down on the bench, close to the doorstep, and tried to talk to Nele. But Nele would not answer her, for she was jealous.

It was not long before Ulenspiegel returned, well washed and clothed in fustian. He looked fine in his Sunday clothes, the little man.

" Are you really going off with this fine lady ? " Nele asked him.

" I shall soon be back," he told her.

" Let me go instead of you," said Nele.

" No," he said, " the roads are muddy."

" Why, little girl," said the lady, who was annoyed and jealous now in her turn, " why do you try to hinder him from coming with me ? "

Nele did not answer, but great tears gushed from her eyes, and she gazed at the fine lady in sadness and in anger.

Then the four of them started off, the dame seated like a queen upon her ambling palfrey, the attendant with his belly that shook with every step, Ulenspiegel holding the lady's horse by the bridle, and Bibulus Schnouffius walking at his side, tail proudly in air.

Thus went they on horseback and on foot for some long while. But Ulenspiegel was not at his ease ; dumb as a fish he sniffed the fine scent of benjamin that floated from the lady, and saw out of the corner of his eye all her beautiful gear, rare jewels and trinkets, and the sweet expression of her face, her bright eyes, and bare neck, and her hair that shone in the sunlight like a hood of gold.

" Why are you so quiet, my little man ? " she asked him.

He answered nothing.

" Do you keep your tongue so deep in your boots that you could not take a message for me ? "

" What is it ? " said Ulenspiegel.

" I would have you leave me here," said the dame, " and go to Koolkercke, from whence this wind is blowing.

There you will find a gentleman dressed in black and red
motley. Tell him that he must not expect me to-day, but
let him come to-morrow evening to my château, by the
postern gate, at ten o' the clock.

" I will not go," said Ulenspiegel.

" Why not ? " asked the lady.

" I will not go, not I," Ulenspiegel said again.

" What can it be," the lady asked him, " what can it be
that inspires you with this unyielding will, you angry little
cock ? "

" I will not go," Ulenspiegel persisted.

" But if I gave you a florin ? "

" No," said he.

" A ducat ? "

" No."

" A carolus ! "

" No," Ulenspiegel repeated, " although "—and this was
added with a sigh—" I should rather see it in my mother's
purse than a mussel-shell ! "

The dame laughed, then suddenly cried out in a loud
voice :

" My bag ! I have lost my little bag ! Beautiful it was and
rare, made of silk, and sown with fine pearls ! It was hanging
from my belt when we were at Damme ! "

Ulenspiegel did not budge, but her attendant came up to
his lady.

" Madame," said he, " whatever else you do, be careful
not to send this young robber to look for it, for so you will
certainly never see it again."

" Who will go then ? " asked the lady.

" I will," he answered, " old as I am."

And away he went.

Midday had struck. It was very hot. The silence was
profound. Ulenspiegel said not a word, but taking off his
new doublet he laid it on the grass in the shade of a lime-tree,

so that the dame might sit down thereon without fear of the damp. He stood close by, heaving a sigh.

She looked up at him, and felt compassion on that shy little figure, and she inquired of him if he was not tired standing there upright on his young legs. He did not answer, but slid gently down at her side. She was desirous of resting him, and she drew his head on to her bare neck, and there it lay so willingly that she would have thought it the sin of cruelty itself had she bade him find some other pillow.

After a while the attendant came back, saying that he had not been able to find the bag.

" I have found it myself," replied the lady, " for when I dismounted from my horse, there it was hanging half open on the stirrup. And now "—this to Ulenspiegel—" show us the way to Dudzeel, please, and tell me your name."

" My patron saint," he replied, " is Monsieur Saint Thylbert, a name which means fleet of foot towards that which is good ; my second name is Claes, and my surname Ulenspiegel. But now, if you would deign to look at yourself in my mirror, you would see that in all the land of Flanders there is not one flower so dazzling in its beauty as is the scented grace of you."

The lady blushed with pleasure, and was not angry with Ulenspiegel.

But Soetkin and Nele sat at home, weeping together, through all this long absence.

XVIII

When Ulenspiegel returned from Dudzeel and came to the entrance of the town, he saw Nele standing there leaning with her back against the toll-gate. She was picking the stones out of a bunch of black grapes, which she munched one by one, and found therefrom, doubtless, much delight and refreshment ; nevertheless, she did not allow anything of her enjoyment to appear on her countenance. On the contrary, she seemed annoyed at something, tearing at the grapes angrily. She looked, indeed, so sad and sorrowful, so sweetly unhappy, that Ulenspiegel felt overcome with that pity which is almost love, and coming up to her from behind, he printed a kiss on the nape of the girl's neck. But all the return she gave him was a great box on the ear.

"Now I shall not be able to see properly any more," he said.

She burst into tears.

"O Nele," says he, "are you going to set up fountains at the entrance of all the villages?"

"Be off with you," says she.

"But I can't go away and leave you crying like this, my little pet."

"I am not your little pet," says Nele; "neither am I crying."

"No, you are not crying, but there is certainly some water coming out of your eyes."

"*Will you go away?*" She turned on him.

"No," he answered.

All the time she was holding her pinafore in her small trembling hand, tearing at the stuff in little spasms of rage, and wetting it with her tears.

"Nele," said Ulenspiegel, "when is it going to be fine again?"

And he smiled at her very lovingly.

"Why do you ask me that?" she said.

"Because when it is fine there is an end of weeping," answered Ulenspiegel.

"Go back to your beautiful lady of the brocaded gown," she said. "Your jokes are good enough for *her*. . . ."

Then Ulenspiegel sang:

> *When I see my love crying*
> *My heart is torn.*
> *When she smiles 'tis honey,*

Pearls when she weeps.
Either way I love her.
And I'll draw a draught of wine,
Good wine from Louvain,
And I'll draw a draught of wine,
When Nele smiles again.

" You villainous man ! " she cried, " making fun of me again ! "

" Nele," said Ulenspiegel, " it is true that I am a man. But I am not a villain. For our family is of noble origin, a family of aldermen, and it carries on its shield *three pint pots argent on a ground bruinbier*. But, Nele, tell me now, is it a fact that in Flanders when a man sows a kiss he always reaps a box on the ear ? "

" I refuse to speak to you," said Nele.

" Then why open your mouth to tell me so ? "

" I am angry," she said.

Ulenspiegel slapped her on the back very lightly with his hand, saying :

" Kiss a naughty girl and she will cuff you ; cuff her, she will cry. Come then, sweet, cry upon my shoulder since I have cuffed you ! "

Nele turned round. He opened his arms, and she threw herself into them.

" You won't go away any more down there, will you Tyl ? " she asked him.

But he did not answer, busy as he was in pressing with his the hand that trembled so pitifully, and in drying with his lips the hot tears that fell from the eyes of Nele, like heavy drops of rain in a storm.

XIX

These were the days when the noble city of Ghent refused to pay the tax which her son, the Emperor Charles, was demanding of her. The fact was it was impossible to pay, for already the city was drained of money by the act of Charles himself.   But it seemed that the city was guilty of a great crime, and Charles resolved to go himself and exact punishment.   For to be whipped by her own son is above all things painful to a mother.

Now, although he was his enemy, Francis Long-Nose was pleased to offer the Emperor a free passage through the land of France.   Charles accepted the offer, and instead of being held as a prisoner, he was fêted and feasted in right royal fashion.   For this is ever a sovereign bond of union between kings : each to aid the other against their own peoples.

Charles stayed a long time at Valenciennes, and still gave no sign of his wrath, so that Mother Ghent began to lay aside her fears, believing that the Emperor her son was going to forgive her, seeing that she had acted within her rights.

But at length Charles arrived under the walls of the city with 4000 horse, together with the Duke of Alba and the Prince of Orange.   The poorer townsfolk and the small business men wished to prevent this filial entry into their city, and would have called to arms 80,000 men of the city and of the country round.   But the merchants, the *hoogh-poorters*, opposed this suggestion, being afraid of the predominance of the people.   Thus Ghent could easily have cut her son to pieces, him and his 4000 horse.   But it seemed she loved him too dearly, and even the small tradesmen themselves were fast regaining their trust in him.

Charles also loved the city, but only for the sake of his coffers that were stored with her money, and which he hoped to store up fuller yet.

Having made himself master of the place, he established military posts everywhere, and ordered that they should patrol the city night and day.   Then, in great state, he pronounced his sentence.

The chief merchants of the city with cords round their necks were to appear before him as he sat on his throne, and to make a formal apology. Ghent itself was declared guilty of the most costly crimes—of disloyalty, disregard of treaties, disobedience, sedition, conspiracy, and high treason. The Emperor declared that all and every privilege—rights, customs, freedoms, and usages—all were to be abolished and annulled ; and he stipulated for the future too, as though he were God himself, that none of his successors on coming to the throne should ever observe any one of these usages again, except only that which was called the Caroline Concession, as granted by him to the city.

The Abbey of St. Bavon he razed to the ground, and in place he erected a fortress whence he could pierce with bullets and at his ease his mother's very heart. Like a good son that is in a hurry for his inheritance, he confiscated all the riches of Ghent, its revenues, its houses, its artillery and munitions of war. Finding it still too well guarded, he destroyed also the Red Tower, the Tower of the *Trou de Crapaud*, the *Braampoort*, the *Steenpoort*, the *Waalpoort*, the *Ketelpoort*, and many another of its gates, all carved as they were and sculptured like jewels in stone.

And afterwards, when strangers came to Ghent, they would ask of one another :

" Can this indeed be Ghent whose marvels were on the lips of all—this city so desolated and brought low ? "

And the people of Ghent would make answer :

" Charles the Emperor has been to the city. He has ravished her sacred zone."

And so saying they would be filled with anger and with shame. And from the ruins of the city gates did the Emperor take away the bricks wherewith to build his castle.

For it was his will that Ghent should be utterly impoverished, that thereby he might make it impossible for her ever to oppose his proud designs, either by her labour or her industry or wealth ; therefore he condemned her to pay that share of the tax of 400,000 caroluses which she had previously refused him, and in addition 150,000 caroluses down, and 6000 more every year in perpetuity. Moreover, in earlier days the city had lent him money upon which he should have paid interest at the rate of 150 pounds gross annually. But he made himself remit by force the notes of credit, and by paying off his debt in this way he actually enriched himself.

Many and many a time had Ghent cherished him and succoured him, but now he struck her on the breast as it were with a dagger, looking for blood, since it seemed he had not there found milk enough.

Last shame of all, he cast his eye upon the bell that is called *Roelandt*; and the man who had sounded the alarm thereon, bidding all the citizens to defend the rights of their city, him he had bound and hung to the clapper of the bell. And he had no pity upon *Roelandt*, the very tongue of his mother, the tongue whereby she spake to all the land of Flanders, *Roelandt* the proud bell that sings of herself this song :

> *When I ring there is a fire*
> *When I peal there is a storm*
> *In the land of Flanders.*

And thinking that his mother had too loud a voice he carried away her bell. And the people of the country round would say that Ghent was dead, now that her son had wrenched away her tongue with his pincers of iron.

XX

In those days, which were days of spring, fresh and clear, when all the earth is in love, Soetkin was chatting by the open window, and Claes humming a tune, while Ulenspiegel was dressing up the dog Bibulus Schnouffius in a judge's bonnet. The dog plied his paws as though desirous of passing judgment upon some one, though in reality it was simply his way of trying to get rid of his ungainly head-gear.

All at once, Ulenspiegel shut the window and ran back into the room. Then he jumped upon the chairs and the table, reaching up towards the ceiling with his hands. Soetkin and Claes soon discovered the cause of this mad behaviour, for there was a tiny little bird, chirruping with fear, and cowering against a beam in the recess of the ceiling, and Ulenspiegel was trying to catch it. He had almost succeeded when Claes spoke out briskly and asked him:

"Why are you jumping about like this?"

"To catch the bird," answered Ulenspiegel, "and put him in a cage, and feed him with seeds, and make him sing for me."

Meantime the bird, crying in an agony of terror, flew back into the room, striking its head against the window-pane. Still Ulenspiegel went on trying to catch it, but suddenly the hand of Claes came down heavily upon his shoulder.

"Catch the bird if you can," said he, "put it in a cage, make it sing for your pleasure; but I also will put you in a cage that is fastened with strong bars of iron, and I will make you sing too. Then you, who like nothing better than to run about, will be able to do so no more; and you will be kept standing in the shade when you are chilly, and in the sun when you are hot. And, one Sunday, we shall all go out and forget to give you your food, and we shall not return again till Thursday, and then maybe we shall find our Tyl all stiff and starved to death."

Soetkin was crying at this picture, but Ulenspiegel started forward.

"What are you going to do?" asked Claes.

"Open the window for the bird to fly out," he answered.

And in fact the bird, which was a goldfinch, flew straight out through the window, and with a cry of joy mounted up into the air like an arrow, and then alighted upon a neigh-

bouring apple-tree, smoothing its wings with its beak, ruffling
its plumage. And all kinds of abuse did it sing in its bird
language, all directed against Ulenspiegel.

Then Claes said :

"O son of mine, take care that you never take away its
liberty from either man or beast, for liberty is the greatest
good in the world. Let every one be free, free to go out into
the sun when it is cold, and into the shade when it is hot.
And let God give judgment on His Sacred Majesty, he who,
not content with denying freedom of belief to the people of
Flanders, has now put all the noble city of Ghent into a cage
of slavery."

XXI

Now Philip was married to Marie of Portugal, and with
her he acquired her lands for the crown of Spain ; and together they had a son, Don Carlos, he who was afterwards
called " the mad " and " the cruel." And Philip had no
love for his wife.

The Queen was lying-in. She kept her bed, and by her side
were the maids of honour, the Duchess of Alba among them.

Oftentimes did Philip leave his wife to go and see the
burning of heretics. And all the gentlemen and ladies of
the Court did likewise. And thus also did the Duchess of
Alba and the other noble ladies whose duty it was to watch
by the Queen in her childbed.

Now at that time the ecclesiastical judges had seized a
certain sculptor of Flanders, a good Roman Catholic, on the
following charge : He had been commissioned, it seems, by a
certain monk to carve a wooden statue of Our Lady for a
certain sum, and on the monk refusing to pay the price which
had been agreed between them, the sculptor had slashed at the
face of the image with his chisel, saying that he would rather
destroy his work than let it go at the price of a piece of dirt.

He was straightway denounced by the monk as an icono-
clast, tortured most piteously and condemned to be burnt

alive. During the torture they had scalded the soles of his feet, so that he cried out as he passed along from the prison to the stake: "Cut my feet off! For God's sake cut my feet off!"

And Philip, hearing these cries from afar, was glad, though smiled he never a smile.

Queen Marie's dames of honour all left her, wishing to be present at the burning, and the last of all to desert her was the said Duchess of Alba, who, hearing the cries of the sculptor, could not forbear to witness the spectacle.

So, in the presence of King Philip and of his lords, princes, counts, equerries, and ladies, the sculptor was bound to the stake by a long chain. And all round the stake was a circle of flaming bundles of straw and fiery torches, the idea being that if he wished, the sculptor could be roasted very gently by keeping close to the stake in the centre of the circle, thus avoiding the full rigour of the fire.

And right curiously did they watch him, naked or almost naked as he was, and trying to stiffen his resolution against the heat of the fire.

Meanwhile Queen Marie was stricken with a great thirst, lying there alone on her bed of childbirth. And seeing the half of a melon on a plate, she dragged herself out of bed, and took hold of the melon and ate it all. But thereafter the cold substance of the melon made her to sweat and to shiver, and she lay upon the floor unable to move.

"Alas!" she cried, "would that there were some one to carry me back into bed that I might get warm again!"

Then it was that she heard the cry of the poor sculptor: "Cut off my feet! Cut off my feet!"

"Ah!" said the Queen, "is that some dog or other baying at my death?"

It was at this very moment that the sculptor, seeing around him none but the faces of Spaniards, his enemies, bethought him of Flanders, the land of valorous men, and he crossed his

42

arms on his breast, and dragging the long chain behind him, walked straight towards the outer circle of the straw and the flaming torches. And standing upright there, still with his arms crossed :

" This," cried he, " this is how the men of Flanders can die in the face of the tyrants of Spain. Cut off *their* feet—not mine—that they may be able no more to run into the way of crime. Flanders for ever ! Flanders for ever ! "

And the ladies clapped their hands, crying him mercy for the sake of his proud look.

And he died.

And Queen Marie shook all over her body, and she cried out, her teeth chattering together with the chill of approaching death. And her arms and legs grew stiff, and she said :

" Put me back into my bed that I may be warmed."

So she died.

And thus it was, according to the prophecy of Katheline the good sorceress, that Philip the King sowed everywhere he went the seeds of death, and blood, and tears.

XXII

But Ulenspiegel and Nele loved each other, and their love was true.

It was now the end of April. All the trees were in bloom, and every plant was swollen with sap, for May was near, the month of the peacock, flowered like a bouquet, the month that sends the nightingales singing aloud in the trees of all the earth.

Oftentimes would Nele and Ulenspiegel wander together along the roads. Nele would lean on the arm of Ulenspiegel, and hang round him with her two hands. Ulenspiegel loved this little game, and often did he pass his arm about Nele's waist, to hold her the better, as he said. And she was happy, but spake not a word.

Softly along the roads blew the wind, wafting the scent from the fields; the sea boomed in the distance, rocking lazily in the sun; Ulenspiegel seemed like some youthful devil, all pride; and Nele like a little saint from Paradise, half shy of her happiness.

She leant her head against Ulenspiegel's shoulder, and her hand was in his, and as they passed along he kissed her forehead, and her cheek, and her sweet lips. But still she spake no word.

After some hours they grew hot and thirsty, and they drank milk at the house of a peasant; and yet they were not refreshed. Then they sat them down on the grass by the side of the ditch, and Nele seemed pale and pensive, and Ulenspiegel looked at her, afraid that something was amiss.

" You are unhappy ? " said she.

" Yes," he admitted.

" But why ? " she asked him.

" I know not," said he. " But these apple-trees and cherry-trees all in flower, this air so warm that one would say it was charged with lightning, these daisies that open their blushing petals to the fields, and oh, the hawthorn, there, close by us in the hedge, all white . . . Will no one tell me why it is that I feel troubled, and always ready to die or to go to sleep ? And my heart beats so strangely when I hear the birds awaken in the trees, and when I see the swallows coming home ! Then I am fain to go away beyond the sun and beyond the moon. And sometimes I am cold, and then again I am hot. Ah, Nele ! would that I were no longer a creature of this low world ! Verily I would give my life a thousand times to her that would love me ! "

Yet Nele spake not at all, but smiling at her ease sat looking at Ulenspiegel.

XXIII

One Day of All Souls, Ulenspiegel went forth from Notre Dame with certain other vagabonds of his own age. Among

44

NELE AND ULENSPIEGEL

them was Lamme Goedzak, who seemed strayed among them like a lamb in the midst of a herd of wolves. Lamme treated them with drinks all round, for his mother, as her custom was on Sundays and feast days, had given him three *patards*.

So he went with his companions to the tavern *In dem Rooden Schildt*—at the sign of the Red Shield. Jan van Liebeke kept the house, and he served them with *dobbel knollaert* from Courtrai.

They began to be warmed with the drink, and the talk turned on the subject of prayer, and Ulenspiegel declared quite openly that, for his part, he thought that Masses for the dead did nobody any good, except the priests who said them.

Now in that company there was a Judas, who went and denounced Ulenspiegel for a heretic. And in spite of the tears of Soetkin, and the entreaties of Claes, Ulenspiegel was seized and taken prisoner. He remained shut up in a cellar for the space of a month and three days without seeing a soul. The jailor himself consumed three-quarters of the ration that was given him for food.

During all this time the authorities were informing themselves as to Ulenspiegel's reputation—whether it was good or whether it was bad. They found that there was not much to be said against him except that he was a lively sort of customer, always railing against his neighbours. But they could not find that he had ever spoken evil of Our Lord God, or of Madame the Virgin, nor yet of the Saints. On this account the sentence passed on him was a light one, for he might easily have been condemned to have his face branded with a hot iron and to be flogged till the blood flowed. But in consideration of his youth, the judges merely sentenced him to walk in his shirt behind the priests barefoot and hatless, and holding a candle in his hand. And this he was to do on the Feast of the Ascension, in the first procession that left the church.

So it was done, and when the procession was on the point

of turning back, Ulenspiegel was made to stop beneath the porch of Notre Dame, and there cry out aloud :

"Thanks be to our Lord Jesus! Thanks be to the reverend priests! Sweet are their prayers unto the souls in purgatory; nay, they are filled with every virtue of refreshment! For each *Ave* is even as a bucket of water poured upon the backs of those who are being punished, and every *Pater* is a tubful!"

And the people heard him with great devotion, and not without a smile.

On Whit-Sunday the same proceeding had to be gone through, and Ulenspiegel followed again in the procession with nothing on but his shirt, and with his head bare, and no shoes on his feet, and holding a candle in his hand. On returning to the church he stood up in the porch, holding the candle most reverently in his hand, and then in a high, clear voice (yet not without sundry waggish grimaces) spake as follows :

" If the prayers of all good Christians are very comforting to the souls in purgatory, how much more so must be those of the Dean of Notre Dame, a holy man and perfect in the performance of every virtue. Verily, his prayers assuage the flames of fire in such wise that they are transformed all of a sudden into ice. But yet be sure that not an atom of it goes to refresh the devils that are in hell."

And again the people hearkened to what he said with great devotion. But some of them smiled, and the Dean smiled too, in his grim ecclesiastical way.

After that, Ulenspiegel was condemned to banishment from the land of Flanders for the space of three years, on condition that he went to Rome on pilgrimage and brought back with him the papal absolution. For this sentence Claes had to pay three florins : but he gave an extra florin to his son, and bought him a pilgrim's habit.

Ulenspiegel was heart-broken when he came to say good-

bye to Claes and Soetkin on the day of his departure. He
embraced them both, and his mother was all in tears ; but
she accompanied him far on his way, and Claes went too,
and many of the townsmen and townswomen.

When they were home again Claes said to his wife :

" Good wife, it is very hard that such a boy should be
condemned to this cruel punishment and all for a few silly
words."

" Why, you are crying, my man ! " said Soetkin.
" Truly, you love him more than you like to show. Yes,
you are sobbing now with a man's sobs, sobs that are like
unto the tears of a lion."

But he answered her not.

As for Nele, she had gone to hide herself in the barn, so
that none might see that she also wept for Ulenspiegel.
But she followed afar after Soetkin and Claes and the other
townsfolk ; and when she saw her lover disappearing in the
distance, she ran after him and threw herself on his neck.

" In Italy you will meet many beautiful ladies," she said.

" I do not know about their being beautiful," he replied,
" but fresh like thee—no. For they are all parched with the
sun."

They walked a long way side by side, and Ulenspiegel
seemed thoughtful, muttering from time to time :

" I'll make 'em pay—I'll make 'em pay for their Masses
for the dead ! "

" What Masses are those you speak of ? " Nele inquired.
" And who is to pay for them ? "

Ulenspiegel answered :

" All the deans, *curés*, clerks, beadles and the rest, both
superior and inferior, who feed us with their trash. See now,
if I had happened to be a strong working man they would
have robbed me of the value of three years' labour by making
me thus to go on this pilgrimage. But as things are, it is the
poor Claes who pays. Ah, but they shall give me back my

47

three years a hundredfold, and with their own money I myself will sing for them their Masses for the dead!"

"Alas, Tyl!" said Nele, "be prudent, or they will have you burnt alive."

"I am fireproof," answered Ulenspiegel.

And they parted from one another, she all in tears, he heart-broken and angry.

XXIV

Once in the open country, Ulenspiegel shook himself like a dog, or like a bird that has regained its liberty, and his heart was cheered by the trees and fields and the bright sunshine.

When he had walked on thus for three days he came to the outskirts of Brussels, and to the wealthy township of Uccle. And there, passing in front of the inn with the sign of the Trumpet, his attention was drawn to a most heavenly odour of fricassee. A little urchin who stood by was also sniffing the delightful perfume of the sauce, and Ulenspiegel asked him in whose honour it was that there rose to heaven such odour of festal incense. The boy made answer that the Guild of the Jolly Face was to meet at the inn that evening after vespers, to celebrate the deliverance of the town by the women and girls of olden time.

Now in the distance Ulenspiegel saw a high pole with a popinjay on the top of it, and the pole was set in the ground, and round it were a company of women armed with bows and arrows. He asked the boy if women were become archers nowadays?

The boy, still sniffing greedily the savour of the sauces, replied that in the days of the Good Duke the very bows that were now being used by those women had been the means of killing over a hundred brigands.

Ulenspiegel desired to know further concerning this matter, but the boy said that he could tell no more, so hungry was he, unless forsooth Ulenspiegel would give him a *patard* with which he might buy food and drink. This Ulenspiegel did, for he felt sorry for him.

No sooner had the boy received the *patard* than he rushed into the tavern like a fox to the hen-house, and presently reappeared in triumph with half a sausage and a large loaf of bread.

And now Ulenspiegel was suddenly aware of a sweet sound of viols and tabors, and soon he saw a number of women dancing together, and among them a woman of great beauty with a chain of gold hanging round her neck.

The boy, who had by this time assuaged his hunger and was grinning with delight, informed Ulenspiegel that the beautiful woman was the Queen of Archery, that her name was Mietje, and that she was wife to Messire Renonckel, alderman of the parish. Then he asked Ulenspiegel to give him six *liards* for a drink. Ulenspiegel gave him the money, and when he had thus eaten and drunk his fill the urchin sat himself down in the sun and fell to picking his teeth with his nails.

When the women archers noticed Ulenspiegel standing there in his pilgrim's habit, they came and began to dance round him in a ring, crying :

" Hail pilgrim, hail ! Do you come from far away, you handsome pilgrim boy ? "

Ulenspiegel, thinking sadly of Nele, thus made answer :

" I come from Flanders, a lovely land and filled with lovesome girls."

" What crime have you committed ? " asked the women, stopping in their dance.

" I dare not confess it, so great it was," said he.

They asked him the reason why it was needful for him to journey thus with a pilgrim's staff and wallet, and those scalloped oysters that are the sign of the pilgrim.

" The reason is," he replied, not quite truthfully, " that I said that Masses for the dead are advantageous to the priests."

"True, they bring many a sounding *denier* to the priests," they answered; "but are they not also of advantage to the souls in purgatory!"

"I have never been there," answered Ulenspiegel.

"Will you come dine with us?" said the prettiest of the archers.

"Willingly would I dine with you," said he, "and dine *off* you into the bargain! You and all your companions in turn, for you are morsels fit for a king, more delicate to swallow than any ortolan or thrush or snipe!"

"Nay," they answered, "but we are not for sale."

"Then perhaps you will *give*?" he asked them.

"Yea, verily," they laughed, "a good box on the ear to such as are too bold. And if needs were we would beat you now like a bundle of corn!"

"Thank you," he said, "I will go without the beating."

"Well then," they said, "come in to dinner."

So he followed them into the inn yard, glad for their fresh young faces. And thereafter he saw the Brethren of the Jolly Face themselves, who were now entering the yard with great ceremony, and by their own jolly appearance living up most conspicuously to the name of their Guild.

They scrutinized Ulenspiegel with some curiosity, till one of the women informed them who he was—a pilgrim they had picked up on the road, and whom, being a good red-face like unto their husbands and their sweethearts, they had invited to share in the entertainment. The men were agreeable to this proposal, and one of them addressed himself to Ulenspiegel:

"Pilgrim on pilgrimage, what say you now to continuing your pilgrimage across some sauce and fricassee?"

"I shall have need of my seven-league boots," answered Ulenspiegel.

Now as he was following them into the festal hall, he noticed twelve blind men coming along the Paris road. And as they passed they were lamenting most piteously

their hunger and thirst. But Ulenspiegel said to himself
that they should dine that night like kings, and all at the
expense of the Dean of Uccle himself, and in memory of the
Masses for the dead.

He accosted them, saying :

" Here are nine florins for you. Come in to dinner. Do
you not smell the good smell of fricassee ? "

" Ah ! " they cried, " for the last half-league, and without
hope ! "

" Now you can eat your fill," said Ulenspiegel, " for you
have nine florins."

But he had not really given them anything.

" The Lord bless you," they said. For being blind, each
man believed his neighbour had been given the money. And
shown the way by Ulenspiegel, they all sat down at a small
table while the Brethren of the Jolly Face took their seats at
a long one, together with their wives and their daughters.

Then, with the complete assurance that comes from the
possession of nine florins :

" Mine host," cried the blind men insolently, " give us
now to eat and to drink of your best."

The landlord, who had heard tell of the nine florins and
thought that they were safe in the blind men's purse, asked
them what they would like for their dinner.

Then they all began to talk at once at the top of their
voices :

" Bacon and peas, hotchpotch of beef and veal, chicken
and lamb ! And where are the sausages—were they made for
the dogs, pray ? And who is he that has smelt out the black
and white puddings in the passage without collaring them
for us ? I used to be able to see them, alas, in the days when
my poor eyes were bright as candles ! And where is the
buttered *koekebakken* of Anderlecht ? Sizzling in the frying-
pan, juicy and crackling, enough to make a fish thirsty for
drink ! Ho there ! But who will bring me eggs and ham, or

51

ham and eggs, twin friends of my palate ? And where are
you, you *choesels*, that float in a heavenly mess of meats and
kidneys, coxcombs, sweetbreads, ox-tails, lamb's feet, with
many onions, pepper, cloves, nutmegs, all in a stew, and three
pints at least of best white wine for sauce ? And who will
bring you to me divine, chitterlings, you that are so good
that one does not utter a word while you are being
swallowed ! And they come straight from Luyleckerland, a
land bursting with fatness and filled with happy lazy folk,
whose passion for good things to eat is never assuaged ! And
where are you, dried leaves of autumns past ? Now quick
there ! Bring me a leg of mutton with broad beans. And for
me, some pig's ears grilled with bread-crumbs. And for me,
a chaplet of ortolans. Verily the snipe shall figure the
Paters, and a fat capon the *Credo*."

Mine host answered quietly :

" I will bring you an omelette made with sixty eggs.
And as sign-posts to guide your spoons, I will plant fifty
black puddings in the midst, all smoking on a veritable
mountain of good cheer ; and from the top of all some *dobbel
peterman* shall flow down like a river on every side."

At this the mouths of the poor blind men began to water
indeed, and they said :

" Then serve us, pray, and that right quickly with the
mountain, the sign-posts, and the river ! "

And the Brethren of the Jolly Face, who were now all
seated at table with their wives, remarked to Ulenspiegel that
this should be called the Day of the Invisible Feast ; for
that the blind men could not see what they were eating, and
thus, poor things, were deprived of half their pleasure.

At last it came—the omelette all garnished with cress and
parsley, carried by mine host himself and four of his cooks—
and the blind men desired to fall to incontinently, and at
once began to set their paws upon it. But mine host was
determined to serve each of them fairly, and, however difficult

it might be, to make sure that each trencher had its just portion.

The women archers were filled with pity to see the blind men gobbling and sighing with joy at what was set before them. For in truth they were half starved, and they swallowed down the puddings as though they had been oysters. And the *dobbel peterman* flowed into their stomachs as it had been a cataract falling down from some lofty mountain.

When at length they had cleared their trenchers, they demanded yet further supplies of *koekebakken*, ortolans, and fricassees. Mine host, however, only provided a great platter of beef and veal and mutton bones, all swimming in a most goodly sauce. But he did not divide it properly. So that when they had well dipped their bread in the sauce, and eke their hands right up to the elbows, yet drew not out anything but bones of cutlet of veal or mutton, each man fell straightway to imagining that his neighbour had got hold of all the meat, and they began to fight among themselves, hitting out most furiously one against another with the bones.

The Brethren of the Jolly Face laughed heartily at this, but being charitably disposed, each put a portion of his own dinner into the blind men's platter. So now if one of the blind went searching for a new bone with which to carry on the fight, he would put his hand belike upon a thrush or chicken or a lark or two ; and all the time the women, holding their heads well backwards, kept pouring into the mouths of the blind long draughts of Brussels wine, and when they reached out with their hands to feel, as blind men will, whence came these rivulets of ambrosia, they would catch oftentimes at a woman's skirt, and try to hold it fast. But quickly the skirt would make its escape.

Thus they laughed and drank, ate and sang, enjoying themselves hugely. Some of them, when they found that women were present, ran through the hall all maddened with amorous desire. But the malicious girls kept out of their way, hiding behind the Brethren of the Jolly Face. And one of them would say : " Come, kiss me ! " And when the blind victim tried to do so he would find himself kissing not a girl at all but the bearded face of a man, who would reward him with a cuff on the cheek as like as not.

And the Brethren of the Jolly Face began to sing, and the blind men sang also, and the merry women smiled with fond delight to see their pleasure. But when the juicy hours were past, it was the turn of the innkeeper, who came forward, saying :

" Now you have eaten your fill, my friends, and drunk your fill. You owe me seven florins."

But each of the blind men swore that he had no purse, and asserted that it was one of the others who carried it. Thereat arose a further dispute, and they began to hit out at one another with feet and hands and heads ; but they mostly missed their mark, striking out at random, while the Brethren of the Jolly Face, entering into the fun, took care to keep them apart, so that their blows rained down upon the empty air—all save one, which happened unfortunately to strike the face of the innkeeper, who straightway fell into a rage and ransacked all their pockets. But he found there nothing but an old scapular, seven *liards*, three breeches-buttons, and a few rosaries.

At last he threatened to throw the whole lot of them into the pig-trough, and leave them there with nothing but bread and water to eat till they paid what they owed.

" Let me go surety for them," said Ulenspiegel.

" Certainly," answered the innkeeper, " if some one will also go surety for you."

This the Brethren of the Jolly Face at once offered to do, but Ulenspiegel refused them.

" No," he said, " the Dean of Uccle shall be my surety. I will go and find him."

To be sure it was those Masses for the dead that he was

THE FEAST OF THE BLIND MEN

thinking of. And when he had found the Dean he told him a story of how the innkeeper of the Trumpet Inn was possessed by the Devil, and how he could talk of nothing but " pigs " and " blind men "—something or other about pigs eating the blind, and the blind eating the pigs under various infamous forms of roast meats and fricassees. While these attacks were on, the innkeeper, so Ulenspiegel affirmed, would break up all the furniture in the inn ; and he begged the Dean to come and deliver the poor man from the wicked devil that possessed him.

The Dean promised to do so, but he said he could not come at the moment (for he was busy with the accounts of the Chapter, trying to make something out of them for himself). Seeing that the Dean was growing impatient, Ulenspiegel said that he would return and bring with him the innkeeper's wife in order that the Dean might speak to her himself.

" Very well," said the Dean.

So Ulenspiegel came again to the innkeeper and said to him :

" I have just seen the Dean, and he is willing to go surety for the blind men. Do you keep watch over them, and let your wife come with me, and the Dean will repeat to her what I have just told you."

" Go, wife," said the innkeeper.

So the innkeeper's wife went with Ulenspiegel to the Dean, who was still at his accounts and busy with the same problem. When, therefore, he saw Ulenspiegel and the woman, he made an impatient gesture that they should withdraw, saying at the same time :

" It is all right. I will come to the help of your husband in a day or two."

And Ulenspiegel went back to the inn and said to himself :

" Seven florins shall he pay ; seven florins. And that shall be the first of my Masses for the dead ! "

55

And Ulenspiegel departed from that place, and the blind men likewise.

XXV

Now in those days Katheline had effected a cure, by means of herbs, on three sheep, an ox, and a pig, all belonging to a certain man named Speelman. She also attempted to cure a cow, the property of one Jan Beloen, but in this she was not successful. Jan Beloen promptly accused her of being a witch, asserting that she had laid a charm on the animal, inasmuch as all the time she was giving the herbs she had caressed it and talked to it, in the Devil's own language, as was evident—for what business has an honest Christian woman to go talking with an animal. . . . ?

Jan Beloen added that he was a neighbour of Speelman's, the man whose ox had been cured, together with three sheep and a pig as aforesaid, and if Katheline had now killed his cow, it was doubtless at the instigation of Speelman, who was jealous at seeing his, Beloen's, land better and more profitably cultivated than his own. Pieter Meulmeester, a man of good life and reputation, and Jan Beloen himself both testified that Katheline was commonly reputed to be a witch by the people of Damme, and that she had certainly killed the cow ; and on this testimony Katheline was arrested and condemned to be tortured until she had confessed her crimes and malpractices.

She was cross-examined by a certain alderman who was notorious for his ill-temper, for he was accustomed to drink brandy all the day long. And he ordered her to be placed on the seat of torture in the presence of himself and the members of the Town Council.

The torturer put her on the seat stark naked, and then shaved off her hair, looking carefully to see that no charm was concealed anywhere about her person. Finding none, he bound her with cords to the seat of torture. And she said :

Katheline at the Torture

" It shames me to be naked before these men.   O Mother Mary, let me die ! "

The torturer then wrapped some damp cloths round her breast and body and legs, and raising the bench upright he proceeded to pour great quantities of hot water down her throat so that her stomach became all swollen.   Then he let the bench down again.

The alderman asked Katheline if she would now acknowledge her crime.   She made a sign in the negative.   And the torturer poured more hot water into her ; but this Katheline brought all up again.

Then by the advice of the doctor she was released.   But she did not speak a word, only beat her breast as much as to say that the hot water had burned her.   When the torturer saw that she was recovered from this first ordeal, he said to her :

" Confess that you are a witch, and that you laid a charm on the cow."

" I will confess no such thing," replied Katheline.   " I am here in your power.   Nevertheless, I tell you that an animal can die of an illness, just as a man can, and in spite of all the help of surgeons and of doctors.   And I swear by Our Lord Christ who was pleased to die upon the Cross for our sins, that I wished to do no harm to this cow, but simply to cure her by well-known remedies."

Thereat the alderman was angry and cried out :

" This devil's drab, she cannot go on lying for ever ! Put her to the second torture."

Then he drank a large glass of brandy.

The torturer meanwhile sat Katheline down on the lid of an oak coffin which was placed on trestles.   Now the coffin-lid was pointed like a roof, and the edge of it was as sharp as a sword.   A great fire was burning in the fireplace, for it was the month of November.   Katheline, seated on the edge of the coffin-lid, had her feet shod in shoes of new leather several sizes too small for her, and then she was placed in

57

front of the fire. When she began to feel the sharp wood of the coffin-lid cutting into her flesh, and when her shoes began to shrink under the heat of the fire, Katheline cried aloud :

"Oh, agony! Will no one give me a draught of black poison ?"

"Put her nearer the fire," said the alderman.

Then he inquired of her :

"How often, pray, have you ridden on a broom to the Witches' Sabbath ? And how many times have you caused the corn to wither in the ear, and the fruit on the tree, and the babe in the womb of its mother ? And turned most loving brothers into sworn enemies, and sisters into rivals full of hatred ?"

Katheline would have answered if she had been able. But she could only move her arms, as if to say "No." But the alderman said :

"I see she will not speak till she has felt her witch's fat all melting in the fire. Put her nearer."

Katheline cried out. But the alderman said :

"You had better ask Satan, your friend, to refresh you."

And now her shoes were beginning to smoke in the heat of the fire, so that she made a gesture as if to try and take them off.

"Ask Satan to help you," said the alderman.

Ten o'clock struck. It was the madman's dinner hour. And he retired with the torturer and the clerk of the court, leaving Katheline alone in front of the fire in the place of torture.

An hour later they returned. Katheline was still sitting there stiff and motionless. The clerk said :

"I think she is dead."

The alderman commanded the torturer to remove Katheline from the coffin-lid, and to take off the shoes from her feet. This he could not do, so that he was forced to cut them, and Katheline's feet were exposed to view, all red and bleeding. The alderman, whose thoughts were still with his dinner, gazed at her without a word. But after a while she came to her senses, and fell upon the ground, nor was she able to get up again in spite of many attempts. Then she said to the alderman:

"Once you desired me for your wife. But now you shall have none of me! *Four times three is the sacred number, and my husband is the thirteenth.*"

The alderman was going to answer her, but she forestalled him:

"Be silent. His hearing is more delicate than that of the archangel in heaven who counts the heart-beats of the just. Why are you so late? *Four times three is the sacred number.* He killeth those who hold me in desire."

The alderman said:

"It seems she welcomes the devil to her bed!"

"The pains of the torture have turned her brain," said the clerk.

So Katheline was taken back into prison. And three days later there was a meeting of the aldermen in the Council Hall; and after some deliberation Katheline was condemned to suffer the ordeal by fire.

She was taken to the grand market of Damme by the torturer and his assistants. There she was made to mount the scaffold. In the square were assembled the provost, the herald, and the judges. The herald sounded his trumpet thrice, then turned towards the crowd and made the following announcement:

"The Council of Damme," he cried, "having taken pity upon the woman Katheline, have decreed that punishment shall not be exacted to the full extremity of the rigour of our laws. Nevertheless, in witness that she is a sorceress, her hair shall be burned, she shall pay a fine of twenty *carolus d'or*, and she shall be banished from the territory of Damme for the space of three years, under penalty of losing one of her limbs."

And at this rough gentleness the people broke into applause.

Then the torturer tied Katheline to the stake, placed on her shorn scalp a wig of tow, and held it in the fire. And the tow burned for a long time, and Katheline cried aloud and wept.

Then they released her, and she was put in a cart and taken away outside the territory of Damme. She could not walk at all, because of her feet that were burned.

XXVI

Ulenspiegel, meanwhile, had arrived in his wanderings at the fish-market at Liége. There he descried a tall young fellow carrying under his arm a net filled with all sorts of poultry, and another net also which he was rapidly filling with haddock, trout, eels, and pike.

Ulenspiegel recognized him as none other than his old friend Lamme Goedzak.

"What are you doing here, Lamme?" he said.

"You must know," Lamme answered, "that many people have lately emigrated from Flanders to this gentle land of Liége. As for me, I follow my loves. And you?"

"I am on the look-out for a master to serve for my daily bread," said Ulenspiegel.

"Bread is a dry sort of nourishment," said Lamme. "You would do better to try a chaplet of ortolans with a thrush for the *Credo*."

"You have plenty of money?" Ulenspiegel inquired.

Lamme Goedzak made answer:

"I have lost my father and mother, and that young sister of mine that used to beat me so. I shall inherit all their property, and now I am living with a one-eyed servant who is very learned in the noble art of making fricassees."

" Would you like me to carry your fish and your poultry for you ? " suggested Ulenspiegel.

" Yes," said Lamme.

And together they began to wander through the market. All at once Lamme said to his companion :

" You are mad. Do you know why ? "

" No," said Ulenspiegel.

" Because you go carrying fish and poultry in your hand instead of in your stomach."

" You are right, Lamme," said Ulenspiegel ; " but since I have lacked bread, ortolans will not even look at me."

" You shall eat your fill of them," said Lamme, " and serve me too, if my cook takes a fancy to you."

While they were walking along, Lamme pointed out to Ulenspiegel a beautiful young girl, who was walking through the market. She wore a silk dress and gazed at Lamme with sweet and gentle eyes. An old man, her father, walked just behind, carrying two nets, one filled with fish, the other with game.

" See that girl ? " said Lamme, pointing at her. " I am going to marry her."'

" Oh ! " said Ulenspiegel, " I know her. She is a Flemish maid from Zotteghem. She lives in the rue Vinave-d'Isle, and the neighbours say that she lets her mother sweep the road in front of the house in her stead, while her own father irons her underclothing."

To this Lamme made no answer, but exclaimed delightedly :

" She looked at me just now ! "

By this time they were come to Lamme's lodging, near the Pont-des-Arches. They knocked at the door, and a one-eyed servant opened to them. Ulenspiegel saw that she was old, scraggy, lank, and fierce of aspect.

Lamme addressed her as *La Sanginne*, and inquired if she would take Ulenspiegel to help in the kitchen.

" I will give him a trial," she said.

" Then take him," said Lamme, " and let him also make trial of the delights of your kitchen."

La Sanginne put three black puddings on the table, a pint of ale, and a large loaf of bread. Ulenspiegel set to with a will, and Lamme began to nibble at one of the puddings.

" Know you," Lamme asked presently, " where it is that our souls abide ? "

" No, Lamme," said Ulenspiegel.

" In our stomachs," Lamme told him, " so they can keep them excavated continually, and for ever renew in our bodies the impulse for life. And who are the best companions for a man ? I'll tell you. The best companions for a man are all good and jolly things to eat, and wine from the Meuse to crown all ! "

" True," said Ulenspiegel. " A pudding is good company to a solitary soul."

" He's still hungry," said Lamme to La Sanginne. " Give him some more." And the woman served him with a second portion of pudding—white this time.

While Ulenspiegel went on eating, Lamme grew thoughtful.

" When I die," said he, " my stomach will die with me, and down there in purgatory they will leave me to fast, and I shall have to carry my poor belly about with me, all empty and limp."

" I like the black ones best," said Ulenspiegel.

" You have eaten six already," said La Sanginne, " and you won't have any more."

" You may be sure," said Lamme, " that you will be well treated here, and you will have just the same to eat as I do."

" I shall remember this promise of yours," said Ulenspiegel. But seeing that what his friend had told him was the truth, Ulenspiegel was well content, and the puddings that he had swallowed gave him such courage that on that very day he polished the kettles and the pots and the pans till they shone like the sun. And he lived happily in that house, frequenting willingly the kitchen and the wine-cellar, and leaving the loft to the cats.

One day La Sanginne had two poulets to roast, and she asked Ulenspiegel to turn the spit while she went to market for some herbs for a seasoning. The two poulets being well roasted, Ulenspiegel took one of them and ate it. When La Sanginne returned from the market she remarked :

" There were two poulets, but now I can only see one."

" Just open your other eye," answered Ulenspiegel, " and you will see the two of them all right ! "

But she was angry, and went to Lamme Goedzak to tell him what had happened. Lamme came down into the kitchen and said to Ulenspiegel :

" Why do you make fun of my serving-maid ? There were certainly two poulets."

" There *were*," said Ulenspiegel, " but when I came you told me that I was to eat and drink just as much as you. There were two poulets. Very well. I have eaten one, and you will eat the other. My pleasure is over. Yours is still to come. Are you not happier than I ? "

" Yes," said Lamme smiling, " but just you do what La Sanginne tells you, and you'll find your work halved."

" I will be careful to do as you say," said Ulenspiegel.

So every time that La Sanginne told him to do anything he did but the half of it. If she asked him to go and draw two pails of water he would only bring back one ; and if she told him to go and fill a pot of ale at the cask, he would pour the half of it down his throat on the way—and so on and so on.

At last La Sanginne grew tired of these goings on, and she told Lamme that either this good-for-nothing fellow must leave the house or she must leave herself.

Lamme descended on Ulenspiegel and told him :

63

" You'll have to go, my son, notwithstanding that you
have looked so much better in health since you have been
here. Listen to that cock crowing. And it's two o'clock
of the afternoon ! That means rain. I am sorry to have to
put you out of doors in bad weather. But there, my son,
you know that La Sanginne is the guardian angel of my life,
with her lovely fricassees. If she were to leave me I might
die a speedy death. I cannot risk it. Go then, my boy,
and God be with you, and here are three florins and this
string of saveloys to liven your journey."

And Ulenspiegel departed, crestfallen and with many
regrets for Lamme and his kitchen.

XXVII

There was a rumour abroad that the Emperor Charles
was going to annul the right of the monks to inherit the estates
of those who happened to die in their convents, a thing which
was very displeasing to the Pope.

One day when Ulenspiegel was come to fish from the banks
of the river Meuse, he was thinking to himself that by the
above action the Emperor would stand to profit both ways,
since he would inherit the said estates, while the family of the
deceased would inherit nothing at all. Pondering these
thoughts, he carefully baited his hook, and then sat down by
the river-side. And he began to nibble at a piece of stale
brown bread, regretting the while that he had no good
Romagna wine wherewith to wash it down. Still, he thought,
one cannot always have everything just as one would like.
And all the time he kept on throwing little pieces of his bread
into the water, saying to himself that no man deserves a meal
who will not share it with his neighbours.

Now it was that a gudgeon came upon the scene, attracted
in the first place by the odour of bread-crumbs ; and he licked
up the bread with his lips and opened his mouth for more,
thinking no doubt in his innocence that the bread would fall

into his gullet of itself. But while gazing thus in the air the gudgeon was suddenly swallowed up by a treacherous pike who had hurled himself upon him like a flash of lightning.

Now the pike played a similar trick upon a carp who was catching flies on the top of the water without any fear of danger. And after this good meal the pike stayed motionless below the surface of the water, disdainful of the smaller fry, who, indeed, were only too glad to swim away from him of their own accord and as fast as ever they could. But while the pike was taking his ease in this manner, a second pike came up; and he was a hungry pike, and his mouth was open wide, for as yet he had not breakfasted. With a bound the new arrival threw himself upon his brother, and a furious combat ensued. They lashed at one another with their fins, the water was red with their blood. The pike that had eaten defended himself but feebly against the assaults of the hungry one; nevertheless, backing a little, he took courage again and threw himself like a bullet against his adversary. The latter awaited this new attack with open jaws, which did not close until more than half of his assailant's head had disappeared between them. Now they tried to free themselves, but could not because of the hooked teeth of the one that had become embedded in the flesh of the other. And so they battled against each other in despair. Nor did they notice, interlocked as they were, the strong fish-hook at the end of a silken cord, which rose towards them from the depths of the water. In another moment it had embedded itself in the body of the pike that had dined, and the two struggling fish found themselves drawn out of the water and laid together on the grass without the least deference.

As he killed them Ulenspiegel said:

"Ha ha, my little pikes, I will call you the Pope and the Emperor, that prey ever one upon the other; but I, forsooth, am the Common Man that shall catch you on his hook, in God's good time, and make an end of your battles!"

65

XXVIII

In the meantime Nele was taking care of Katheline, who was still out of her mind and who called continually upon Hanske, her ice-cold lover. But sometimes Nele would leave her mother safely guarded in the house of some kindly neighbour, and herself would wander far and wide and all alone, even unto Antwerp, searching ever, among the ships on the river, or along the dusty roads, for Ulenspiegel.

And at home, also, in the house of Claes, it was evil days. Claes worked sadly on his land alone, for there was not enough work for two. And Soetkin stayed in the cottage by herself, cooking the beans which formed their daily fare in a hundred different ways, so that she might have something to enliven her husband's appetite. And she sang and laughed all the time, so that he might not be grieved by seeing her unhappy.

One day a man on horseback drew up in front of the cottage. He was dressed all in black, he was very thin, and very sad of countenance.

" Is any one within ? " he asked.

" God bless your sadness," answered Soetkin, " but am I a phantom, that seeing me here you must yet inquire if there is any one within ? "

" Where is your father ? " asked the horseman.

" If my father's name is Claes, he is over there," Soetkin told him. " You will find him sowing corn."

The horseman departed in the direction in which she had pointed, and Soetkin also went her way ruefully, for this was the sixth time that she had had to go to the baker's to buy bread with no money to pay for it.

On returning empty-handed to the cottage, Soetkin was amazed to see Claes coming down the road triumphantly seated on the horse of the man in black. He looked very proud of himself, and the man in black walked by his side holding the horse's bridle. Hanging at his side, Claes held a leathern bag which appeared to be full of things. Dismounting from the horse, Claes embraced his companion, gave him a playful pat upon the back, and then, shaking the bag, cried out in a loud voice :

" Long life to Josse, my brother, the good hermit of Meyborg ! May God keep him in joy and fatness, in happiness and health ! Our Josse, patron of plenty, and of all abundance, and rich soups ! "

And so saying he took up the sack and deposited it upon the table. But Soetkin said sadly :

" My good man, we shall not eat this day. The baker has refused to give me any bread."

" Bread ? " cried Claes, opening the sack and letting a river of golden coins roll out on the table. " Bread ? Here is bread and butter, meat, wine, beer ! Here are hams, marrowbones, pasties, ortolans, fatted poulets, castrelins, all just as you might find them in the houses of the rich ! Bread indeed ! Here are casks of beer and kegs of wine ! Mad must be the baker who will refuse to give us bread. Verily we will deal at his shop no more ! "

" But, my good man ! " said Soetkin amazed.

" Nay, listen," said Claes, " and make the most of your good fortune. For these are the facts. Katheline, it seems, has lately been to Meyborg in Germany, and Nele with her, on a visit to my eldest brother Josse, who dwells there as a hermit. Nele told my brother how that we were living in poverty, notwithstanding that we work so hard. And now, if we are to believe this good messenger "—and here Claes pointed to the black horseman—" Josse has left the holy Roman religion and abandoned himself to the heresy of Luther."

The man in black made answer :

" It is they that are heretics, they who follow the cult of the Scarlet Woman. For the Pope is a cheat and a trader in holy things."

"Oh!" cried Soetkin, "speak not so loud, sir. You will have us burned alive, all three."

"Well," continued Claes, "it appears that Josse has made known to this good messenger that inasmuch as he is going to fight in the army of Frederic of Saxony, and is bringing him fifty armed men fully equipped, he has no need of much money to leave it to the hands of some wretch of a landsknecht, now that he himself is going to the war. Therefore, says he, take it to my brother Claes, and render to him, with my blessing, these seven hundred florins. Tell him to live virtuously, and to ponder the salvation of his soul."

"Yea, verily," said the horseman, "now is the time. For God will reward every man according to his works, and every man according to his merit."

"Good sir," said Claes, "it is not forbidden, I trust, to rejoice in the meantime at this good news? Deign, then, to stay with us, and we will celebrate our fortune with a nice dinner of tripe, well boiled, and a knuckle of that ham which I saw just now at the pork-butcher's. Of a truth, it looked so plump and tasty that my teeth almost shot out of my mouth to close thereon."

"Alas!" said the stranger, "the foolish make merry while the eye of the Lord is yet upon them."

"Come now, messenger," said Claes, "will you eat and drink with us or will you not?"

The man answered: "It will be time enough for the faithful to think about such earthly joys when mighty Babylon has fallen."

Seeing Claes and Soetkin cross themselves, he made as though to leave them. But Claes said to him:

"Since you persist in leaving us without accepting of our hospitality, will you at least give to my brother the kiss of peace on my behalf, and look after him well at the wars."

"That will I," said the man.

And he departed from them, while Soetkin went to make her preparations for celebrating their good fortune.

Now it was quickly noised abroad through the town that Claes that was once so poor had now become rich through the generosity of his brother Josse. And the Dean of Damme was heard to say that it was Katheline no doubt who had laid a charm on Josse, and he said this because Claes, although he had received a large sum of money from his brother, had given not so much as a single vestment to Notre Dame. But Claes and Soetkin were happy again, Claes working in the fields or looking after his business of charcoal-burning, while Soetkin attended to her home right valiantly. Yet still was she sorrowful at heart, scanning ever with her eyes the open road if perchance she might see her son Ulenspiegel returning back to her. And thus it was these three lived on and experienced the happiness which comes from God while waiting for that which was going to come to them from men.

XXIX

The Emperor Charles had received a letter from England, from Philip, who was now married to the Queen of that country.

"SIR AND FATHER," the letter ran,—"It is matter of sore displeasure to me that I should have to live in a country like this where the accursed heretics swarm like fleas and worms and locusts. Fire and sword are needed to remove them from the trunk of that tree of life which is our Holy Mother the Church. And, as if this were not trouble enough, I have also to put up with being regarded not as a King but merely as the husband of the Queen ; for in very truth apart from her I am destitute of all authority. And the English make mock of me, spreading broadcast the most shameful pamphlets which assert that I am being bribed by the Pope to afflict their country with every kind of impious burning and persecution. Nor can I discover who it is that writes these pamphlets, nor yet who prints them. And when I try to raise from the people some necessary contribution (for in their malice and wickedness they often leave me without any money at all), they answer by advising me, in coarse lampoons, to ask of Satan in whose pay I am. Parliament makes excuses for fear of my sting, but I can get nothing out of them. And meanwhile the walls of London are covered with the grossest pictures representing me as a parricide who is ready to strike down your Majesty for the sake of my inheritance. But well you know, my Lord and Father, that notwithstanding all the hopes of a legitimate ambition, I most certainly desire that your Majesty may enjoy yet long and glorious years of rule. Furthermore, there are circulating through the city certain engravings on copper which show me torturing animals and laughing the while. But well you know, Sire, that if ever it has happened to me to taste this profane pleasure, I have surely never laughed thereat. But they try to make out that this innocent sport is a sort of crime, despite the fact that animals have no souls, and although it is assuredly permitted to all men, especially if they be of Royal birth, to make use of brute beasts even unto death for purposes of honest recreation. But in this land of England the people are so fond of animals that they treat their animals better than their own servants. The stables and dog-kennels are kept like palaces, and I have known great lords who pass the night on the same litter with their horse. To crown all, my noble Wife and Queen is barren, and these people have the outrageous effrontery to declare that I am to blame and not she, who is in other respects a most jealous and intractable woman, and amorous to excess. Sir and Father, I pray daily that the Lord God may have me in his grace, and I live in hopes that another throne may be given me, even though it be with the Turk, what time I still await that other glorious throne to which I shall be one day called by the honour of being the son of your very Glorious and Victorious Majesty. (Signed) PHLE."

To this letter the Emperor made reply in the following terms :

"SIR AND SON,—You have bitter enemies, I do not dispute it ; but you must try to endure them without vexation in anticipation of the yet more brilliant crown that shall be yours hereafter. I have already made it widely known that I am determined to retire from my lordship over the Low Countries and other of my dominions, for I am growing old and gouty, and I know that I shall not long be able to withstand King Henry the Second of France, for Fortune ever favours the young. You should remember also that so long as you are master of England, you will be as a thorn in the side of our enemy France. Truly I suffered a nasty defeat at Metz, and lost there near forty thousand men. I was compelled to retreat before the King of Saxony. If God does not soon see fit by a stroke of His good and divine will to re-establish me in the force and vigour of my prime, I am inclined, Sir and Son, to quit my kingdoms altogether and to leave them to you.

" Have patience therefore, and do your duty meanwhile against the heretics, sparing none of them, man, woman, girl, or child, for I am credibly informed that Madame your Queen has been minded to treat them mercifully, and this is a great grief to me.

" Your affectionate father,
"(Signed) CHARLES."

XXX

Ulenspiegel had been long upon the road. His feet were bleeding, but in the district of the bishopric of Mayence he met a wagon full of pilgrims who invited him to join them, and they carried him with them to Rome.

When they arrived at the city Ulenspiegel got down from the wagon, and straightway noticed a charming-looking woman standing at the door of an inn. She smiled when she saw him looking at her.

Taking this kindly humour of hers for a good omen :

" Hostess," says he, " will you give asile, pray, to a poor pilgrim on pilgrimage who has carried his full time and is about to be delivered of his sins ? "

" We give asile to all such as pay us for it," said the woman.

" I have a hundred ducats in my purse," said Ulenspiegel (who, in fact, had no more than one), " and I would dearly like to spend the first of them in your pleasant company and over a bottle of old Roman wine."

" Wine is not dear in these holy parts," she answered. " Come in and drink your fill. It will only cost you a *soldo*."

And they twain drank together for so long, and emptied so many bottles of wine and all to the tune of such pleasant conversation, that the hostess was constrained to order her servant to serve the customers in her place, while she and Ulenspiegel retired into a room at the back of the inn, a marble chamber, cool as a winter's day, where, leaning her head on her new friend's shoulder, she demanded of him who he might be.

And Ulenspiegel answered her :

" I am Lord of Geeland, Count of Gavergeëten, Baron of Tuchtendeel. I was born at Damme, in Flanders, and I hold there for my estate five and twenty acres of moonlight."

" What land is that whence you come ? " the hostess asked him, drinking from Ulenspiegel's tankard.

" It is a misty land," he told her, " a land of illusion, where are sown the seeds of false hopes and of castles in the air. But you, sweet hostess mine, were born in no such land of moonlight, you with your amber skin and your eyes that shine like pearls. For bright is the sunshine that has coloured that browned gold of your hair, and it is Lady Venus herself who, without a single pang of jealousy, has formed your soft shoulders, and your prancing breasts, your rounded arms, your delicate sweet hands. Say, shall we sup together this night ? "

" Fine pilgrim that you are from Flanders," says she, " say, why are you come hither ? "

" To have a talk with the Pope," said Ulenspiegel.

" Heavens ! " she cried, clasping her hands together, " and that is something that even myself, a native of the country, have never been able to do ! "

" Yet shall I," said Ulenspiegel.

" But know you where the Pope lives, what he is like, what are his habits and his ways of life ? "

" I heard all about him on the way," answered Ulenspiegel. " His name is Julius III. Wanton he is, and gay and dissolute, a good talker, that never falters for a clever repartee. I have also heard that he has taken an extraordinary fancy to a little dirty beggar of a man—a dark fellow and a rude who used to wander about with a monkey asking for alms. He came to the Pope, and the Pope, it seems, has made a Cardinal of him, and now gets quite ill if a single day passes without their meeting."

" Have some more to drink," said the landlady, " and do not speak so loud."

" I have also heard," continued Ulenspiegel, " that one day he swore like a soldier, *Al dispetto di Dio, potta di Dio*, and all because they did not bring him the cold peacock that he had ordered to be kept for his supper. And he excused himself, saying, ' If my Master was angered over an apple, I, who am the vicar of God, can certainly swear an oath about a pheasant ! ' You see, my pet, I know the Pope very well, and understand just what sort of a man he is ! "

73

" Oh dear," she said, " pray be careful and do not tell this to any one else. But still, and in spite of all you tell me, I maintain that you will not get to see him."

" I shall," said Ulenspiegel.

" I will wager you a hundred florins."

" They are mine ! " said Ulenspiegel.

The very next day, tired as he was, he ran through all the city and found out that the Pope was to say Mass that morning at the Church of St. John Lateran. Thither Ulenspiegel repaired, and took up a position as prominently in the Pope's view as he could. And every time that the Pope elevated chalice or Host, Ulenspiegel turned his back to the altar. Now one of the cardinals was officiating with the Pope, swarthy of countenance he was, malicious and corpulent ; and on his shoulder he carried a monkey. He reported Ulenspiegel's behaviour to the Pope, who straightway after Mass sent four terrible-looking soldiers (such as one finds in those warlike lands) to seize the pilgrim.

" What religion do you profess ? " the Pope asked him.

" Most Holy Father," answered Ulenspiegel, " my religion is the same as my landlady's."

The Pope had the woman fetched.

" What is your religion ? " he asked her.

" The same as your Holiness's," she told him.

" That also is mine," said Ulenspiegel.

The Pope asked him why he turned his back upon the Holy Sacrament.

" I felt myself unworthy to look upon it face to face," he answered.

" You are a pilgrim ? " said the Pope.

" Yes," answered Ulenspiegel, " and I am come from Flanders to beg remission of my sins."

The Pope absolved and blessed him, and Ulenspiegel departed in the company of his landlady, who paid over to him his hundred florins. And with this good store of money he departed from Rome and set out to return again to the land of Flanders.

But he had to pay seven ducats for the certificate of his pardon, all scribed upon parchment.

XXXI

In those days there came to Damme two brothers of the Premonstratensian Order, sellers of indulgences. And over their monastic robes they wore beautiful jackets bordered with lace.

When it was fine they stood outside the porch of the church, and under the porch when it was wet, and there they stuck up their tariff; and this was the scale of charges : for six *liards* a hundred years' indulgence, for one *patard* two hundred years, three hundred years for half a sovereign, four hundred years for seven florins, and so on according to the price—indulgences plenary or semi-plenary, and pardons for all the most terrible crimes.

And they gave to their patrons, in exchange for payment, little parchment certificates on which were written out the number of years of indulgence, and below was the following inscription :

> *Who wants not to be*
> *Stewed, roasted, fricasseed,*
> *Burning in hell for evermore,*
> *Indulgences let him buy.*
> *Pardon and forgiveness,*
> *For a little money,*
> *God will return to him.*

And the eager purchasers came thronging round the monks. One of whom never left off addressing his audience. This brother had a blooming countenance, and displayed three chins at least, and a portentous belly, all without the least embarrassment.

75

"Unhappy ones!" he cried, fixing with his eye now one, now another of the crowd. "Unhappy ones! Let me show you a picture. Behold! You are in hell! The fire burns you most cruelly. You are boiling in that cauldron full of oil wherein are prepared the *olie-koekjes* of Astarte. You are nothing better than a sausage on the frying-pan of Lucifer, or a leg of mutton on the spit of Guilguiroth, biggest of all the devils. And first they cut you up in little pieces. Ah, woe is me! Behold this sinner who despised indulgences! Behold this plate of daintiness! 'Tis he! 'Tis he! His wicked body thus reduced by damnation. And for sauce, brimstone and pitch and tar! Thus are those poor sinners eaten alive to be born again continually to their pain! And here in all reality is the place of tears and of grinding of teeth. Have mercy, God of mercy! For now, poor damned one, you are in hell, and you suffer unspeakable woes. And yet if any there were to subscribe a *denier* for you, straightway one of your hands would find relief; and let but some other give a half a *denier* and your two hands would be freed entirely from the pain of the fire. But as for the remainder of your body, let some one only give a florin, and there falls the dew of indulgence over all! O freshness of delight! And now for ten days, a hundred days, a thousand years maybe, according as one pays, no more roast meat, no more *olie-koekjes*, no more fricassees for you! And even if it is not for yourself, is there no one else, there in the secret depths of the fire, no one else for whom you would wish to gain relief—one of your parents perhaps, a dear wife, or some lovely girl with whom you have committed wilful sin?"

And as he spoke these words, the monk jogged the elbow of his brother that stood by holding in his hands a silver bowl. And that brother, lowering his eyes at this signal, shook the bowl unctuously, as if inviting contributions.

Whereat the preacher continued in this wise: "Or perhaps you have a son or a daughter, maybe, in the midst

THE MONK'S SERMON

of this terrible fire, or some beloved little child? Hark, how they cry aloud, and weep, and call to you by name. Can you remain deaf to their pitiful voices? You cannot. Even a heart of ice must melt, though it cost you a carolus! And behold, at the very sound of the carolus as it strikes this vile metal" (and here his comrade shook the plate again), "a space opens out in the midst of the fire, and the tormented soul ascends to some volcano mouth where it meets the air, the fresh, free air! Where are the pains of the fire now? For the sea is close at hand, and straight into the sea the soul plunges. She swims on her back, on her stomach, floats upon the waves, dives beneath them. Oh, listen how she sings aloud in her joy! See how she rolls about in the water! The very angels gaze down upon her from heaven and are glad. Eagerly they await her coming; but not yet, not yet has she had her fill of the sea. If she might only turn into a fish! She knoweth not how there are prepared for her up aloft sweet baths, perfumed and scented, with fine bits of sugar-candy floating therein, all white and fresh like bits of ice. Now a shark appears. She fears it not at all, but clambers upon its back, and sits there all unnoticed, hoping he will take her with him down into the depths of the sea. And now she goes to greet the little water-angels that feed on *waterzoey* from coral cauldrons, and on freshest oysters from plates of mother-of-pearl. And she is welcomed and fêted and made much of, but still the angels in heaven beckon her on high, till at last, refreshed and happy, you may see her rise aloft, singing like a lark, up to the highest heaven where God sits in glory on his throne. There she finds again all her earthly friends and loved ones (save only those, forsooth, that in this life have spoken ill of indulgences and of our Holy Mother Church and who burn now for their sin upon the floor of hell. And so for ever and for ever and for ever to all ages, in an all-consuming eternity). But that other soul, now dear to God, refreshes herself in soft baths and crunches sugar-candy.

Buy then, my brothers, buy your indulgences. We sell them for *crusats*, for florins, or for English sovereigns. Even copper coin is not refused. Buy then, buy! This is the Holy Mart! And we have indulgences adapted to the poor man's purse as well as to the rich man's. Only, I am sorry to say, my brothers, no credit is allowed. For to buy without paying cash is a crime most grievous in the eyes of Our Lord."

Hereupon the monk who had kept silent shook his platter, and the florins, *crusats*, *patards*, *sols*, and *deniers* fell into it as thick as hail.

Claes, feeling himself rich, paid a florin for an indulgence of ten thousand years; and the monks delivered to him a piece of parchment in exchange.

At last, seeing that there was no one left in Damme but the miserly folk who would not buy indulgences at any price, the two monks left the village and proceeded on their way to Heyst.

XXXII

In those days the country round Liége was in a disturbed and dangerous state by reason of the heresy hunts, and Lamme Goedzak came again to live in Damme. He was married now, and his wife followed him willingly because the people of Liége, who had a mocking nature, used to make fun of her husband's meekness.

Lamme often visited Claes, who, since coming into his fortune, was always to be found at the tavern of the *Blauwe Torre*, and had even appropriated one of the tables for himself and his boon companions. This table was next to the one where sat the Dean of the Fishmongers, Josse Grypstuiver by name, drinking sparingly from his half-pint tankard. For he was a miser, a stingy fellow who thought the world of himself, and lived for the most part on smoked herrings, and thought more of money than of the safety of his own soul. Now Claes carried in his pocket that piece of parchment whereon was inscribed the tale of his ten-thousand-year indulgence.

One evening Claes was drinking at the *Blauwe Torre* in the company of Lamme Goedzak, Jan van Roosebeke, and Matthys van Assche, Josse Grypstuiver also being present. Claes had been imbibing freely, and Jan Roosebeke was remonstrating with him, saying that it was sin to drink so much. But Claes replied that a pint too much meant nothing more serious than an extra half-day in purgatory.

" Besides," said he, " I have a ten-thousand-year indulgence in my pocket ! Is there any one here that would like a hundred years of them, I wonder, so that he may indulge his stomach without fear of the consequences ? "

Every one shouted at once :

" How much are you selling them at ? "

" For a pint of beer," Claes answered, " I will give you one hundred days, but for a *muske conyn* you shall have a hundred and fifty ! "

Some of the revellers gave Claes a pint of beer, others a piece of ham, and for each and all Claes cut off a little strip of his parchment. It was not Claes, forsooth, who consumed the price of his indulgences, but Lamme Goedzak ; and he gorged himself so that he began to swell visibly ; and all the time Claes went on distributing his merchandise up and down the tavern.

The man Grypstuiver turned a sour face towards him, and asked if he had an indulgence for ten days.

" No," said Claes, " that's too small a piece to cut."

Every one laughed, and Grypstuiver ate his anger as best he could. Then Claes went home, followed by Lamme, walking as if his legs were made of wool.

XXXIII

Towards the end of the third year of her banishment, Katheline returned to her home in Damme. And continually she cried aloud in her madness : " Fire, fire ! My head is on fire ! My soul is knocking, make a hole, she wants to get out ! " And if ever she saw an ox or a sheep she would run from it as if in terror. And she would sit on the bench at the back of her cottage, under the lime-trees, wagging her head and staring at the people of Damme as they passed by. But she did not recognize them, and they called her " The mad-woman."

Meanwhile Ulenspiegel went wandering along the roads and pathways of the world, and one day he met a donkey on the highway, harnessed with leather and studs of brass, and its head ornamented with tassels and plumes of scarlet wool. . . .

Some old women were standing round the donkey in a circle, all talking at once and telling each other how that no one could tame the donkey for that he was a terrible animal and had belonged to the Baron of Raix, who was a magician and had been burned alive for having sacrificed eight children to the devil. " And he ran away so fast," said the old women, " that none could catch him. And without a doubt he is under the protection of Satan. For a while ago he seemed tired, resting by the wayside, and the village constables came to seize him. But he suddenly kicked out with his hind legs and brayed in such fearful fashion that they durst not to go near him. And that was no bray of an ass, but the bray of the devil himself. So the constables left him to browse among the thistles, and passed no sentence upon him, nor did they burn him alive for a sorcerer as they should have done. Verily these men have no courage."

Notwithstanding this brave talk, the donkey had only to prick up his ears or flick his sides with his tail, to send the women running away from him with cries of terror. Then back they would come, chattering and jabbering, but ever ready to be off again if the donkey showed the least sign of movement. Ulenspiegel could not help laughing at the sight,

" Ah ! " said he, " talk and curiosity ! They flow like an everlasting river from the mouths of women—and especially *old* women, for with the young the flow is less continuous by reason of their amorous occupations."

Then, considering the donkey :

" This sorcerer-beast," said he to himself, " is a sprightly ass without a doubt, and a good goer. What if I were to take him for my own, to ride, or maybe sell him ? "

Without another word Ulenspiegel went and got a feed of oats, and returning, offered them to the donkey. But while he was eating of those viands Ulenspiegel jumped nimbly upon his back, and taking the reins, turned him first to the north, then to the east, and lastly to the west. Then, when he had gone from them a little way, he raised his hand as if in blessing on those aged dames. But they, almost fainting with fear, fell upon their knees before him. And that evening when they met together again, the tale was told of how an angel with a felt hat trimmed with a pheasant's feather had come and blessed them, and had taken off the magician's donkey by special favour of God.

And Ulenspiegel, astride of his ass, went his way through the green fields, where the horse pranced about at liberty, where the cows and heifers grazed at their ease or lay resting in the sunshine. And he called the ass Jef.

At last Jef came to a stop, and began, as happy as could be, to make his dinner off the thistles which grew in that place in great abundance. But anon he shivered all over, and flicked his sides with his tail in the hope of ridding himself of the greedy horse-flies who, like himself, were trying to get their dinner, not off the thistles, but off his own flesh.

Ulenspiegel, who himself began to feel the pangs of hunger, grew very melancholy.

" Happy indeed would you be, friend donkey, with your good dinner of fine thistles if there was no one to disturb you in your pleasures, and to remind you that you also are mortal, born, that is to say, to the endurance of all kinds of villainies."

Thus did Ulenspiegel address his steed, and thus continued:

" For even as you have this gadfly of yours to worry you, so also hath His Holiness the Pope a gadfly of his own, even master Martin Luther ; and His Sacred Majesty the Emperor, hath he not my Lord of France for his tormentor—Francis, first of that name, the King with the very long nose and a sword that is longer still ? And forsooth, donkey mine, it is certainly permitted that I also, poor little man wandering all alone, may have my gadfly too.

" Alas ! Woe is me ! All my pockets have holes in them, and by the said apertures do all my fine ducats and florins and *daelders* ramble away, flying like a crowd of mice before the mouth of the cat that would devour them. I wonder why it is that money will have nothing to do with me—me that am so fond of money ? Verily Fortune is no woman, whatever they may say, for she loves none but greedy misers that shut her up in their coffers, tie her up in sacks, close her down under twenty keys and never let her show herself at the window by so much as the little tip of her gilded nose ! This, then, is the gadfly that preys upon me and makes me itch, and tickles me without ever so much as raising a laugh. But there, you are not listening to me at all, friend donkey ! And you think of nothing but your food. You gobbling gobbler, your long ears are deaf to the cry of an empty stomach ! But you *shall* listen to me. I insist ! "

And he belaboured the ass as hard as he could, till the brute began to bray.

" Come, come, now that you have given us a song ! " cried Ulenspiegel. But the donkey would not advance by more than a single step, and seemed determined to go on eating thistles until he had consumed all that grew by the roadside. And of these there was an abundance.

When Ulenspiegel saw what was happening he dismounted

and cut off a bunch of thistles ; then, mounting the ass again, he placed the bunch of thistles just in front of the animal's nose. And in this way, leading the donkey by the nose, he arrived before long in the land of the Landgrave of Hesse.

" Friend donkey," he said as they went along, " you, verily, go running after a bunch of thistles, the meagre fare with which I have provided you ; but you leave behind the lovely road that is filled with all kinds of most delicate herbs. And thus do all men, scenting out, some of them, the bouquet called Fame which Fortune puts under their nose, others the bouquet of Gain, and yet others the bouquet that is called Love. But at the end of the journey they discover, like you, that they have been pursuing things that are of little account, and that they have left behind all that is worth anything—health, and work, repose, happiness, and home."

In such discourse with his donkey Ulenspiegel came at last to the palace of the Landgrave.

There two Captains of Artillery were playing dice upon the steps of the palace, and one of them, a red-haired man of gigantic stature, soon noticed Ulenspiegel as he approached modestly upon his ass, gazing down upon them and their game.

" What do you want," said the Captain, " you, fellow, with your starved pilgrim's face ? "

" I am extremely hungry," answered Ulenspiegel, " and if I am a pilgrim, it is against my will."

" And you are hungry," replied the Captain, " go, eat the next gallows cord you come to, for such cords are prepared for vagabonds like you."

" Sir Captain," answered Ulenspiegel, " only give me the fine golden cord you wear on your hat, and I will go straightway and hang myself by the teeth from that fat ham which I see hanging over there at the cook-shop."

The Captain asked him where he came from. Ulenspiegel told him, " From Flanders."

" What do you want ? "

" To show His Highness the Landgrave one of my pictures. For I am a painter."

" If it is a painter that you are," said the Captain, " and from Flanders, come in, and I will lead you to my master."

When he had been brought before the Landgrave, Ulenspiegel saluted thrice and again.

" May your Highness deign," said he, " to excuse my presumption in daring to come and lay before these noble feet a picture I have made for your Highness, wherein I have had the honour to portray Our Lady the Virgin in her royal attire."

And then after a moment's pause :

" It may be that my picture may please your Highness," he continued, " and in that case I am sufficiently presumptuous to hope that I might aspire even unto this fine chair of velvet, where sat in his lifetime the painter that is lately deceased and ever to be regretted by your Magnanimity."

Now the picture which Ulenspiegel showed him was very beautiful, and when the Landgrave had inspected it, he told Ulenspiegel to sit down upon the chair, for that he would certainly make him his Court Painter. And the Landgrave kissed him on both cheeks, most joyously, and Ulenspiegel sat down on the chair.

" Of a truth you are a very talkative fellow," said the Landgrave, looking him up and down.

" May it please your Lordship," answered Ulenspiegel, " Jef—my donkey—has dined most excellently well on thistles, but as for me I have seen nothing but misery these three days past, and have had nothing to nourish me but the mists of expectation."

" You shall soon have some better fare than that," answered the Landgrave. " But where is this donkey of yours ? "

" I left him on the Grande Place," Ulenspiegel said, " opposite the palace ; and I should be most obliged if he could be given lodging for the night—some straw and a little fodder."

The Landgrave immediately gave instructions to one of his pages that Ulenspiegel's donkey should be treated even as his own.

The hour for supper soon arrived, and the meal was like a wedding festival. Hot meats smoked in the dishes, wine flowed like water, while Ulenspiegel and the Landgrave grew both as red as burning coals. Ulenspiegel also became very merry, but His Highness was somewhat pensive even in his cups.

" Our painter," said he suddenly, " will have to paint our portrait. For it is a great satisfaction to a mortal prince to bequeath to his descendants the memory of his countenance."

" Sir Landgrave," answered Ulenspiegel, " your will is my pleasure. Nevertheless, I cannot help feeling sorry at the thought that if your Lordship is painted by himself he will feel lonely, perhaps, all there in solitary state through the ages to come. Surely he should be accompanied by his noble wife, Madame the Landgravine, by her lords and ladies, and by his captains and most warlike officers of State. In the midst of these, my Lord and his Lady will shine like twin suns surrounded by lanterns."

" Well, painter mine, and how much shall I have to pay you for this mighty work ? "

" One hundred florins, either now or later, just as you will."

" Here they are, in advance," said the Landgrave.

" Most compassionate master," said Ulenspiegel as he took the money, " you have filled my lamp with oil, and now it shall burn bright in your honour."

On the next day Ulenspiegel asked the Landgrave to let him see those persons who were to have the honour of being painted. And first there came before him the Duke of Lüneburg, commander of the infantry of the Landgrave. He was a stout man who carried with difficulty his great paunch

85

swollen with food. He went up to Ulenspiegel and whispered in his ear :

" When you paint my portrait see that you take off half my fat at least. Else will I order my soldiers to have you hung."

The Duke passed on. And next there came a noble lady with a hump on her back and a bosom as flat as a sword-blade.

" Sir painter," said she, " unless you remove the hump on my back and give me a couple of others in the place where they should be, verily I will have you drawn and quartered as if you were a prisoner."

The lady went away, and now there appeared a young maid of honour, fair, fresh, and comely, only that she lacked three teeth under her upper lip.

" Sir painter," said she, " if you do not paint me smiling and showing through my parted lips a perfect set of teeth, I'll have you chopped up into small pieces at the hands of my gallant. There he is, look at him."

And she pointed to that Captain of Artillery who a while ago had been playing dice on the palace steps. And she went her way.

The procession continued, until at last Ulenspiegel was left alone with the Landgrave.

The Landgrave said to him :

" My friend, let me warn you that if your painting has the misfortune to be inaccurate or false to all these various physiognomies by so much as a single feature, I will have your throat cut as if you were a chicken."

" If I am to have my head cut off," thought Ulenspiegel, " if I am to be drawn and quartered, chopped up into small pieces, and finally hung, I should do better to paint no portrait at all. I must consider what is best to be done."

" And where is the hall," he asked the Landgrave, " which I am to adorn with all these likenesses ! "

" Follow me," said the Landgrave. And he brought him to a large room with great bare walls.

" This is the hall," he said.

" I should be very grateful," said Ulenspiegel, " if some curtains could be hung right along the walls, so that my paintings may be protected from the flies and the dust."

" Certainly," said the Landgrave.

When the curtains had been hung as directed, Ulenspiegel asked if he might have three apprentices to help him with the mixing of his colours.

This was done, and for thirty days Ulenspiegel and the apprentices spent the whole of their time feasting and carousing together, with every extravagance of meat and drink. And the Landgrave looked on at it all. But at last on the thirty-first day he came and thrust his nose in at the door of the chamber where Ulenspiegel had begged him not to enter.

" Well, Tyl," he said, " and where are the portraits ? "

" They are not finished," answered Ulenspiegel.

" When shall I be able to see them ? "

" Not just yet," said Ulenspiegel.

On the six-and-thirtieth day the Landgrave again thrust his nose inside the door.

" Well, Tyl," he inquired, " how now ? "

" Ah, Sir Landgrave," said Ulenspiegel, " the portraits are getting on."

On the sixtieth day the Landgrave grew very angry, and coming right into the room :

" Show me the pictures at once ! " he cried.

" I will do so," answered Ulenspiegel, " but pray have the kindness not to draw the curtain until you have summoned hither the lords and captains and ladies of your court."

" Very well," said the Landgrave, and at his command the aforesaid notabilities appeared. Ulenspiegel took up his stand in front of the curtain, which was still carefully drawn.

" My Lord Landgrave," he said, " and you, Madame the

Landgravine, and you my Lord of Lüneburg, and you others, fine ladies and valiant captains, know that behind this curtain have I portrayed to the best of my abilities your faces, every one warlike or gentle as the case may be. It will be quite easy for each one of you to recognize himself. And that you are anxious to see yourselves is only natural. But I pray you have patience and suffer me to speak a word or two before the curtain is drawn. Know this, fair ladies and valiant captains ; all you that are of noble blood shall behold my paintings and rejoice. But if there be among you any that is of low or humble birth, such an one will see nothing but a blank wall. So there ! And now, have the goodness to open wide your noble eyes."

And so saying, Ulenspiegel drew the curtain.

" Remember," said he again, " only they of noble birth can see my pictures, whether they be lords or ladies." And again, presently : " He of low birth is blind to my pictures. But he who clearly sees, that man is a nobleman without a doubt."

At that every one present opened wide his eyes, pretending —you may be sure—to see, and feigning to recognize the various faces and pointing themselves out to one another, though in reality they beheld nothing at all but a bare wall. And for this they were each and all secretly ashamed.

Suddenly the court jester, who was standing by, jumped three feet in the air and jaggled his bells.

" Take me for a villain," he cried, " a most villainous villain, but I verily will affirm and assert and say with trumpets and fanfares that there I see a wall, a blank, white wall, and nothing but a wall, so help me God and his saints ! "

Ulenspiegel said :

" When fools 'gin talking, time for wise men to be walking."

And he was about to leave the palace when the Landgrave stopped him.

" Fool in your folly," said he, " you make boast that you go through the world praising what is good and fair and making mock of foolery, and you have dared to make open game of so many and so high-born ladies, and of their yet more noble lords, bringing ridicule on the pride of their nobility ! Of a truth I tell you that the day will come when you will hang for your free speech."

" If the cord is of gold," said Ulenspiegel, " it will break with dread at my approach."

" Stay," said the Landgrave. " Here is the first bit of your rope," and he gave him fifteen florins.

" All thanks to you," said Ulenspiegel, " and I promise you that every tavern on the road shall have a thread of it, a thread of that gold which makes Crœsuses of all those rascally tavern-keepers."

And off he went on his donkey, holding his head up high in air, with the plume in his cap wagging joyously in the breeze.

XXXIV

Now was the season of yellowing leaves, and the winds of autumn were beginning to blow. Sometimes for an hour or two it seemed that Katheline was come into her right mind again, and at such times Claes would say that the merciful spirit of God had come to visit her. Then it was that she had power to throw a charm upon Nele, by signs and incantations, so that the girl was able to see whatever was happening all over the world, in the public squares of the cities, or on the highways, or in the houses themselves.

To-day Katheline was in one of these moods of right-mindedness, and she was eating *olie-koekje* with Claes, Soetkin, and Nele. Claes said :

" This is the day of His Majesty the Emperor's abdication. Nele, my dear, do you think you could see as far as Brussels in Brabant ? "

" If Katheline wishes me to," said Nele.

Thereupon Katheline caused her to sit down on a bench, and making sundry passes with her hands, she muttered her incantations, which soon sent the girl off into a trance.

Then Katheline said to her :

" Make your way into the little house which is called the Park House, and is the favourite residence of the Emperor Charles the Fifth."

Whereupon Nele began to speak, in a low voice, as though she were half suffocated.

" I am standing in a small room painted green. There is a man in the room. He is about fifty-four years of age, and he has a bald head and a protruding chin with a white beard growing upon it. His grey eyes have a wicked, crafty look, filled with cruelty and false kindness. And this is the man they call ' His Most Sacred Majesty.' He suffers from a catarrh and always keeps coughing. Beside him is another, a young man with an ugly face like that of a hydrocephalous monkey. I saw him once at Antwerp. He is King Philip. At the present moment he is being rebuked by His Sacred Majesty for having slept out last night away from home. Doubtless, says His Majesty, he was at some brothel in company of a trollop of the town. His hair, it seems, smells of the tavern, no place, that, for a King to seek his pleasures in, he who may have his choice of all the sweetest bodies in the world, of skin like satin fresh from perfumed baths, and of hands of high-born ladies, very amorous. Such as these, says His Majesty, are more fit for him, surely, than some half-mad wench that is come, scarcely washed, from the arms of a drunken soldier. For there is not one among all the ladies, the most noble, the most beautiful, whether virgin, wife, or widow, that would resist King Philip ! And they would be proud to give him of their love—not by a greasy glimmer of stinking tallow, but by the light of scented tapers made of finest wax.

" The King replies that he will obey His Sacred Majesty in all things. Whereupon His Sacred Majesty has a fit of

90

coughing and drinks some draughts of hippocras.   After which
he addresses his son, sorrowfully, in these words :

" ' You must know, my son, that very soon I am to give
to the world the mighty spectacle of the abdication of my
throne in the favour of you, my son.   And I shall speak
before a great crowd of people, coughing and hiccuping as I
am—for all my life I have eaten too heartily.   And very
hard-hearted must you be if you shed no tears when you hear
what I shall have to say."

" ' I shall shed many tears,' " answers King Philip.

" And now His Sacred Majesty is speaking to his valet, a
man named Dubois.

" ' Bring me some sugar dipped in Madeira,' he cries.   ' I
have the hiccups.   Pray heaven they do not attack me when
I am making my speech before all those people.   Oh, that
goose I had last night for dinner !   Will it never pass ?   I
think I had better take a glass of Orleans wine ?   No, it is
too harsh.   Or perhaps if I ate some anchovies ?   No, they
are oily.   Dubois, there, give me some Roman wine ! '

" Dubois does as he is told, then dresses his master in a
robe of crimson velvet, wraps a golden cloak about him,
girds on his sword, places the globe and sceptre in his hands,
and on his head the crown.   Thus arrayed, His Sacred
Majesty goes forth from the Park House, riding on a little
mule and followed by King Philip and many notables.   Presently they arrive at a large building called the Palace, and
they come to a room wherein is a tall thin man, most richly
dressed.   He is the Prince of Orange, William, surnamed the
Silent.

" ' Do I look well, Cousin William ? ' His Sacred Majesty
inquires.

" But the man makes no answer, till at length His Sacred
Majesty speaks again, half mused, half angry.

" ' Still silent, cousin ?   Still without a word ?—even
when you have the chance of telling the truth to a grey-beard !

91

Come now, shall I abdicate or stay upon my throne, O silent one ? '

" ' Most Sacred Majesty,' replies the thin man, ' at the approach of winter even the strongest oaks let fall their leaves.'

" Three o'clock strikes.

" ' Lend me your shoulder, silent one, that I may lean upon it.'

" And, so saying, His Most Sacred Majesty leads the way into a great room wherein is a canopy, and under the canopy a dais covered with a carpet of crimson silk. On the dais are three chairs. His Sacred Majesty seats himself on the midmost one, which is more ornamented than the others and surmounted by the imperial crown. King Philip takes the second chair, and the third is occupied by a woman, who is no doubt the Queen. On either side are long benches covered with tapestry, and sitting upon them are men dressed in red robes and wearing round their necks the image of a golden sheep. Behind stand various personages who would seem to be princes and lords. Opposite these, and at the bottom of the dais, there is a row of bare benches which are occupied by men dressed in plain cloth. I hear it said that these men are clothed and seated so modestly because it is themselves that have to pay all the costs. At the entrance of His Sacred Majesty these people all stand up, but when he has sat down he makes a sign and they sit also.

" Now a very aged man is talking of his gout interminably. After which the woman, who seems to be a Queen, presents a roll of parchment to His Majesty. His Sacred Majesty reads what is written thereon in a low voice, coughing all the time, and then he begins to speak for himself.

" ' Many and long are the journeys that I have made through Spain and Italy and the Netherlands, through England and through Africa, all for God's glory, for the renown of my arms, and the good of my peoples.'

92

" And so on, and so on, till at last he comes to tell of his growing weakness and fatigue, and of his determination to relinquish the crown of Spain, together with the counties, duchies, and marquisates of all those countries, and of his desire to hand them over to his son. Thereafter he begins to weep, and every one weeps with him, and King Philip gets up from his chair and falls upon his knees before his father.

" ' Most Sacred Majesty,' he cries, ' am I indeed to receive this crown from your hands while yet you are so strong to wear it ? '

" Then His Majesty whispers into his son's ear that he should speak some kindly words to those men who are seated upon the tapestried chairs. Whereupon King Philip turns towards them, and without rising addresses them in a sharp tone of voice.

" ' I understand French fairly well,' he says, ' but not well enough to be able to talk to any one in that language. But the Bishop of Arras, Monsieur Grandvelle, he will say something to you on my behalf.'

" ' That is not the way to speak to them, my son,' says His Sacred Majesty.

" And in truth the whole assembly begins to murmur, seeing the young King so proud and unbending. The woman, she who is the Queen, then makes an oration, and is followed by an aged professor, who, on sitting down, receives a wave of the hand from His Sacred Majesty by way of thanks. These ceremonies and harangues being finished, His Sacred Majesty makes a declaration to the effect that his subjects are released from their oath of fidelity, signs the deeds drawn up to ratify his abdication, and then, rising from his throne, places his son upon it in his stead. Every one in the hall weeps. Then they return again to the Park House.

" Once more His Sacred Majesty and his son Philip are alone together in the green chamber. As soon as the doors are shut His Sacred Majesty goes off into a peal of laughter, and begins talking to King Philip, who keeps quite solemn all the time.

"'Did you notice,' says the Emperor, laughing and hiccuping at the same time, 'how little was needed to move these good people to tears? Heavens, how they wept! You would have thought it was the deluge! That fat Maes who made the long speech, why, he cried like a calf! Even you appeared to be affected—but not quite sufficiently, perhaps. Really there is no doubt that these are the best of all the entertainments which one can provide for the populace. For just as we nobles are wont to cherish most those mistresses who cost us most, so also it is with the people. The more we make them pay the more they love us. That is why I have tolerated the reformed religion in Germany while punishing it severely in the Low Countries. If, however, the German princes had been Catholics I would have made myself a Lutheran so that I might confiscate their property. Verily they all believe in the integrity of my zeal for the Roman faith, and when I leave them they are full of regrets. Yet for heresy there have perished at my hands fifty thousand of their bravest men and of their tenderest maidens, in the Netherlands alone. But still they grieve at my departure. And without making any count of what has been got from confiscations, I have raised in taxes more than the wealth of all the Indies or Peru; yet they are sorry to lose me. And I have torn up the Peace of Cadzant, brought the city of Ghent under subjection, suppressed every one who might be dangerous to me, put down all liberties, freedoms, and privileges, and placed them under the authority of the royal officers; but yet do these good people think they are still free inasmuch as I allow them to shoot with the crossbow, and to carry in procession the banners of their guilds. Willingly do they submit themselves to the hand of their master, finding happiness in a cage, and singing his praises while he is with them, and weeping when he departs. My son, be you to

FATHER AND SON

them even as I have been, kindly in words but harsh in deed. Lick that which you have no need to bite, and never leave off swearing to maintain liberties, freedoms, and privileges, however little you may scruple to destroy those liberties if they show signs of becoming dangerous. For such things as these are like iron if handled timidly, but brittle as glass if grappled with a strong hand. Therefore you should root out all heresy, not because it differs from the Roman religion, but because, if allowed to flourish, it would mean the end of our rule in all the Netherlands. For they that attack the Pope with his three crowns would finish by denying the authority of the temporal princes who wear but one. So, then, you should follow my example, and regard all claims to freedom of conscience as crimes of high treason to be punished by immediate confiscation. Hereby you will inherit great riches, as I also have done all my life long ; and when you come to die or to abdicate, everybody will say, 'Ah me, the good and noble prince!' and many are the tears that will be shed!"

"And now I hear no more," said Nele, "for His Sacred Majesty has laid him down to sleep. And King Philip, that proud and haughty prince, stands gazing at him with loveless eyes."

And when she had thus spoken, Nele was awakened from her trance by Katheline. And Claes gazed thoughtfully into the fire as it flamed and lit up all the chimney.

XXXV

It was the month of April. The weather had been mild, but now there was come a sharp frost and a sky grey and overcast as it were the sky of All Souls' Day. The third year of Ulenspiegel's banishment had long since passed, and Nele was waiting day after day for the return of her lover.

"Alas!" she cried, "there will be snow on the pear-trees, and snow upon the flowering jasmines, and on all the poor

95

plants that have bloomed in confidence of the mildness and
the warmth of an early spring. Already from the sky little
snowflakes are falling on the roads. And on my poor heart
as well the snow is falling.

"Where, oh where are the bright rays of sunshine that
should be playing now on our happy spring-time faces—and
upon red roofs that were used to grow the redder for that
warmth, and on window-panes that flashed as they caught
that sunny brightness ? Where indeed are those flaming
beams that kindled earth to life again, and the sky, and the
birds, and the insects ? Alas ! For day and night am I
chilled by sorrow and long waiting. Oh where, where are
you, my lover Ulenspiegel ? "

XXXVI

That Sunday there was held at Bruges the Procession of
the Holy Blood. Claes told his wife that she and Nele
ought to go and see the procession, and that if they did so, it
was not impossible they might find Ulenspiegel in the city.
As for himself, he would stay behind and look after the
cottage and be ready to welcome their pilgrim if he should
return.

So the two women went off together. Claes remained at
home and sat himself down on the doorstep and gazed into
the deserted village street. All was quiet as the grave,
except now and again for the crystal sound of the bell of some
village church, or, rising and falling with every little gust of
wind from Bruges, the far-off music of the carillon and the
sound of the guns and fireworks that were being let off in
honour of the Holy Blood. But in spite of all these sounds
of joy, Claes was filled with sadness, scanning the grey mist
that hung over the fields for a sight of his son, and trying to
hear his footfall in the jolly rustling of leaves and gay concert
of birds as they sang among the trees. Suddenly he noticed
a man coming down towards him on the road from Mal-

deghem. It was a man tall of stature, but it was not Ulen-spiegel. And presently Claes saw him come to a stand beside a field of carrots, and bend down to eat of the vegetables as if he were starving for food.

"There's a hungry man sure," said Claes to himself.

But after a while the man continued his walk, and passed out of view ; to reappear a little later at the corner of the rue Héron. Claes recognized him at once as the messenger who had brought the seven hundred ducats from his brother Josse. He went to meet him, and asked him in.

"Blessed are they that are kind to the wandering traveller," said the man, and readily accepted the proffered invitation.

Now on the window-ledge of the cottage window lay some bread-crumbs which Soetkin kept ready for the birds of the neighbourhood, who had learnt to come there during the winter for their food. The man took these crumbs and ate them.

"You must be hungry and thirsty," said Claes.

"Eight days ago was I robbed by thieves," the man replied, "and since then I have had nothing to eat but the carrots I have found in the fields and roots in the forest."

"Well then," said Claes, "I am thinking it is time you had a good round meal." And so saying he opened the bread-pan. "Look," he continued, "here is a dishful of peas, and here are eggs, puddings, hams, sausages from Ghent, *waterzoey*, a hotchpotch of fish. And down below in the cellar there slumbers our good wine from Louvain, made after the manner of Burgundy wine, all clear and red as rubies. Only the glasses are wanting now to rouse it from its sleep. And to crown all, let us put a faggot to the fire. Already I can hear the pudding singing in the grill ! And that's a song of right good cheer, my friend ! "

Claes kept turning the puddings, and as he did so he inquired of the stranger whether he had seen his son, Ulenspiegel.

97

" No," was the answer.

" Then perhaps you bring me news of my brother ? " Claes said, as he placed the puddings, now well grilled, upon the table, together with a ham omelette, some cheese, and two big tankards of gleaming Louvain wine, both red and white.

The man said :

" Your brother Josse has been done to death upon the rack at Sippenaken near to Aix. And all because he was a heretic, and bore arms against the Emperor."

Claes was like one mad, and he shook all over, for his wrath was great.

" Wicked brutes ! " he cried. " O Josse ! My poor Josse ! "

Then the stranger spoke again, but in a voice that held no sweetness.

" Not in this world, my friend, is to be found just cause either for joy or for sorrow." And he fell to his food. But after a while he spoke again.

" You must know that I was able to be of some assistance to your brother while he was in prison, by pretending that I was one of his relatives, a peasant from Nieswieler. I am now come hither in obedience to his command that if I was not killed for the Faith like him, I should go to you, and charge you in his name to live in the faith and peace of our Saviour, practising all works of mercy, and educating your son in secret in the law of Christ. 'That money,' he said, ' which I gave to my brother was money taken from the poor and ignorant. Let Claes make use of it in rearing Tyl in the knowledge of God and of His word."

And when he had thus spoken, the messenger gave Claes the kiss of peace. And Claes made moan and lamentation, saying :

" Dead upon the rack ! Alas ! My poor Josse ! " And his grief was so great that he could not put it from him. Nevertheless, when he saw that the messenger was consumed with thirst and held out his glass for more wine, Claes poured out again. But he himself ate and drank without pleasure.

Now Soetkin and Nele remained away for seven days ; and all this time the messenger stayed beneath the roof of Claes, and every night they heard Katheline howling in her cottage over the way :

" Fire ! Fire ! Make a hole ! My soul wants to get out ! "

And Claes went to her, comforting her with gentle words, and afterwards returned to his own house.

At the end of the seven days the messenger departed. Claes offered him money, but he would only accept two caroluses with which to feed himself and find lodging on his way back home.

XXXVI

When Nele and Soetkin returned from Bruges, they found Claes in the kitchen, sitting on the floor like a tailor, sewing buttons on an old pair of breeches. Titus Bibulus Schnouffius barked his welcome ; Claes smiled, and Nele smiled in answer. But Soetkin did not take her eyes from the road, gazing continually in hopes to see her beloved Ulenspiegel.

All of a sudden she broke silence. " Look," she cried, " here is the Provost-Marshal. He is coming along the road with four sergeants of the peace. They cannot be wanting any one from here, surely ! And yet there are two of them turning off by the cottage ! "

Claes looked up from his work.

" And the other two have stopped at the front," Soetkin said.

Then Claes got up.

" Who can they want to arrest in this road ? " his wife continued, and then : " O Christ ! They are coming in here."

" Look to the money ! " cried Claes. " The caroluses are hidden away behind the fireplace." And with these words he ran out of the kitchen into the garden. Nele understood what he meant, and saw that he was going to try and make his escape over the hedge. But the sergeants seized him by the collar, and now he was hitting out at them in a hopeless endeavour to break free.

"He is innocent!" Nele cried aloud amid her tears. "He is innocent! Do not hurt him. It is Claes, my father! O Ulenspiegel, where are you? Where are you? If you were only here you would kill them both!"

And she threw herself on one of the sergeants and tore at his face with her nails. Then she cried out again: "They will kill him!" and fell down upon the grass in the garden, and rolled there in her despair.

Katheline, hearing the noise, had come out from her cottage, and stood up straight and immovable, gazing at the piteous scene. Then she spoke, wagging her head:

"Fire! Fire! Make a hole! My soul wants to get out!"

Soetkin meanwhile, who had seen nothing of all this, was talking to the sergeants who had entered the cottage.

"Kind sirs," she began, "what is it that you are looking for in our poor dwelling? If it is my son you want, he is far away. Do you feel equal to a long journey?"

And she felt quite pleased at the way she was handling the matter. But it was at this very moment that Nele began to cry aloud for help, and when Soetkin had made her way into the garden, it was to see her husband seized by the collar and fighting on the pathway near the hedge.

"Hit hard and kill them!" she cried, and then: "O Ulenspiegel, where are you?"

And she was about to go to the assistance of her man when one of the sergeants caught hold of her, not indeed without some danger to himself. And Claes was fighting and hitting out so forcibly that he would certainly have escaped had not the two sergeants with whom Soetkin had been talking come out to aid their fellows in the nick of time. So at last they were able to tie the hands of Claes together, and to carry him back to the kitchen, whither Nele and Soetkin had already come, crying and sobbing.

"Sir Provost," Soetkin said, "what crime has he committed that you are binding my poor husband thus with cords?"

"He is a heretic," said one of the sergeants.

"Heretic!" cried Soetkin, looking towards her husband. "You a heretic! These devils are lying!"

Claes answered:

"I resign myself into God's keeping."

And they took him away. Nele and Soetkin followed behind, in tears, believing that they also would be summoned before the judge. They were joined by many of their friends and neighbours, but when these heard that it was on a charge of heresy that Claes was walking thus in chains, fear came upon them and they returned incontinently to their houses, closing their doors behind them. Only a few young girls had the courage to approach Claes and say to him:

"Whither are you going to, Charcoal-burner, in these bonds!"

"I go unto the grace of God, my girls," he answered them.

So they took him away to the town gaol, and Nele and Soetkin sat themselves down upon the threshold. And towards evening Soetkin besought Nele to leave her and to go and see if Ulenspiegel had perchance returned.

XXXVII

The news spread quickly through the neighbourhood that a man had been taken prisoner on a charge of heresy, and that the inquisitor Titelman, Dean of Renaix, surnamed the Inquisitor without Pity, had been appointed judge. Now at this time Ulenspiegel was living at Koolkerke, in the intimate favour of a farmer's widow, a sweet and gentle person who refused him nothing of what was hers to give. He was

very happy there, petted and made much of, until one day a
treacherous rival, an alderman of the village, lay in wait for
him early in the morning when he was coming out of the
tavern, and would have beaten him with a wooden club.
But Ulenspiegel, thinking to cool his rival's anger, threw him
into a duck-pond that was full of water, and the alderman
scrambled out as best he could, green as a toad and dripping
like a sponge.

As a result of this mighty deed Ulenspiegel found it
convenient to depart from Koolkerke, and off he went to
Damme as fast as his legs would carry him, fearing the
vengeance of the alderman.

The night fell cold, and Ulenspiegel ran quickly. For he
was longing to be home again, and already he saw in imagination Nele sewing by the fire, Soetkin getting ready the supper,
Claes binding up his sticks, and Schnouffius gnawing at a
bone.

A tramping pedlar met him on the road and asked
him whither he was off to so fast and at that time of
night.

" To my home in Damme," Ulenspiegel told him.

The tramp said :

" That town is no longer safe. They are arresting the
Reformers there." And he passed on.

Presently Ulenspiegel arrived at the inn of the *Roode
Schildt* and went in for a glass of *dobbel kuyt*. The innkeeper
said to him :

" Are you not the son of Claes ? "

" I am," said Ulenspiegel.

" Make haste then," said the innkeeper, " for the hour of
evil fortune has sounded for your father."

Ulenspiegel asked him what he meant by these words,
and the innkeeper told him that he would know soon enough.
So Ulenspiegel left the inn and continued on his way, running
apace.

102

The Return of Ulenspiegel

When he arrived at the outskirts of Damme, the dogs that stood by the doorways came running round his legs, jumping up at him, yelping and barking. Hearing this noise, the women also came out of their houses, and when they saw who it was they all began talking at once.

" Whence come you ? " they cried. " And have you any news of your father ? And do you know where your mother is ? Is she in prison too ? Alas ! Heaven send they do not bring him to the stake ! "

Ulenspiegel ran on faster than ever. He met Nele.

" Tyl," she said, " you must not go home. They have set guards in our house in the name of His Majesty."

Ulenspiegel stopped running.

" Nele," he said, " is it true that Claes, my father, is in prison ? "

" It is true," Nele said, " and Soetkin sits weeping at the gaol door."

Then the heart of the prodigal son swelled with grief, and he said : " I must go to them."

" No," said Nele. " First you must do what Claes told me, just before he was taken away. ' Look to the money,' he said, ' it is hidden at the back of the grate. You must make sure of that first of everything, for it is the inheritance of poor Soetkin.' "

But Ulenspiegel would not hear aught and ran on quickly to the gaol. There he found Soetkin sitting at the gate. She embraced him with many tears, and they cried on one another's neck.

Knowing that they were there, the populace began to crowd in front of the prison. Then the sergeants arrived and told Soetkin and Ulenspiegel that they were to go away at once. So mother and son returned to Nele's cottage, which was next door to their own, and was being guarded by one of the foot-soldiers who had been sent for from Bruges in case there might be trouble during the trial and execution of Claes.

For it was well known that the people of Damme loved him exceedingly.

The soldier was sitting on the pavement in front of the door, draining the last drops of brandy from a flask. Finding it was all gone he threw the flask away and was amusing himself by dislodging the stones on the path with the point of his dagger.

Soetkin went in to Katheline, crying most bitterly.

But Katheline said: "Fire! Fire! Make a hole! My soul wants to get out!" And she kept wagging her head.

XXXVIII

Borgstorm, the great bell of Damme, had summoned the judges to judgment. It was four o'clock, and now they were collected together at the *Vierschare*, around the Tree of Justice.

Claes was brought before them. Seated upon the dais was the high bailiff of Damme, and by his side, opposite Claes, the mayor, the alderman, and the clerk of the court.

The populace ran together at the sound of the bell. A great crowd they were, and many of them were saying that the judges were there to do—not justice—but merely the will of His Imperial Majesty. . . .

After certain preliminaries, the high bailiff began to make proclamation of the acts and deeds for which Claes had been summoned before that tribunal.

"The informer," he said, "had been staying by chance at Damme, not wishing to spend all his money at Bruges in feasting and festivity as is too often the case during these sacred occasions. On a time, then, when he was taking the air soberly on his own doorstep, he saw a man walking towards him along the rue Héron. This man Claes also saw, and went up to him and greeted him. The stranger, who was dressed all in black, entered the house of Claes, leaving the door into the street half open. Curious to find out who the man was,

104

the informer went into the vestibule, and heard Claes talking
to the stranger in the kitchen. The talk was all about a
certain Josse, the brother of Claes, who it seems had been
made prisoner among the army of the Reformers, and had
suffered the punishment of being broken alive on the wheel
of torture, not far from Aix. The stranger said that he had
brought Claes a sum of money which his brother had desired
to leave him, which money having been gained from the
ignorant and poverty-stricken, it behoved Claes to spend it
in bringing up his own son in the Reformed Faith. He also
urged Claes to quit the bosom of our Holy Mother Church,
and spake also many other impious words to which the only
reply vouchsafed by Claes was this : ' The cruel brutes !
Alas, my poor Josse ! ' So did the prisoner blaspheme
against our Holy Father the Pope and against His Royal
Majesty, accusing them of cruelty in that they rightly had
punished heresy as a crime of treason against God and man.
When the stranger had finished the meal that Claes put before
him, our agent heard Claes cry out again : ' Alas, poor Josse !
May God keep thee in his glory ! How cruel they were to
thee ! ' And thus did he accuse God himself of impiety by
this suggestion that He could receive a heretic into His
heaven. Nor did Claes ever cease to cry aloud : ' Alas !
Alas ! My poor Josse ! ' The stranger then, launching out
into a frenzy, like a preacher beginning his sermon, fell to
revile most shamefully our Holy Mother the Church. ' She
will fall,' he shouted, ' she will fall, the mighty Babylon, the
whore of Rome, and she will become the abode of demons,
and the haunt of every bird accursed.' And Claes meanwhile
continued the same old cry : ' Cruel brutes ! Alas, poor
Josse ! ' And the stranger went on in the same way as he
had begun, saying : ' Verily an angel shall appear that shall
take a stone that is great as a millstone, and shall cast it
into the sea, crying : " Thus shall it be done to Babylon the
mighty, and she shall be no more seen." ' Whereupon, ' Sir,'

says Claes, ' your mouth is full of bitterness ; but tell me, when cometh that kingdom in which they that are gentle of heart shall be able to dwell in peace upon the earth ? ' ' Never,' answered the stranger, ' while yet my Lord Antichrist rules, that is the Pope, who is to-day the enemy to all truth.' ' Ah,' said Claes, ' you speak with little respect of the Holy Father. But he, surely, is ignorant of the cruel punishments which are meted out to poor Reformers.' ' Not at all,' answered the stranger, ' and far from it, for it is he who initiates the decrees and causes them to be put into force by the Emperor, now by the King. The latter enjoys all the benefits of confiscation, inherits the property of the dead, and finds it easy to bring charges of heresy against those who have any wealth.' Claes said : ' Indeed I know that such things are freely spoken of in the land of Flanders, and one may well believe them, for the flesh of man is weak, even though the flesh be royal flesh. O my poor Josse ! ' And by this did Claes give to understand that heretics are punished because of a vile desire on the part of His Majesty for filthy lucre. The stranger wished to argue the matter further, but Claes said : ' Please, sir, do not let us continue this conversation, for if it were overheard I might easily find myself involved in some awkward inquiry.' Then Claes got up to go to the cellar, whence he presently returned with a pot of beer. ' I am going to shut the door,' said he, and after that the informer heard nothing more, for he had to make his way out of the house as quickly as he could. Not till it was night was the door again opened, and then the stranger came forth. But he soon returned, knocking at the door and calling to Claes : ' It is very cold, and I know not where I am to lodge this night. Give me shelter, pray. No one has seen me. The town is deserted.' Claes welcomed him in, lit a lantern, and last of all he was seen to be leading the heretic up the staircase into a little attic room with a window that looked out on to the country."

106

The Dean of the Fishmongers

At this Claes cried out : " And who could have reported all this but you, you wicked fishmonger ! I saw you on Sunday, standing at your door, as straight as a post, gazing up, like the hypocrite you are, at the swallows in their flight ! "

And as he spoke, he pointed with his finger at Josse Grypstuiver, the Dean of the Fishmongers, who showed his ugly phiz in the crowd of people. And the fishmonger gave an evil smile when he saw Claes betraying himself in this way. And the people in the crowd, men, women, and maids, looked one at the other and said : " Poor good man, his words will be the death of him without a doubt."

But the clerk continued his depositions.

" Claes and the heretic stayed talking together for a long time that night, and so for six other nights, during which time the stranger was seen to make many gestures of menace or of benediction, and to lift up his hands to heaven as do his fellow-heretics. And Claes appeared to approve of what he said. And there is no doubt that throughout these days and nights they were speaking together oppro-briously of the Mass, of the confessional, of indulgences, and of the Royal Majesty. . . ."

" No one heard it," said Claes, " and I cannot be accused in this way without any evidence."

The clerk answered :

" There is something else that was overheard. The even-ing that the stranger left your roof, seven days after he had first come to you, you went with him as far as the end of Katheline's field. There he asked you what you had done with the wicked idols "—here the bailiff crossed himself— " of Madame the Virgin, and of St. Nicholas and St. Martin. You replied that you had broken them all up and thrown them into the well. They were, in fact, found in the well last night, and the pieces are now in the torture-chamber."

At these words Claes appeared to be quite overcome.

The bailiff asked if he had nothing to answer. Claes made a sign with his head in the negative.

The bailiff asked him if he would not recant the accursed thoughts which had led him to break the images, and the impious delusion whereby he had spoken such evil words against Pope and Emperor, who were both divine personages.

Claes replied that his body was the Emperor's, but that his soul was Christ's, whose law he desired to obey. The bailiff asked him if this law were the same as that of Holy Mother Church. Claes answered:

" The law of Christ is written in the Holy Gospel."

When ordered to answer the question as to whether the Pope is the representative of God on earth, he answered, " No."

When asked if he believed that it was forbidden to adore images of Our Lady and of the saints, he replied that such was idolatry. Questioned as to whether the practice of auricular confession was a good and salutary thing, he answered: " Christ said, confess your sins one to another."

He spoke out bravely, though at the same time it was evident that he was ill at ease and in his heart afraid.

At length, eight o'clock having sounded and evening coming on, the members of the tribunal retired, deferring their judgment until the morrow.

XXXIX

The next day the great bell, *Borgstorm*, clanged out its summons to the judges of the tribunal. When they were all assembled at the *Vierschare*, seated upon the four benches that were set around the lime-tree, Claes was cross-examined afresh, and asked if he was willing to recant his errors.

But Claes lifted his hand towards heaven:

" The Lord Christ beholdeth me from on high," he said, " and when my son Ulenspiegel was born I also gazed upon

108

His Sun. Where is Ulenspiegel now ? Where is he now, the vagabond ? O Soetkin, sweet wife, will you be brave in the day of trouble ? "

Then looking at the lime-tree he cursed it, saying : " South wind and drouth, I adjure you to make the trees of our fathers perish one and all where they stand, rather than that beneath their shade freedom of conscience shall be judged to death ! O Ulenspiegel, my son, where are you ? Harsh was I unto you in days gone by. But now, good sirs, take pity on me, and be merciful to me in your judgment, even as Our Lord would be merciful."

And all that heard him wept, save only the judges.

Then Claes asked them a second time if they would not pardon him, saying :

" Truly I was always a hard-working man, and one that gained little for all his toil. I was good to the poor and kind to every one. And if I have left the Roman Church it is only in obedience to the spirit of God that spake to me. I ask for no grace except that the pain of fire may be commuted to a sentence of perpetual banishment from the land of Flanders. Banishment for life ! A sufficient punishment that, surely ! "

And all they that were present cried aloud :

" Have pity upon him ! Have mercy ! "

But Josse Grypstuiver held his peace.

Now the bailiff made a sign to the company that they should keep silence, adding that the placards contained a clause which expressly forbade the petitioning of mercy for heretics. But he said that if Claes would abjure his heresy he should be executed by hanging instead of by burning. And the people murmured :

" What matters burning or hanging, they both mean death ! "

And the women wept and the men murmured under their breath.

Claes said :

" I will abjure nothing. Do to my body whatsoever is pleasing to your mercy."

Then spoke the Dean of Renaix, Titelman by name :

" It is intolerable that these vermin of heretics should raise up their heads in this way before their judges. After all, the burning of the body is but a passing pain, and torture is necessary for the saving of souls, and for the recantation of error, lest the people be given the dangerous spectacle of heretics dying in a state of final impenitence."

At these words the women wept still more, and the men said : " In those cases where the crime is confessed punishment may be rightly inflicted, but torture is illegal ! "

The tribunal decided that since indeed it was a fact that the ordinances did not order torture to be applied in such cases, there was no occasion to insist that Claes should suffer it. He was asked once more if he would not recant.

" I cannot," he answered.

Then, in accordance with the ordinances, sentence was passed upon him. He was declared guilty of simony in that he had taken part in the sale of indulgences, and he was also declared to be a heretic and a harbourer of heretics, and as such he was condemned to be burned alive before the hoardings of the Town Hall. His body was to be left hanging on the stake for the space of two days as a warning to others, and afterwards it was to be interred in the place set apart for the bodies of executed criminals. To the informer, Josse Grypstuiver (whose name had never been mentioned throughout the whole trial), the tribunal ordered to be paid the sum of fifty florins calculated on the first hundred florins of the inheritance of the deceased, and a tenth part of the remainder.

When he heard the sentence that had been passed upon him, Claes turned to the Dean of the Fishmongers.

" You will come to a bad end," he said, " you wicked man

hat for a paltry sum of money have turned a happy wife
nto a widow, and a joyous son into a grieving orphan."

The judges suffered Claes to speak in this way for they
ilso, all except Titelman, could not help despising from the
)ottom of their hearts the Dean of the Fishmongers for the
nformation he had given. Grypstuiver himself went pale
vith shame and anger.

And Claes was led back to his prison.

XL

On the morrow (which was the day before the execution of
Claes) the decision of the court was made known to Nele, to
Jlenspiegel, and Soetkin. They asked the judges for leave
.o visit Claes in prison, which permission was granted in the
:ase of the wife and the son only.

On entering the prison cell they found Claes tied to the
vall by a long chain. A small fire was burning in the grate
)ecause of the damp. For it is custom and law in Flanders
:hat they who are condemned to death shall be gently treated
ind be given bread and meat to eat, or cheese and wine.
;till gaolers are a greedy race, and oftentimes the law is
)roken, there being many prison guards who themselves
at up the greater part of the nourishment provided for the
)oor prisoners, or keep the best morsels for themselves.

Claes embraced Ulenspiegel and Soetkin, crying the while.
3ut he was the first to dry his eyes, for he put control upon
iimself, being a man and the head of the family. Soetkin,
iowever, went on crying, and Ulenspiegel kept muttering
nder his breath :

" I must break these wicked chains ! "

And Soetkin said through her tears :

" I shall go to King Philip. He surely will have mercy ! "

But Claes answered that this would be no use since
he King was wont to possess himself of the property of
hose who died as martyrs. . . . He said also :

111

" My wife and child, my best beloved, it is with sadness and sorrow that I am about to leave this world. If I have some natural apprehension for my own bodily sufferings, I am no less concerned when I think of you and of how poor and wretched you will be when I am gone, for the King will certainly seize for himself all your goods."

Ulenspiegel made answer, speaking in a low voice for fear of being overheard :

" Yesterday Nele and I hid all the money."

" I am glad," Claes answered ; " the informer will not laugh when he comes to count his plunder."

" I had rather he died than had a penny of it," said Soetkin with a look of hate in her eyes now dry of tears. But Claes, who was still thinking about the caroluses, said to Ulenspiegel :

" That was clever of you, Tyl, my lad ; now Soetkin need not be afraid of going hungry in the old age of her widowhood."

And Claes embraced her, pressing her close to his breast, and she wept all the more bitterly as she thought how soon she was to lose his tender protection.

Claes looked at Ulenspiegel and said :

" My son, it was wrong of you to go running off along the high roads of the world like any ruffian. You must not do that any more, my boy. You must not leave her alone at home, my widow in her sorrow. For now it is your duty to protect her and take care of her—you, a man."

" I will, father," said Ulenspiegel.

" O my poor husband ! " cried Soetkin embracing him again. " What crime can we have committed ? Nay, we lived our life peaceably together, lowly and humbly, loving each other well—how well Thou, Lord, knowest ! Early in the morning we rose for work, and at eventide, rendering our thanks to Thee, we ate our daily bread. Oh, would that I could come at this King, and tear him with my nails ! For in nothing, O Lord God, have we offended ! "

112

But here the gaoler entered and said that it was time for them to depart.

Soetkin begged to be allowed to stay, and Claes felt her poor face burning hot as it touched his, and her tears falling in floods and wetting all his cheek, and her poor body shaking and trembling in his arms. He, too, entreated the gaoler that she might be suffered to remain with him. But the gaoler was obdurate, and removed Soetkin by force from the arms of Claes.

" Take care of her," Claes said to Ulenspiegel.

He promised, and son and mother left the room together, she supported in his arms.

XLI

The next day, which was the day of the execution, the neighbours, out of pity for their suffering, came and shut up Soetkin and Nele and Ulenspiegel in Katheline's cottage. For they could not bear that they should see the terrible sight of the burning. Yet it had been forgotten that the far-off cries of the tormented one would reach the cottage, and that those within would be able to see through the windows the flames of the fire.

Katheline, meanwhile, went wandering through the town, wagging her head and crying out continually :

" Make a hole ! Make a hole ! My soul wants to get out ! "

At nine of the clock Claes was led out of his prison. He was dressed in a shirt only, and his hands were tied behind his back. In accordance with the sentence that had been passed upon him, the pile was set up in the rue Notre Dame, with a stake in the midst, just in front of the hoarding of the Town Hall. When they arrived there the executioner and his assistants had not yet completed the work of stacking the wood. Claes stood patiently in the midst of his tormentors watching while the work was finished, and all the time the provost on his horse, with the officers of the tribunal and the filite foot-soldiers that had been summoned from Bruges, had the greatest difficulty in keeping order among the people. For they murmured one to another, saying that it was cruelty thus to do to death unjustly a man like Claes, a poor man and already old in years, and one that was so gentle, so forgiving, and such a good and steady workman.

Suddenly they all fell upon their knees and began to pray, for the bells of Notre Dame were heard tolling for the dead.

Katheline also was among the crowd, right in the front, mad as she was. Fixing her eye on Claes and the pile of wood, she wagged her head and cried continually:

"Fire! Fire! Dig a hole! My soul wants to get out!"

When Nele and Soetkin heard the sound of the tolling they crossed themselves. But Ulenspiegel did not cross himself, saying that he would never pray to God after the same fashion as those hangmen. But he ran about the cottage, trying to force open the doors or jump from the windows. But they were shut and fastened well.

Suddenly Soetkin hid her face in her apron.

"The smoke!" she cried.

And in very fact, the three mourners could see, mounting high to heaven, a great eddy of smoke; all black it was, the smoke of the funeral pile whereon was Claes, tied to a stake, the smoke of that fire which the executioner had just set burning in the name of the Father and of the Son and of the Holy Ghost.

Claes looked around for Soetkin or Ulenspiegel. But not seeing them anywhere in the crowd he felt happier and more at ease, thinking that they would not know how he suffered. And all the time there was a silence like death, except for the sound of Claes' voice praying, and the crackling of the wood, the murmuring of men, the weeping of the women, the voice of Katheline as she cried: "Put out the fire! Make a hole! My soul wants to get out!" and over all, the bells of Notre Dame tolling for the dead.

The Death of Claes

Suddenly Soetkin's face went as white as snow, and her body trembled all over. She did not utter a sound, but pointed to the sky with her finger. For there a long, straight flame of fire had risen above the pyre, and now was leaping high above the roofs of the lower houses. It was a flame of pain and cruelty to Claes, for following the caprice of the breeze, it preyed upon his legs, or touched his head so that it smoked, licking and singeing his hair.

Ulenspiegel took Soetkin in his arms and tried to tear her away from the window. Then they heard a sharp cry, the cry which came from Claes when one side of his body was burnt by the dancing flames. But then he was silent again, weeping to himself. And his breast was all wet with his tears.

Thereafter Soetkin and Ulenspiegel heard a great noise as of many voices. This was the townsfolk, their wives and their children, who now began to cry and shout out all together :

" He was not sentenced to be burnt by a slow fire, but by a quick fire ! Executioner, stir up the faggots !"

The executioner did so. But the fire did not flame up quick enough to please the mob.

" Kill him !" they shouted. " Put him out of his misery !" And they began to throw missiles at the provost.

Soetkin cried aloud : " The flame ! The great flame !"

And in very truth they saw now a great red flame, mounting heavenwards, in the midst of the smoke.

" He is about to die," said the widow. " O Lord, of your mercy receive the soul of this innocent. Where is the King, that I may go and tear out his heart with my nails ?"

And all the while the bells of Notre Dame kept tolling for the dead. Yet again did Soetkin hear a great cry from her husband ; but mercifully she was spared the sight of his body writhing in the agony of the fire, and his twisted face, and his head that he turned from side to side and beat upon the wood of the stake. Meanwhile the crowd continued to shout and to hiss, and the boys threw stones, until all of a sudden the whole pile of wood caught alight, and the voice of Claes was heard crying out from the midst of the flame and smoke:

"Soetkin! Tyl!"

And then his head fell down upon his breast as though it were made of lead.

And there came a cry, most piteous and piercing, from the cottage of Katheline; and after that there was silence, except for the poor mad woman wagging her head and saying:

"My soul wants to get out!"

Claes was dead. The fire burned itself away, smouldering at the foot of the stake whereon the poor body still hung by its neck.

And the bells of Notre Dame tolled for the dead.

XLII

In Katheline's cottage Soetkin stood leaning against the wall, with her head hanging down and her hands clasped together. She held Ulenspiegel in her arms, speechless and without a tear. Neither did Ulenspiegel say anything. It made him afraid to feel the burning fever that raged in the body of his mother.

The neighbours, returning from the place of execution, came to the cottage and told how Claes had made an end of his sufferings.

"He is in glory," said the widow.

"Pray for him," said Nele, putting her rosary into the hands of Ulenspiegel. But he would make no use of it, giving as his reason that the beads had been blessed by the Pope.

At last night came, and Ulenspiegel urged his mother to go to bed, telling her that he himself would sit up and keep watch in the room. But Soetkin said that there was no need for him to do that. Let him sleep also, for the young have

116

need of a good night's rest. So Nele prepared two beds for them in the kitchen, and after that she left them.

Mother and son stayed up together while what remained of the wood fire burned itself out in the grate. Then Soetkin retired to her bed, and Ulenspiegel did likewise, listening to his mother sobbing to herself under the bedclothes.

Outside in the silence of the night the wind made a murmuring sound in the trees by the canal. It was like the far-off sound of waves, and it meant that autumn was coming soon. Also, there were great eddies of dust that beat against the cottage windows.

Now it seemed to Ulenspiegel that he saw the figure of a man going to and fro in the room, and he thought he heard the sound of footsteps coming and going in the kitchen. But when he looked he no longer saw the man, and listening he no longer heard those footsteps, but only the sound of the wind as it whistled in the chimney and Soetkin crying under the bedclothes.

Then once again he heard those footsteps, and just behind him, near his head, a soft sigh.

"Who is it?" he said.

No one answered, but quite distinctly came the sound of three taps on the table. Ulenspiegel was afraid, and began to tremble. "Who is it?" he said again. No one answered, but once more there came the three taps upon the table, and after that he felt two arms hugging him round, and over him there leant a man's body with skin all wrinkled and a great hole in its breast that gave forth a smell of burning.

"Father," said Ulenspiegel, "is it you, and is this your poor body that weighs thus upon me?"

He received no answer to his question, and although the shadow seemed still quite close, it was from outside the cottage that he heard a voice crying out to him by name, "Tyl! Tyl!"

Suddenly Soetkin got out of bed and came over to where Ulenspiegel was lying.

" Do you hear something ? " she said.

" Yes," he answered, " it is father calling to me."

" I too," said Soetkin, " I have felt a cold body beside me in my bed, and the mattress has moved, and the curtains. And I heard a voice that spoke my name : ' Soetkin !' it said, a voice soft as a whisper. And I heard a step near by, light as the sound of a gnat's wings." Then she addressed herself to the spirit of Claes : " If there is aught that you desire in that heaven where God guards you in his glory, you must tell me, my man, that we may know what you would have us do."

All of a sudden a mighty gust of wind came blowing upon the door, and it burst wide open and straightway the room was filled with dust ; and from afar, Soetkin and Ulenspiegel could hear the sound of the cawing of many ravens.

They went out of the cottage, and came together to the place of torture. . . .

It was a black night, save where the clouds—coursing in the sky like stags before the keen north wind—were parted here and there so as to disclose the glittering face of some star.

By the remnants of the pile strode a sergeant of the commune, up and down, keeping guard. Soetkin and Ulenspiegel heard his steps as they resounded on the hardened ground, and together with that sound there came the cry of a raven, calling his fellows, doubtless; for from far away there came the sound of other caws in answer.

As Soetkin and Ulenspiegel approached the pile the raven swooped down upon the shoulder of Claes, and they could hear its beak pecking upon the body. And soon the other ravens followed. Ulenspiegel would have thrown himself upon the pile and beaten them off had not the sergeant come up and prevented him.

" Are you a sorcerer," cried the man, " that comes hither for the hands of the dead as a talisman, and yet do you not know that the hands of a man that has been burnt to death

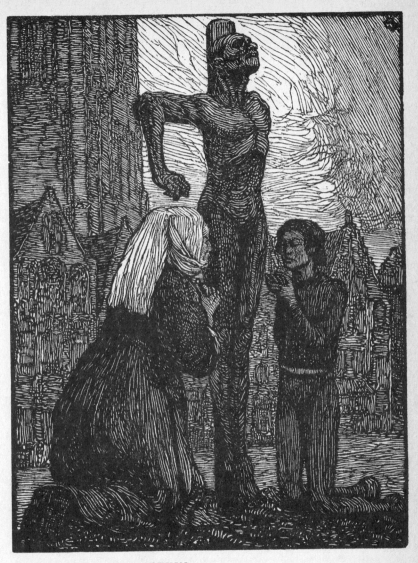

ULENSPIEGEL AND SOETKIN
BY THE DEAD BODY OF CLAES

possess no power of invisibility, but only hands of one who has been hanged—such as you yourself will be one of these days?"

"Sir," Ulenspiegel replied, "I am no sorcerer, but the orphaned son of the man tied to this stake here. And this woman is the dead man's widow. We only wish to kiss him once again, and to take away a few of his ashes in his memory. Give us leave, sir, pray, for you are certainly no foreign soldier, but a son of this land."

"Very well," said the sergeant.

So the orphan and the widow made their way over the charred wood and approached the body. Weeping, they both kissed the face of Claes.

Then Ulenspiegel found the place where the heart had been, a great hole hollowed out by the flames, and therefrom he took a few ashes. Then Soetkin and he knelt down and said a prayer, and when the sky began to turn pale in the dawn they were still kneeling there together. But the sergeant drove them off, for he was afraid that he would be punished for his kindness.

When they were home again Soetkin took a piece of red silk, and a piece of black silk, and she made a little bag to contain the ashes. And on the little bag she sewed two ribbons so that Ulenspiegel could always carry it suspended round his neck. And she gave it to him with these words:

"These ashes are the heart of my husband. This red ribbon is his blood. This black one is our sorrow. Always upon your breast let them lie, and call down thereby the fire of vengeance upon his torturers."

"Amen," said Ulenspiegel.

And the widow embraced her orphan, and the sun rose.

XLIII

In that year, being the fifty-eighth year of the century, Katheline came into Soetkin's house and spake as follows:

The Legend of Tyl Ulenspiegel

" " Last night, being anointed with balm, I was transported to the tower of Notre Dame, and I beheld the elemental spirits that carry the prayers of men to the angels, and they in their turn, flying up towards the highest heaven, bring them to the Throne of God. And everywhere the sky was strewn with glittering stars. Suddenly I saw the figure of a man that seemed all blackened and charred, rising from a funeral pile. Mounting up towards me, this figure took its place beside me on the tower. I saw that it was Claes, just as he was in life, dressed in his charcoal-burner's clothes. He asked me what I was doing there on the tower of Notre Dame. 'And you,' I asked in my turn, 'whither are you off to, flying in the air like a bird?' 'I am going,' he answered, 'to judgment. Hear you not the angel's trump that summons me?' I was quite close to him, and could feel the very substance of his spiritual body—not hard and resisting to the touch like the bodies of those that are alive, but so rarefied that to come up against it was like advancing into a kind of warm mist. And at my feet stretched out on every side the land of Flanders, with a few lights shining here and there, and I said to myself: 'They that rise early and work late, surely they are the blessed of God!' And all the time I could hear the angel's trumpet calling through the night. And presently I saw another shade mounting up towards me from the land of Spain. This was an old man and decrepit, with a protruding chin, and quince jam all oozing from the corners of his lips.

" On its back it wore a cloak of crimson velvet lined with ermine, and on its head an imperial crown, and it kept nibbling a piece of anchovy which it carried in one hand, while in the other hand it clutched a tankard of beer. I could see that this spirit was tired out and had come to the tower of Notre Dame to rest itself. Kneeling down, I addressed it in these words: 'Most Imperial Majesty, of a truth I revere you, yet I know not who you are. Whence

come you ? And what was your position in the world ? '
' I come,' answered the shade, ' from Saint Juste in the
country of Estramadoure. I was the Emperor Charles the
Fifth.' ' But,' said I, ' whither, pray, are you going on such a
cold night as this, and over these clouds that are all heavy
and charged with hail ? ' ' I go,' answered the shade, ' to
judgment.'

" Just as the Emperor was about to finish his anchovy
and drink up his tankard of beer, the angel's trumpet sounded,
and straightway he had to betake himself to the air again,
grumbling at this sudden interruption of his repast. High
aloft he mounted through space, I following close behind ;
and as he went he hiccuped with fatigue, and coughed
asthmatically, even vomited now and again ; for death had
come upon him at a time when he was suffering from a fit of
indigestion. Thus ceaselessly we soared aloft like arrows
shot from a bow of cornel-wood. The stars glimmered all
around us, and time and again we saw them detach themselves
and fall headlong, tracing long strokes of fire upon the sky.
Once more the angel's trump resounded, very shrill and
powerful. Each fanfare seemed to cleave for itself a pathway
through the cloudy air, scattering the mists asunder like a
hurricane that has begun to blow from near at hand. And
by this means our track was marked out clearly for us, till
at length, when we had been carried up and up a thousand
leagues and more, we beheld Christ Himself in His glory,
seated upon a throne of stars. And at His right hand was
the angel who records the deeds of men upon a register of
brass, and at His left hand stood Mary His Mother, she that
for ever implores mercy for poor sinners.

" Claes and the Emperor knelt down together before the
throne. And the angel took off the crown from the head of
the Emperor, and cast it away.

" ' There is only one Emperor here,' he said. It is ' Christ ! '

" His Sacred Majesty could not conceal his annoyance ;

yet managed to assume a humble tone of voice as he begged
to be allowed to keep his anchovy and his tankard of beer,
for that he had come a long way and was very hungry.

"'Hungry you have been all your life,' said the angel,
'nevertheless, you may go on with your eating and drinking
if you want to.'

"The Emperor emptied the tankard of beer and took a
nibble at the anchovy. Then Christ addressed him with
these words :

"'Do you present yourself to judgment with a clean soul ?'

"'I trust so, dear Lord,' answered Charles the Emperor,
'for I have confessed my sins and am well shriven.'

"'And you, Claes ? You do not seem to be trembling
like the Emperor.'

"'My Lord Jesus,' answered Claes, 'there is no soul that
is clean, and how should I be afraid of you, you that are
sovereign good and sovereign justice. Nevertheless, I am
afraid of my sins, for they are many.'

"'Speak, carrion !' said the angel, addressing himself to
the Emperor.

"'I, Lord,' said Charles, in an embarrassed tone of voice,
'I am he that was anointed with oil by your priests, and
crowned King of Castile, Emperor of Germany, and King of
the Romans. It has ever been my first care to maintain
that power which was given me by you, and to that end I
have done my best by hanging and by sword, by burning and
by burying alive, by pit and by fire to keep down all Reformers
and Protestants.'

"But the angel said :

"'O you false and dyspeptic man, you are trying to
deceive us. In Germany, forsooth, you were tolerant enough
of the Protestants, seeing that there you had good cause to be
afraid of them. But in the Netherlands you beheaded,
burned, hanged, and buried them alive, for there your only
fear was lest you might fail to inherit sufficient of their

property—so rich and plenteous, like the honey made by busy bees. And there perished at your hands one hundred thousand souls, not at all because you loved the Lord Christ, but because you were a despot, a tyrant, a waster of your country, and one that loved himself first of all, and after that, nothing but meat, fish, wine, and beer, for you were always as greedy as a dog and as thirsty as a sponge.'

"When the angel had made an end, Christ commanded that Claes should speak, but now the angel rose from his place, saying : ' This man has nothing to answer. He was a good, hard-working man, as are all the poor people of Flanders, willing either for work or play ; one that kept faith with his masters and trusted his masters to keep faith with him. But he possessed a certain amount of money, and it was for this reason that an accusation was brought against him, and inasmuch as he had harboured in his house a heretic, he was condemned to be burnt alive.'

" ' Alas ! ' cried Mary, ' the poor martyr ! But here in heaven there are springs of fresh water, fountains of milk, and exquisite wine which will refresh you, and I myself will lead you there, good charcoal-burner ! '

"And now the angel's trumpet sounded yet again, and I saw a man, naked and very beautiful, rising from the abyss. On his head was an iron crown, and on the rim of the crown these words inscribed : ' Sorrowful till the day of judgment.'

" He approached the throne and said to Christ :

" ' Thy slave I am until that day when I shall be Thy master ! '

" ' O Satan,' said Mary, ' the day will come when there shall be neither slave nor master any more, and when Christ who is Love, and Satan who is Pride, shall stand forth together as the One Lord both of Power and of Knowledge.'

" ' Woman,' said Satan, ' thou art all goodness and all beauty.'

" Then addressing himself to Christ, and pointing at the

123

same time towards the Emperor, Satan demanded what was to be done with him.   Christ answered:

" 'Take this crowned wormling and put him in a room wherein you have collected together all instruments of torture which were in use under his rule.   And each time that some innocent wretch is made to suffer the torture of water, whereby the bodies of men swell up like bladders; or the torture of the candles, whereby the soles of their feet or their armpits are burned and scorched; or the torture of the *strappado*, whereby their limbs are broken; or the torture of the four wagons that drags them asunder—and every time that a free soul breathes out its last upon the funeral pile let this man also endure in his turn these same deaths and tortures, to the end that he may learn in his own person what evil may be wrought in the world by an unjust man who has power over his fellows.   Let him languish in prison, let him meet death upon the scaffold, let him mourn in exile, far from his native land, let him be scorned, abused, and flogged with many whips.   Let him know what it is to be rich and see all his property eaten up by the tax-gatherer, let him be accused by informers and ruined by confiscations.   Turn him into an ass that he may know what it is to be gentle by nature and at the same time ill-treated and badly fed; let him be a poor man that asks for alms and is answered only with abuse; let him be a workman that labours too long and eats too little; and then, when he has thus well suffered both in his body and his soul, turn him into a dog that he may be beaten, an Indian slave that he may be sold to the highest bidder, a soldier that he may fight for another and be killed without knowing why.   And then, at the end of three hundred years, when he has exhausted all sufferings and all miseries, make a free man of him, and if in that state of life he is good like Claes here, you may lay at last his body to rest in some quiet corner of earth that is shady in the noonday heat and open to the morning sun, and there beneath a beautiful tree and covered with fresh sward, he shall find eternal repose. And his friends shall come to his grave to moisten it with their tears, and to sow violets there, which are called the flowers of remembrance.'

" But Mary said : 'Have mercy upon him, O my Son ; he knew not what he did, and we know how power hardens the heart.'

" ' There is no mercy for him,' said Christ.

" ' Alas ! ' cried His Sacred Majesty, ' woe is me ! Would that I had but a single glass of Andalusian wine ! '

" ' Come,' said Satan, ' it is past the time for wine or meat or poultry ! '

" And away he carried off the soul of the poor Emperor, down to the nethermost hell, still nibbling as he went his piece of anchovy. For this Satan suffered him to do out of pity.

" Thereafter I saw that Our Lady conducted Claes away and up into the highest heaven, where is nothing but stars hanging from the roof like clusters of grapes. And there the angels washed him clean, and he became all beautiful and young, and they gave him *rystpap* to drink in silver ladles. And then the heavens closed."

" Claes is in glory," said the widow.

" His ashes beat against my heart," said Ulenspiegel.

XLIV

During all the three and twenty days that followed, Katheline grew paler and paler, and thin and all dried up as though devoured not only by the madness that consumed her but by some interior fire that was even deadlier still. No more did she cry out as of old : " Fire ! Fire ! Dig a hole ! My soul wants to get out ! " But she was continually transported into a kind of ecstasy, in which she spake to Nele many strange words.

" A wife I am," she said, " and a wife you also ought to be.

My husband is a handsome man. A hairy man is he, hot with love. But his knees and his arms, they are cold!" And Soetkin looked at her sadly, wondering what new kind of madness this might be. But Katheline continued:

"Three times three are nine, the sacred number. He whose eyes glitter in the night like the eyes of a cat—he only it is that sees the mystery."

One evening when Katheline was talking in this way, Soetkin made a gesture of misgiving. But Katheline said:

"Under Saturn, four and three mean misfortune. But under Venus, it is the marriage number. Cold arms! Cold knees! Heart of fire!"

Soetkin answered:

"It is wrong to talk in this way of these wicked pagan idols."

But Katheline only crossed herself and said:

"Blessed be the grey horseman. Nele must have a husband—a handsome husband that carries a sword, a dusky husband with a shining face!"

"Yes," cried Ulenspiegel, "a very fricassee of a husband, for whom I will make a sauce with my knife!"

Nele looked at her lover with eyes that were moist with pleasure to see him so jealous.

"None of your husbands for me!" she said.

But Katheline made answer:

"When cometh he? He that is clad in grey, and booted and spurred?"

Soetkin bade them say a prayer to God for the poor afflicted one, whereupon Katheline in her madness ordered Ulenspiegel go and fetch four quarts of *dobbel kuyt* what time she made ready some *heete-koeken*, as pancakes are called in Flanders.

Soetkin asked her why she wished to make festival on a Saturday like the Jews.

"Because the butter is ready," said Katheline.

So Ulenspiegel stood up and took in his hand the big pot of English pewter that held just four quarts.

" Mother," he asked, " what shall I do ? "

" Go," said Katheline.

Soetkin did not like to say anything more, for she was not mistress of the house. So she told her son to go and do as Katheline had bidden him. Ulenspiegel ran to the tavern and brought back with him the four quarts of *dobbel kuyt*. And soon the kitchen reeked with the good smell of pancakes, and every one felt hungry, even the poor afflicted Katheline.

Ulenspiegel ate heartily, and drank heartily also, for Katheline had given him a full tankard, saying, with a malicious look, that it behoved him to drink more than the others seeing that he was the only male and the head of the house. Afterwards she asked him to give them a song.

But Ulenspiegel did not sing, and Nele was all tearful, seeing Soetkin so pale, and as it were all sunken into herself. Katheline alone of them all appeared to be happy.

When the meal was over Soetkin and Ulenspiegel went up into the loft to bed. Katheline and Nele stayed behind, for they slept together in the kitchen.

All was quiet until the second hour after midnight. Ulenspiegel had already been asleep for a long time because of all the beer he had been drinking. But Soetkin, as her custom was, lay on with eyes wide open, praying Our Lady to send her sleep, but with no avail.

All of a sudden she heard the cry of a sea-eagle, and from the kitchen came a like cry, in answer. Then, from far off in the country somewhere, other cries resounded, always as it seemed in answer to that cry in the kitchen just below.

Soetkin tried to think it was only the night-birds calling to one another, and endeavoured to distract her attention from those sounds. But presently she heard a neighing of horses and a noise as of iron sabots beating along the high road. Then it was that she opened the window of the loft and saw that in very fact there were a couple of horses saddled just outside the cottage, pawing the ground and nibbling the grass that grew by the side of the road. Thereafter she heard the voice of a woman crying out in fear, and a man's voice threatening, followed by the sound of blows, more cries, a door shutting with a bang, and then steps running up the ladder in mortal fear:

All his time Ulenspiegel was snoring away in his bed, hearing nothing, till the door of the loft opened and Nele came in, out of breath, sobbing, and with scarcely anything on. As hastily as she could the girl dragged against the door a table, some chairs, an old heating stove, any bit of furniture that was to hand. With these she made a rough-and-ready barricade. Meanwhile, outside, the last stars were paling in the heavens and the cocks beginning to crow.

Ulenspiegel had turned over in his bed at the noise Nele was making, but now he had gone to sleep again. Nele, meanwhile, had thrown herself on to Soetkin's neck.

" Soetkin," she said, " I am afraid. Light the candle, do !"

Soetkin did so, and all the time Nele never left off moaning. By the light of the candle Soetkin looked the girl up and down. Her shift was torn at the shoulder and in front, and there were traces of blood upon her neck and cheek, such as might be left by the scratch of a finger-nail.

" Whence have you come ? And what are these wounds ? " Soetkin asked her.

Trembling and groaning all the time, the girl made answer :

" For mercy's sake, Soetkin, do not bring us to the stake ! "

Ulenspiegel meanwhile had awakened from his sleep, and was blinking his eyes in the sudden light of the candle. Soetkin said :

" Who is it down there ? "

" Not so loud ! " Nele whispered. " It is the husband Katheline desired for me."

All at once Soetkin and Nele heard Katheline cry out in a

loud voice, and their legs gave way beneath them in their terror.

" He is beating her," said Nele, " he is beating her because of me ! "

" Who is it in the house ? " cried Ulenspiegel, jumping out of bed. And then, rubbing his eyes, he went stalking up and down the room till at last he found a heavy poker that stood in the corner. He took hold of it, but Nele tried to dissuade him, telling him that there was no one there. But he paid no attention, running to the door and throwing to one side the chairs and tables and the stove that Nele had piled up in front of it. All this time Katheline was crying out from the kitchen, and Nele and Soetkin held Ulenspiegel —the one by the waist, the other by the legs—and tried to prevent him from descending the stairs. " Don't go down," they told him. " Don't go down, Ulenspiegel. There are devils down there."

" Forsooth," says he, " Nele's devil-husband ! Him verily will I join in marriage to this long poker of mine ! A marriage of iron and flesh ! Let me go ! "

But they did not loose their hold, hanging on as they were to the landing rail.

And all the time Ulenspiegel was trying to drag them down the staircase, and they the more frightened as they came nearer to the devils below. And they could avail naught against him, so that at last, descending now by leaps and bounds like a snowball that falls from the top of a mountain, he came into the kitchen. And there was Katheline, all exhausted and pale in the light of dawn.

" Hanske," she was saying, " O Hanske, why must you leave me ? Is it my fault if Nele is naughty ? "

Ulenspiegel did not take any notice of her, but straightway opened the door of the shed, and finding no one there, rushed out into the yard, and thence into the high road. Far away he descried two horses galloping off and disappearing in the mist. He ran after them hoping to overtake them, but he could not, for they went like a south wind that scours the dry autumn leaves.

Ulenspiegel was angry with disappointment, and he came back into the cottage grieving sore in his heart and muttering between his teeth :

" They have done their worst on her ! They have done their worst ! . . ."

And he looked on Nele with eyes that burned with an evil flame. But Nele, all trembling, stood up before Katheline and the widow.

" No ! " she cried. " No, Tyl, my lover ! No ! "

And as she spoke she looked him straight in the face, so sadly and so frankly that Ulenspiegel saw clearly that what she said was true. Then he spake again, and questioned her :

" But whence came those cries, and whither went those men ? Why is your shift all torn on the shoulder and the back ? And why do you bear on forehead and cheek these marks of a man's nails ? "

" I will tell you," she said, " but be careful that you do not have us burned at the stake for what I shall tell you. You must know that Katheline—whom God save from Hell— hath had these three-and-twenty days a devil for her lover. He is dressed all in black, he is booted and spurred. His face gleams with a flame of fire like what one sees in summer-time when it is hot, on the waves of the sea."

And Katheline whimpered : "Why, oh why, have you left me, Hanske, my pet ? Nele is naughty ! "

But Nele went on with her story :

" The devil announces his approach in a voice that is like the crying of a sea-eagle. Every Saturday my mother receives him in the kitchen. And she says that his kisses are cold and that his body is like snow. One time he brought her some florins, but he took from her all the other money that she had."

130

All this time Soetkin kept on praying for Katheline, with clasped hands. But Katheline spake joyfully :

"My body is mine no more. My mind is mine no more. O Hanske, my pet, take me with you yet once again, I beg you, to the Witches' Sabbath. Only Nele will never come. Nele is naughty, I tell you."

But Nele went on with her story :

"At dawn," she said, "the devil would go away, and the next day my mother would relate to me a hundred strange things. But, Tyl dear, you must not look at me with those cruel eyes. . . . Yesterday, for instance, she told me that a splendid prince, clad in grey, Hilbert by name, was anxious to take me in marriage, and that he was coming here himself that I might see him. I told her that I wanted no husband, handsome or plain. Nevertheless, by weight of her maternal authority she persuaded me to stay up for him, for she certainly keeps all her wits about her in whatever pertains to her amours. Well, we were half undressed, ready to go to bed ; and I had gone off to sleep sitting on that chair. It seems that I did not wake up when they came in, and the first thing I knew was that some one was embracing me and kissing me on the neck. And then, by the bright light of the moon, I beheld a face that shone like the crests of the waves of a July sea when there is thunder in the air, and I heard a low voice speaking to me and saying : 'I am your husband, Hilbert. Be mine ! I will make thee rich.' And from the face of him that spake these words there came an odour like the odour of fish. Quickly I pushed that face away from me, but the man tried to take me by force, and although I had the strength of ten against him, he managed to tear my shift and scratch my face, crying out the while that if only I would give myself to him he would make me rich. 'Yes,' I answered, 'as rich as my mother, whom you have deprived of her last *liard* !' At that he redoubled his violence, but he could not do anything against me. And at last, since he was more disgusting than a corpse, I scratched him in the eye with my nails so sharply that he cried out with pain, and I was able to make my escape and run up here to Soetkin."

And all this while Katheline kept on with her " Nele is naughty. And why did you go away so soon, O Hanske, my pet ? "

But Soetkin asked her where she had been while wicked men were attempting the honour of her child.

" It is Nele that is naughty," Katheline replied. " As for me, I was in company of my black master, when the devil in grey comes to us, with his face all bloody. ' Come away,' he cries, ' come away, my boy, this is an evil house ; for the men, it seems, are of a mind to fight with one to the death, and the women carry knives at the tips of their fingers.' And there and then they ran off to their horses, and disappeared in the mist. Ah, Nele, Nele ! She is a naughty lass, I tell you ! "

XLV

On the following day, while they were making a meal of hot milk, Soetkin said to Katheline :

" You see how misfortune is already driving me from this world ; and yet you, it seems, would like to drive me away all the faster by your accursed sorceries ! "

But Katheline only went on repeating :

" Nele is naughty. Come back, Hanske, my pet ! "

It was the following Wednesday when the two devils came again. Ever since the preceding Saturday Nele had slept out at the house of a widow woman named Van den Houte, saying, by way of excusing herself, that she could not stay with Katheline because of that young rogue Ulenspiegel.

Now Katheline welcomed her black master and her master's friend out in the *keet*, which is to say the laundry or bakehouse adjoining the cottage. And there did they feast and regale themselves with old wine and with smoked ox tongue, which viands were always prepared and ready in that place for them. And the black devil said to Katheline :

" You must know, Katheline, that we are engaged in a mighty work, and to accomplish it we have need of a large sum of money. Give us, I pray you, what you can."

When she only offered them a florin they threatened to kill her. But when she had raised the amount to a couple of golden caroluses and seven *deniers* they let her off.

" Come not again on Saturdays," she told them, " for Ulenspiegel has discovered that your custom it is to come on that day, and he will certainly be waiting for you and will beat you to death, and that would be the death of me as well."

" We will come next Tuesday," they told her.

Now on that day Nele and Ulenspiegel went to sleep without any anxiety, thinking that the devils only came to the cottage on Saturdays. But Katheline got out of bed secretly and went into the yard to see if her friends had arrived. She was very impatient, for since seeing Hanske again her madness had abated, for hers was a lover's madness, as they say.

But to-night she could nowhere see her friends, and she was greatly distressed, so that when, presently, she heard the cry of the sea-eagle coming as it seemed from the open country in the direction of Sluys, she went out towards that cry, making her way across the field by the side of a tall dike that was constructed of sticks and grass. She had not gone far when she heard the two devils conversing together at the other side of the dike. And one of them said :

" Half shall be mine."

And the other answered :

" No. Nothing of the kind. What is Katheline's belongs to me. All of it."

Then they blasphemed together most terribly, disputing as to which of the two should be possessed of the property and the love of Katheline and of Nele into the bargain. Paralysed

133

with fear, daring neither to speak nor to move, Katheline presently heard them fall to fighting with one another. And then one of the devils cried aloud :

" Ah ! The cold steel ! "

And after that there came the sound of a death-rattle, and of a body falling heavily.

Terrified as she was, Katheline returned to the cottage.

At two of the morning she heard once more the cry of the sea-eagle, but this time close at hand in the yard. She went to the door and opened it, and saw her devil lover standing there all alone.

She asked him what he had done with his friend.

" He will not come again," he told her.

Then he kissed her and caressed her, and his kisses seemed colder than ever before. When the time came for him to depart, he asked her to give him twenty florins. This was all that she had, but she gave him seventeen.

The next day she could not control her curiosity, and walked out along by the dike. But she found nothing, except at one place a mark on the grass about the size of a man's coffin ; and the grass was wet underfoot and red with blood. But that evening rain fell, washing the blood away.

On the following Wednesday Katheline heard yet again the cry of the sea-eagle in the yard.

XLVI

Now whenever any money was needed to pay for the expenses of Katheline's household, Ulenspiegel was accustomed to go by night to the hole by the well wherein had been hidden the money left by Claes. He would lift up the stone that covered the top of the well and would take out a carolus.

One evening the two women were busy with their spinning, while Ulenspiegel sat carving a chest which had been commissioned from him by the town bailiff. And upon the side of the chest he was carving a hunting scene. Very beautiful it was and cleverly carved, with a pack of hounds running in pairs closely following one another, chasing their quarry.

Katheline was there, and Nele asked Soetkin absent-mindedly if she had found a safe hiding-place for her treasure. Thinking no harm, the widow answered that it would be hard to find a safer place than the side of the well wall.

Near midnight of the following Thursday Soetkin was awakened by Bibulus Schnouffius, who was barking fiercely. But soon he was quiet again, and Soetkin, thinking that it was a false alarm, turned over and went to sleep.

The next day when Nele and Ulenspiegel rose at dawn they were surprised to find no Katheline in the kitchen, neither was the fire lit, nor was there any milk boiling on the fire as usual. They were surprised at this and went out to see if perchance she was in the yard. And there they found her, all dishevelled in her linen shift, notwithstanding that it was drizzling with rain, and she was all damp and shivering, and stood there, not daring to come in.

Ulenspiegel went up to her and asked her what she was doing half naked there in the rain?

"Ah!" she said. "Yes, yes. Strange things have happened! Strange, wonderful things!"

And as she spoke she pointed to the ground, and they saw the dog lying there with its throat cut, all dead and stiff.

Ulenspiegel's thoughts ran at once to the treasure. He hastened to the hole by the well, and found as he had feared that it was empty, and all around the earth scattered about far and wide.

He ran back to Katheline and struck her with his hand.

"Where are the caroluses?" he cried.

"Yes! Yes! Strange things have been happening!" she answered.

"Have Nele tried to protect her mother from the wrath of Ulenspiegel.

At this mercy, have pity," she cried, "O Ulenspiegel!"

135

Then he stopped beating the wretched woman, and at the same moment Soetkin appeared on the scene and wanted to know what was the matter.

Ulenspiegel showed her the dog with its throat cut and the empty hole. Soetkin turned pale, and cried out most sorrowfully: " O God, thou hast brought me low indeed!"

And Nele, seeing how gentle Soetkin was, wept also and was very sorrowful. But Katheline, flourishing a piece of parchment that she held in her hand, began to speak in this wise : " Yes, yes. Strange things and wonderful have come to pass this night! For he came to me, my good one, my beautiful. And no longer did his face display that ghastly glitter which makes me so afraid. And it was with a great tenderness in his voice that he addressed me. Yes, I was overcome with love for him, and my heart was melted within me. ' I am a rich man,' he told me, ' and soon I will bring thee a thousand florins in gold.' ' So be it,' I answered him. ' I rejoice for your sake rather than for mine, Hanske, my pet.' ' But is there no one else in your cottage,' he asked, ' that you love, perhaps, and would rejoice to see enriched by me also ? ' ' No,' I replied. ' They that live here have no need of any help of thine.' ' You are proud, it seems,' he answered. ' Soetkin and Ulenspiegel, are they then so rich as to need nothing ? ' ' They live without the help of any,' I told him. ' In spite of the confiscations ? ' he asked. But then I laughed aloud, and said that he knew that they would not be such simpletons as to hide their treasure in the house where it could be easily found. ' Nor yet in the cellar ? ' he persisted. ' Of course not,' I told him. ' Nor yet in the yard ? ' To that I answered not a word. ' Ah,' he said, ' that would indeed be a piece of imprudence.' ' Not so imprudent as all that,' I answered, ' for neither walls nor water have tongues.' And at that he began laughing to himself. Presently he went away, earlier it was than usual. But first he gave me a powder, telling me that

136

if I took it I should be spirited away to the finest of all the Sabbaths. I accompanied him a little way just as I was, as far as the door of the yard, and I seemed half asleep, and soon I found myself, even as he had told me, at the Witches' Sabbath, and I did not return from thence until the morning. Then it was that I found myself here as you see me, and discovered the dog with his throat cut, and the empty hole. And this is a heavy blow to me, to me that loved him so tenderly, and had given to him my very soul. But whatsoever I have shall be yours, and I will labour with my hands and my feet to keep you alive, never fear."

But Soetkin said :

" I am become even as the corn beneath the grindstone. God and this devil robber are heavy upon me both at once."

" *Robber* do you call him ? " cried Katheline. " Speak not so. He is a devil, a devil I say ! And for proof I will show to you this parchment which he left behind him in the yard, and on it is written, ' Forget not to serve me, and behold, in three times two weeks and five days I will render thee back again twice as much again as the treasure I have now taken from thee. Doubt not, or else thou wilt surely die.' And oh," cried Katheline, " of a surety he will keep his word ! "

" Poor mad thing," said Soetkin.

And this was the only word of reproach that she uttered.

XLVII

Six months passed, and the devil lover came no more. Nevertheless Katheline did not live without hope of seeing her Hanske again.

Soetkin meanwhile had given up her work altogether, and was always to be found sitting huddled up in front of the fire ; and her cough never left her. Nele provided the choicest and most sweetly smelling herbs, but no remedy had any power over her. As for Ulenspiegel, he never left the cottage for fear that his mother might die while he was out.

At last there came a time when the widow could neither eat nor drink without being sick. The surgeon (who also carried on the trade of a barber) came to bleed her, and when the blood had been taken away she was so enfeebled that she could not leave her chair. And at last the evening came when she cried out, all wasted with pain :

" Claes ! Husband ! And Tyl, my son ! Thanks be to God for He taketh me ! "

And with a sigh she died.

Katheline did not dare to watch by that bed of death, so Nele and Ulenspiegel kept watch together, and all night long they prayed for her that was gone.

As the dawn broke a swallow came flying in by the open window.

Nele said : " The bird of souls ! It is a good omen. Soetkin is in heaven ! "

The swallow flew three times round the room, and departed with a cry. Then there came a second swallow, larger it was and darker than the first. It fluttered around Ulenspiegel, and he said :

" Father and mother, the ashes beat upon my breast. Whatsoever you command me, that will I do."

And the second swallow went off with a cry, just as the first had done. And Ulenspiegel saw thousands of swallows skimming over the fields. And the sun rose.

And Soetkin was buried in the cemetery of the poor.

XLVIII

After the death of Soetkin Ulenspiegel grew dreamy, sorrowful, and angry, and he would wander about the fields, hearing nothing, taking what food or drink was put before him, and never choosing for himself. And oftentimes he rose from his bed in the middle of the night and went out into the country alone.

In vain did the gentle voice of Nele urge him not to

138

despair, in vain did Katheline assure him that Soetkin was now in Paradise with Claes. To both alike Tyl answered :

" The ashes beat upon my breast."

And he was as one mad, and Nele was sorrowful because of him.

Meanwhile, Grypstuiver the fishmonger dwelt alone in his house, like a parricide, daring only to come out in the evening. For if any man or woman passed him on the road they would shout after him and call him " murderer." And the little children ran away when they saw him, for they had been told that he was a hangman. So he wandered about by himself, not venturing to enter any of the taverns that are in Damme, for the finger of scorn was pointed at him, and if ever he stood in the bar for a minute, they that were drinking there left the tavern.

The result was that no innkeeper desired him as a customer any more, and whenever he presented himself at their houses they would shut the door on him. The fishmonger would make a humble remonstrance, but they answered that they had a licence to sell wine certainly, but that they were not obliged to sell it against their will.

The fishmonger grew impatient at this, and in future when he wanted a drink he would go to the *In 't Roode Valck*— at the sign of the Red Falcon—a little cabaret outside the town on the banks of the Sluys canal. There they served him, for they were hard up at that inn, and glad to get anything from any one. But even so, the innkeeper never entered into conversation with him, nor did his wife either. Now in that house there were also two children and a dog ; but when the fishmonger made as though he would kiss the children they ran away, and the dog, when he called him, tried to bite him.

One evening Ulenspiegel was standing on his doorstep in a dream, and Mathyssen, the cooper, happening to pass by, saw him standing there, and said to him :

" If you worked with your hands belike you would forget this grievous blow."

But Ulenspiegel answered: "The ashes of Claes beat upon my breast."

"Ah!" said Mathyssen, "there lives a man who is sadder even than you are—Grypstuiver the fishmonger. None speaks to him, and all avoid him, so much so that when he wants his pint of *bruinbier* he is forced to go out all alone to the poor folk of the *Roode Valck*. Verily he is well punished."

"The ashes beat . . ." Ulenpiegel answered him again.

And the same evening, when the bells of Notre Dame were sounding the ninth hour, Ulenspiegel sallied forth towards the *Roode Valck*, but failing to find the fishmonger there as he had expected, he went wandering along under the trees that grow by the canal-side. It was a bright moonlight night.

Presently he saw the figure of the murderer coming towards him. He passed close in front of Ulenspiegel, who could hear what he was saying, for the fishmonger was talking to himself, as is the custom of they who live much alone.

"Where have they hidden it?" he muttered. "Where have they hidden the money?" But Ulenspiegel answered the question for him by giving him a great blow in the face.

"Alas!" cried the fishmonger as he felt the hand of Ulenspiegel upon him. "Alas, I know you! You are his son! But have pity on me. Have pity! For I am weak and aged, and what I did to your father was not done out of malice, but in the service of His Majesty. Only deign to forgive me, and I will give you back again all the goods that I have bought, and you shall not pay me a penny. You shall have everything, and half a florin over and above, for I am not a rich man. No, you must not think that I am rich!"

And he was about to kneel down in front of Ulenspiegel. But seeing him so ugly, so craven, and so base, Ulenspiegel took hold of him and threw him into the canal.

And he went away.

XLIX

And from many a funeral pyre there ascended to heaven the smoke from the flesh of the victims, and Ulenspiegel, thinking ever upon Claes and Soetkin, wept in his loneliness.

At last, one evening, he went to find Katheline, thinking to inquire of her some way of remedy or revenge.

She was alone with Nele, sewing by the light of the lamp. At the sound which Ulenspiegel made as he came in, Katheline raised her head slowly like one that is awakened from a heavy sleep.

He said: "The ashes of Claes beat upon my breast, and I am fain to do somewhat to save this land of Flanders. But what can I do? I have entreated the great God of earth and heaven, but he has answered me nothing."

Katheline said: "The great God cannot hear you. First of all you should have recourse to the spirits of the elemental world, for they, uniting in themselves two natures, both celestial and terrestrial, are enabled to receive the plaints of men and hand them on unto the angels, who themselves in their turn carry them up thereafter to the Throne."

"Help me," he said, " only help me now, and I will repay you with my blood if need be."

"I can help you," said Katheline, "on one condition only: that a girl who loves you is willing to take you with her to the Sabbath of the Spirits of Spring, which is the Easter of Fruitfulness."

"I will take him," said Nele.

Whereupon Katheline took a crystal goblet and poured into it a certain mixture of a greyish colour, and she gave it to them both to drink, and rubbed their temples with this mixture, and their nostrils likewise, and the palms of their hands, and their wrists, and she also caused them to eat a pinch of white powder, and then she told them to gaze the one at the other in such manner that their two souls might become one.

Ulenspiegel looked at Nele, and straightway the sweet eyes of the girl illumined in him a mighty flame, and because of the mixture he had taken he felt as it were a thousand crabs nipping his skin all over him.

After that Nele and Ulenspiegel undressed, and very beautiful they looked in the lamplight, he in the pride of his manly strength, and she in all her youthful grace and sweetness. But they were not able to see one another, for already it was as though they were asleep. Then Katheline rested the neck of Nele upon the arm of Ulenspiegel, and taking his hand she placed it upon the young girl's heart. And there they stayed, all naked, lying side by side. And to both of them it seemed that their bodies, where they touched, were made of tender fire, like the sun itself in the month of roses.

Then, as they afterwards related, they climbed together on to the window-sill, whence they threw themselves out into space, and felt the air all round them, buoying them up as the waters buoy up the ships at sea.

Thereafter they lost all consciousness, seeing naught of earth where slept poor mortals, nor yet of heaven whose clouds were rolling now beneath their feet; for now they had set their feet upon Sirius, the frozen star, and from thence again they were flung upon the Pole.

There it was that a fearful sight awaited them, a giant all naked, the Giant Winter. His hair was wild and tawny, and he was seated on an ice-floe, with his back resting against a wall of ice. Near by in the pools of water there disported a host of bears and seals, bellowing all round him. In a hoarse voice the giant summoned to his presence the hail-storms and the snow-storms and the icy showers; also there came at his behest the grey clouds and brown odorous mists, and the winds among whom is the sharp north wind, he that blows the strongest of all. Such were the terrors that raged together in that place of bane.

But smiling in the midst, the giant reclined on a bed of

142

flowers that had been withered by his own hand, and of leaves dried by his very breath. Then, leaning down and scratching the ground with his finger-nails, and biting it with his teeth, the giant began to burrow a great pit. For he wanted to discover the heart of the earth to devour it, and to put the blackened coal where once there had been shady forests, and chaff where once had been corn, and barren sand in place of fruitful soil. But old earth's heart was made of fire, so that he dared not touch it but recoiled therefrom in dread.

There he sat like a king upon his throne, draining his horn of oil. All round him were his bears and seals, and the skeletons of those whom he had killed on the high seas or on the dry land or in the cottages of the poor. He listened joyfully to the roaring of the bears, to the braying of the seals, and to the sound made by the skeletons of men and animals as the bones clicked together beneath the claws of the crows and vultures that came for the last remaining piece of flesh that might still adhere to them. And sweet also to his ears was the noise the ice-floes made as they were driven one against another by the waves of that dreary sea.

And when he spoke, the voice of the giant was even as the roaring of a hurricane or as the noise of winter storms, or as the wind howling in the chimneys.

" I am cold and afraid," said Ulenspiegel.

" He is powerless against immortal souls," said Nele.

Even as she spoke a great commotion arose among the seals, who began to rush back into the sea with all haste. And it was apparent that the bears also were afraid for they lay back their ears and began to bellow most piteously. As for the crows and ravens, they cawed as though they were in terror of their lives, and started off to hide themselves among the clouds.

And now it was that Nele and Ulenspiegel first began to hear a sound as of a mighty battering-ram beating upon the farther side of that glassy wall against which Giant Winter had been reclining. And the wall cracked visibly and shook to its founda-

143

tions. But of all this Giant Winter heard nothing at all, for he went on baying and bellowing most joyfully, filling and emptying again and again his bowl of oil, and continuing his search for the heart of the earth, that he might freeze it to nothing, although, forsooth, whenever he found that fiery centre he always lacked the courage so much as to take it in his hand!

Meanwhile the blows of the battering-ram resounded heavier and louder, and the crack in the wall of ice grew broader every second, and all around the giant, the rain of icicles ceased not to fall in myriad fragments. And the bears roared ceaselessly and piteously, and the seals sent up their plaintive cries from the dreary waste of water.

Suddenly the wall gave way, and from the bright sky beyond it a man descended. Naked he was, most beautiful of aspect, holding in one of his hands a hatchet of pure gold. This was Lucifer, the light-bringer, Lord of the Spring.

When Giant Winter saw him he immediately cast away his bowl of oil and entreated the new-comer to spare at least his life. But at the first warm breath of Spring, Giant Winter lost all his strength, and Lucifer was able to bind him with a chain of diamonds, and tie him securely to the Pole.

Then, standing still, the Lord of the Spring most tenderly and amorously cried aloud, and from the heavens there descended a woman, naked also, and most fair, most beautiful. She stood beside her lord, and spake to him:

"You are my conqueror, strong man."

And thus he answered her:

"If you are hungry, eat; if you are thirsty, drink; if you are afraid, come near to me. I am your mate."

"I have no hunger, no thirst, but for thee alone," she said.

Then the Lord of the Spring called out yet seven times and again. Most tremendous was his voice, and there was a mighty din of thunder and lightning, and behind him there came into being a kind of dais all made of suns and stars. And the lord and his lady sat them down on two thrones.

The Girl-Flowers

Then these twain, their countenances remaining still and motionless, and without the least tremor to spoil the calmness of their majesty and their power, both together cried aloud. And at that sound there was a movement in the earth like that of a countless multitude of worms, and not in the earth only but in the hard stone and in the ice-floes also. And Nele and Ulenspiegel heard a sound like that which might be made by gigantic birds trying to crack with their beaks the great imprisoning egg-shells wherein they were concealed. And amid this great commotion of the earth, heaving and subsiding like the waves of the sea, there appeared forms like those of eggs.

And suddenly, on all sides, trees emerged, their bare branches all entangled together, and their stems shaking and tottering together like drunken men, which began to separate themselves the one from the other, leaving empty spaces of earth between. And now from the ever restless soil there emerged the Spirits of Earth, and from the depths of the forest the Spirits of the Woods, and from the neighbouring sea, now cleared of ice, the Spirits of the Water.

And Nele and Ulenspiegel could discern the guardian spirits of all these wonders. Dwarfs there were, men of the woods that lived like trees and carried, instead of mouths and stomachs, little clusters of roots sprouting from below the face to the end that they might suck their nourishment from the bosom of mother earth. Lords of the mines there were as well, they that know no speech, and are destitute of heart or entrails, and move about like glittering automatons. There came also the dwarfs of flesh and bone, little fellows with lizards' tails and the heads of toads, and a lantern on their head for head-gear. These are they that leap by night upon the shoulder of the drunken wayfarer or the tired traveller, and then jump down again, waving their lanterns the while so as to lead into marsh or ditch that hapless wight who thinks the light he sees is a candle set to beacon his way home.

There came too the Girl-Flower spirits, blossoms they of

145

womanly health and strength. Naked they were and unashamed, glorying in their beauty, and having nothing to cover them but their hair. The eyes of these maids shone liquid like mother-of-pearl seen through water ; the flesh of their bodies was firm, white, and glittering in the sunshine ; and from half-opened ruby lips their breath wafted down more balmy than jasmine.

These are the maids that wander at eventide in the parks or gardens of the world, or belike in the shady paths of some woodland glade. Amorous they are, searching ever for some soul of man to possess it for themselves. And whenever some mortal lad and lass come walking their way, they try to kill the girl, but failing in this they breathe a breath of love upon the doubting damsel, so that she fears no longer to abandon herself to the delights of love, but gives herself to her lover. For then the Girl-Flower is permitted to take her share of the kisses.

Besides all this, Nele and Ulenspiegel could see descending now far from heaven the Guardian Spirits of the Stars, the Spirits of the Winds, of the Breezes, and of the Rain : young, winged men that fertilize the earth. And there appeared from every point in the heavens the soul-birds, the dear swallows. At their coming the light itself seemed to grow brighter, and the girl-flowers, the lords of the rocks, the princes of the mines, the men of the woods, the spirits of water, fire, and earth, all cried out with one voice, "O Light, O sap of Spring, Glory to the Spirit of Spring ! " And though the sound of all this shouting was more powerful than the noise of a raging sea, or of a thunder-storm, or of a hurricane let loose, yet it seemed most solemn music to the ears of Nele and Ulenspiegel, who stood, motionless and dumb, curled up behind the gnarled and wrinkled stem of a mighty oak.

But sights more terrible yet awaited them, for now the spirits took their places by thousands upon the backs of gigantic spiders, and toads with trunks like those of elephants, and serpents all intertwined, and crocodiles that stood upright on

146

their tails and held a whole bevy of spirits in their mouths. Snakes, too, there were that carried more than thirty dwarfs at a time, both male and female, sitting astride on their writhing bodies ; and thousands upon thousands of insects, more huge than Goliath himself, armed with swords, lances, jagged scythes, seven-pronged forks, and every other kind of murderous and horrifying implement. Great was the uproar, and stern the battle which they fought amongst themselves, the strong eating up the weak and getting fat thereon, thus demonstrating how death is ever born from life, and life from death.

And out of all this throng of spirits, confused and serried, there came a sound as of a deep rumbling of thunder, or of a hundred looms, of weavers, fullers, and locksmiths, all working together in full swing.

And suddenly the Spirits of the Sap made their appearance on the scene. Short they were, and squat, and their loins were as large as the great barrel of Heidelberg itself. And their thighs were fat like hogsheads of wine, and their muscles so strangely strong and powerful that one would have said that their bodies were made of naught but eggs, eggs big and little, joined up to one another, and covered over with a kind of ruddy skin, strong and glistening like their scanty beards and tawny hair. And they carried great tankards or goblets that were filled with a strange liquor.

When the other spirits saw them coming, there at once arose among them a great flutter of joy. The trees and the plants became the victims of a strange restlessness, and the thirsty earth opened in a thousand fissures that it might drink of the liquor.

And the Spirits of the Sap poured out their wine, and at the same moment everything began to bud, and to grow green, and to come into flower ; and the sward was alive with buzzing insects, and the sky was filled with birds and butter-flies. The spirits, meanwhile, continued pouring out their sap, and those below them received the wine as they best were able : the girl-flowers opening their mouths and leaping upon the tawny cup-bearers and kissing them for more ; others clasping their hands in prayer ; yet others, in their delight, allowing the precious liquid to rain upon them as it would ; but all alike, hungry and thirsty, flying, standing still, running, or motionless, all greedy for the wine, and more alive for every drop they were able to get. And none was there so old, whether he were plain or handsome, but he was filled with fresh force and with new and lusty youth.

And with great shouting and laughing they pursued each other among the trees like squirrels, or in the air like birds, each male seeking his female, and acting out beneath God's open sky the sacred task of nature.

And the Spirits of the Sap brought to the King and Queen a mighty bowl brimming with their wine. And the King and the Queen drank thereof, and embraced one another. And the King, holding the Queen fast in his arms, threw the dregs of that bowl far away upon the trees and flowers and all the other spirits that were there. And loud did he raise his voice, crying :

" Glory to Life ! Glory to the free air ! Glory to Force ! "

And all with one voice cried aloud : " Glory to Nature ! Glory to Life ! "

And Ulenspiegel took Nele in his arms. And thus entwined, a dance began, an eddying dance like that of leaves in a whirlwind ; and in that vortex everything was swinging together, both trees and plants, and insects, the butterflies, heaven and earth itself, the King and his Queen, the girl-flowers and the lords of the mines, spirits of the water, hunchbacked dwarfs, lords of the rocks, men of the woods, will-o'-the-wisps, guardian spirits of the stars, and the thousand thousand terrible insects all commingled with their lances, their jagged swords, their seven-pronged forks. A giddy dance it was, rolling in the space which it filled, a dance

148

wherein the very sun and moon took part, and the stars and planets, the clouds, and the winds.

And in that whirlwind the oak to which Nele and Ulenspiegel were clinging rolled over on its side, and Ulenspiegel said to Nele:

" We are going to die, little one. . . ."

These words of Ulenspiegel one of the spirits overheard, and seeing that they were mortals:

" Men !" he cried. " Men, here ? "

And he dragged them from the tree to which they clung, and cast them into the very midst of the crowd. But they fell softly on the backs of the spirits, who passed them on one to another, bidding them welcome in such terms as these:

" All hail to man ! All hail, worms of the earth ! Who is there now would like to see a young mortal, a boy or a little girl ? Poor wights that are come to pay us a visit ! "

Nele and Ulenspiegel flew from one to the other, crying " Mercy ! " But the spirits payed no attention to them, and they were suffered to go on flying about, legs in air, heads downwards, whirling about like feathers in a winter wind. And all the time the spirits were saying:

" Hail to the little men and little women ! Come dance like us ! " Now the girl-flowers desired to separate Nele from Ulenspiegel, and they would have beaten her to death had not the King of the Spring stopped the dance suddenly with a single gesture.

" Bring them to me," he cried; " bring before me these two lice ! " So they were separated the one from the other, each girl-flower doing all she could to tear Ulenspiegel from her rival, saying:

" Tyl, Tyl, wouldst not die to have me ? "

" I shall die soon enough," answered Ulenspiegel.

And the dwarfish spirits of the woods that carried Nele

149

said to her also : " Why are you not a spirit like us that we might take you ? "

And Nele answered : " Only have patience."

So they came at length before the throne of the King, and when they saw his golden axe and his crown of iron they began to tremble with fear. And he asked them :

" Wherefore have you come to see me, poor little things ? "
But they answered him not at all.

" I know you," added the King, " you bud of a witch, and you also, shoot of a charcoal-burner. By power of sorcery have you penetrated into this laboratory of Nature, yet now your lips are closed like capon stuffed with bread-crumbs ! "

Nele trembled as she gazed upon the awful aspect of that spirit. But the manly courage of Ulenspiegel revived, and he made answer bravely :

" The ashes of Claes beat upon my breast. For, Most Divine Highness, Death now goes gathering his harvest through all the land of Flanders, mowing down the bravest of her men and the sweetest of her women in the name of His Holiness the Pope. And the privileges of my country are broken, her charters annulled, she is wasted by famine, her weavers and cloth-workers abandon her to look for work in other lands. And soon must she die if none comes to her aid. Your Highness, I am naught indeed but a poor little chit of a man that has come into the world like any other, and I have lived as I was able, imperfect, limited on every side, ignorant, neither virtuous nor chaste, and most unworthy of any grace, human or divine. Yet my mother Soetkin died as the result of torture and grief, and Claes was burned in a terrible fire, and I have sworn to avenge them. Once I have been able to do this. But now I long to see the miserable soil of my native land made happy, the soil where the bones of my parents lie scattered ; and I have asked of God the death of our persecutors, but not yet has He heard my prayer. This is why, all weary of my complaining, I have

150

evoked your presence by the power of Katheline's charm, and this is why we are come to you, I and my trembling comrade here, to fall at your feet and to beg you, Most Divine Highness, to save our poor land!"

To this the King and his illustrious companion as with one voice made answer :

> *By battle and fire,*
> *By death and sword,*
>   *Seek the Seven.*
>
> *In death and blood,*
> *Ruin and tears,*
>   *Find the Seven.*
>
> *Ugly, cruel, wicked, deformed,*
> *Very scourge of the whole earth,*
>   *Burn the Seven.*
>
> *Listen now, attend and see,*
> *Tell us, poor thing, are you not glad ?*
>   *Find the Seven.*

And all the spirits sang now together :

> *In death and blood,*
> *In ruin and tears,*
>   *Find the Seven.*
>
> *Listen now, attend and see,*
> *Tell us, poor thing, are you not glad ?*
>   *Find the Seven.*

But Ulenspiegel only said :

"Your Highness, and you my Lords Spirits, I understand nothing of your language. You are mocking me, without a doubt."

But the spirits, without listening to him at all, went on with their singing :

> *When the North*
> *Shall kiss the West,*
> *Then shall be the end of ruin.*
> *Find the Seven,*
> *And the Cincture.*

And they sang with such an effect of unanimity and such a terrifying force of sound that the very earth trembled and the heavens shuddered. And the birds twittered, the owls hooted, the sparrows chirruped with fear, the sea-eagles wailed aloud, flying hither and thither in their dismay. And all the animals of the earth, lions, snakes, bears, stags, roe-bucks, wolves, dogs, and cats, roared, hissed, belled, howled, barked, and miawed most terribly.

And the spirits kept on singing :

> *Listen now, attend and see,*
> *Love the Seven,*
> *And the Cincture.*

And the cocks crowed, and all the spirits vanished away, excepting only one wicked lord of the mines, who took Nele and Ulenspiegel each in one of his arms, and cast them most roughly into the void.

Then they awoke and found themselves lying by each other, as if they had been asleep, and they shivered in the chill morning air.

And Ulenspiegel beheld the sweet body of Nele, all golden in the light of the rising sun.

HERE BEGINS THE SECOND BOOK OF THE LEGEND OF THE GLORIOUS JOYOUS AND HEROIC ADVENTURES OF TYL ULENSPIEGEL AND LAMME GOEDZAK IN THE LAND OF FLANDERS AND ELSEWHERE

I

ONE morning in September Ulenspiegel took his staff,
three florins that had been given him by Katheline,
a piece of pig's liver and a slice of bread, and set out
to go from Damme to Antwerp, seeking the Seven. Nele
he left asleep.

On the way he met a dog who followed after him, smelling
around because of the liver, and jumping up at his legs.
Ulenspiegel would have driven off the dog, but seeing the
persistence of the animal, he thus addressed him :

" My dear dog, you are certainly ill-advised to leave your
home, where you would find awaiting you an excellent meal
of patties and other fine remains (to say nothing of the
marrow-bones), to follow, as you are now doing, a mere ad-
venturer of the road, a vagabond that is like to lack so much
as a root to give you for nourishment. Follow my advice,
most imprudent little dog, and return to your innkeeper.
And for the future, take good care to avoid the rain and snow,
the hail, the drizzling mists, the glassy frosts and other
such wretched fare as is alone reserved for the back of the
poor wanderer. Keep close at home, rather, in a corner of
the hearth, and warm yourself, curled up in front of the
cheerful fire. But leave to me the long wandering in mud
and dust, in cold and heat, to be roasted to-day, to-morrow
frozen, plenished on Friday but on Sunday famished for
want of food. For, trust me, little dog, the wise thing is to
return at once like a sensible and experienced little dog to
the place whence you came."

But it would seem that the animal did not hear a single
word of what Ulenspiegel was saying, for he continued to
wag his tail and jump his highest, barking all the while, in
his desire for food. Ulenspiegel imagined that all this was
just a sign of friendliness, and gave no thought to the liver
which he carried in his scrip.

By the Wayside

So on and on he walked, with the dog following behind. And when they had gone in this way the better part of a league, they saw a cart on the roadside with a donkey harnessed thereto, holding his head down. On a bank, at the side of the road, between two clumps of thistles, reclined a man. He was very fat, and in one hand he held the knuckle-end of a leg of mutton, and in the other hand a bottle. He gnawed the knuckle-bone and drank from the bottle, but when he was doing neither of these things he would fall to weeping and groaning.

Ulenspiegel stopped on his way, and the dog stopped too, but quickly jumped up on to the bank, smelling doubtless a good odour of liver and mutton. There he sat on his hind legs by the fat man's side, and began to paw at the stranger's doublet, as much as to say, " Please give me a share of your meal ! " But the man elbowed him off, and holding up the knuckle-bone in the air began to moan aloud most piteously. The dog did likewise in the eagerness of his desire, while the donkey (who was weary of being tied to the cart and thus prevented from getting at the thistles) set up, in his turn, a most piercing bray.

" What's the matter now, Jan ? " the man inquired of his donkey.

" Nothing," said Ulenspiegel, answering for him, " except that he would fain make his breakfast off those thistles that grow there on either side of you, like the thistles that are carved on the rood-screen at Tessenderloo, below the figure of Our Lord. Nor would this dog here, I'm thinking, be any the less inclined to join his jaws together on the bone you have got there. But in the meanwhile I will give him a piece of this liver of mine."

The man looked up at Ulenspiegel, who straightway recognized him as none other than his friend Lamme Goedzak of Damme.

" Lamme," he cried, " you here ? And what are you

155

doing, eating and drinking and moaning ? Has some soldier or other been so impertinent as to box your ears, or what's the matter ? Tell me."

" Alas ! " said Lamme, " my wife ! "

And he would have emptied his bottle of wine there and then had not Ulenspiegel laid a hand on his arm and suggested that it were fairer that the drink should be given to him that had none. " Besides," he added, " to drink thus distractedly profits naught but one's kidneys."

" Well said," answered Lamme, handing his friend the bottle, " but will you drink, I wonder, to any better purpose ? "

Ulenspiegel took the bottle, drank his fill, then handed it back again.

" Call me a Spaniard," he said, " if I've left enough to make a minnow drunk ! "

Lamme inspected the bottle. Then, without ever ceasing to groan, he rummaged in his wallet and produced another bottle, and another piece of sausage which he cut up in slices and began to munch in the most melancholy fashion.

" Do you *never* stop eating, Lamme ? " asked Ulenspiegel.

"Often, my son," he replied. " But now I am eating to drive away sad thoughts. Where are you, wife of mine ? " And as he spoke, Lamme wiped away a tear. After which he cut himself ten slices of sausage.

" Lamme," said Ulenspiegel, " you should not eat so quickly, taking no thought at all for the poor pilgrim."

Lamme, who was still whimpering, gave four of the slices to Ulenspiegel, who ate them up immediately, and was much affected by their good flavour. But Lamme said, eating and crying all at the same time :

" O wife, O goodly wife of mine ! How sweet she was, how beautiful she was ! Light as a butterfly, nimble as the lightning, and with a voice like a skylark ! For all that, she

156

was overfond of fine clothes. Alas, but how well she looked in them! And surely, the flowers also, are they not fond of rich apparel? Oh, if you had seen her, my son—her little hands, so nimble to caress, such hands as you never could have suffered to come in contact with saucepan or frying-pan! And her complexion, which was clear as the day, would surely have been burnt by standing over the kitchen fire. And what eyes she had! Only to look at them was to be melted quite with tenderness. Alas, I have lost her! Go on eating, Tyl; it is good Ghent sausage."

"But why has she left you?" asked Ulenspiegel.

"How should I know?" Lamme replied. "Alas! gone for ever are those days when I used to go to her home a-courting! Then, verily, she would fly away from me, half in love and half in fear! And her arms were bare, as like as not (beautiful arms they were, so round and white), but if she saw me looking at them she would cover them quickly with the sleeve of her gown.

"At other times, again, she would gladly lend herself to my caresses, and I would kiss her closed eyes, and that lovely neck of hers, so large and firm. She would shiver all over, uttering little cries of love, and then, leaning her head backwards, she would give me a playful slap upon my nose. Thereafter she would laugh and I would cry aloud, and we would wrestle together right amorously, and there was naught betwixt us but laughter and fun. But there, there. Is any wine left in the bottle, Tyl?"

Tyl gave him what remained.

"This ham does great good to my stomach," he said.

"To mine also," answered Lamme, "but I shall never see my dear one again. She has fled away from Damme. What say you, will you come with me in my cart to look for her?"

"That will I," answered Ulenspiegel.

So they got up into the donkey-cart, and the donkey set up a most melancholy bray to celebrate their departure.

As for the dog, he had already made off, well filled, without a word to any one.

II

While the cart went lumbering along on the top of the dike, with the pond on one side and the canal on the other, Ulenspiegel sat brooding on the past and cherishing in his bosom the ashes of Claes. He pondered deeply upon that vision he had seen, and asked himself if indeed it were true or false, and if those spirits of Nature had been making mock of him, or if perchance they had been revealing to him under a figure those things that must be done if the land of his fathers were to be restored. In vain did he turn the matter over and over in his mind, for he could not discover what was meant by those words, the " Seven " and the "Cincture." He called to mind the late Emperor Charles V, the present King, the Governess of the Netherlands, the Pope of Rome, the Grand Inquisitor, and last of all, the General of the Jesuits —six great persecutors of his country whom most willingly would he have burned alive had he been able. But he was forced to conclude that none of these was the personage indicated, for that they were all too obviously worthy of being burnt, and would be in another place. And he could only go on repeating to himself those words of the Lord of the Spring :

> *When the North*
> *Shall kiss the West,*
> *Then shall be the end of ruin.*
> *Love the Seven,*
> *And the Cincture.*

"Alas !" he cried, "in death, in blood, in tears, find the Seven, burn the Seven, love the Seven ! What does it all
158

mean? My poor brain reels, for who, pray, would ever want
to burn that which he loved?"

The cart by this time had progressed a good way along
the road, when all at once a sound was heard of some one
stepping along the sand, and of a voice singing:

> *Oh, have ye seen him, ye that pass,*
> *The lover I have lost, alas!*
> *Feckless he wandereth, knowing no tie—*
> > *Have ye seen him pass by?*
>
> *As tender lamb the eagle seizeth,*
> *So on my poor heart he feedeth.*
> *Beardless his chin, though to manhood nigh—*
> > *Have ye seen him pass by?*
>
> *If ye find him, ye may tell*
> *Weary with following faints his Nele.*
> *O Tyl, my beloved, hear me, I cry!*
> > *Have ye seen him pass by?*
>
> *Languisheth ever the faithful dove,*
> *Seeking, seeking her fickle love.*
> *So, far more so, languish I—*
> > *Have ye seen him pass by?*

Ulenspiegel gave Lamme a blow on his great belly, and
told him to hold his breath.

"That," said Lamme, "is a very difficult thing, I fear,
for a man of my corpulence."

But Ulenspiegel, paying no further attention to his companion, hid himself behind the canvas hood of the cart, and
began to sing in the voice of a man with a bad cold that has
drunk well:

> *In a shaky old cart with age all green,*
> *Your feckless sweetheart I have seen;*
> *And a glutton rides with him, like pig in sty—*
> > *I have seen him pass by.*

"Tyl," said Lamme, "you have a wry tongue in your cheek this morning!"

But Tyl put his head out of a hole in the hood:

"Nele, don't you know me?" he said.

And Nele, for it was none other than she herself, was filled with fear, crying and laughing all at the same time, and her cheeks were wet as she answered him:

"I see you, and I know you, you wretch, you traitor!"

"Nele," said Ulenspiegel, "if you want to give me a beating, you will find a stick in the cart here. It is heavy enough in all conscience, and knotted so that it will leave its mark right enough."

"Tyl," said Nele, "are you seeking the Seven?"

"Even so," Tyl told her.

Now Nele carried with her a bag, or satchel, that was so full it seemed likely to burst. This satchel she offered to Tyl, saying:

"I thought it was unwholesome, Tyl, that a man should go on a journey without a good fat goose, and a ham, and some Ghent sausages. So take them, and when you eat of them think of me."

While Ulenspiegel stood gazing at Nele, quite oblivious of the satchel which she was holding out to him, Lamme poked out his head from another hole in the hood, and began to address the girl in his turn.

"O girl most wise," he said, "O girl most prudent, if he refuses such a gift it must be from pure absence of mind. But you had much better give into my own keeping that goose of yours, that ham, and those fine sausages. I will take care of them, I promise you!"

"And who," asked Nele of her lover, "who may this red-face be?"

"A victim of the married state," Tyl told her, "that is wasting away with sorrow, and would soon, in fact, shrink away to nothing, like an overbaked apple, were it not that

160

he recuperated his strength from time to time and all the time by taking nourishment."

" Alas, my son," sighed Lamme, " what you say is only too true."

Now it was very hot, and Nele had covered her head with her apron because of the sun. Ulenspiegel looked upon her, and conceived a sudden desire to be alone with her. He turned to Lamme, and pointed to a woman that was walking some way off in a field.

" Do you see that woman ? " he said.

" I see her," said Lamme.

" Do you recognize her ? "

" Heavens ! " cried Lamme, " can it be my wife ? In truth she is dressed like no common country wench ! "

" Can you still be doutful, you old mole ? "

" But supposing it were not her after all ? " said Lamme.

" You would be none the worse off," Ulenspiegel told him, " for over there to the left, towards the north, I know a tavern that sells most excellent *bruinbier*. We will join you there, and here meanwhile is some salt ham that will provide an excellent relish to your thirst."

So Lamme got down from the cart, and made off as fast as his legs would carry him in the direction of the woman in the field.

Ulenspiegel said to Nele : " Why will you not come near me ? "

Then he helped her to climb up beside him on to the cart, and made her sit close by his side. He removed her apron from her head and the cloak from her shoulders, and then when he had kissed her a hundred times at least, he asked her :

" Where were you going to, beloved ? "

She answered him nothing, but seemed carried away in a sort of ecstasy. Ulenspiegel, in like rapture, said to her :

" Anyway you are here now ! And truly the wild hedge-row is dun beside the sweet pink colouring of your skin, and though you are no queen, behold I will make a crown of kisses all for you ! O sweet arms of my love, so tender, so rosy, and made for nothing but to hold me in their embrace ! Ah, little girl, little love, how dare I touch you ? These rough hands of mine, will they not tarnish the purity of your white shoulder ? Yea verily, for the lightsome butterfly may flit to rest upon the crimson carnation, but I, clumsy bumpkin that I am, how can I rest myself without tarnishing the living whiteness that is you ? God is in heaven, the king is on his throne, the sun rides triumphing in the sky, but am I a god, or a king, or the sun himself that I may come so close to you ? O tresses softer than silk ! O Nele, I fear to touch your hair, so clumsy am I, lest I tear it, lest I shred it all to pieces. But have no fear, my love. Your foot, your sweet foot ! What makes it so white ? Do you bathe it in milk ? ”

Nele would have risen from his side, but,

“What are you afraid of ? ” he asked her. “It is not the sun alone that shines upon us now and paints you all gold. Do not cast down your eyes, but look straight into mine, and behold the pure fire that flames there. And listen, my love, hearken to me, dearest. Now is midday, the silent hour. The labourer is at home, eating his dinner of soup. Shall we not also feed upon our love ? Oh why, oh why have I not yet a thousand years wherein to tell at your knees my rosary of Indian pearls ! ”

“ Golden Tongue ! ” she said.

But my Lord the Sun blazed down upon the white hood of the cart, and a lark sang high over the clover, and Nele leant her head upon the shoulder of Ulenspiegel.

III

After a while Lamme came back to the cart, great drops of sweat pouring off him, and he, puffing and blowing like a dolphin.

162

A False Start

"Alas!" he cried, "I was born under an evil star. For no sooner had I run and caught up with this woman than I found that she was not a woman at all, but an old hag rather, as indeed I could see at once by her face—forty-five years old at the very least! And to judge by her head-gear she had never been married. For all that, she inquired of me in a harsh voice what I was doing there, carrying my great fat belly about in the clover! I told her as politely as I could that I was looking for my wife who had lately left me, and that I had run after her by mistake.

"At that the old girl told me that the only thing for me to do was to return at once whence I came, and that if my wife had left me she had indeed done well, seeing that all men are thieves and rascals, heretics, unfaithful, poisoners, and deceivers of women; and she threatened to set her dog on me if I did not make off at once. Which in truth I did incontinently, for that I perceived a great mastiff lying there growling at her feet. When, therefore, I had reached the boundary of the field, I sat me down to rest myself and to eat a bit of ham. And I was between two clover-fields. Suddenly I heard a great noise just behind me, and turning round I saw the old girl's mastiff, no longer now in menacing mood but wagging his tail as sweetly as possible and as much as to say that he was hungry and would like a piece of my ham. I was for throwing him some small bits when all at once his mistress appeared on the scene, and shouted out fiercely:

"'Seize the man! Seize him with your fangs, my son!'

"I started to run away, the great mastiff hanging on to me by my breeks. And now he had bitten off a piece of them, together with a gobbet of my own flesh. The pain made me angry and I turned and gave him such a smart stroke with my stick upon his front paws that I must have broken one of them at least. At that he fell down, crying out in his dog language: 'Mercy! Mercy!' the which I granted him. Meanwhile his mistress, finding no stones to throw at me, had

163

begun to threaten me with pieces of earth and bits of grass. So I made good my retreat. And is it not a sorry thing, and a thing most unjust and most cruel, that because a girl has not been good-looking enough to find some one to marry her, she must needs go and take her revenge on a poor innocent like me ? "

IV

Some while after these happenings, when Nele had returned to her home with Katheline, Lamme and Ulenspiegel came to Bruges. They were at the place called Minne-Water, the Lake of Love—though the learned folk would have it to be derived from Minre-Water, that is, the Water belonging to the order of monks who are called Minims. Be this as it may, here on the bank of the lake, Lamme and Ulenspiegel sat themselves down, watching those that passed in front of them under the trees. The green branches hung over the pathway like a vault of foliage, and below there sauntered both men and women, youths and maids, clasping each other's hands, with flowers on their heads, walking so close together and gazing so tenderly into each other's eyes that they seemed to see nothing else in all the world save themselves alone.

As he watched them, the thoughts of Ulenspiegel were far away with Nele, and his thoughts were sad thoughts. Yet his words were of another colour, bidding Lamme come off with him to the tavern for a drink. But Lamme paid no attention to what Tyl was saying, for he himself was absorbed no less by the sight of those loving pairs.

" In the old days," he said, " we too, my wife and I, were wont to go a-courting, while others, just as we are now, would watch us, alone and companionless by the lake-side."

" Come and have a drink ! " said Ulenspiegel, " Belike we will find the Seven at the bottom of a pint of beer."

" That's but a drunkard's notion," answered Lamme, " for you know quite well that the Seven are giants, and taller than the roof of the Church of St. Sauver itself ! "

164

At the Sign of the Blue Lantern

The thoughts of Ulenspiegel were still with Nele, but none
the less did he hope to find, perchance, good quarters in some
inn, a good supper, and a comely hostess into the bargain.
Again, therefore, did he urge his companion to come along
with him and drink. But Lamme would not listen to him,
gazing sadly at the tower of Notre Dame, and addressing
himself in prayer to Our Lady somewhat in this wise :

"O Blessed Lady, patroness of all lawful unions, suffer
me, I pray, to see yet once again the white neck, the soft and
tender neck, of my love ! "

"Come and drink ! " cried Ulenspiegel. "Belike you will
find her displaying these charms of hers to the drinkers in the
tavern."

"How dare you harbour such a thought ! " cried Lamme.

"Come and drink ! " repeated Ulenspiegel. "Your wife
has turned innkeeper without a doubt."

And thus conversing, they repaired to the *Marché du
Samedi*, and entered into the *Blauwe Lanteern*—at the sign
of the Blue Lantern. And there they found a right jolly-
looking innkeeper.

The donkey meanwhile was unharnessed from the cart,
and was put up in the stables and provided with a good feed
of oats. Our travellers themselves ordered supper, and when
they had eaten their fill, they went to bed and slept soundly
till morning, only to wake up and eat again. And Lamme,
who was wellnigh bursting with all that he had eaten, said
that he could hear in his stomach a sound like the music of
the spheres.

Now when the time came to pay the bill, mine host came
to Lamme and told him that the total amounted to six
patards.

"*He* has the money," said Lamme, pointing to Ulenspiegel.

"No such thing," said Ulenspiegel.

"What about that half-florin ? " said Lamme.

"I haven't got it," said Ulenspiegel.

"Here's a nice way of going on!" cried the innkeeper. "I shall strip your doublet and shirt from the two of you!"

Suddenly Lamme took courage of all he had been drinking:

"And if I choose to eat and to drink," he cried, "yea, to eat and to drink the worth of twenty-seven florins, and more, do you think I shall not do so? Do you think that this belly of mine is not the equal of a penny? God's life! Up to now I have fed on ortolans. But you, never have *you* carried anything of that sort under your belt of greasy hide. For you, you bad man, must needs carry your suet in the collar of your doublet, far otherwise than I that bear three inches at least of delicate fat on this good belly of mine."

At this the innkeeper fell into a passion of rage, and though he was a stammerer he began to talk at a great rate, and the greater his haste the more he stammered and spluttered like a dog that has just come out of the water. Ulenspiegel began to throw pellets of bread at him, and Lamme, growing more and more excited, continued his harangue in the following strain:

"And now, what do you say? For here have I enough, and more than enough, to pay you for those three lean chickens forsooth, and those four mangy poulets, to say nothing of that big simpleton of a peacock that parades his paltry tail in the stable yard. And if your very skin was not more dry than that of an ancient cock, if your bones even now were not falling to very dust within your breast, still should I have the wherewithal to eat you up, you and your slobbering servant there—your one-eyed serving-maid and your cook, whose arms are not long enough to scratch himself though he had the itch! And do you see," he continued, "do you see this fine bird of yours that for the sake of half a florin would have deprived us of our doublet and our shirt? Say, what is your own wardrobe worth, preposterous chatterbox that you are; and I will give you three *liards* in exchange for the lot!"

But the innkeeper, who by this time was beside himself with rage, stammered and spluttered more and more, while Ulenspiegel went on throwing pellets of bread in his face, till Lamme at last cried out again in a voice brave as a lion's :

" What's the value, think you, skinny-face, of a fine donkey with a splendid nose, long ears, large chest, and legs as strong as iron ? Twenty-eight florins at the least, is it not so, most seedy of innkeepers ? And how many old nails have you, pray, locked fast away in your coffer, with which to pay the price of so fine an animal ? "

More than ever did the innkeeper puff and blow, yet dared not budge an inch from where he stood. And Lamme said again :

" And what is the value, think you, of a fine cart of ash-wood, finely painted in crimson, and furnished with a hood of Courtrai cloth for protection from sun and rain ? Twenty-four florins at the least, is it not so ? And how much is twenty-four florins added to twenty-eight florins ? Answer that, you miser that cannot even count ! And now, since it is market day, and since your paltry tavern happens to be full of peasants that are come to market, behold I will put up my cart to auction and my donkey too, and I will sell them here, now, and at once ! "

Which, in very truth, he did. For all they that were there knew very well who Lamme was. And he actually realized from the sale of his donkey and cart as much as forty-four florins and ten *patards*. And he jingled the money under the innkeeper's nose, and said to him :

" Scent you not the savour of festivities to be ? "

" Yea," answered mine host. But under his breath he swore that if ever Lamme came to him and offered to sell him his very skin, he would buy it for a *liard* and make of it an amulet for a charm against extravagance.

Meanwhile there was a sweet and gentle-looking young woman that stood in the yard without, and she came up

167

oftentimes to the window and looked at Lamme, but withdrew her pretty face each time that he might have seen her. And the same evening, when Lamme was going up to bed, stumbling about on the staircase without any light (for he had been drinking not wisely), he was aware of a woman that put her arms round him, and greedily kissed his cheek and mouth and his nose even, and moistened his face with amorous tears, and then left him.

But Lamme, who was thoroughly drowsed by all that he had been drinking, lay down straightway and went to sleep ; and on the morrow he departed to Ghent together with Ulenspiegel. There he went seeking his wife in all the *cabarets* and taverns of the town. But at nightfall he rejoined Ulenspiegel at the sign of the Singing Swan.

V

Now King Philip was obstinate as a mule, and he thought that his own will ought to dominate the entire world as if it had been the will of God himself. And his will was this : that our country, little accustomed as it was to obedience, should now curb itself under an ancient yoke without obtaining any reforms at all. And the be-all and the end-all of his desire was the aggrandizement of that Holy Mother of his, the Catholic Church, Apostolic and Roman, One, Entire, Universal, changeless and unalterable, and this was his will for no other reason at all than just the fact that it *was* his will. And in this he was like some woman without sense, that tosses about all night upon her bed as though it were a bed of thorns, endlessly tortured by her own imaginings.

" Yes," he would say, " O most Holy Saint Philip, and you, O my Lord God, if only I could turn the Low Countries into a common grave, and cast therein all the inhabitants of that country, then surely they would return to Thee, my most blessed Patron, and to Thee, my Lady Virgin Mary, and to ye, my good masters, the saints and saintesses of Paradise ! "

Odd Behaviour of Ulenspiegel

And he really tried to do as he said; so that he was more Roman than the Pope and more Catholic than the Councils!

And the people of Flanders and of the Low Countries began to grow anxious again, and to think that they could discern in the distance this crowned spider, working in the sombre house of the Escurial, reaching out his long claws with their nippers open, and spreading wide the web in which he might enwrap them all and suck them white of their blood.

Ulenspiegel, for his part, went spreading the alarm wherever he could, and stirring up the people against the ravishers of his country and the murderers of his parents.

One day, therefore, when he was in the *Marché du Vendredi*, near by the *Dulle-Griet*—the Great Canon—Ulenspiegel lay flat down on his stomach in the middle of the road. A charcoal-burner who happened to be passing came up and asked him what he was doing there.

" I am giving my nose a wetting," Ulenspiegel told him, " so that I may discover where this great wind is coming from."

Next a carpenter came along.

" Do you take the pavement for a mattress ? " he asked.

" Before long," said Ulenspiegel, " there are some that will be taking it for a counterpane."

A monk came up and stopped by his side.

" What does this booby here ? "

" He entreats your blessing, lying flat at your feet," said Ulenspiegel. The monk gave his blessing and went away. But Ulenspiegel continued where he was with his head pressed to the earth, till at last a peasant came along and asked him what he was listening for. " Do you hear some noise or other ? " he said.

" Yes," replied Ulenspiegel. " I hear the wood beginning to grow, that wood whence many a faggot shall be made for the burning of poor heretics."

"Do you hear aught else?" inquired a sergeant of the commune.

"Yes," said Ulenspiegel, "I hear the men-at-arms that are on their way from Spain. If you have anything you wish to save, bury it now, for in a little while our cities will not be safe from thieves any more."

"The man is mad," said the sergeant.

And the people of the town thought so too.

VI

Now in those days, day in, day out, King Philip of Spain was used to spend his time fingering old papers and scribbling and writing on leaves of parchment. To these alone did he confide the secrets of his cruel heart, for he loved no man living, and knew that none loved him. For he desired to direct his great empire by himself alone, and like a weary Atlas he was bowed under that weight. Melancholy and phlegmatic by nature, this excess of work was consuming a body that was already none too strong. Hating as he did every happy face, he had begun to hate our land of Flanders, for its gaiety if for nothing else. And he hated our merchants just because they were wealthy and luxurious, and he hated our nobility just because they were free in speech and frank in manner, and because of the high ardour of their bravery and their jovial bearing. Neither had he forgotten the tale that was told how, as early as the year 1380, the Cardinal de Cousa had pointed out the abuses of the Church, and had preached the need of reformation, since which time the revolt against the Pope and the power of Rome had begun to be manifest in our land, and was now, under different forms and sects, rife in every head like water boiling in a kettle with the lid on.

And although, under the Emperor Charles, the Papal Inquisition had already been the death, by burning, burying alive, or hanging, of so many as a hundred thousand

Christians, and although the property of these unfortunates
had gone into the coffers of the Emperor and the King like
rain falling into a sink, Philip decided that this was not
enough, and now imposed on the country a new College of
Bishops, and aspired to introduce into Flanders all the horrors
of the Spanish Inquisition.

And the Town Heralds sounded their trumpets and
their timbrels, and declaimed a proclamation to the effect
that all heretics, whether men, women, or girls, should be done
to death. Those who would recant their heresies were to be
hanged, but those who were obstinate were to be burnt at the
stake. The women and girls were to be buried alive, and the
executioner was to dance upon their dead bodies.

And the flame of resistance began to burn and run through
all the country.

VII

It was the fifth of April, just before Easter, and the Counts
Louis of Nassau, de Culembourg, and de Brederode (he that
was surnamed Hercule the Toper) were entering the courtyard
of the palace of Brussels, together with three hundred gentlemen. They were come to seek an audience of the Governess
of the Netherlands, Madame the Duchess of Parma, and were
mounting the great stairway of the palace four by four.

Coming at length into the hall where my Lady was seated
they presented their petition, which entreated her to use her
influence with King Philip for the abolition of all those decrees
which concerned religion and the introduction into Flanders
of the Spanish Inquisition. This petition, which afterwards
became known as " The Compromise," also declared that in
our already disaffected country such a policy as the introduction of the Inquisition could only result in troubles of all
kinds, ruin to the country, and universal misery.

Berlaymont, who later on was to prove so treacherous and
baneful to the land of his birth, stood close by Her Highness,

and mocked at the poverty of certain of the confederate nobles who had come to visit her.

"Have no fear, my Lady," he told her, "they are nothing but beggars!"

And by these words he implied either that the said nobles had been ruined in the service of the King, or else that they were eager to emulate the luxury of the great Lords of Spain. And thus it was that later on these same nobles endeavoured to bring ridicule upon the words of Berlaymont by saying that "they held it indeed an honour to be esteemed and spoken of as beggars—beggars for the good service of the King and the advantage of these lands." And from that time they began to wear round their necks a golden medal carved with an effigy of the King. And on the obverse side of the medal were two hands clasped upon a beggar's wallet, with these words writ thereunder: "To the King, faithful even unto beggary." On their hats and bonnets they carried also little golden ornaments made in the form of beggars' hats and platters.

And all this time Lamme went carrying his portly form about the town, seeking the wife that he never found.

VIII

One morning Ulenspiegel said to Lamme:

"Come with me. Let us go and present our compliments to a certain high noble I wot of, a most renowned and powerful personage!"

"Will he tell us where my wife is?" asked Lamme.

"Certainly," answered Ulenspiegel, "if he knows."

And away they went to Brederode, surnamed Hercule the Toper. And they found him in the courtyard of his house.

"What do you want with me?" he demanded of Ulenspiegel.

"To speak with you, my Lord."

"Speak then," said Brederode.

"You are a handsome, brave, and powerful nobleman," said Ulenspiegel. "Time was when you were able to flatten out a Frenchman in full armour as though he were no better than a mussel in its shell. But if you are brave and powerful you are also well-informed. Can you tell us, therefore, why you wear this medal inscribed with these words : 'To the King, faithful even unto beggary' ? "

"Yes," Lamme put in, "pray tell us why, my Lord ! "

But Brederode made no answer, and only looked very hard at Ulenspiegel, who thereupon continued his discourse in this wise.

"And why, pray, do you, you other noble Lords, seek to be faithful to the King even unto beggary ? Is it for the great good that he wishes you ? Or for the fair friendship that he bears you ? How is it that instead of being faithful to the King even unto beggary you do not so act rather that the brute himself may be despoiled of his country, and thus be made faithful for ever to beggary himself ? "

And Lamme nodded his head to show his agreement with what his friend had said :

Brederode looked at Ulenspiegel with his keen glance, and smiled with pleasure at his handsome appearance.

"Either you are a spy of King Philip," he said, " or else a good man of Flanders ; and for whichever you are I will pay you your due."

So saying he led Ulenspiegel to his pantry, and Lamme followed close behind. When they were come there, Brederode pulled Ulenspiegel's ear till the blood flowed.

"This for the spy," he said.

But Ulenspiegel remained quite quiet and said nothing.

Then Brederode, pointing to a pipkin of cinnamon wine, bade his butler bring it to him.

"Drink," said Brederode, " this for the good Fleming."

"Ah ! " cried Ulenspiegel, " good Fleming means sweet

tongue for cinnamon! Verily the saints themselves do not know the likes of it!"

When he had drunk half the tankard he passed the remainder to Lamme.

"And who," said Brederode, "who is this *papzak*, this belly-carrier that needs must be recompensed for having done nothing?"

"This," said Ulenspiegel, "is my friend Lamme Goedzak, and whenever he drinks mulled wine he thinks that he is going to find the wife he has lost."

"That's so," said Lamme, sucking up the wine from the goblet most devotedly.

"And where may you be going to now?" asked Brederode.

"In quest of the Seven," said Ulenspiegel, "the Seven that shall save the land of Flanders."

"And who may they be?" asked Brederode.

"When I have found them," said Ulenspiegel, "then I will tell you."

But Lamme, who was grown sprightly with what he had been drinking, suggested to Ulenspiegel that they should go there and then to the moon, to see if his wife perchance was there.

"All right," said Ulenspiegel, "if you'll provide a ladder!"

And it was May, the green month of May, and Ulenspiegel said to Lamme:

"O Lamme, behold the lovely month of May! Ah, the bright blue of the sky! The joy of the swallows! And behold, the branches of the trees, how they are all red with sap, and the very earth is in love! Verily this is now the time both to hang and to burn for the Faith. For they are ready, the good little Inquisitors. Ah, what noble faces they have! And theirs is the power to correct us and to punish us and to degrade, and hand us over to the secular judges, or to imprison us—O the fine month of May!—and to

174

*" AH ! THE LOVELY
MONTH OF MAY ! "*

take us captive, and to proceed to trial against us without serving any writ, and to burn, hang, behead us, and to dig the grave of premature death for our women and our girls. In the trees the chaffinch is singing! But upon him that is rich and wealthy the good Inquisitors have cast a favourable eye! And it is the King himself that shall enter into their inheritance. Then go, my girls, dance in the meadows to the sound of bagpipes and shawms. O the fine month of May!"

And the ashes of Claes beat upon the breast of Ulenspiegel.

"On, on!" said he to Lamme. "Happy are they that shall keep heart high and sword drawn in the dark days that are coming!"

IX

Lamme and Ulenspiegel, each mounted upon a donkey given him by Simon Simonsen, one of the followers of the Prince of Orange, went riding far and wide, warning the people concerning the bloodthirsty designs of King Philip, and always on the look-out for any news from Spain. They frequented all the markets and fairs of the countryside, selling vegetables and habited like peasants.

One day as they were returning from the market at Brussels, they passed a stone house on the Quai aux Briques, and there, in a room on the ground floor, they beheld a beautiful dame dressed all in satin. She had a high complexion, a lively look in her eyes, and her neck was most fair to behold. By her side was a young, fresh-looking cook, to whom she was addressing words like these:

"Clean me this saucepan, will you! No rusty sauce for me!"

"As for me," cried Ulenspiegel, poking in his nose at the window, "any kind of soup is good enough! For a hungry man cannot afford to be particular."

The lady turned towards him:

"And who," she said, "who is this little man, I wonder, that must needs concern himself with my soup?"

" Alas, my lovely lady," said Ulenspiegel, " if only you will consent to make soup in my company, I will teach you how to prepare a traveller's relish of a sort that is quite unknown to lovely ladies who stay at home."

And then, smacking his lips :

" I am hungry," he said.

" Hungry for what ? " she asked him.

" For you."

" Sure, he's a nice enough looking fellow," said the cook to her mistress. " Let him come in a while and tell us his adventures."

" But there are two of them ! " said the lady.

" I'll look after the other," said the cook.

" Madame," said Ulenspiegel, " it is true that there are two of us, I and my poor friend Lamme here, whose back cannot support so much as the weight of a hundred pounds, yet who carries in his stomach five hundred pounds at the least of food and drink, and that right willingly ! "

" My son," Lamme said, " do not make mock of me, unfortunate that I am, for my belly costs a deal to fill."

" To-day, at any rate, it shall not cost you so much as a *liard*," said the lady. " Come in, both of you."

" But what about these donkeys of ours ? " said Lamme.

" There is no lack of fodder," answered the lady, " in the stable of Monsieur le Comte de Meghen ! "

Thereupon the cook left her saucepan, and led Lamme and Ulenspiegel into the stable yard, they still riding on their donkeys, who now began to bray inordinately.

" Hark," cried Ulenspiegel, " hearken to the fanfare with which they greet their coming nourishment. They are blowing their trumpets for joy, the poor beasts ! "

But when they were dismounted, Ulenspiegel said to the cook :

" Come now, my dear, tell me, if you were a she-ass would you choose for your mate a donkey like me ? "

176

" If I were a woman," the cook replied, " I would desire a fellow that had a merry countenance."

" What are you then," asked Lamme, " being neither woman nor she-ass ? "

" I am a maid," quoth she, " and that is neither woman nor she-ass into the bargain. Now do you understand, fat-belly ? "

Meantime the lady was inviting Ulenspiegel to drink a pint of *bruinbier* and to partake of some ham, a *gigot*, a *pâté*, and some salad. Ulenspiegel clapped his hands.

" Ham ! " he cried, " that's good to eat ; and *bruinbier* is a drink divine. *Gigot* is food fit for the Gods ! And the thought of a *pâté* is enough to send one's tongue a-tremble in one's mouth for joy ! A rich salad is worthy victual for a king, forsooth. But blessed above all men shall that man be to whom it is given to dine off thy loveliness, O lady mine !"

" How the fellow does run on ! " she exclaimed. And then : " Eat first, you rogue."

" Shall we not say grace ere we consume all these dainties ? " said Ulenspiegel.

" Nay," answered the lady.

But Lamme began to make moan, complaining that he was hungry.

" Eat, then, your fill," said the beautiful dame, " for well I see that you have no other thoughts but of meats well cooked."

" And fresh withal," Lamme added, " even as was my wife."

At this the cook grew moody ; nevertheless they ate and drank their fill, and that night also did the beautiful dame give his supper to Ulenspiegel, and so the next day, and the days that followed.

As for the donkeys, they were given double feeds, and for Lamme there was always a double ration. And throughout a whole week he never once went outside the kitchen, playing the wanton with many a dish of food, but never with the cook, for he was thinking of his wife all the time.

This annoyed the girl, and she went so far as to say that it was not worth while to cumber the earth if one thought of nothing but one's belly.

But all this time Ulenspiegel and the beautiful dame were passing the time together in right friendly wise, till one day she said to him :

"Tyl, I think you have no principles at all. Who are you ? "

"I am," said he, "a son that Chance begat one day on High Adventure."

"You are not afraid to speak well of yourself," she told him.

"That's for fear that others will praise me."

"Would you go so far as to help such of your brethren who have suffered for the Faith ? "

"The ashes of Claes beat upon my breast."

"There is something splendid about you, Tyl, when you say that," she told him, " but who is this Claes ? "

"He was my father," answered Ulenspiegel, "that was burnt alive for the Faith."

"Verily you are not at all like my husband, the Count de Meghen," she said, "for he, if he could, would bleed to death the country that I love. For you must know that I was born in the glorious city of Antwerp. And now I will make known to you that the Count has entered into an agreement with the Councillor of Brabant to bring into that very city of Antwerp a regiment of infantry."

"I must inform the citizens of this," said Ulenspiegel. "Behold, I will go there immediately, swift as a ghost."

He departed there and then ; and by the following morning the citizens of Antwerp were in arms. But Ulenspiegel and Lamme, having sent their donkeys to a farmer that was a friend of Simon Simonsen, were themselves obliged to go into

178

hiding for fear of the Count de Meghen, who was seeking for them everywhere to have them hanged; for it had been reported to him that there were two heretics that had drunk of his wine and eaten of his meat. And he was jealous and spoke concerning this matter to his lovely dame, who ground her teeth in anger, and wept and swooned seventeen times. The cook behaved in a similar fashion, but swooned not so often, and swore by her hope of Paradise and by the eternal salvation of her soul, that neither she nor her mistress had done anything wrong unless it had been to give what was left of their dinner to a couple of poor pilgrims who, mounted on two wretched donkeys, had stopped for a moment at the kitchen window.

All that day there was a great shedding of tears, so that the floors of the house became quite damp with them. And when he saw this, Monsieur de Meghen felt reassured that he was being told the truth and nothing but the truth.

Lamme did not dare to show himself again there, for the cook always jeered at him, calling after him, " My wife ! " And for this cause he was very sorry for himself, thinking of all the good food that he was missing. But Ulenspiegel continued his visits to the beautiful dame, entering the house by the rue Sainte-Catherine, and hiding himself in the storeroom. And he always took care to bring back to Lamme some dainty morsel.

Now one evening the Count de Meghen informed his lady that before morning dawned he was resolved to lead his men-at-arms into the city of Bois-le-Duc. When he had told her this he went to sleep. But the beautiful dame went straightway to the storeroom, and apprised Ulenspiegel of what had happened.

X

Ulenspiegel, in the garb of a pilgrim, and with no provision of food or money, departed incontinently for Bois-le-Duc, with the intention of warning the citizens. He reckoned

179

to find a horse at the house of Jeroen Praet, the brother of Simon Simonsen, for whom he carried letters from the Prince. From thence he would go by side roads to Bois-le-Duc as fast as his horse would carry him.

As he was crossing the road he spied a company of soldiers coming towards him. This gave him a great fright because of the letters which he carried ; but being resolved to put the best face on the misadventure, he awaited the arrival of the soldiers with all the courage at his command, standing still by the roadside telling his beads. When the soldiers came up with him he joined them, and soon discovered that they also were going to Bois-le-Duc.

At the head of the troop marched a company of Walloons led by a captain, Lamotte by name, with his bodyguard of six halberdiers. Then followed the other officers each according to rank, and with a smaller bodyguard : the provost with his halberdiers and two bailiffs, the chief watchman with the baggage-carriers, the executioner with his assistants, and a band of drums and fifes making a great row. Thereafter came a company of Flemish soldiers, two hundred strong, with their captain and his ensign-bearers. They were divided into two divisions, each of one hundred men, under the command of two sergeants, and in squads of ten under the command of corporals. The provost and his lieutenants were likewise preceded by a band of drums and fifes, beating and screaming.

Behind these, again, came two open wagons wherein rode the loving companions of the soldiers, pealing with laughter, twittering like birds, singing like nightingales, eating, drinking, dancing, standing, lying down, or sitting astride—all gay and pretty girls.

Many of them were dressed like foot-soldiers, but in fine white cloth which was cut away at the arms and legs and at the neck so as to show their sweet white flesh. And on their heads they wore bonnets of fine linen trimmed with

180

gold and surmounted with magnificent ostrich plumes that fluttered in the wind. Their belts were of cloth of gold crimped with red satin, from which hung the scabbards of their daggers, made of cloth of gold. And their shoes, their stockings, their hose, their doublets, shoulder-knots and fitments were all of gold and white silk. Others there were, dressed also in the uniform of infantrymen but with uniforms of divers colours, blue, green, scarlet, sky-blue, and crimson, cut away and embroidered or emblazoned according to their fancy. But on the arm of each and all was to be seen the coloured band that indicated her calling.

The girls were in charge of a sergeant who did his best to keep them in order, but they made no pretence of obeying him, but bombarded him with japes and sweet grimaces so that he found it hard to keep his countenance.

Ulenspiegel meanwhile, in his dress of a pilgrim and telling his beads, went marching along by the side of the two ensign-bearers and their guard, for all the world like a little boat by the side of a big ship. Suddenly Lamotte inquired of him whither he was going.

"Sir Captain," answered Ulenspiegel, who was growing hungry, "you must know that I am one that has committed a grievous sin, for which I have been condemned by the Chapter of Notre Dame to journey to Rome on foot and to ask pardon there from the Holy Father. This he has granted, and now I am shriven and suffered to return to my own country on the one condition that I am to preach the Holy Mysteries to whatsoever soldiers I may encounter on the way ; and they for their part are enjoined to give me bread and wine in return for my preaching. And thus by my sermons do I sustain my wretched life. Would you now give me permission to fulfil my vow at the next halt ? "

"I will," said Monsieur de Lamotte.

After this, Ulenspiegel began to mingle with the Walloons and Flemings in right brotherly fashion, but all the time he

181

kept fingering those letters which he kept concealed under his doublet. And the girls began to cry out to him :

"Come hither, handsome pilgrim, come hither and show us the strength of your pilgrim's oyster-shells !"

And Ulenspiegel drew nigh to them with modest mien, and said :

"O my sisters in God, pray you do not make mock of the poor pilgrim that wendeth up hill and down dale preaching ever the Holy Faith to the soldiers."

But with his eyes he feasted himself upon the sight of their sweet charms. And the wanton girls, thrusting their lively faces betwixt the canvas curtains of the wagons, cried out to him yet the more :

"Surely you are too young a man to go preaching to soldiers ? Climb up into our wagon and we will teach thee more gentle subjects of conversation !"

And right willingly would Ulenspiegel have done as they bade him, but he dared not, by reason of the letters which he carried. And already two of the girls were leaning out of the wagon trying to hoist him up with their white, round arms. But the sergeant was jealous.

"Be off with you, or else I'll off with your head !" he threatened.

So Ulenspiegel removed himself away, but not without a sly look behind him at the fresh young beauty of those joysome girls, all golden in the sun which now shone brightly.

They came at last to Berchem, where Philip de Lannoy, Lord of Beauvoir, ordered a halt. For he it was that was in command of the Flemings.

Now in that place was an oak-tree, of medium height, but despoiled of all its branches save one only, a big branch that was broken off short in the middle ; for only a month before an Anabaptist had been hanged there by the neck.

Here then the soldiers came to a halt, and the keepers of the canteen came up and began to sell to them bread, wine, beer, with meats of every kind. And to the gay girls they sold all manner of sugared sweets, and castrelins, and almonds, and tartlets, the which when Ulenspiegel saw, he felt hungrier than ever.

All at once Ulenspiegel climbed up like a monkey into the tree, and seated himself astride on the big branch, seven feet above the ground at the least. And then, when he had given himself a few strokes from his pilgrim's scourge, he began his sermon, while the soldiers and their gay girls sat round him in a circle.

" It is written," he began, " that whosoever giveth to the poor, the same lendeth to God. Very well then, O soldiers present here to-day, and you, fair ladies, sweet comrades in love of all these valiant warriors, do you lend now to God. That is to say, give me, I beg you, some of your bread, meat, wine, beer, if you please, and eke your tartlets, and I promise you that God, who is very rich, shall give you back in exchange many pieces of ortolan, rivers of malmsey wine, mountains of sugar-candy, and great pieces of that lovely *rystpap* which they eat in Paradise from silver spoons."

Then, changing to a more sorrowful tone, he continued :

" Behold now, with what cruel tortures do I strive to merit pardon for my sins ! Will you do nothing to assuage the smarting pain of this scourge by which my back is lacerated till the blood flows ? "

" Who is this madman ? " cried the soldiers.

" My friends," answered Ulenspiegel, " I am no madman but one that is repentant even to the point of starvation. For while my soul weeps for its sins, my stomach weeps for want of food. Good soldiers, and you, fair damosels, I see you well provided with ham and goose, with fat sausages and wine and beer and all manner of tartlets. Will you not give so much as a morsel to the wandering pilgrim ? "

" Yes, yes, we will," cried the Flemish soldiers, " for the preacher hath a merry countenance."

And now they all began to throw him chunks of bread as though they had been balls, and Ulenspiegel did not cease from talking and from eating, astride as he was on the branch.

"Hunger," he said, "makes a man hard of heart and little apt for prayer, yet a piece of ham removes that evil disposition in no time."

"Look out for your head," shouted a sergeant as he threw him a bottle half full of wine. Ulenspiegel caught the bottle in mid-air, and began to drink in little gulps, talking all the while.

"If hunger, sharp and raging, is bane to the poor body of a pilgrim, there is something else that is equally harmful to his soul ; nothing less than his fear that the generosity of his soldier friends may lead him on to drunkenness. For as a general rule the pilgrim is a right sober fellow, but when, as now, one soldier gives him a slice of ham, and another a bottle of beer, he is mightily afraid lest by drinking thus upon an empty, or nearly empty, stomach he may lose his head."

And even as he spoke, he caught hold of the leg of a goose that came whizzing to him through the air.

"This truly is a miracle," he cried, "that one should go fishing in the air for a bird of the field ! And see ! Hey, presto ! it has disappeared, bone and all ! Verily, what is it that is greedier than dry sand ? I will tell you. A barren woman and a hungry man."

Scarcely had he spoken than he clapped his hand to his face, for two tartlets had flattened themselves, one on his eye, the other on his cheek. The gay girls who had thrown them laughed aloud, but Ulenspiegel made answer :

"Many thanks, my pretties, many thanks for thus embracing me with this jammy accolade."

Nevertheless the tartlets had fallen to the ground.

And then suddenly the drums began to beat, the fifes screamed, and the soldiers fell in again.

Monsieur de Beauvoir ordered Ulenspiegel to come down

from his tree and to march by the side of the soldiers. Ulenspiegel would willingly have been parted from them by a hundred leagues, for he had gathered from the remarks let fall by certain thin-faced foot-soldiers that he was already under suspicion, and that he ran danger of being arrested for a spy; and if this was so, he knew that they would most certainly search his pockets, and have him hanged when they found the letters which he carried. So in a little while he purposely let himself stumble into the ditch which ran by the wayside, and as he fell he cried out loudly:

"Mercy, soldiers, mercy! My leg is broken, and now I cannot walk any more. You must let me get up into the cart with the girls!"

But to this he knew that the jealous sergeant would never consent.

The girls, meanwhile, cried out from the carts:

" Come, come, jolly pilgrim, and we will succour you, and caress and make much of you, and cure you all in a day."

" I know it," said Ulenspiegel, " for a woman's hand is balm celestial for all and every wound."

But the jealous sergeant consulted with Monsieur de Lamotte, saying:

" Sir, I suspect that this pilgrim is playing some trick upon us with his tale of a broken leg. All he wants is to have the chance of getting up into the cart with the girls. Order him rather to be left behind on the road."

" Very well," answered Monsieur de Lamotte.

So Ulenspiegel was left where he was in the ditch.

Some soldiers, who really believed that his leg was broken, were sorry for him because of his gaiety, and they left with him a two days' ration of food and wine. And the girls would have got down and run to his assistance, but as this was forbidden they threw him all that was left of their castrelins.

As soon as the soldiers had disappeared in the distance Ulenspiegel, still in his pilgrim's dress, recovered his liberty, purchased a horse, and rode like the wind by roads and by-paths to Bois-le-Duc.

When he told them the news of the approach of Monsieur de Lamotte, the townspeople flew to arms to the number of eight hundred men, and they chose out their leaders, and sent off Ulenspiegel, disguised as a charcoal-burner, to Antwerp to summon help from Hercule Brederode, surnamed the Toper.

And the soldiers of de Lamotte and de Beauvoir were able to gain no entry into Bois-le-Duc, most vigilant of cities, most valiant in defence.

XI

One day Simon Simonsen said to Ulenspiegel :

" Hearken, brother mine, and tell me, are you a brave man think you ? "

" Brave enough," answered Ulenspiegel, " to whip a Spaniard to death, to kill an assassin, or to murder a murderer."

" Do you think you could hide yourself in a chimney and wait there patiently so as to overhear what was being said in the room below ? "

God has given me strong legs," answered Ulenspiegel, " and a supple back, and in virtue of these gifts I could stand a long time in whatever position I would, like a cat."

" Have you patience and a good memory ? " asked Simon.

" The ashes of Claes beat upon my breast," answered Ulenspiegel.

" Very well then," said Simon, " you will take this playing card, folded as you see it, and you will go to Dender-monde to a house, a drawing of which I will give you, and you will knock at the door twice loudly and once softly. Some one will open to you and will ask if you are the chimney-sweep ; you will answer that you are he and that you have not lost the card. Then you will show the card to him who opened the door. After that, Tyl, you must do as best you can. For great are the evils that are a-planning against the

186

land of Flanders. And you will be conducted to a chimney that has been swept and cleaned against your arrival, and in it you will find a series of strong cramp-irons made ready for you to climb by, and a little wooden shelf securely fastened to the side of the chimney for a seat; and when he that has opened the door shall direct you, you will climb up into your hiding-place, and there remain. In the chamber below, and in front of the chimney where you will be hidden, a conference is to be held between certain noble Lords : William the Silent, Prince of Orange, and the Counts d'Egmont, de Hoorn, de Hoogstraeten, and Ludwig of Nassau, the brother of William. And we Reformers desire to find out whether these noble Lords are able and willing to undertake the saving of our country."

Well, on the first day of April, Ulenspiegel did as he had been bidden and took up his place in the chimney. Luckily for him there was no fire in the grate, and it seemed that the absence of smoke would not make it any the less easy for him to hear properly. After a little while the door of the room was opened, and Ulenspiegel was pierced through and through by a draught of cold wind blowing up the chimney. But he endured the wind with patience, telling himself that it would serve to keep him alert and attentive.

After a while he could hear my Lords of Orange, Egmont and the rest making their entrance into the room. They began by speaking of the fears they felt, of the wrath of the King and of the maladministration of the revenue and finances of the country. One of them spoke in a sharp, clear, and haughty tone of voice, which Ulenspiegel recognized as that of my Lord of Egmont; just as he recognized de Hoogstraeten by his husky tones, and de Hoorn by his loud voice, the Count Ludwig of Nassau by his firm and soldierly manner of speech, and William the Silent by that slow, deliberate way of enunciating his words as if they had all been thought out beforehand and weighed in a balance.

187

The Count d'Egmont asked why they had been summoned to this second conference when they had had plenty of time at Hellegat to come to a decision on what they meant to do. De Hoorn replied that the days passed quickly, that the King was growing angry, and that they must be careful to lose no time.

Then spake William the Silent.

" The country is in danger. It must be defended against the attack of a foreign army."

At this d'Egmont grew excited, and said that he was indeed astonished to hear that the King his master had thought it necessary to send an army when all was so peaceful by reason of the watchful care of their noble Lordships, and of himself especially.

But William the Silent made answer :

" King Philip already has an army in the Low Countries consisting of not less than fourteen regiments of artillery, and they are under the control of him who commanded them at Gravelines, a general to whom all the soldiers are devoted."

D'Egmont said that he could scarcely believe it.

" I will say no more," said William, " but there are certain letters which shall be read to you and to the assembled Lords, and to begin with, letters from the poor prisoner, Monsieur de Montigny."

And in these letters it was told how that the King was extremely vexed with what was happening in the Low Countries, and that when the hour was come he had determined to punish the fomenters of disturbance.

It was at this juncture that the Count d'Egmont complained of the cold, and desired to have the fire lit ; the which was done while the two Lords continued their discussion of those letters. Now it was a big fire of wood, but it did not burn well on account of that big obstruction which was hidden in the chimney, and the room became quickly full of smoke.

Then the Count de Hoogstraeten began to read (for all that he was coughing continually because of the smoke) certain letters which had been intercepted on their way from Alava, the Spanish ambassador, to the Governess of the Netherlands.

" The ambassador," he said, " writes that all the evil that has happened in the Low Countries was the work of three men : the Lords of Orange, Egmont, and Hoorn. But it were desirable, he adds, to appear well disposed to these three, and to tell them that the King recognizes that it is thanks to them that their lands have been kept loyal to him. As for the two others, Montigny and de Berghes, let them alone where they are."

" Ah ! " said Ulenspiegel, " I had rather a smoky chimney in the land of Flanders than a damp prison in the land of Spain ; for garrotters grow between damp walls."

But the Count de Hoogstraeten continued :

" The said ambassador adds that on one occasion the King, being in the city of Madrid, spoke these words : ' By all accounts that come from the Low Countries it is evident that our royal reputation is diminished, and we are ready therefore to abandon all our other possessions rather than leave such a rebellion unpunished. We are decided to proceed to the Netherlands in person, and to claim the assistance of the Pope and of the Emperor. For beneath the present evil is concealed a future good. We shall reclaim the Low Countries to absolute obedience, and according to our own will we shall modify the constitution of that State, its religion and its government."

" Ah, King Philip," said Ulenspiegel, " if only I could modify yours to mine ! Verily you would suffer, under the blows of my trusty Flemish stick, a wondrous modification of your thighs and arms and legs ! I would fix your head in the middle of your back with a couple of nails, and as you viewed from this position the charnel-house you have created,

189

you should sing at your good ease a pretty song of tyrannous modification ! ”

Now wine was brought, and de Hoogstraeten rose upon his feet and said :

“ I drink to our country ! ” and every one followed his example, and when he had finished the toast he threw his empty tankard down on the table, and said : “ Now sounds an evil hour for the nobility of Belgium. Let us take counsel as to how we may best defend ourselves.”

He awaited some response, and looked at d’Egmont, but he uttered not a word, and it was left to William of Orange to break the silence.

“ We can offer resistance,” he said, “ provided that the Count d’Egmont—who at Saint-Quentin and at Gravelines has twice made France to tremble and who holds complete sway over the Flemish soldiery—provided that he, I repeat, is willing to come to our assistance in our endeavour to prevent the Spaniard from entering the fatherland.”

To this my Lord of Egmont made answer :

“ I have too much respect for the King to think that it is right that we should take up arms against him like rebels. Let those who fear his wrath retire before it. I shall remain where I am, for I have no means of living if I am deprived of his help.”

“ Philip knows how to avenge himself most cruelly,” said William the Silent.

“ I trust him,” answered d’Egmont.

“ You would trust him with your heads ? ” asked Ludwig of Nassau.

“ Head, body, and soul,” replied d’Egmont.

“ Friend, faithful and true, I will do likewise,” said de Hoorn.

But William said :

“ It behoves us to be far-sighted, and not to wait for things to happen.”

190

And then my Lord of Egmont spoke again, very excitedly.

" I have arrested twenty-two Reformers at Grammont," he said, " and if their preachings come to an end, and if punishment is meted out to the iconoclasts, the anger of the King will be appeased."

But William said :

" These are mere hopes."

" Let us arm ourselves with trust," said d'Egmont.

" Let us arm ourselves with trust," echoed de Hoorn.

" It is cold steel rather than trust that should be our weapons," replied de Hoogstraeten.

Whereupon William the Silent made a sign to the effect that he wished to depart.

" Adieu, Prince without a country," said the Count d'Egmont.

" Adieu, Prince without a head," answered William.

" The sheep are for the butcher," said Ludwig of Nassau, " but glory waits the soldier that saves the land of his fathers."

" That I cannot," said d'Egmont, " neither do I desire to."

" May the blood of the victims fall once again upon the head of the flatterer," said Ulenspiegel.

And then those Lords retired.

Whereupon did Ulenspiegel come down from his chimney, and go straightway to carry the news to Praet. And the latter said : " D'Egmont is nothing better than a traitor. But God is with the Prince."

The Duke! The Duke at Brussels! Where are the safes and coffers that have wings?

XII

William the Silent went in the way by God appointed. As for the two Counts, they had already given themselves up to the Duke of Alba, who offered pardon to William as well if only he would appear before him.

At this news Ulenspiegel said to Lamme:

"My good friend, what do you think now? The Duke has sent out a summons through Dubois, the Attorney-General, by which the Prince of Orange, Ludwig his brother, de Hoogstraeten, Van den Bergh, Culembourg, de Brederode, and other friends of the Prince are cited to appear before him within forty days; and if they do this they are assured of justice and mercy. But listen, Lamme, and I will tell you a story. One day there was a Jew of Amsterdam who summoned one of his enemies to come down and join him in the street, for the Jew was standing on the pavement, but his enemy was looking out of a window just above. 'Come down at once,' said the Jew, 'and I will give you such a blow on the head as will squash it down into your chest, so that your two eyes will look out from your sides like the eyes of a thief from betwixt prison-bars.' But the other answered: 'Even if you promised me a hundred times as much, still I would not come down.' Even so may the Prince of Orange and his friends make reply to him that summons them!"

And so they did, refusing point-blank to appear before the Duke. But the Counts d'Egmont and de Hoorn were not of this mind. And their failure to do their duty brought them nearer to their doom.

XIII

One day in June, a fine warm day it was, a scaffold was set up in the market square at Brussels, in front of the Town Hall. The scaffold was draped in black, and close to it were two tall posts tipped with steel. On the scaffold were a couple of black cushions and a little table with a silver cross thereon.

And on this scaffold were beheaded the noble Counts d'Egmont and de Hoorn. And the King entered into their inheritance. And it was of the Count d'Egmont that the ambassador of Francis spake, saying:

" This day have I seen a man beheaded who twice made the Kingdom of France to tremble."

And the heads of the two Counts were placed upon the posts with the iron tips. And Ulenspiegel said to Lamme :

" With a black cloth have they covered both their flesh and their blood. Verily, blessed now are they who keep heart high and sword drawn in the dark days that are coming ! "

XIV

In those days William the Silent gathered together an army and invaded the country of the Netherlands from three sides.

And Ulenspiegel was at a meeting of his countrymen at Marenhout. And they were wild with anger and he addressed them in this wise :

" Know you, my friends, that King Philip has taken counsel with the Holy Inquisition, and by their advice he has declared all the inhabitants of the Netherlands to be guilty of high treason. And the charge against them is one of heresy, namely, that either they are heretics themselves, or else that they have put no obstacles in the way of the spread of heretical doctrine. And for this execrable crime the King has condemned them all, without regard to age or sex, to suffer the appropriate penalties—all except a few here and there that are exempted by name. And there is no hope of grace or pardon. And the King will enter into their inheritance. For the scythes of Death are busy through all the wide land that borders the North Sea : the Duchy of Emden, the river-land of Amise, and the countries of Westphalia and of Cleves, of Juliers and Liége, together with the Bishoprics of Cologne and Treves and the lands of France and Lorraine. The scythes of Death are busy over more than three hundred leagues of our soil, and in two hundred of our walled towns, in a hundred and fifty boroughs, in the countrysides and villages and level lands of the whole country. And the

King is taking all for his own. And I tell you," Ulenspiegel continued, " that eleven thousand executioners will not be too many for this business. But the Duke of Alba calls them soldiers. And all the land of our fathers is become a charnel-house. Fugitive are all the arts of peace, and all the crafts and industries abandon us now to enrich those foreign lands which still permit a man to worship at home the God of conscience. But here the scythes of Death are busy, and the King takes all for his own.

" Our country, as you know, had gained various privileges by gifts of money to princes when they were in need. But now these privileges have all been annulled. And as the result of many an agreement made between ourselves and our overlords we had hoped to enjoy the wealth that came to us as the fruit of our labours Yet were we deceived. The stone-mason builded for the incendiary, the labourer laboured for the thief. And the King takes all for his own.

" Blood and tears ! Everywhere naught but blood and tears ! For the scythes of Death are busy—busy at the places of execution and at the trees that serve for gallows by the roadsides ; and at many an open grave wherein are thrown the living bodies of our maids. And they are busy in the prison dungeons and within those circles of faggots that flame around the victims, scorching them little by little to death ; or in the huts of straw where they fall suffocated in the fire and the smoke. And the King takes all for his own. And this, forsooth, by the will of the Pope of Rome. The very cities teem with spies that await their share of the plunder. The richer one is the more likely one is to be found guilty. And the King takes all for his own.

" But never shall the valiant men of Flanders suffer themselves to be butchered thus like lambs. For among those who fly away for refuge there are some who carry arms, and these are hiding in the woods. . . .

194

Let the Monks pay

"The monks verily have denounced them and hold themselves free to kill them and take possession of their goods. But by night and day these refugees, banded together like wild beasts, rush down upon the monasteries and seize the money that has been stolen from the poor, and take it away under the form of candlesticks and reliquaries of gold and silver, ciboria and patens, and other precious vessels of the kind. . . . Do I not speak truth, my friends? And they drink therefrom that wine which the monks had been keeping for themselves. And when melted down or mortgaged, these vessels will serve to provide money for the Holy War. Long live the Beggarmen!

"And even now they begin to harass the soldiers of the King, killing and plundering, then back into their lairs. And in the woods by day and night are to be seen the fires which have been lit during the hours of darkness, flaring up or dying down and ever breaking out in some fresh place. These are the fires of our banquetings. All for us the game of the woods, both furred and feathered. We are the masters here. And the peasants load us with bread and bacon whenever we are in need. Look at them Lamme; fierce and talkative, resolute and proud of bearing, they wander through the woods. And they are armed with hatchets and halberds, and with long swords and *bragmarts*, with arquebuses, pikes, lances, and crossbows. For any kind of weapon is good enough for such brave men, and they need no officers to lead them. Long live the Beggarmen!"

And Ulenspiegel sang this song:

> *Beat the drum!   Beat the drum!*
> *Drums of war!*
> *Slit the carcass of the Duke,*
> *Flog him on his hangman's face!*
> *To the death with the murderer!*

> *Beat the drum !   Beat the drum !*
>   *Drums of war !*
> *With the victims of his wrath*
> *Foul corruption let him share !*
>   *But long live the Beggarmen !*

> *Christ from Heaven look Thou down,*
>   *Look upon thy soldiers true,*
> *That risk hanging, fire, and sword*
>   *For thy Word !*
>   *And for their dear Fatherland !*
> *Beat the drum !   Beat the drum !*
>   *Drums of war !*

And all drank the toast and cried aloud :

"Long live the Beggarmen !"

And Ulenspiegel drank in his turn from a golden goblet that had once belonged to some monk or other, and proudly he gazed on the wild faces of the brave Beggarmen that stood before him.

"Men," he cried, "wild beasts rather that are my comrades, be you wolves lions, or tigers in very deed, and eat up all the cursed dogs of this King of Blood !"

"Long live the Beggarmen !" they shouted, and yet again they sang the song of

> *Beat the drum ! Beat the drum !*
>   *Drums of war !*

XV

William the Silent, with his army, was at the gates of Liége. But before crossing the Meuse he made sundry marches and counter-marches, leading the Duke astray, for all his vigilance.

Ulenspiegel applied himself most diligently to his duties as a soldier, worked his arquebus most skilfully, and kept his eyes and ears wide open.

In the Camp of the Prince of Orange

Now at that time there arrived in the camp certain
gentlemen of Flanders and Brabant, and these lived in
friendly fashion with the colonels and captains of the Prince's
following.

But soon there came into being two parties in the camp,
who began to dispute one with the other continually, some
saying that William was a traitor, others that such accusation
was a gross libel on the Prince, and that they who had made it
should be forced to eat their words. Suspicion grew and grew
like a spot of oil, and at length they came to blows—
small companies of six, eight, or a dozen men fighting together
in single combat, with all kinds of weapons and sometimes
with arquebuses even.

One day the Prince, hearing the noise, came to see what
was going on, and walked straight in between the combatants. It chanced that a piece of shot hit his sword and
struck it from his side. He stopped the combat, and visited
the whole camp, intending to put an end once for all to these
combats and to these cries of " Death to William ! " " Death
to the war ! "

Now the day after this adventure, Ulenspiegel had been
to the house of a Walloon maiden to sing to her some Flemish
love-songs of his. And it was near midnight, and very
misty, and Ulenspiegel, being just about to leave the house,
thought he heard the cawing of a crow, three times repeated.
And the sound came from the door of a cottage close by.
And from far off came other cawings, three times repeated,
as if in answer. Presently a peasant made his appearance at
the doorway of the cottage, and at the same time Ulenspiegel
heard steps on the road. Two men came up to the peasant
and began to talk to him in the Spanish tongue. The peasant
spoke to them, also in Spanish :

" Well ? And how goes it ? " asked the cottager.

" Well, indeed," the two men answered. " We have been
spreading rumours on behalf of the King, and it is thanks to us

that the captains and their soldiers are everywhere suspicious and talking among themselves in this wise :

"'The Prince, so the gossip goes—is resisting the King for vile ambition and for nothing else. For by this means he thinks to make himself feared so that he may acquire cities and overlordships as the price of peace. For five hundred thousand florins he would leave in the lurch all the brave nobles who have come out to fight for their country. And it is a fact that the Duke has offered him a complete amnesty, and has promised to restore both him and his chief officers in their possessions, if only the Prince will return to the obedience of the King, and will negotiate with him alone.'

"But they that remain faithful to the Prince make answer to us in this wise :

"'By no means will William have aught to do with the proposals of the Duke. For these are but snares and treachery. For the Prince must surely call to mind what happened to d'Egmont and de Hoorn. And it is well known that the Cardinal de Granville said at Rome, when the two Counts had been taken : "The two gudgeon, verily, have been caught, but the pike has been allowed to escape." For nothing has been taken while William still remains at large.'"

"Is the camp divided in twain then ?" asked the peasant.

"It is," replied the two men, "and the division grows greater every day. But whom are those letters for ?"

Whereupon they all entered into the cottage. A lantern was lit inside, and looking through a crack in the door Ulenspiegel could see them unsealing two letters. These they read with every appearance of enjoyment, and then they all fell to drinking honey-wine. After which the two men came out of the cottage and said to the peasant, still speaking in Spanish :

"The camp split in two, and the Prince captured—that will be worth a dozen glasses, eh ?"

198

"Those men," said Ulenspiegel to himself, "cannot longer be allowed to live."

But even now they were disappearing in the thick mist, with the lantern which the peasant had brought for them. The light of the lantern shone out intermittently, as if continually intercepted by some dark body. From this Ulenspiegel concluded that the two men must be walking one behind the other.

He raised his arquebus to his shoulder and fired. Then he saw the lantern raised and lowered several times, as if the man who carried it was looking at his fallen comrade, trying to discover where he had been hit and the nature of the wound.

Yet again did Ulenspiegel raise his arquebus, and then when the lantern began to steady itself and to retreat speedily towards the camp, he fired again. Now the lantern swayed, fell to the ground and went out, leaving all in darkness.

Ulenspiegel ran on to the camp, and there he soon encountered the provost with a number of soldiers who had been awakened by the noise of the firing. Ulenspiegel accosted them, saying: "I am the huntsman. Go you now and find the game."

"Brave Fleming," said the provost, "methinks you are a man that knows other ways of talking besides with your tongue."

"Words of the tongue they are but so much wind," answered Ulenspiegel. "But words of lead—they know how to find for themselves a lasting habitation in the carcass of a traitor! Come then, follow me."

And so saying he led them to the place where the two men had fallen. And in very deed the soldiers saw by the light of their lanterns two bodies stretched out on the ground. One was dead, and the other at the last gasp, holding his hand to his heart, and in his hand a letter all crumpled in the agony of death. The soldiers lifted the two bodies, whose clothes clearly showed them to be the bodies of gentlemen, and straightway carried them, still by the light of their lanterns, to the Prince.

Now William was about to hold a council with Frederick of Hollenhausen, the Margrave of Hesse, and other nobles. But the soldiers, who had now been joined by a company of other troopers in green and yellow jackets, stood before the tent, demanding with shouts and cries that the Prince should give them audience.

At length William of Orange came out to them, and the provost began to clear his throat and make other preliminaries for the accusation of Ulenspiegel. But the latter cut in before him, saying :

" My Lord, I had thought to kill two crows, but I have killed two traitors in their stead—two noblemen—belonging to your suite."

Then he told the story of all that he had seen and heard and done. William did not utter a word, but the two bodies were carefully examined in the presence of Ulenspiegel himself and William the Silent, together with Frederick of Hollenhausen, the Margrave of Hesse, Dietrich of Schoonenbergh, Count Albert of Nassau, the Count de Hoogstraeten, and Antoine de Lailang, Governor of Malines. And the soldiers stood by, with Lamme Goedzak, his great belly all of a tremble. Sealed letters were found on the persons of the deceased gentlemen, which had been sent by Granvelles and Noircames, and engaged the recipients to sow division in the Prince's entourage, and by that means to diminish his power and to compel him to yield, so that he might ultimately be delivered up to the Duke and beheaded according to his deserts. " The right procedure is," continued the letter, " to act at first with caution and to use allusive phrases only, so that the army may be led to think that the Prince has already come to a secret understanding with the Duke, for his own advantage. This will arouse the anger of his captains and soldiers, and they will assuredly take him prisoner." Now as a reward for this service it appeared that notes to the value of some five hundred ducats were being sent them on the Fugger Bank at Antwerp, and they were promised a thousand more as soon as the four hundred thousand ducats which were already on their way from Spain had arrived in Zeeland.

The whole plot having been now unmasked, the Prince turned in silence towards the gentlemen, Lords, and soldiers who stood round him. Many of these men he knew to be suspicious of him already, nevertheless, he pointed at the two bodies without speaking a word, intending by this gesture to reproach them for their mistrust. And at this every one present there exclaimed and shouted aloud :

" Long live the Prince of Orange ! The Prince is faithful and true !" And such was their anger that they were desirous to throw the two dead bodies to the dogs ; but William forbade them, saying :

" It is not these two poor corpses that deserve to be thrown to the dogs so much as that littleness of mind which must needs be suspicious of the purest intentions."

And the Lords and soldiers cried out again :

" Long live the Prince ! Long live the Prince of Orange, the friend of our country ! "

And the sound of their voices was like the noise of thunder threatening injustice. And the Prince pointed to the two corpses and ordered that they should be given Christian burial.

" And I," demanded Ulenspiegel, " what shall be done to me, faithful and true ? If I have done evil let me be beaten, but if good—why then let me be suitably rewarded ! "

Then the Prince addressed him, saying :

" This soldier is to receive fifty strokes from the green wood in my presence for having killed two gentlemen without orders, to the contempt of all discipline. At the same time let him receive a reward of thirty florins for having used his eyes and ears to some purpose."

" My Lord," answered Ulenspiegel, " give me the thirty florins first, and I shall then be able to support my beating with equanimity."

" Yes, yes," murmured Lamme Goedzak, " give him the thirty florins first, and then he will bear the rest with equanimity."

" One thing more," said Ulenspiegel, " since my soul is admittedly free from fault, is there any real reason why I must be cleansed with the wood of the oak or washed with the branch of the cherry-tree ? "

" No," murmured Lamme again, " Ulenspiegel surely has no need to be washed or cleansed. For his soul is without stain. Do not wash it, my masters, do not wash it."

But when Ulenspiegel had received the thirty florins the provost ordered him to give himself up to the *Stock-meester*.

" Behold, my Lords," said Lamme, " behold how piteous he looks. There's no love lost between the hard wood and him—my beloved Ulenspiegel."

But Ulenspiegel answered :

" Of a truth I love a fine ash-tree in full leaf, growing up towards the sun in all its native verdure, but I agree I loathe like poison these heavy cudgels of wood with their sap still oozing out of them, stripped of their branches and without any leaves or twigs growing thereon, for they are rough to look upon and hard to feel."

" Are you ready ? " demanded the provost.

" Ready ? " Ulenspiegel repeated. " Ready for what ? Ready to be flogged do you mean ? No, I cannot, nor will I, be flogged by you, Mr. *Stock-meester*. You have a red beard certainly, and your appearance is formidable. Nevertheless, I am sure that you have a kind heart and would have no desire to thrash a poor fellow like me. And now to tell you the truth I should be loath to do such a thing myself, much

less to see any one else do it. For the back of a Christian
is a sacred thing, as sacred as his breast which holds the
lungs, those trusty organs whereby we breathe the goodly
air of God. And think how bitter would be your remorse
if a too brutal blow from your cudgel should chance to break
me in pieces ! "

" Make haste," said the *Stock-meester.*

" My Lord," said Ulenspiegel, addressing himself to the
Prince, " believe me, there is no need for all this hurry. First
of all the wood of the cudgel ought to be allowed to dry. For
I have heard that wood while still green is like to communicate
a mortal poison to any flesh with which it comes in contact.
Would your Highness desire to see me die such an ugly death ?
My Lord, my back I hold most pitifully at your service.
Have it flogged, if you must, with rods and lashed with
whips. But unless you wish to see me dead, spare me, I
pray you, from the wood while it is still green."

" Have mercy on him, Prince," cried my Lords of Hoogstraeten and of Schoonenbergh both together ; while the
others all began to smile compassionately. Lamme also
put in a word of his own, " Have mercy, my Lord. Green
wood is poison, neither more nor less than rank poison ! "

The Prince said :

" Very well."

Thereupon Ulenspiegel leapt in the air again and again,
and smote Lamme on his belly and compelled him to dance
too, saying : " Join me now in praising the good Duke who
has delivered me from the green wood."

And Lamme did his best to dance, but could not very well
because of his belly. And Ulenspiegel gave him to eat and
to drink as much as he was able.

XVI

It was now at the end of October. The Prince was in want of money, and his army of food. The soldiers too began to murmur, and he marched them towards the French frontier to offer battle to the Duke. But the Duke would not fight.

Leaving Quesnoy-le-Comte to go to Cambrésis, the Prince's army fell in with ten companies of Germans and eight Spanish ensigns and three cohorts of cavalry. They at once joined battle, and in the midst of the *mêlée* was Ruffele Henricis, the Duke's son, crying out at the top of his voice :

" No quarter ! No quarter ! Long live the Pope ! "

Now Don Henricis found himself opposite to a company of arquebusiers which was led by Ulenspiegel, and he threw himself upon them with all his men. Ulenspiegel said to his sergeant :

" I will cut out this murderer's tongue for him ! "

" Very good," said the sergeant.

And Ulenspiegel took careful aim, and his bullet shattered the tongue and the entire jaw-bone of Don Ruffele Henricis, son of the Duke. At the same time Ulenspiegel brought down the son of the Marquess Delmares, and in a little while more the eight ensigns and the three cohorts of cavalry were thoroughly worsted.

After this victory Ulenspiegel went seeking for Lamme everywhere through the camp, but he could not find him.

" Alas," he said, " he is gone ! Lamme is gone ; my friend, my great fat friend ! In his warlike ardour he must have forgotten how heavy his belly was, and tried to follow the Spaniards in their flight. Out of breath he must have fallen like a sack on the wayside. And then the enemy will have picked him up for ransom—a ransom of good Christian fat ! O Lamme, my friend, where are you ? Where are you, my great fat friend ? "

Tyl is sent on a Mission

Ulenspiegel sought him everywhere but found him not and had to nurse his grief in silence.

And now November was come, the month of snow-storms, and Ulenspiegel, having been ordered to report himself before William, found the Prince brooding in silence, and biting the lacings of his coat of mail.

" Listen to me," the Prince said presently, " and give me your whole attention."

Ulenspiegel answered : " My ears are like the gates of a prison. One enters easily but to get out again is a different matter."

" Very good," said William, " but now I would have you go for me to Namur, and to Flanders, Hainaut, Sud-Brabant, Antwerp, Nord-Brabant, and to Gueldre, Overyssel, and the North of Holland, telling the people everywhere that, although it seems that the fates on land are hostile to our most Holy and Christian Cause, we will yet continue the struggle by sea, no matter what the evil powers that are arrayed against us. For God holds the issue in His own good providence, whether in success or failure. And when you are come to Amsterdam you will render an account of all that you have done to Paul Bruys who is my trusty vassal. Here are three passports, signed by the Duke of Alba himself, which were found on certain bodies of the dead at Quesnoy-le-Comte. My secretary has filled them in afresh. And it may be that on your journey you will meet some good companion in whom you can trust. Let him go with you. And those are to be accounted trustworthy who know how to answer the song of the lark with a warlike cockcrow. Here are fifty florins. Be valiant and faithful."

" The ashes of Claes beat upon my heart," answered Ulenspiegel.

And he went his way.

XVII

Now the passports were countersigned both by the King and the Duke, and they authorized the bearer to carry any kind of arms at his convenience. So Ulenspiegel took with him his trusty arquebus as well as a good supply of cartridges and dry gunpowder. He dressed himself in a short cloak and a shabby doublet and hose made after the Spanish fashion, and thus accoutred, with a plumed cap on his head and a sword at his side, he made his departure from the Prince's army where it lay at the French frontier, and set out for Maestricht.

The roitelets, those heralds of bad weather, were flying around the houses seeking asile from the storm, and on the third day snow fell. Many times during the journey did Ulenspiegel have to show his safe-conduct. But they always let him pass, and so he came at length to the confines of Liége. He was plodding along over a level heath, and a fierce wind was driving the swirling snowflakes against his face, and in front and on every side the heath stretched out all white under the snow that fell in eddies, which themselves were whirled about hither and thither in the squalls of wind. And there were three wolves that began to follow him. But one of them he killed with a shot from his arquebus, and the other two flung themselves upon their wounded comrade, and then made off into the woods, each carrying a piece of the corpse.

Delivered from this peril, Ulenspiegel peered about him, fearing lest there might be other bands of wolves in that country, but he saw nothing except, in the far distance, certain objects that looked like grey statues moving slowly along in the falling snow. Behind these again, Ulenspiegel could descry the dark figures of a couple of soldiers on horseback. To see the better what all this might portend, Ulen-

206

spiegel climbed up into a tree, and there the wind brought
to him a far-off sound of lamentation. "It may be," Ulenspiegel said to himself, "these people are pilgrims, clad in
white habits; for I can scarcely distinguish their figures
against the snow." But after a little while he saw that they
were men running, quite naked, and that behind them were
two German troopers in black uniforms riding on horses.
And they were driving the poor wretches in front of them
with whips. Ulenspiegel took aim with his arquebus. Now
he could distinguish the individual figures of that mournful
company—old men and young men naked, shivering, and
quaking with cold, hardly able to stand some of them, but
running all, for fear of the cruel whips of the two soldiers who,
themselves being warmly clad and red with brandy and good
food, took pleasure in lashing the bodies of naked men to
make them run the faster.

Ulenspiegel said: "You shall be avenged, ashes of
Claes!" And he killed one of the soldiers outright with a
bullet from his arquebus. The soldier fell from his horse,
and his companion took fright, not knowing whence the
shot had come. But concluding that his assailant must be
hiding somewhere in the wood, he decided to make good his
escape, together with the horse of his dead companion. The
man contrived to get hold of the horse's bridle, but while he
himself was dismounting to plunder the body of the dead, he
was hit by a bullet in the neck and fell to the ground.

As for the naked prisoners, they imagined that some
angel from heaven, who was also forsooth a fine marksman,
had descended from the sky to aid them, and they all fell
down upon their knees in the snow. At this Ulenspiegel
descended from his tree, and was at once recognized by the
company who had previously served with him as soldiers
in the armies of the Prince. They said to him:

"O Ulenspiegel, we are come from France, and we were
being driven in this piteous plight to Maestricht, where the

Duke is, to be treated there as rebel prisoners because we cannot pay our ransom, and are therefore condemned in advance to be tortured, cut into pieces, or sent to row like caitiffs and criminals in the galleys of the King."

Ulenspiegel gave his *opperst-kleed* to the oldest of the soldiers, saying :

"Come with me, my friends. I will accompany you as far as Mézières ; but first of all let us strip these two dead soldiers and take possession of their horses." Thereupon the doublets, hose, boots, head-gear, and body-armour of the soldiers were divided up among the sick and feeble, and Ulenspiegel said :

"We shall soon be entering the wood, where the air is thicker and more gentle. You had better run, my brothers."

Suddenly one of the men fell down on the ground, crying : " I am hungry and cold, and I am going to God to bear witness that the Pope is Antichrist on earth." And he died, and the others agreed to carry the body with them that it might be given Christian burial.

While thus proceeding along the road, they met a peasant driving a cart with a canvas hood. Seeing the men all naked, the peasant had compassion on them and invited them to ride in his cart. There they found some hay to lie on, and some empty sacks to cover them withal. And they were warmed and gave thanks to God. Ulenspiegel rode beside the cart on one of the two horses that had belonged to the German troopers, leading the other by the bridle.

At Mézières they all alighted. Good hot soup and beer and bread and cheese were handed round, with some meat for the older men and women. And they were nobly entertained ; and they were clothed and armed again, all at the expense of the commune. And every one joined in giving thanks and praise to Ulenspiegel, who received it gladly. Ulenspiegel also sold the horses of the German troopers for eight-and-forty florins, out of which he distributed thirty florins among the Frenchmen.

Thereafter he took the road again, and as he walked solitarily along he said to himself:

" Verily now do I wander through a land of ruin, blood, and tears. Nevertheless, I find nothing. Those spirits lied to me without a doubt. For where is Lamme ? Where is Nele ! Where are the Seven ? "

And he heard a voice speaking to him as though in a whisper :

" In death, in ruin, and in tears, seek ! "

And he went his way.

XVIII

It was the month of March when Ulenspiegel came to Namur. There he found Lamme, who, having conceived a violent passion for the fish of the Meuse, and for the trout especially, had hired a boat and spent all day fishing in the river by permission of the commune. But for this privilege he had been obliged to pay the sum of fifty florins to the Guild of the Fishmongers.

Some of his fish he sold. But the rest he ate himself, and by this means he gained a finer belly than ever, and a small sack of money. When he saw his friend and comrade walking along the banks of the Meuse and about to enter the town, Lamme was mightily rejoiced and pushed his boat to the shore, and there springing on to the bank rushed up to Ulenspiegel, blowing and puffing and stammering for joy.

" Here you are," he cried, " here you are at last, my son. And where are you off to ? What are you after ? You are not dead, then ? And have you seen my wife ? You'll feed off the fish of the Meuse, which are the best to be found anywhere on this base earth ! And let me tell you something. The people here make such sauces as will tempt you to dip your fingers into the dish right up to your shoulder !

209

Ah, but how proud and splendid you look! On your cheeks is the very bloom of battle. And here you are! It's you, it's really you, my son! My Ulenspiegel! You jolly vagabond!" Then in a lower tone of voice he added:

"And how many Spaniards have you killed? You have not seen my wife by any chance, in the carts with those other hussies? Ah, but the wine of the Meuse! You must taste it. And have you been wounded, my son? You must rest here a while, so fresh and cheery as you are, and vigilant as a young eagle. But our eels! You must taste our eels. No muddy taste about *them*! Come, kiss me, my second self! Praise be to God! How glad I am!"

And Lamme danced and leapt in the air, puffing and blowing and compelling Ulenspiegel to dance too.

Thereafter they walked towards Namur. At the gate of the city Ulenspiegel showed his passport signed by the Duke. And Lamme conducted him to his house. While their repast was being prepared he made Ulenspiegel tell him all his adventures and then recounted his own, telling how he had left the army to follow a girl whom he thought was his wife. It was in pursuit of her, it seemed, that he had come at last to Namur. And he kept on asking Ulenspiegel:

"Are you sure you have not seen her anywhere?"

"I have seen many other beautiful women," answered Ulenspiegel, "and in this town especially, where it seems they are all most amorous. . . ."

"It is so," said Lamme, "nevertheless I have remained faithful. For my sad heart is heavy with but a single recollection."

"Even as your belly is heavy with countless platterfuls!" said Ulenspiegel.

"When I am unhappy I have to eat," Lamme replied.

"Your unhappiness knows no end?" demanded Ulenspiegel.

"Alas, no!" said Lamme.

And helping himself to another trout :

" Look," he cried, " look how lovely and firm he is.
This flesh is as pink as the flesh of my wife. But to-morrow
we will leave Namur. I have a purseful of florins, and we
will buy a donkey for each of us, and so we will go riding away
to the land of Flanders ! "

" You will be giving up a great deal," said Ulenspiegel.

" Never mind," said Lamme. " My heart draws me back
to Damme. For it was there that my love loved me well.
And it may be that she also has returned thither."

" We will set out to-morrow," said Ulenspiegel, " since
such is your desire."

And in fact they set forth as Lamme had said, each on a
donkey ; and so they rode along side by side.

XIX

Nele all this time was living at Damme, sorrowful and
alone, with Katheline, who still continued to call amorously
for her cold devil who never came.

" Ah ! " she would say, " you are rich, Hanske my pet ; and
you could easily give me back those seven hundred caroluses.
Then Soetkin would live again and come to earth once more,
and Claes in heaven would laugh for joy. Easily could you
do this, and you would ! Put out the fire ! My soul wants to
get out ! "

And with her finger she would point without ceasing to
the place on her head where the flaming tow had burned
her.

Katheline was very impoverished, but the neighbours
helped her by sending in beans and bread and meat, according
as they were able. The commune also gave her a certain
amount of money, and Nele did sewing for the wealthy
bourgeois, and went to their houses to mend their linen,
earning in this way a florin or two every week. But Katheline kept on with her eternal " Make a hole ! Let out my soul !

She is knocking to be let out! And he will give me back the seven hundred caroluses!"

And Nele wept to hear her.

XX

In the meantime Ulenspiegel and Lamme continued their wanderings. Under the protection of their passports, they entered one day into a little tavern built against the rocks of the Sambre, the which rocks are covered with trees here and there, and on the sign of the tavern was written mine host's name—MARLAIRE. When they had drunk many a flask of wine—wine of the Meuse, rather like Burgundy—and when they had eaten a large plate of fish, they fell talking to the innkeeper, who was a keen Papist but as talkative as he was pious because of the wine he had been drinking. And he kept on winking his eye maliciously. Ulenspiegel had a suspicion that all this winking portended something mysterious, and he made the fellow drink yet more, with the result that he fell to dancing and shouting with laughter, till at last he sat himself down at the table again, and, "Good Catholics," says he, "I drink to you."

"And to you we drink also," answered Lamme and Ulenspiegel.

"And I drink to the extinction of all heresy and rebellion."

"We will join you in that toast," answered Lamme and Ulenspiegel, who kept on filling up the goblets which mine host could never suffer to remain full.

"You are good fellows," said the innkeeper. "Let me drink to the health of your noble Generosities. For you must know that I derive some profit from all the wine that is drunk here. But where are your passports?"

"Here they are," replied Ulenspiegel.

"With the Duke's signature and all," said the innkeeper. "Here's a health to the Duke."

The Discreet Innkeeper

" To the Duke," echoed Lamme and Ulenspiegel. And mine host went on talking :

" Answer me now, do you know what it is that they catch rats and mice in ? Why in rat-traps to be sure, and mouse-traps. Who is the mouse then ? The great heretic of Orange —and orange he is in very truth, like the flames of hell ! But God is on our side. They will come. Ho ho ! A toast ! Pour out the wine ; I bake and burn with thirst. Come, drink, my masters. Fine little Protestant evangelists . . . I said *little*. Fine valiant little fellows they are, and brave soldiers, sturdy as oaks . . . I drink to them ! Are you not going with them to the camp of the great heretic ? I have certain passports signed by him. . . . You will see."

" We are going to the camp," answered Ulenspiegel.

" Yes, they will do their work well. And one fine night, if the opportunity presents itself "—and here the innkeeper whistled, and made a gesture as of one man cutting another's throat—" cold steel, I tell you. It's that that shall prevent the black bird of Nassau from singing any more. Come, drink again."

" You're a gay fellow," said Ulenspiegel, " in spite of being married."

The innkeeper said :

" I am neither married nor have I ever been. The secrets of Princes are safe with me. Drink ! But if I had a wife she would steal my secrets from under my pillow to get me hanged and herself made widow before the time. Long live God ! They will come. . . . But where are the new passports ? On my heart of a Christian. Drink ! They are there, there I tell you. One hundred paces along the road near by Marche-les-Dames. Do you see them ? Drink again ! "

" Drink ? " said Ulenspiegel. " Yes, I drink and drink and drink. To the King, to the Duke, to the Protestant preachers, and to *Vent d'acier*—Wind of Lead. And I drink to thee and

213

to me, to the wine and the bottle that holds it. But why? It is you that have stopped drinking!"

And at each new toast Ulenspiegel filled up the glass of the innkeeper, who emptied it straightway.

Ulenspiegel looked at him for some time, then rose and said to Lamme: "Come, Lamme, it is time for us to be off. He is asleep." But when they were outside, "He has no wife," Ulenspiegel continued. "We are safe. The night is at hand. Did you hear what the rascal said? And do you rightly understand who these three preachers are? Do you realize that they are to come along the bank of the Meuse from Marche-les-Dames, and that it will be our part to await them on the road? And then for *Vent d'acier*—Wind of Lead —to start his whistling?"

"Yes," said Lamme.

"It is for us to save the Prince's life," said Ulenspiegel.

"Yes," said Lamme.

"Wait," said Ulenspiegel. "You take my arquebus, and go and hide in the undergrowth among the rocks. Load it with two shots, and shoot when you hear me caw and crow."

"I will," said Lamme.

And so saying he disappeared into the undergrowth. And Ulenspiegel could hear quite clearly the click of the gun as Lamme loaded it.

"Do you see them coming?" he asked presently.

"I see them," answered Lamme. "There are three of them, marching together like soldiers, and one of them is much taller than the others."

Ulenspiegel sat himself down by the side of the road, with his legs stretched out in front of him, muttering his prayers on a rosary, just like beggars do. And he held his hat between his knees. And when the three evangelists passed in front of him, he held out his hat as though asking for alms; but they gave him nothing. Then Ulenspiegel got up and addressed them most piteously:

" Kind sirs," he said, " do not refuse a *patard* to a poor quarryman who has recently had an accident and broken his back by falling down a mine. The people in this part of the world are hard of heart, and they have not been willing to give me anything to relieve my distress. Alas ! Give me but a *patard*, and I will say many prayers for you. And God will keep you happy, all your lives long, kind friends ! "

" My son," said one of the evangelists, " there can be no happiness for us in this world so long as the Pope and the Inquisition remain in power."

Ulenspiegel heaved another sigh :

" Alas ! What are you saying, my lords ? Do not speak so loud, if it please you. But give me a *patard*."

" My son," replied one of the evangelists, he that was the smallest of the three, and of a very warlike countenance, " we poor martyrs carry no *patards* save only just enough to keep us going on our journey."

At this Ulenspiegel threw himself on to his knees in front of them.

" Give me your blessing then," he said.

The three evangelists laid their hands upon the head of Ulenspiegel, albeit with little signs of devotion.

Now Ulenspiegel noticed that although they were lean of figure, these men all had very fat stomachs, so he rose from his knees, and then pretended to stumble, knocking against the body of the tall evangelist as he did so. At that a merry tinkle of coin was distinctly audible. Thereupon Ulenspiegel raised himself to his full height and drew his dagger.

" My good man," he said, " it is cold and I am but poorly clad ; but methinks you have too much about you. Give me some of your wool, that I may get a cloak made for me. I am a Beggarman. Long live the Beggarmen ! " The tall evangelist made answer :

" You cock of a Beggarman, you carry your crest proudly forsooth, and we are going to cut it off for you ! "

"Cut it off then," cried Ulenspiegel, giving ground, "but let me warn you that trusty Wind of Lead is going to sing for you or ever he sings for the Prince my master! Beggar I am! Long live the Beggarmen!"

The three evangelists were astounded and cried out to each other: "How does he know? We are betrayed! Kill him! Long live the Mass!" And each man drew forth from beneath his hose a sharp dagger. But Ulenspiegel, without waiting for them to attack him, gave ground towards the bushes where Lamme was hidden, and when he judged that the three evangelists were within range of the arquebus, he cried out: "Crows, black crows, the Wind of Lead is going to whistle. I sing your bitter end!"

Then he cawed like a crow. And a shot rang out from the bushes, and the tall evangelist fell prone on the earth. The next moment followed a second shot, which accounted in the same way for the second.

And from among the bushes Ulenspiegel saw the jolly face of Lamme, and his arm raised as he hastily reloaded his arquebus. And from the midst of the dark shrubbery a puff of blue smoke mounted into the air.

There now remained but one evangelist, and he was in a furious rage, and tried to cut at Ulenspiegel with all his might. But Ulenspiegel cried:

"Wind of Steel or Wind of Lead, which matters it? Either way you shall quit this world for another, you shameless murderer!"

And he attacked the foe and defended himself most bravely. So they stood on the roadway, inflexible, face to face, giving and parrying blows. Now Ulenspiegel was covered with blood, for his opponent was an experienced fencer, and had wounded him on the hands and on the legs. But Ulenspiegel attacked and defended himself like a lion. Still the blood which began to flow from his head blinded him, and he retreated continually, trying to wipe away the

blood with his left hand but every moment feeling weaker.
And he would most certainly have been killed had not Lamme
brought down the third evangelist with another shot from
his arquebus.

And Ulenspiegel saw him fall, and heard him vomit forth
blasphemies and blood, and the white froth of death. And
once again the blue smoke drifted up above the dark
shrubbery, in the midst of which Lamme displayed yet again
his jolly face.

"Have you finished him off?" he asked.

"Yes, my son," replied Ulenspiegel, "but come. . . ."

Lamme, then, coming out of his hiding-place, saw Ulenspiegel all covered with blood. He ran like a stag, in spite of
his fat belly, and came to Ulenspiegel where he sat by the
three dead men.

"He is wounded!" Lamme cried. "My gentle friend is
wounded by the rascally murderer." And then, with a
vicious kick at the jaw of the evangelist who lay nearest to
him: "You cannot answer me, Ulenspiegel? Are you going
to die, my son? Where is the ointment! Ha! I remember
now. It is at the bottom of his satchel under the sausages.
Can't you hear me speak, Ulenspiegel? Alas! there is no warm
water here to wash your wound, and no way of getting any.
The water of the Sambre will have to do instead. But speak
to me, my friend. You are not so badly hurt after all, surely.
A little water—there, it's cold, isn't it? But he is waking up.
It's I, your friend; and your enemies are all dead! Oh,
where is some linen? Some linen to bind up his wounds.
There isn't any. What am I to do? Ah! my shirt, that
must serve."

Presently Ulenspiegel opened his eyes and raised himself
from the ground with his teeth all chattering because of
the cold.

"And here you are standing up already!" Lamme exclaimed.

" It is a balm of much virtue," said Ulenspiegel.

" Balm of valiance," answered Lamme.

And then, taking the bodies of the evangelists one by one, he cast them into a hole in the rocks, leaving their weapons and their clothes upon them. But he took their cloaks.

And all around in the sky the crows were beginning to caw to each other, in anticipation of the feast. And the Sambre flowed by like a river of steel under the grey sky.

And the snow fell, washing the blood away.

Yet they felt ill at ease, and Lamme said :

" I had rather kill a chicken than a man."

And they mounted again upon their donkeys. And when they arrived at the gates of Huy, the blood was still trickling from the head of Ulenspiegel, so they dismounted and pretended to have a quarrel, and to use their daggers on one another, with the utmost ferocity as it seemed. But when they had finished their duel, they remounted their donkeys and came into the town, showing their passports at the city gates.

The women, seeing Ulenspiegel wounded and bleeding while Lamme rode his donkey as though he had been the victor, threw many a glance of tender commiseration upon Ulenspiegel, and pointed their fingers at Lamme, saying : " That is the rascal who wounded his friend."

Lamme all this time was anxiously scrutinizing the crowd, hoping to discover his wife among them ; but all was in vain, and he was sad at heart.

XXI

" Where are you going now ? " said Lamme.

" To Maestricht," answered Ulenspiegel.

" But stay, my son. I have heard that the army of the Duke is camped all round the city and that he himself is within. Our passports will be of no use to us there. Even if they satisfy the Spanish soldiers, we shall still be arrested in the city and put through an examination. And in the

LAMME SUCCOURS
ULENSPIEGEL

meantime they will become aware of the death of the evangelists and our days on this earth will be numbered."

To this Ulenspiegel made answer:

" The crows and the owls and the vultures will make short work of their repast.   Already no doubt the dead bodies have become unrecognizable.   As for our passports, there is no reason why they should not remain effective.   But if the murder of the evangelists becomes known we should be arrested as you say.   Nevertheless, whatever happens we shall have to go to Maestricht and pass through Landen on the way."

" We shall be captured," said Lamme.

" We shall get through," answered Ulenspiegel.

Conversing in this wise they came to the inn of *La Pie*, where they found a good supper awaiting them, and good quarters for the night, both for themselves and for the donkeys; and on the morrow they took the road again for Landen.

Not far from that town they came to a large farm.   There Ulenspiegel whistled like a lark, and from the interior came the sound of a warlike cockcrow in answer.   After that a jolly-looking farmer appeared at the door of the farmhouse, and greeted them as friends and good Beggarmen, and bade them welcome.

" Who is this man ? " Lamme inquired.

" His name is Thomas Utenhove," said Ulenspiegel, " and he is a valiant Protestant.   The man-servants and maid-servants that work on the farm are fellows with him in the cause of freedom of conscience."

Then Utenhove said :

" You are the envoys of the Prince ?   Come in then, eat and drink with me."

And the ham was crackling in the frying-pan, the sausages likewise, and the wine flowed and the glasses were filled again.   And Lamme drank like dry sand, and ate his fill. And the boys and girls of the farm came one after another and thrust their noses into the half-open door to gaze on him as he worked away so hard. But the men were jealous, saying that they also would be able to eat and drink as bravely if they had the chance.

When all was finished, Thomas Utenhove said:

"One hundred of our peasants will be leaving us this week under pretext of going to work on the dikes at Bruges and thereabouts. They will be setting out in small bands of five or six at a time, and all by different routes. At Bruges they will find certain barges waiting for them to take them by sea to Emden."

"Will these men be provided with arms and with money?" inquired Ulenspiegel.

"Each man will carry ten florins and a heavy cutlass."

"God and the Prince will reward you," said Ulenspiegel.

"But tell me," said the farmer, "is Edzard, Count of Frise, still friendly to the Prince?"

"He feigns not to be," answered Ulenspiegel. "Nevertheless, he is giving harbourage all the time to the Prince's ships at Emden." And then he added: "We are on the way to Maestricht."

"You cannot go there," said the farmer. "The Duke's army is camped in front of the town and all round it."

With that he conducted his visitors up into the loft, whence they could see the standards of enemy cavalry and infantry moving about in the distance over the plain.

Ulenspiegel said:

"I have a plan to get through, if only they who have authority in this place would give me leave to get married. But for wife I should need a sweet and a gentle and comely lass who would be willing to marry me—if not for always, then for a week at least."

Lamme gasped with astonishment.

"Don't do it, my son," he cried. "She will only leave you, and then, all alone, you will burn with the fire of love; and the bed where now you sleep so sweetly will seem to you nothing better than a bed of prickly holly leaves, and gentle sleep will shun you for evermore."

" Still I must marry," replied Ulenspiegel. And then to Thomas Utenhove: " Come now, find me a wife; rich or poor, I don't care which! And I will take her to church, and our marriage shall be blessed by the priest. And he shall give us our marriage lines. Though, to be sure, we shall not hold them valid as being given by the hand of a Papist and an Inquisitor. Nevertheless they will be good enough for our purpose, and we will prepare ourselves, as is the custom, for our wedding trip."

" But what about the wife ? "

" That's your look-out," answered Ulenspiegel. " But when you have found her I shall take two wagons and decorate them with wreaths of fir branches and holly and paper flowers, and in the wagons themselves I shall dispose the men whom you wish to be conveyed to the Prince of Orange."

" But your wife ? " persisted Thomas Utenhove. " Where will you find her ? "

" Here, I doubt not," answered Ulenspiegel. " And then I shall harness two of your own horses to one of the wagons, and our two donkeys to the other. In the first wagon will ride my wife and myself, together with my friend Lamme here, and the witnesses of our nuptials. In the second wagon will follow the musicians, the players upon the drum, the fife, and the shawm. And then, with all our joyous wedding-flags a-flying, and with music playing, and we ourselves singing and drinking each other's healths, we shall ride along at the trot by the high road that leads to the *Galgen-veld*—the Field of the Gallows—which for us indeed will be the Field of Liberty."

" I will do all in my power to help you," said Thomas Utenhove, " but the women and girls will want to follow their men-folk.

"We will go where God wills," said a pretty-looking girl who had thrust in her head at the half-opened door.

"You can have four wagons if need be," said Thomas Utenhove, "and by that means we should be able to convey as many as five-and-twenty men."

"The Duke will be nicely fooled," said Ulenspiegel.

"And the Prince's fleet will gain the service of some fine soldiers," added Thomas Utenhove.

Then he caused a bell to be rung to summon his footman and his servants, and when they were all assembled he said to them:

"All you that are from the land of Zeeland, women as well as men, listen now to me. Ulenspiegel, who is hither come from Flanders, has a plan to convey you through the enemy's lines, disguised as the followers in a wedding procession."

And thereat the men and women of Zeeland cried out with one accord:

"We are ready, even unto the death!"

And the men said one to another:

"What joy it will be to exchange this land of slavery for the freedom of the sea!"

And the women and girls said likewise:

"Let us follow our husbands and our lovers; we belong to Zeeland and there we shall find asile!"

Now Ulenspiegel had noticed a young and pretty maid, and he addressed her jokingly:

"I would you were my wife!"

But she blushed and answered him:

"I would have thee for my husband—but at the church only, remember!"

The women laughed and said among themselves:

"She is in love with Hans Utenhove, the master's son. He will go along with her, doubtless."

"You say truly," Hans replied.

A Bride for Ulenspiegel

And his father said :

" You have my permission."

Then all the men put on their best clothes, their doublets and hose of velvet, and the great *opperst-kleed* over all. As for the women, they wore black petticoats and pleated shoes. Round their necks they wore a white ruff, their bodices were embroidered in gold, scarlet, and blue ; their skirts were of black wool with broad stripes of black velvet thereon, and their stockings were of black wool, and their shoes of velvet with silver buckles.

Thereupon Thomas Utenhove went to the church and put into the hands of the priest a couple of *ryckdaelders*, asking him at the same time to join in marriage Thylbert the son of Claes (that is Ulenspiegel) and Tannekin Pieters. And this the curé consented to do.

Ulenspiegel then went to church, followed by the wedding procession. And there, in the presence of the priest, Tannekin was made his wife.

And she looked so pretty and so sweet, so complaisant and so tender, that right willingly would he have eaten her up as she had been a ripe apple of love. And he told her so, not daring to do more for the respect he felt for her gentle loveliness. But she pouted her lips, and bade him leave her alone, for that Hans was watching him and would kill him without a doubt.

And a certain damsel was jealous, and said to Ulenspiegel :

" Seek elsewhere for a lover. Do you not see that she is afraid of her own man ? "

Lamme clapped his hands together and cried :

" You cannot have them all, you rascal ! "

So Ulenspiegel, making the best of his misfortune, returned to the farm with the wedding guests. And there he drank and sang and made merry, clinking many a glass with the damsel that was jealous. And at this Hans was glad, but

223

not so Tannekin, nor yet the youth that was betrothed to the damsel.

At noon, while the sun shone down from a clear sky and a fresh breeze was blowing, the wedding carriages started off. They were decorated with flowers and every kind of greenery, with flags flying, and drums and fifes, bagpipes and shawms playing most joyfully.

Now it happened that in the camp of the Duke of Alba there was another fête in progress ; and the sentries of the guard, having sounded the alarm, ran to the Duke, crying :

" The enemy is at hand. We have heard the noise of drums and fifes, and we have seen their banners in the distance. There is a strong force of cavalry that is hoping to draw you into some ambush. The main body, doubtless, is not far off."

The Duke at once sent to warn the colonels and captains, and himself ordered the army to be massed in battle array, and dispatched certain scouting parties on reconnaissance.

Then it was that there came on the scene the four carriages, making straight for the Duke's gunners. And in the chariots were none but men and women dancing and drinking and playing most joyously on fifes and drums and bagpipes and shawms. And wondrous was the din that came from all those instruments.

When the procession had been brought to a halt, the Duke himself came up, attracted by the noise, and he saw the newly married bride where she stood in one of the four chariots ; and beside her was Ulenspiegel, the bridegroom, covered with flowers ; and all the other peasants, both men and women, who had by now got down from the chariots and were dancing all round them and offering drink to the soldiers.

The Duke and his friends were much astonished at the simplicity of these peasants who sang and made merry when all around them was an army ready to do battle.

And now they that remained in the chariots were giving all the wine to the soldiers, and they in their turn were

224

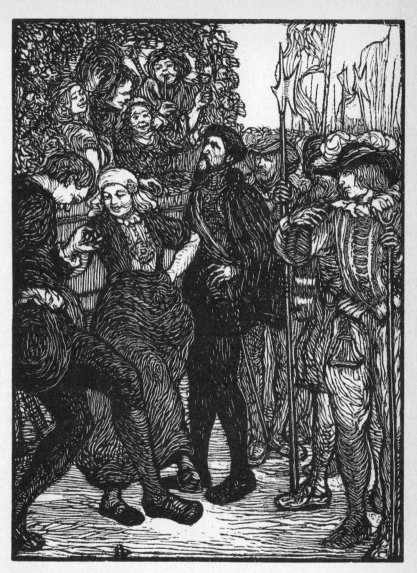

THE MOCK MARRIAGE

fêted by them and made much of; till at last, when the
wine began to run out, the peasants continued on their way
again. The drums and fifes and bagpipes struck up once
more and the cavalcade moved off without any let or
hindrance. And the soldiers, in high good humour, let off a
volley from their guns in honour of the festal occasion.

And thus they came to Maestricht, where Ulenspiegel
took counsel with the agents of the Reformers as to the best
way of sending ships loaded with arms and munitions to
the assistance of the Prince's fleet.

And from there they went to Landen and to other places,
disguised as working men.

The Duke was not long in learning the trick that had been
played on him, and there came into his hands a lampoon
which was in circulation at the time, with this refrain:

> *Bloody Duke,*
> *Silly Duke,*
> *Hast thou seen the Bride?*

And every time that the Duke made a mistake in his general-
ship the soldiers would sing:

> *The Duke he can't see clearly;*
> *He has seen the Bride!*

XXII

Now in those days the Duke divided his army into two
parts, one of which he ordered to march towards the Duchy
of Luxemburg and the other to the Marquisate of Namur.

"These tactics of the military are all one to me," said
Ulenspiegel to Lamme, "let us go on our way with confidence."

They were walking along the banks of the Meuse, near
the town of Maestricht, and Lamme saw that Ulenspiegel
gazed attentively at all the boats that were sailing on the
river. Suddenly he came to a stand before one of these

boats upon whose prow was carved the figure of a mermaid. And the mermaid carried a shield and on it in gold upon a black ground were blazoned the letters J.H.S., being the monogram of Our Lord and Saviour Jesus Christ. Ulenspiegel signed to Lamme that he should stand still, and then he began to sing like a lark most joyously.

A man appeared on the boat and began to crow like a cock. At this Ulenspiegel set up a noise like a donkey's bray, which the man immediately echoed with interest. And the two donkeys of Lamme and Ulenspiegel lay back their ears and joined in the chorus with their own natural voices. Sundry women and men were passing along that way, the latter riding on the backs of the horses which were tugging the barges along the tow-path. And Ulenspiegel said to Lamme:

" This boatman is making mock of us and our good steeds. What do you say to going and attacking him on his boat ? "

" Let us rather entice him over to the bank," replied Lamme.

But a woman who happened to be passing at the moment said :

" If you don't want to come back with your arms cut off, your backs broken, and your noses in pieces, let me advise you to let this Stercke Pier bray at his ease."

" Ee—aw ! Ee—aw ! Ee—aw ! " went the boatman.

" Let him sing," continued the woman. " Only the other day he showed us how he could lift on his shoulders a truck of heavy barrels of beer, and hold back yet another truck that was being dragged forwards by a strong horse. And at the inn there "—and as she spoke she pointed to the tavern of the *Blauwe Torre*—" it was there one day that he threw his knife at a plank of oak-wood twelve inches thick and pierced it at a distance of twenty paces ! "

" Ee—aw ! Ee—aw ! Ee—aw ! " went the boatman, and now he was joined by a youngster of twelve or so, who climbed on to the bridge of the boat, and began to bray in like manner.

But Ulenspiegel answered the woman :

"He's nothing to us, your Peter the Strong! For however strong he is, we are stronger! See my friend Lamme here. He could eat up two men like that without so much as a hiccup!"

"What's this you're saying, my son?" demanded Lamme.

"The truth," answered Ulenspiegel. "And do not let your modesty contradict me. For of a truth, good people, women and working men of Maestricht, I tell you that before long you shall see my friend here belabouring and beating to nothing this famous Stercke Pier of yours!"

"Be quiet," said Lamme.

"Your strength is famous far and wide," answered Ulenspiegel. "You cannot conceal it."

"Ee—aw!" went the boatman. "Ee—aw!" went the boy.

Suddenly Ulenspiegel began again to sing like a lark very melodiously, and the men and women and workmen standing by were enchanted, and began to ask him where he had learnt the art of whistling so divinely.

"In Paradise," answered Ulenspiegel, "whence I come." Then he addressed himself to the boatman, who was still continuing his braying and mocking :

"Why do you stay there on your boat, you good-for-nothing? Haven't you the courage to come and jeer at us and our steeds from the dry land?"

"Haven't you the courage for *that*?" said Lamme.

"Ee—aw! Ee—aw!" went the boatman. "Come, my good bray-masters, come up rather into my boat."

Then Ulenspiegel whispered to Lamme to do exactly as he did. But to the boatman he said aloud :

"If you are Stercke Pier, I am Tyl Ulenspiegel. And these two here are our donkeys, Jef and Jan, and they know how to bray better than you do, for that is their natural way of talking. As for coming on to your leaky decks, it is the last thing we wish to do. Your boat is like a tub, and each time that a wave comes along it shivers, and it knows no other way of walking save sideways-on like a crab."

" Yes, like a crab ! " said Lamme.

To which the boatman made answer :

" What are you croaking there between your teeth, great block of fat ? "

At this Lamme fell into a rage, crying :

" You are no Christian to make mock of my infirmity. My fat is my own, let me tell you, and is the result of the good food I eat, whereas you, old bag of bones that you are, you have never lived upon aught better than smoked herrings and old candle-wicks if one may judge anything from the lean flesh that shows through the tears in your measly hose."

" Ee—aw ! Ee—aw ! ' ' cried the boatman, and Lamme would have got down from his donkey to collect stones to throw at him had not Ulenspiegel said him nay.

The boatman now began to whisper something into the ear of the lad who was still " ee—awing " at his side, and a moment later the lad unfastened a little boat which lay by the side of the big one, and with the end of the boat-hook shoved himself cleverly off towards the river-bank. When the boy was quite close to the bank he drew himself up proudly and threw down this challenge :

" My master wants to know if you will have the courage to come on to his boat and join with him in a battle of fist and feet. And these good men and women shall be the arbiters."

" Certainly," said Ulenspiegel in a dignified tone of voice.

" We accept the challenge," said Lamme haughtily.

It was midday. The workmen who laboured on the dike and the road-menders and the builders of ships were about to take their repast of beans and boiled beef which had been brought them by their women-folk or their children. All

228

these, then, who stood around began to laugh and to clap
their hands at the prospect of a fight, looking forward with
joy to the chance of seeing the head of one of the combatants
broken, or his body thrown in pieces into the river.

" My son," said Lamme under his breath, " the boatman will assuredly throw us into the water."

" Let him throw you in if he wants to," said Ulenspiegel.

" The big one is afraid," said the crowd of workmen.

Lamme, who was still sitting his donkey, turned round and
gave them a look of anger, but they jeered at him the more.

" Come on," said Lamme. " Let us to the boat, and
then they shall see if I am afraid."

At these words the jeers broke out again, and Ulenspiegel
said :

" Come, let us to the boat ! "

When, therefore, they had dismounted from their donkeys
they threw the bridles to the boatman's lad, who caressed the
animals in friendly wise and led them to a place where he saw
some thistles growing. At the same time Ulenspiegel seized
hold of the boat-hook, made Lamme get into the skiff, and
then steered straight for the big boat. There he mounted
on to the deck by the help of a rope, and Lamme climbed up
in front of him, puffing and blowing.

Arrived on the bridge of the boat, Ulenspiegel leant down
as if to lace up his boots, and at the same time he spoke a word
into the boatman's ear, who straightway laughed and gave
Lamme a curious look. Then he began to roar out at him
every kind of insult, calling him worthless rogue, a man
bloated with vicious fat, prison-bred, *pap-eter*, and at the
same time inquiring of him how many tons of oil they gave
him when he was bled.

All of a sudden, without waiting to reply, Lamme threw
himself like a mad bull upon the boatman, knocked him down,
and began to beat him with all his might. The boatman,
however, did not receive much injury, forasmuch as Lamme's

229

arms were but weak on account of their fatness. And the boatman suffered himself to be thus dealt with despite the fact that he was making a great pretence at resistance all the time. And the men and women who were watching the battle from the bank were astonished, and exclaimed to each other: "Who would have thought that this fat man could be so fiery!"

And they clapped their hands while Lamme continued to belabour the boatman most unmercifully. But the latter took care only to protect his face. Suddenly Lamme was seen to be kneeling upon the breast of Stercke Pier, with one hand on his adversary's throat, and the other raised to strike.

"Cry for mercy," he said furiously, "or else I shall make you pass through the planks of your tub."

At this the boatman began to cough, thereby signifying that he could not speak, and demanded mercy with a sign of his hand.

Then Lamme was seen to pick up his adversary in a most generous manner, who thereupon, standing upright and turning his back towards the onlookers, put out his tongue at Ulenspiegel. Now the latter was rocking with laughter to see Lamme shaking the feather on his cap so proudly and walking about in triumph upon the deck of the boat.

And the men and women, boys and girls, who were watching from the bank applauded their loudest and cried out: "Long live the conqueror of Stercke Pier! He is a man of iron! Did you see how he cuffed him with his fist, and how he threw him down on his back with a blow of his hand? But see, they are now about to drink together to make the peace! Stercke Pier is coming up from the hold with wine and sausages!" And in very truth, Stercke Pier might now have been seen coming on deck with two tankards and a quart of white Meuse wine. And Lamme and the boatman made their peace. After which Lamme asked his new friend

230

what sort of fricassees they were that were being cooked in the hold of the ship ; for at one end of the deck was a chimney whence rose a column of thick black smoke. And the boatman made answer :

" Since you are men of valiant heart, knowing well the song of the lark, the bird of freedom, and the warlike clarion of the cock, and the bray of the ass withal, come you with me and I will show you my kitchen."

And so saying he led the way into the hold, where, removing certain planks from the floor, he disclosed some mighty piles of gun-barrels, together with a quantity of iron lances, halberds, sword-blades, and a great heap of powder and shot.

" Where shall I take them ? " he asked.

" To Emden, through the North Sea," said Ulenspiegel, " good Beggarman that you are ! "

" The sea is big," said the boatman.

" Big for battle," said Ulenspiegel.

" God is with us," said the boatman.

" Who then can be against us ? " cried Ulenspiegel.

And when they had thus spoken, the boatman conducted Lamme and Ulenspiegel on deck, with many words of cheer and good counsel. Then they rowed to the bank, where they mounted again upon their donkeys and set off towards Liége.

" My son," said Lamme whilst they were ambling gently along, " pray tell me why did that man, strong as he was, allow himself to be beaten by me so cruelly ? "

" To the end," answered Ulenspiegel, " that wherever we go, the fear of your prowess may go before us. That indeed will prove a more powerful escort than twenty landsknechts. For who would dare to measure his strength with Lamme the mighty, Lamme the conqueror ? Lamme the matchless bull among men, that overcame in the sight of all beholders the famous Stercke Pier—Peter the Strong—and threw him to the ground like a feather ? "

" You say well, my son," said Lamme, drawing himself up in the saddle.

" And I say what is true," answered Ulenspiegel, " for did you not notice the faces that looked out so curiously from the houses on the outskirts of this village ? They were pointing at the terrible figure of Lamme the Conqueror! And do you see these men who are gazing on you even now with such envy, and these sorry cowards who uncover as you pass ? Answer to their salute, O Lamme, my sweet one, nor be disdainful of the populace. Behold, the very children know your name and whisper it with terror."

And Lamme passed along proudly, saluting right and left like a king. And the fame of his valour followed him from village to village and from town to town, as far as Liége, Chocquier, La Neuville, Vesin, and Namur, to which place, however, our travellers gave a wide berth because of the three evangelists. And so they wended along by the banks of river and canal, and everywhere the song of the lark answered the song of the cock. And wherever they went they found that in the sacred cause of Liberty weapons were being forged and armour furbished for the ships that stood by along the coast to carry away.

And Lamme, preceded everywhere by his glorious reputation, began himself to believe in his own prowess, and growing proud and warlike he let his beard grow too. And Ulenspiegel called him Lamme the Lion. But Lamme did not continue in this purpose longer than the fourth day, because the hairs of his beard began to tickle him. And he passed a razor over the surface of his victorious countenance, so that it appeared thereafter like his own face once more, round and full as the sun, ablaze with the flame of good nourishment. And thus they came at length to Harlebeke.

LAMME THE VICTOR

At Courtrai

XXIII

At Harlebeke Lamme renewed his provision of *olie-koekjes*, eating seven-and-twenty of them on the spot and putting thirty away into his basket. The same evening they came to Courtrai and dismounted from their donkeys at the tavern of the Bee that was kept by one Gilis Van den Ende, who himself came to the inn door as soon as he heard the singing of the lark.

At once the new arrivals found that everything was made like sugar and honey for them; for mine host, as soon as he had seen the letter from the Prince, presented Ulenspiegel with fifty caroluses on the Prince's behalf, nor would he accept any payment at all for the turkey which he served for their dinner, nor yet for the *dobbel clauwaert* which he gave them to drink. He warned them also that there were many spies in Courtrai, and that it behoved both Ulenspiegel and his companion to keep a close watch on what they said during their stay in the city.

"We shall be careful," said Ulenspiegel and Lamme. And so saying they came out of the tavern.

The gables of the houses were all gilded in the rays of the setting sun. The birds sang in the lime-trees, and Lamme and Ulenspiegel wandered at their ease along the streets of the town. All at once Lamme said:

"I asked Martin Van den Ende if by chance he had seen any one at all resembling my wife in Courtrai, and he told me that there were a number of women that were accustomed to meet together of an evening at the sign of the Rainbow, a house that is kept by a woman called La Stevenyne, just outside the town on the road to Bruges. I shall go there."

"I will meet you anon," said Ulenspiegel. "But now I would see the sights of the town. If I meet your wife I will send her on to you. Meanwhile remember what the innkeeper said, and keep your own counsel if you value your own skin."

" I will be careful," said Lamme.

Ulenspiegel walked about by himself till the sun set and night began to come on quickly. He had come to the *Pierpot-Straetje*—the Alley of the Pot of Stone—and there he heard the sound of a viola being played most melodiously, and presently he noticed a white figure that beckoned to him from a distance, then retreated, playing the viola all the time. It was a woman, and she sang like a seraphim, a sweet, slow song, stopping now and then to look behind her with a beckoning gesture, then retreating again. But Ulenspiegel ran quickly and overtook her, and was about to speak to her when she sealed his lips with a hand all scented with benjamin.

" Are you a working man or a nobleman ? " she asked.

" I am Ulenspiegel."

" Are you rich ? "

" Rich enough for you."

" But you have not seen me ! " And she opened the lantern she carried so as to let the light shine straight upon her face.

" You are beautiful," said Ulenspiegel.

" Then come with me," she said.

And she brought him to the house of La Stevenyne, on the road to Bruges, at the sign of the Rainbow.

They entered a large room where a great number of girls were assembled, who all looked up jealously at Ulenspiegel's companion as she came in. And suddenly Ulenspiegel saw Lamme, sitting there in a corner by a little table whereon was a candle, a ham, and a pot of beer. By his side were a couple of girls, who were endeavouring to get a share in the ham and the beer ; but Lamme was trying to prevent them. As soon as he noticed Ulenspiegel he jumped up, crying :

" Blessed be God who has given back to me my friend ! Bring more drink, *baesine* ! "

At this Ulenspiegel drew out his purse, saying :

234

" Yes, bring us to drink to the value of what is in here ! "
and he jingled the money that was in the purse.

" No, by heaven ! " cried Lamme, seizing the purse.
" It's I that shall pay, not you."

Ulenspiegel would have recovered the purse by force, but
Lamme kept tight hold. As they were struggling together,
the one to keep the purse, the other to get it back again,
Lamme whispered by fits and starts into Ulenspiegel's ear :

" Listen. *Constables. Here . . . four of them . . . in the
little room with three girls.* Two outside waiting for you and
for me. . . . I tried to go out . . . prevented. . . . The
girl over there in the brocaded gown is a spy . . . Stevenyne a
spy ! "

And all the time they were fighting Ulenspiegel listened
attentively, though he kept on crying aloud :

" Give me back my purse, you rascal ! "

And they seized each other by the neck and by the
shoulders, and rolled together on the floor, while Lamme
went on with his tidings to Ulenspiegel. Suddenly there
appeared on the scene mine host of the tavern of the Bee ;
and he was followed by seven other men, with whom, however,
he apparently had no connexion. As he came in he crowed
like a cock and Ulenspiegel whistled like a lark. Then, seeing
Ulenspiegel and Lamme still struggling on the floor, he
inquired of La Stevenyne who they might be. " Two rascals,"
she told him, " who ought to be parted from each other
instead of being allowed to make all this disturbance ere they
are brought to the gallows."

" If any one tries to separate us," said Ulenspiegel, " we
will make him eat of these paving-stones."

" Yes," said Lamme, " we will make him eat these paving-
stones ! "

Then Ulenspiegel whispered something in Lamme's ear.
" *The innkeeper is come to rescue us.*" And presently the
innkeeper, who must have divined some mystery was afoot,

joined the *mêlée* on the floor with his head down, and Lamme attacked him in the ear with these words :

" You have come to rescue us ?   How will you do it ? "

The innkeeper made pretence of pulling Ulenspiegel by the ears, but managed to say to him the while, under his breath :

" These seven men are on your side . . . they are strong men . . . butchers. . . . I must be off . . . too well known in the town . . . but when I have gone . . . *'T is van te beven de klinkaert.* . . . Break up everything. . . ."

" I understand," said Ulenspiegel, rising at the same time from the floor and kicking out at the innkeeper.   The latter struck Ulenspiegel in his turn and Ulenspiegel said :

" You hit hard, my hearty ! "

" As hard as a hail-storm," said the innkeeper.   And quickly seizing the purse from Lamme he handed it back to Ulenspiegel.

" You may stand me a drink, you rogue, now you are come into your right mind again."

" I'll stand you one, you scandalous scamp," replied Ulenspiegel.

" See how insolent he is," said La Stevenyne.

" As insolent as you are beautiful," answered Ulenspiegel.

Now La Stevenyne was sixty years old at least, and her face was like the fruit of the medlar, but all yellow with bile, and she had a large port-wine stain on her left cheek.

When the innkeeper had had his drink, he paid the bill and departed.   The seven butchers meanwhile made sundry knowing grimaces at the constables and La Stevenyne.   One of them indicated by a gesture that he held Ulenspiegel for a simpleton, and that he would be able to do for him very easily.   But all the time that he was putting out his tongue in mockery to La Stevenyne, who herself was grinning and laughing, he whispered in Ulenspiegel's ear :

" *'T is van te beven de klinkaert*—it is time to rattle the glasses." Then, in his ordinary tone of voice, and pointing at the constables:

"Gentle Reformer," he said, "we are all on your side. Stand us some food and drink, won't you?"

And La Stevenyne laughed with pleasure, and put out her tongue at Ulenspiegel when his back was turned. And La Gilline, she of the brocaded gown, she also put out her tongue at Ulenspiegel, and the girls all began to whisper one to another: "Behold the spy that by her beauty draweth men to the torture and bringeth them at last to a death more cruel even than torture. Above seven-and-twenty Protestants hath she betrayed already. Gilline is her name, and now she is in a rapture of joy as she thinks of the reward she will get for her information—the first hundred caroluses, to wit, from the estate of each of her victims. But she will not laugh when she bethinketh her that she must share one-half of the spoil with La Stevenyne!"

And every one there present—the constables, the butchers, and the girls themselves—put out their tongues in mockery of Ulenspiegel. And Lamme sweated great drops of sweat, and became red with anger like the crest of a cock. But he would not let himself say a word.

"Come, stand us food and drink," said the butchers and the constables.

"Very well," said Ulenspiegel, jingling yet again the money in his purse. "Bring us meat and drink, my sweet Stevenyne; bring us drink in glasses that can sing!"

At this the girls began to laugh anew; but La Stevenyne went down to the cellar and brought back with her ham, sausages, black-pudding omelettes, and some of those singing glasses, that are so called because they are mounted on tall stems and can be made to resound like a bell when some one strikes them. Then Ulenspiegel said:

"Let him who is hungry eat, and he who is thirsty let him drink!" And the constables, the girls, the butchers, Gilline,

237

and La Stevenyne applauded these words of Ulenspiegel, clapping their hands and stamping their feet; and then they all sat down to the feast. Ulenspiegel, Lamme, and the seven butchers sat at the big table of honour, the constables and the girls at two smaller tables; and they ate and drank right heartily. And the constables invited their two comrades, who had been waiting outside the house, to come in and join them.

La Stevenyne said with a snigger:

" Remember, no one can leave till he has paid me."

And she went and locked all the doors, and put the keys in her pocket.

At this La Gilline raised her glass.

" The bird is in its cage," she cried. " Let us drink."

But two of the girls, whose names were Gena and Margot, said to her:

" Is this yet another man that you are going to lure to his death, you wicked one ? "

" I know not," said Gilline; " let us drink."

But the girls would not drink with her.

And Gilline took her viola and sang in French this song:

Au son de la viole,
Je chante nuit et jour ;
Je suis la fille-folle,
La vendeuse d'amour.

Astarté de mes hanches
Fit les lignes de feu ;
J'ai les épaules blanches,
Et mon beau corps est Dieu.

Je suis froide ou brûlante,
Tendre au doux nonchaloir :
Tiède, éperdue, ardente,
Mon homme, à ton vouloir.

Caged

Vois, je vends tout : mes charmes,
Mon âme et mes yeux bleus ;
Bonheur, rires et larmes,
Et la Mort si tu veux.

Au son de la viole,
Je chante nuit et jour ;
Je suis la fille-folle,
La vendeuse d'amour.

As she sang this song La Gilline looked so beautiful, so
soft and fragrant, that all the men, the constables and the
butchers, Lamme and Ulenspiegel himself, sat smiling there,
quite melted and overcome by her charm.

All at once La Gilline gave a loud laugh and fixed her gaze
on Ulenspiegel :

" And it's thus that the birds are caged," she said.   And
the spell of her charm was broken.

Ulenspiegel, Lamme, and the butchers looked at one
another.

" Well now," said La Stevenyne, " are you going to pay
the bill, my Lord Ulenspiegel ? "

" We shall pay nothing in advance," said he.

" Then I shall pay myself later on—out of your inheritance," said La Stevenyne.   After that :

" Let us drink ! " she cried.

" Let us drink ! " cried the constables.

" Let us drink ! " cried La Stevenyne.   " The doors are
shut ; the windows are strongly barred ; the birds are in
their cage.   Let us drink ! "

" Let us drink then," said Ulenspiegel.   " And bring us
wine of the best to crown the banquet."

La Stevenyne brought in more wine.   And now they
were all seated, drinking and eating, the constables and the
girls together.   But the seven butchers were at the same table

with Ulenspiegel and Lamme, and they kept on throwing pieces of ham, and sausages, omelettes, and bottles of wine to the table of the girls, who themselves caught the food in mid-flight as carp catch the flies that buzz on the surface of a fish-pond. And La Stevenyne laughed and grinned, and pointed to the packets of candles which hung over the counter. And these were the candles that the gay girls were used to purchase, five to the pound. Then La Stevenyne said to Ulenspiegel:

"On his way to the stake it is the custom for the condemned man to carry a wax candle. Shall I make you a present of one?"

"Let us drink!" said Ulenspiegel.

But La Gilline said: "Look at Ulenspiegel's eyes. They are shining like the eyes of a swan that is about to die."

"Wouldn't you like to eat one of the candles?" said La Stevenyne. "They would serve you in hell to lighten your eternal damnation."

"I see clearly enough to admire your ugly mug," said Ulenspiegel.

Suddenly he struck the stem of his wine-glass and clapped his hands together with a rhythm like that an upholsterer uses when he beats the wool of a mattress with his stick.

"'*T is van te beven de klinkaert*," he said; "it is time to make the glasses shiver—the glasses which resound. . . ."

And this, in Flanders, is the signal that the drinkers make when they are angry, and when they are like to ransack and despoil in their wrath the houses of ill fame. So even now did Ulenspiegel raise his glass and drink, and then did he made it vibrate upon the table, crying yet again:

"'*T is vante beven de klinkaert*."

And the seven butchers did likewise.

Then a great stillness fell upon the company. La Gilline grew pale; La Stevenyne looked astonished. The constables said:

" Are the seven with them too ? " But the butchers winked their eyes and reassured them ; yet all the time they continued without ceasing, and louder and louder as Ulenspiegel led them :

" *'T is van te beven de klinkaert. 'T is van te beven de klinkaert.*"

La Stevenyne took another draught of wine to give herself courage.

Then Ulenspiegel struck his fist on the table in that regular rhythm which the upholsterers use as they beat their mattresses ; and the seven did likewise ; and the glasses, jugs, trenchers, flagons, and goblets began to dance upon the table, slowly at first, but beginning soon to knock against each other, and to break and to heel over on one side as they fell. And all the time echoed and re-echoed, more sternly menacing, with every monotonous repetition :

" *'T is van te beven de klinkaert.*"

"Alas ! " said La Stevenyne, " they will break everything." And her teeth seemed to show farther out from her lips than ever. And the hot blood of their fury and of their anger began to flame in the souls of the seven butchers, and in the souls of Lamme and Ulenspiegel. Till at last, without ceasing once their melancholy and monotonous chant, all they that were sitting at Ulenspiegel's table took their glasses, and brake them upon the table, and at the same moment they drew their cutlasses and leapt upon the chairs. And they made such a din with their song that all the windows in the house shook. Then like a band of infuriated devils they went round the room, visiting each table in turn, crying without ceasing :

" *'T is van te beven de klinkaert.*"

And the constables rose up trembling with terror and seized their ropes and chains. But the butchers, together with Lamme and Ulenspiegel, thrust their knives quickly back into their cases, and sprang up to run nimbly through the chamber, hitting out right and left with their chairs as though they had been cudgels. And they spared nothing there except the girls, for everything else they brake in pieces —furniture, windows, chests, plates, pots, trenchers, glasses, and flagons, hitting out at the constables without mercy, and crying out all the time in the rhythm of the mattress-beaters : "'*T is van te beven de klinkaert. 'T is van te beven de klinkaert.*" And Ulenspiegel, who had given La Stevenyne a blow on the nose with his fist, and had taken all her keys and put them into his satchel, was now amusing himself by forcing her to eat those candles of hers. And the girls laughed at the sight of her as she sneezed with anger and tried to spit out the candles—but in vain, for her mouth was too full. And all the time Ulenspiegel and the seven butchers did not cease the rhythm of their dire refrain : " '*T is van te beven de klinkaert.*" But at last Ulenspiegel made a sign, and when silence had at last been restored he spake, saying :

" You are here, my friends, in our power. It is a dark night and the River Lys is close at hand, where a man drowns easily if he is once pushed in. And the gates of Courtrai are shut." Then turning to the seven butchers :

" You are bound for Peteghen, to join the Beggar-men ? "

" We were ready to go there when the news came to us that you were here."

" And from Peteghen you were going to the sea ? "

" Yes," they said.

" Do you think there are one or two among these constables whom it would be safe to release for our service ? "

" There are two," they said, " Niklaes and Joos by name, who have never as yet been guilty of persecuting the poor Reformers."

" You can trust us ! " said Niklaes and Joos.

" Very well then," said Ulenspiegel. " Here are twenty caroluses for you, twice as much, that is, as you would have

242

" 'T IS VAN TE BEVEN
DE KLINKAERT "

got for an act of shameful betrayal." And at that the other
five constables cried out as one man :

"Twenty florins ! We will serve the Prince for twenty
florins. The King's pay is bad. Only give us half as much and
we will tell the judge any tale you please." But Lamme and
the butchers kept muttering under their breath :

" '*T is van te beven de klinkaert.* '*T is van te beven de
klinkaert.*"

"In order that you may be kept from too much talking,"
Ulenspiegel continued, "the seven will lead you in hand-
cuffs to Peteghen, and there you will be given over into the
hands of the Beggarmen. The florins will be handed to you
at sea, and if you prove brave in battle you will have your
share of the spoil. If you attempt to desert you will be
hanged."

"We will serve him who pays us," they said.

" '*T is van te beven de klinkaert !* '*T is van te beven de
klinkaert,*" murmured the seven.

"You will also take with you," said Ulenspiegel, " La
Gilline, La Stevenyne and the girls. If any one of them
tries to escape you will sew her in a sack and throw her
into the river."

"He has not killed me yet !" cried La Gilline, jumping
up from her corner and brandishing her viola in the air.
And she began to sing :

> *Sanglant était mon rêve.*
> *Le rêve de mon cœur.*
> *Je suis la fille d'Eve*
> *Et de Satan vainqueur.*

But La Stevenyne and the others seemed as if they were
going to cry.

"Do not be afraid, my sweets," said Ulenspiegel. "You
are so pretty and so tender that all men will love to caress you
wherever you go, and after every victory you will have your

share in the spoils." But the three girls turned upon La Gilline :

" You that were her daughter, her breadwinner, sharing with La Stevenyne the shameful rewards of her espionage, do you still dare to flaunt yourself before us and to insult us with your dress of brocade ? Verily it is the blood of the victims and nothing else that has clothed you so richly. But now let us take her dress from her, so she may be like to us."

" That shall not be," said Ulenspiegel.

And the girls looked jealously at Ulenspiegel, saying :

" He is mad about her, like all the rest."

And La Gilline played upon her viola and sang, and the seven butchers departed for Peteghen, taking with them the constables and the girls. And they passed along by the River Lys. And as they went they kept muttering :

" *'T is van te beven de klinkaert! 'T is van te beven de klinkaert!* " And at break of day they came to the camp, and sang out like the lark and were answered straightway by a cockcrow. The girls and the constables were put under a strong guard, but in spite of these precautions La Gilline was found dead at noon on the third day, her heart pierced by a long needle. The three girls accused La Stevenyne of having done this deed, and she was brought before the captain. There she confessed that she had committed the crime out of jealousy and anger at the way the girl had treated her. And La Stevenyne was hanged and buried in the wood.

La Gilline also was buried, and prayers were said over her sweet body.

XXIV

Warm was the air, and not a breath of wind was wafted from the calm sea. The trees on the Damme canal were motionless, and the grasshoppers were busy in the meadows, while from many a church and abbey the men came into the fields to fetch that " thirteenth part of the harvest " which was claimed by the curés and the abbés who lived round about.

244

Tyl comes Home

From the depths of a blue and blazing sky the sun poured
down his heat, and Nature slept beneath that radiance like
some beautiful girl that has swooned away beneath the
caresses of her lover.

From far off, Lamme and Ulenspiegel descried the high,
square, massive tower of Notre Dame, and Lamme said:

"There, my son, is the home both of your loves and of
your sorrows." But Ulenspiegel made no answer.

"In a little while," continued Lamme, "I shall be seeing
my old home, and perhaps my wife!" But Ulenspiegel did
not answer.

"You man of wood," said Lamme, "you heart of stone,
will nothing move you—neither the near approach to the
place where you passed your childhood, nor yet the dear
memory of poor Claes and Soetkin, the two martyrs? What!
You are not sad, neither are you merry; who can it be that
has thus hardened your heart? Look at me, how anxious
and uneasy I am, and how my belly heaves with nervousness;
look at me I say!"

But Lamme looked at Ulenspiegel and saw that his face
was drawn and pale, and his lips were trembling with tears, and
he said not a word. And now Lamme also held his peace.

They walked along in this way without speaking till
they came to Damme, which they entered by the rue
Héron; and they saw no one about because of the heat.
Only the dogs lay on their sides on the doorsteps of many a
house, gasping, with their tongues out, while Lamme and
Ulenspiegel passed right in front of the Town Hall where
Claes had been burnt to death; and here the lips of Ulenspiegel trembled the more, and his tears dried up. And at
last they were come to the house of Claes himself, which was
now occupied by a master charcoal-burner. Ulenspiegel
entered in and said:

"Do you recognize me? I would wish to rest here
a while."

245

The master charcoal-burner answered :

" I recognize you. You are the son of the victim. You are free in this house to go wheresoever you will."

Ulenspiegel went into the kitchen, and then upstairs into the room of Claes and Soetkin, and there he shed many tears.

When he had come down again, the master charcoal-burner said to him : " Here is bread, cheese, and beer. If you are hungry, eat. If you are thirsty, drink."

But Ulenspiegel made a gesture to the effect that he was neither hungry nor thirsty, and he left the house and came with Lamme to Katheline's cottage, and there they tethered their donkeys and straightway entered in. It was the hour of the midday meal. On the table was a dish of broad beans in their pods together with some white beans. Katheline was busy eating, while Nele was standing by her ready to pour into Katheline's plate some vinegar sauce which she had just taken off the fire. When Ulenspiegel came into the room Nele was so startled that she put the sauce, and the pot and all, into Katheline's platter. And Katheline kept on wagging her head, and picking out the broad beans with her spoon from the trencher, striking her forehead the while and crying ever like one mad :

" Put out the fire ! My head is burning ! "

And the smell of the vinegar made Lamme feel hungry. But Ulenspiegel stood still where he was, gazing at Nele and smiling for love of her despite his great sorrow.

And Nele, without a word of greeting, flung her arms round his neck. And she also seemed like one bereft of sense. For she cried and laughed, and blushing as she was with her great and sweet happiness, she could only say : " Tyl ! Tyl ! "

Ulenspiegel, happy now in his turn, gazed into her eyes. Then she let go of him and stepped back a pace or two, gazed at him joyfully in her turn, and then threw herself on him again, clasping her arms round his neck, and so many times

246

and again. And he suffered her gladly, powerless to tear himself away from her, till at last she fell into a chair, tired out and like one bereft of her senses, and she said without shame :

"Tyl! Tyl, my beloved! Here you are come back to me again!"

Lamme meanwhile was standing at the door; but when Nele had recovered herself a little, she pointed to him, saying :

"Where have I seen this fat man?"

"He is my friend," Ulenspiegel told her. "He goes seeking his wife in my company."

"I know you," said Nele to Lamme. "You used to live in the rue Héron. You are seeking for your wife? Well, I have seen her. She is living at Bruges in all piety and devotion, and when I asked her why she had left her husband so unkindly, she answered that it was by the Holy Will of God and at the command of Holy Penance, and that she could never live with her husband again."

At these words Lamme was sad, but his eyes wandered to the beans and vinegar. And outside the larks sang as they flew upwards into the sky, and all Nature swooned away under the caress of her Lord the Sun. And Katheline kept stirring with her spoon that pot of beans and sauce.

XXV

Now, in those days a damsel some fifteen years of age was going from Heyst to Knokke, alone in the middle of the day, by the sand-dunes. No one had any fear for her for they knew that the wolves and wicked spirits of the damned go biting their victims only in the night. The damsel carried a satchel wherein were forty-eight gold coins of the value of four florins carolus, being the sum owed by the girl's mother, Toria Pieterson, who lived at Heyst, to her uncle, Jan Rapen of Knokke, on account of a sale. The girl's name was Betkin, and she was wearing her best clothes, and she went on her way most happily.

The same evening, seeing that she did not return, her mother became anxious, but reassured herself with the thought that the girl must have stayed the night with her uncle.

On the morrow, certain fishermen on their way back from the sea with a boat-load of fish, drew their boat on to the beach and unloaded their catch, which they would sell at auction by the cart-load at the *Minque* of Heyst. They went up the road along the dunes, all strewn with shells, and presently came upon a young girl, stripped naked even to her chemise, with traces of blood all about her. Coming nearer they found upon her neck the horrid marks of long sharp teeth. She was lying on her back with her eyes wide open gazing up into the sky, and her mouth was open also as if with the cry of death itself !

Covering the girl's body with an *opperst-kleed* they brought it to Heyst, to the Town Hall, and there quickly assembled the aldermen and the leech, who declared that the long teeth that had made those marks were no teeth of a wolf as known in nature, but rather of some wicked and devilish werwolf, and that it behoved them now to pray God one and all that he would deliver the land of Flanders.

And in all that country, and notably at Damme, at Heyst, and at Knokke, prayers and orisons were ordered to be made.

But Ulenspiegel went to the town bailiff and said to him : " I will go and kill the werwolf."

" What gives you this confidence ? " asked the bailiff.

" The ashes beat upon my heart," Ulenspiegel replied. " Only give me leave to labour a while at the forge of the commune."

" Very well," said the bailiff.

Ulenspiegel, without telling a word concerning his project to any man or woman in Damme, betook him to the forge,

248

THE DEATH OF BETKIN

and there, in secret, he fashioned a fine and a strong trap
such as those traps which are made to catch wild beasts.

On the following day, which was a Saturday, day beloved
of werwolves, Ulenspiegel armed himself with a letter from
the bailiff to the curé of Heyst, together with the trap which
he carried under his cloak, as well as a good crossbow and a
well-sharpened cutlass. Thus provided, he departed on his
way, saying to those in Damme :

" I am going out to hunt the seagulls, and of their down
will I make a soft pillow for madame the wife of the bailiff."

Now before he reached Heyst, he came out on to the sea-
shore. The sea was rough and boisterous, and he heard the
great waves growling like thunder, and the wind that blew
from England whistling in the rigging of the boats that were
stranded on the beach. A fisherman said to him :

" This bad wind will be our ruin. Last night the sea was
calm, but at sunrise she suddenly swelled with anger. And
to-day we shall not be able to go out fishing." Ulenspiegel
was pleased at this, for he knew that now he would be sure of
some assistance if need arose. At Heyst he went straight
to the curé and presented the letter that the bailiff had given
him. The curé said :

" You are a brave man, but let me tell you that no one
goes along the dunes on Saturday nights without being bitten
by the werwolf and left dead on the sands. Even the men
who are at work on the dikes never go there except in a party.
The evening is coming on. Do you not hear the werwolf
howling in his valley ? Perchance he will come again into
the cemetery, even as he came last night, howling most
horribly through all the hours of darkness ! God be with you,
my son. But go not there." And the curé crossed himself.

" The ashes beat upon my heart," answered Ulenspiegel.
The curé said :

" Because you have so brave a spirit I will help you."

" Monsieur le Curé," said Ulenspiegel, " you will be

doing a great kindness, as well to me as to this poor desolated land of ours, if you will go to Toria, the dead girl's mother, and to her two brothers also, and tell them that the wolf is near at hand, and that I am going out to wait for it and kill it."

The curé said :

" If you want to know where you should lie in wait, let me advise you to keep along by the path which leads to the cemetery. It runs between two hedges of broom. It is so narrow two men could scarcely walk abreast."

" I understand," said Ulenspiegel. " And you, brave curé, will you tell the girl's mother and her husband and her brothers to come themselves and wait together in the church about the hour of the curfew. There, if they hear a cry like the cry of a seagull, it will mean that I have seen the werwolf. Then they must sound the *wacharm* on the bell, and come fast to my assistance. And if there are any other brave men . . ."

" There are none, my son," replied the curé. " The fishermen are less afraid of the plague and of death itself than of the werwolf. Do not go, I beseech you."

Ulenspiegel answered :

" The ashes beat upon my heart."

And the curé said to him :

" I will do as you bid. God bless you. Are you hungry or thirsty ? "

" Both," answered Ulenspiegel.

The curé gave him some beer, some bread, and some cheese, and Ulenspiegel when he had eaten and drunk went his way.

And as he walked along he raised his eyes and beheld Claes, his father, seated in glory at the side of God in heaven where the moon shone so brightly. And thereafter he gazed upon the sea and upon the clouds, and he heard the wind that came blowing stormily from England.

" Alas ! " he cried, " O Dusky Clouds that pass along so rapidly yonder in the sky, be you now for a vengeance on the murderer. And you, O Wind that whistles so sadly in the gorse along the dunes and in the rigging of the ships, be you now the voice of the victims that cry to God that he should help me on in this enterprise."

And so saying he came down into the valley, stumbling as if he had been a drunken man ; and he began to sing, hiccuping all the time, staggering from side to side, yawning, spitting, and then standing still and pretending to be sick. But all the time he was keeping his eyes wide open, and peering this way and that, for he had heard the sharp sound as of a wolf howling. Then, as he stood there vomiting like a dog, he descried the long outline of a wolf moving towards the cemetery in the bright light of the moon.

At that he lurched on again, and came into the path between the hedges of broom. There he pretended to fall down, and as he did so, he placed his trap upon the side from which the wolf was coming. Then he loaded his crossbow, and went forward about ten paces, standing up again in a drunken posture. He still went on staggering to right and to left, nor did he cease to retch and to hiccup, but all the time his mind was taut as a bowstring, and he was all eyes and ears for what might be going to happen. Yet he saw nothing save the dark clouds racing in the sky, and again that large and heavy form of blackness coming down the path towards him. Neither did he hear aught but the dismal wailing of the wind, and the angry thunder of the sea, and the sound that the shells on the path gave forth beneath a heavy step that tapped upon them. Feigning to be about to sit down, Ulenspiegel fell forwards on to the path, very heavily like a drunken man. After that he heard as it were a piece of iron clinking close to his ear, and then the sound of the trap shutting, and a human voice that cried out in the darkness.

"The werwolf," said Ulenspiegel to himself. "He's got his front paws caught in the trap. Now he is howling and trying to run away, dragging the trap with him. But he shall not escape." And he drew his crossbow and shot an arrow at the legs of the werwolf.

"He's wounded now," said Ulenspiegel, "and he has fallen down."

· Thereupon he whistled like a seagull, and straightway the church bell clanged out from the village and a boy's shrill voice was heard crying from afar off:

"Awake! Awake, you sleepers! The werwolf is caught."

"Praise be to God," said Ulenspiegel.

Now the first to arrive on the scene of the capture were Toria the mother of Betkin, and Lansaen her husband, and her two brothers Josse and Michael. And they brought lanterns with them.

"You have caught him?" they asked.

"Look on the path," answered Ulenspiegel.

"Praise be to God," they exclaimed, crossing themselves.

"Who is it that is calling out the news in the village?" asked Ulenspiegel.

"It is my eldest boy," Lansaen answered. "The youngster is running through the village knocking on all the doors and crying out that the wolf is caught. Praise be to thee!"

"The ashes beat upon my heart," answered Ulenspiegel.

Suddenly the werwolf began to speak:

"Have mercy on me! Have mercy, Ulenspiegel!"

"This wolf can talk!" they exclaimed, crossing themselves again. "He is a devil in very truth, and knows Ulenspiegel's name already!"

"Have mercy! Have mercy!" the voice cried again. "I am no wolf. Order the bell to stop ringing. For thus it is that it tolls for the dead. And my wrists are torn by the trap. I am old and I am bleeding. Have mercy! And what is this—this shrill voice of a child awakening all the village? Oh pray, have mercy!"

252

The Wolf that talked

"I have heard your voice before," said Ulenspiegel passionately. "You are the fishmonger. The murderer of Claes, the vampire that preys upon poor maids! Have no fear, good mother and father. This is none other than the Dean of the Fishmongers on whose account poor Soetkin died of grief." And with one hand he held the man fast by the neck, and with the other he drew out his cutlass.

But Toria the mother of Betkin prevented him.

"Take him alive," cried she. "Take him alive. Let him pay!"

Meanwhile there were many fisherfolk, men and women of Heyst, who were come out at the news that the werwolf was taken and that he was no devil but a man. Some of these carried lanterns and flaming torches, and all of them cried aloud when they saw him:

"Thief! Murderer! Where hide you the gold that you have stolen from your poor victims?"

"He shall repay it all," said Toria. And she would have beaten him in her rage had she not fallen down there and then upon the sand in a mad fury like unto one dead. And they left her there until she came to herself.

And Ulenspiegel, sad at heart, beheld the clouds racing like mad things in the sky, and out at sea the white crests of the waves, and on the ground at his feet the white face of the fishmonger that looked up at him in the light of the lantern with cruel eyes. And the ashes beat upon his heart.

And they walked for four hours, and came to Damme where was a great crowd assembled that already was aware of what had happened. Every one desired to see the fishmonger, and they pressed round the fishermen and fisherwives, crying out and singing and dancing and saying: "The werwolf is caught! He is caught, the murderer! Blessed be Ulenspiegel! Long live our brother Ulenspiegel!—*Lange leve onsen broeder Ulenspiegel.*" And it was like a popular rising. And when the crowd passed in front of the bailiff's

253

house, he came out, hearing the noise, and said to Ulenspiegel:

"You are the conqueror; all praise to you!"

"It was the ashes of Claes that beat upon my heart," said Ulenspiegel.

Then the bailiff said:

"Half the murderer's fortune shall be yours."

"Let it be given to his victims," answered Ulenspiegel.

Now Lamme and Nele were there too—Nele laughing and crying with joy and kissing her lover; Lamme jumping heavily and striking his belly while he cried out at the same time:

"Brave, trusty, and true! My comrade, my well-beloved! You cannot match him anywhere, you other men of the flat country."

But the fisherfolk laughed and made mock of Lamme.

XXVI

The great bell, the *Borgstorm*, rang out on the morrow to summon to the *Vierschare* the aldermen and the clerks of the court. There they sat on four banks of turf under the noble lime-tree which was called the Tree of Justice. And round about stood the common people. When he was examined the fishmonger would confess nothing. All he did was to repeat continually:

"I am poor and old, have mercy upon me."

But the people howled at him, saying:

"You are an old wolf, destroyer of children; have no pity, sir judges."

"Let him pay! Let him pay!" cried Toria.

But the fishmonger entreated again most piteously:

"I am poor. Leave me alone."

Then, since he would not say anything of his own free will, he was condemned to be tortured until he should confess how he had committed the murders, whence he came, and

254

where he had hidden the remains of the victims and their money.

So now he was brought to the torture chamber, and on his feet were put the iron shoes of torture, and the bailiff asked him how it was that Satan had inspired him with designs so black and crimes so abominable. Then at last he made answer:

" Satan is myself, my essential nature. Even as a child, ugly as I was and unskilled in all bodily exercises, I was regarded as a simpleton by every one and was continually being beaten. Neither girl nor boy had any pity for me, and as I grew up no woman would have anything to do with me, not even for payment. So I conceived a hatred for the whole human race, and for this reason I betrayed the man Claes who was beloved by all. Thereafter I was attracted more than ever by the idea of living like a wolf, and I dreamed of tearing flesh with my teeth. And I killed two wolves in the woods of Raveschoet and Maldeghem, and I sewed together their two skins as a covering. And by day and by night I wandered along the sand-dunes, and especially on Saturdays—the day of the market at Bruges."

Then the bailiff said:

" Repent and pray to God."

But the fishmonger blasphemed, saying:

" It is God himself who willed me to be as I am. I did all in spite of myself, led on by the will of nature. Evil tigers that you are, you will punish me unjustly."

But he was condemned to die the death, and Toria cried aloud: " Justice is done. He shall pay the penalty."

And all the people cried:

" *Lang leven de Heeren van de wet!*—Long live the Officers of the Law!"

The next morning at early dawn, as they were bringing him to the place of punishment, he saw Ulenspiegel standing near the pile and he pointed his finger at him, crying:

The Legend of Tyl Ulenspiegel

" There is a man who ought to die no less than I. For ten years ago it was that he threw me into the Damme canal because I had denounced his father. But in that I had acted as a loyal subject to His Most Catholic Majesty."

And the bells of Notre Dame tolled for the dead.

" For you also the bells are tolling," said he to Ulenspiegel. " You will be hanged. For you have committed murder."

" Is this true ? " demanded the bailiff.

Ulenspiegel answered :

" I threw into the water the man who denounced Claes and was the cause of his death. The ashes of my father beat upon my heart."

And the women that were in the crowd said to him :

" Why confess it, Ulenspiegel ? No one saw the deed. But now you also will die the death."

And the prisoner laughed aloud, leaping in the air with a bitter joy.

" He will die," he said. " He will leave this earth for hell. He will die. God is just."

" He shall not die," said the bailiff, " for after the lapse of ten years no murderer can lawfully be brought to punishment in the land of Flanders. Ulenspiegel did a wicked act, but it was done for love of his father : and for such a deed as that Ulenspiegel shall not be summoned to trial."

" Long live the law ! " cried the crowd. " *Lang leven de wet!* "

And the bells of Notre Dame tolled for the dead. And the prisoner ground his teeth and hung his head, and now for the first time he let fall a tear. And his hand was cut off and his tongue pierced with a red-hot iron, and he was burned alive in a slow fire in front of the Town Hall.

And Toria cried out :

" He is paying the penalty ! He is paying the penalty ! See how they writhe—those arms and those legs which helped him to his murdering ! See how it smokes, the body of this brute ! Burning is the hair of him, all pallid like the hair

256

of a hyena, and burning is his pallid face. He pays! He pays!"

And the fishmonger died, howling like a wolf.

And the bells of Notre Dame tolled for the dead.

And once more did Lamme and Ulenspiegel ride away on their donkeys. And Nele stayed behind in sorrow with Katheline, who never stopped her ceaseless refrain:

"Put out the fire! My head is burning! Come back, come back to me, Hanske, my pet."

XXVII

Ulenspiegel and Lamme had come to Heyst-on-the-Dunes, and behold a fleet of fishing-boats that were come hither from Ostend and from Blankenberghe and Knokke. Filled they were with men-at-arms, the followers of the Beggarmen of Zeeland, who carried on their hats a silver crescent with this inscription: "Serve rather the Turk than the Pope."

Ulenspiegel is glad; he whistles like the lark and from every side there comes to answer him the warlike cock-crow. And Lamme and Ulenspiegel go aboard one of the ships and are carried to Emden and thence to Wieringen, where their ship is hemmed in by the ice. For by now it is the month of February.

Now all around the ship there was to be seen the most joyous sight imaginable: men all clad in velvet, sledging and skating on the ice; and women skating too, with skirts and jackets broidered with pearl and gold, blue and scarlet. And the boys and girls came and went hither and thither, laughing and following one another in line, or two by two in couples, singing the song of love upon the ice, and running to eat and drink at the stalls decorated with flags, where one could buy all kinds of brandy-wine and oranges and figs and eggs and hot vegetables with *heete-koeken*—pancakes, that is, with vegetables flavoured with vinegar. And all around them the sailing sledges made the ice to resound under the press of their sharp runners.

Lamme, who was still searching everywhere for his wife, wandered about on his skates like the rest of that happy crowd, but he kept falling down time and again.

Ulenspiegel, meanwhile, to satisfy his hunger and thirst, was wont to resort to a little tavern on the quay where the prices were not high, and where he used to have many a talk with the old lady who kept it.

One Sunday about nine o'clock he went to the inn and asked them to give him some dinner. A charming-looking young woman came forward to serve him.

"Dear me," he cried, "you rejuvenated hostess! Wherever are those old wrinkles of yours gone to? And your mouth has found all its teeth again, and they are white with the whiteness of youth itself! And your lips are red like cherries! Is it for me this smile of yours so sweet and roguish?"

"Nay, nay," she said. "But what can I get you?"

"Yourself," he said.

The woman answered:

"That would be too big a meal for a lean little man like you. Will not some other kind of meat do for you?"

When Ulenspiegel made no answer:

"What have you done," she said, "with that handsome, well-set-up, but rather corpulent gentleman I have so often seen in your company?"

"Do you mean Lamme?" queried Ulenspiegel.

"Yes. What have you done with him?" she repeated.

"He is busy eating," answered Ulenspiegel, "eating anything he can set his teeth upon—hard-boiled eggs from the street stalls, smoked eels and salted fish: and all this, forsooth, to help him find his wife. But why are you not she, my sweet? Would you like fifty florins? Would you like a collar of gold?"

258

But she crossed herself, saying :

" I am not to be bought, nor yet taken."

" Do you love no one ? " said Ulenspiegel.

" I love you as my neighbour ; but above all I love Our
Lord and Our Lady, they that command me to live an honest
life. Hard indeed and oftentimes burdensome are the duties
that are laid on us poor women. Nevertheless God gives us
his aid. Yet some there are who succumb to temptation.
But this fat friend of yours, come, tell me, is he well and
happy ? "

Ulenspiegel answered :

" He is gay when he is eating, but sad and pensive when
he is empty. I will get him to come and see you."

" Do not do that," she said; " he would weep and so
should I."

" Have you ever seen his wife ? " asked Ulenspiegel.

" She sinned with him once," the woman answered, " and
was condemned therefor to a cruel punishment. She knows
that he goes a-seafaring in the cause of the heretics, and this
is a cruel thought for a Christian heart. But protect him,
I pray you, if he is attacked, and nurse him if he is wounded :
his wife ordered me thus to entreat you."

" Lamme is my brother and my friend," answered
Ulenspiegel.

" Ah ! " she said. " But why will you not return to the
bosom of our Holy Mother Church ? "

" She eats up her children," answered Ulenspiegel. And
he departed.

But one morning in March, while still the cold winds of
winter kept the ice frozen, so that the ship of the Beggarmen
could not make away, Ulenspiegel came again to the tavern.
And the pretty *baesine* said to him (and there was great
emotion and sorrow in her voice) :

" Poor Lamme ! Poor Ulenspiegel ! "

" Why do you pity us so ? " he asked her.

" Alas ! alas ! " she cried. " Why will you not believe in the Mass ?   And you did, you would go straight to Paradise without a doubt, and I might be able to save you in this life also."

Seeing her go to the door and listen there attentively, Ulenspiegel said to her :

" Is it the snow that you hear falling ? "

" No," she said.

" What then ? "

" It is death that comes like a thief in the night."

" Death," exclaimed Ulenspiegel.   " I do not understand you.   Come back and tell me."

" *They are there*," she said.

" Who are ? "

" Who ? " she said.   " Why, the soldiers of Simonen Bol, who are about to come in the name of the Duke and throw themselves upon you all.   And if they treat you well while you are here, it is only as men treat the oxen they mean to kill.   Oh why," she cried all in tears, " why did I not know all this before, so that I could have warned you ! "

" You must not cry," said Ulenspiegel, " and you must stay where you are ! "

" Do not betray me," she said.

Ulenspiegel went out of the house, ran as fast as he could, and went round to all the booths and taverns in the place, whispering to the sailors and soldiers these words : " The Spaniards are coming."

At that they ran every one to the ship, and prepared with all the haste they knew whatever things were necessary for battle.   Then they waited for the evening.   While they were waiting thus, Ulenspiegel said to Lamme :

" Do you see that pretty-looking woman on the quay there, in a black dress embroidered with scarlet ? "

" It's all one to me," answered Lamme.   " I am cold and I want to go to sleep."

And he threw his great cloak around his head, and became like a man who was deaf.

But presently Ulenspiegel recognized the woman and cried out to her from the vessel :

" Would you like to come with us ? "

" Even to the death," she answered, " but I cannot . . ."

Then she came nearer to the ship.

" Take this ointment," she said. " It is for you and that fat friend of yours who goes to sleep when he ought to be awake."

And she withdrew herself, crying :

" Lamme ! Lamme ! May God keep you from harm and bring you back safe."

And she uncovered her face.

" My wife ! My wife ! " cried Lamme.

And he would have jumped down to her.

" Your faithful wife ! " she said, running the while as fast as ever she could.

Lamme would have leaped down from the deck on to the ice, but he was restrained by a soldier who caught him by his cloak, and the provost addressed him, saying :

" You will be hanged if you leave the ship."

Yet again did Lamme try to throw himself down, but an old Beggarman held him back, telling him that the ice was damp and that he would get his feet wet. And Lamme sat down on the deck weeping and crying ever :

" My wife ! My wife ! Let me go and find my wife ! "

" You will see her again," said Ulenspiegel. " She loves you, but she loves God more."

" Mad devil-woman that she is ! " cried Lamme. " If she loves God more than her husband, why does she show herself to me so sweet and so desirable ? And if she loves me, why does she leave me ? "

" Can you see clearly to the bottom of a deep well ? " demanded Ulenspiegel.

In the meanwhile the followers of Simonen Bol had appeared on the scene with a large force of artillery. They shot at the ship, which promptly repaid them in similar coin. And the bullets broke up the ice all around. And towards evening a warm rain began to fall, and the west wind blew from the Atlantic, and the sea grew angry beneath its covering of ice, and the ice was broken into huge blocks which could be seen rising and falling to hurl themselves one against the other, not without danger to the ship, which, nevertheless, as dawn began to dissipate the clouds of night, opened its sails like a bird of freedom and sailed out towards the open sea.

There they were joined by the fleet of Messire de Lumey de la Marche, Admiral of Holland and Zeeland ; and on that day the ship of Messire Très-Long captured a vessel from Biscay that carried a cargo of mercury, gunpowder, wine, and spices. And the vessel was cleaned to its marrow, emptied of its men and its booty, even as the bone of an ox is cleaned by the teeth of a lion. And the Beggarmen took La Brièle, a strong naval base, well called the Garden of Liberty.

XXVIII

It was at the beginning of May. The sky was clear, the ship sailed proudly on the billows, and Ulenspiegel sang this song :

The ashes beat on my heart,
The murderers are come ;
With daggers have they struck at us,
Fiercely, with fire and sword have they struck at us,
They have bribed us most vilely and spied on us,
Where are love and fidelity now ?
In exchange for those sweetest of virtues,
Betrayal and fraud have they heaped on us.
Yet may they that have murdered be murdered themselves !
Beat, beat, drum of war !

"THE ASHES OF CLAES
BEAT UPON MY HEART"

The Song of Ulenspiegel

Long live the Beggarmen!   Loud beat the drum!
La Brièle has fallen,
Flushing too, the key to the Scheldt!
God is good, for Camp-veere is taken,
Taken the place where the guns of all Zeeland were stored!
Now cannon-balls, powder, and bullets are ours,
Bullets of iron, bullets of brass.
God is with us—against us, then, who?

The drum!   Beat the drum of glory and war!
Long live the Beggarmen!   Beat the drum!

And again Ulenspiegel lifted up his voice and sang:

O Duke!   Hark to the voice of the People,
Murmuring so strong in the distance,
Like the sea that swells in the season of tempest!
Enough of silver and gold and of blood,
Of ruins enough!   Beat the drum!   Beat the drum!
The sword is drawn.

Duke!   Duke of Alba, Duke of Blood,
Behold the stalls and the shops, they are closed.
Brewers and bakers, grocers and butchers,
Refuse one and all to do business for nothing.
When you pass who'll salute you?
None.   Do you feel, then, the pestilent mist
Of hate and scorn closing around you?

For the fair land of Flanders,
The gay land of Brabant,
Now are sad as a churchyard.
And where once in the days of our liberty
Sounded the violas, screamed the fifes and the bagpipes,
Now there is silence and death.
Beat the drum, the drum of war.

263

And now, 'stead of all the glad faces
Of those that drank and made love to the sound of sweet singing,
Now is naught but pale faces
Of they that await in dumb resignation
The blade of the sword of injustice.
Beat the drum, the drum of war.

O land of our fathers, suffering, belovèd,
Bow not your head 'neath the foot of the murderer!
And you, busy bees, fling yourselves now
In swarms 'gainst the hornets of Spain.
And you bodies of women and girls
That are buried alive
Cry to Christ: Vengeance!

Wander by night in the fields, poor souls,
Cry to God!
Every arm now trembles to strike.
The sword is drawn.
Duke, we will tear out your entrails,
Yea, we will whip you in the face!
Beat the drum. The sword is drawn.
Beat the drum. Long live the Beggarmen!

And all the sailors and soldiers on the ship of Ulenspiegel, and they also that were on the ships near by, took up the refrain and sang out also:

The sword is drawn. Long live the Beggarmen!

And the sound of their voices was like the growl of the thunder of deliverance.

XXIX

It was the month of January, the cruel month that freezes the calf in the womb of the cow. Snow had fallen

over all the land, and then frozen hard. The boys went out
to snare with bird-lime the sparrows that came to seek what
nourishment they could find on the hardened snow; and
whatever they took they brought back to their cottages.
Against the grey, bright sky the skeletons of the trees de-
tached themselves in motionless outline, and their branches
were covered as it were with cushions of snow, and the roofs
of the cottages likewise, and the tops of the walls where
showed the footprints of the cats who themselves went out
hunting for sparrows in the snow. Far and wide the fields
were hidden under that wonderful white fleece which warms
the earth against the bitter cold of winter. The smoke of
houses and cottages showed black as it mounted heavenwards,
and over everything there brooded a great stillness.

And Katheline and Nele lived alone in their cottage, and
Katheline wagged her head, crying continually:

" Hans, my heart is yours. But you must give back those
seven hundred caroluses. Put out the fire! My head is burning! Alas! Where are your kisses cold as snow?" And she
stood watching at the window.

Suddenly a horseman rode past at the gallop, crying:
" Here comes the bailiff, the high bailiff of Damme!"

And he went on to the Town Hall, crying out all the time,
so as to gather together the burghers and the aldermen.
And thereafter in the silence that ensued Nele could hear
two blasts of a trumpet, and straightway all the people of
Damme came running to their doors thinking that it must
be no less a personage than His Royal Majesty himself whose
arrival was announced by such a fanfare. And Katheline
also went to her door with Nele, and in the distance she could
see a troop of splendid horsemen riding all together, and at
their head a magnificent figure in a cloak of black velvet
edged with sable. And she knew him at once for the high
bailiff of Damme.

Now behind him there rode a company of youthful Lords

clad in long cloaks, and they rode along gaily, and their coats were adorned with buttons and trimmings of gold, and their hats with long ostrich plumes waving gaily in the wind. And they seemed one and all to be good comrades and friends of the high bailiff; and conspicuous among them was a thin-faced gentleman dressed in green velvet and gold trimmings, and like the others his cloak was of black velvet and his hat also was adorned with black plumes. And his nose was like a vulture's beak, his mouth compressed and thin, and his beard was red and his face pale, and very proud was his bearing.

While the company of gentlemen was passing before the cottage, Katheline suddenly ran forward and leapt at the bridle of the pale horseman, and cried out, mad with joy as it seemed:

"Hans! My beloved, I knew you would come back! Oh, you are beautiful like this, all clad in velvet and gold, shining like a sun against the snow! Have you brought me those seven hundred caroluses? Shall I hear you again crying like the sea-eagle?"

The high bailiff brought the cavalcade to a stand, and the pale gentleman said:

"What does this beggar-woman want with me?"

But Katheline, still holding the horse by the bridle, made answer: 'You must be dreaming, Hans. Wake up from your dream! I have cried for you so long. O nights of love, my beloved! O kisses of snow, O body of ice! See, this is your child!"

And she pointed to Nele, who was gazing at the man with terror, for now he had raised his whip as though he were about to strike at Katheline. But Katheline still continued her entreaties, weeping all the time:

"Ah! Do you not remember? Have pity on your servant! Take her with you whithersoever you will! Put out the fire! Hans, have pity!"

"Get out of the way!" he said. And he urged on his

266

steed so quickly that Katheline was forced to loose hold of the bridle, and she fell on to the road, and the horse went over her, leaving a bleeding wound upon her forehead. Then the bailiff inquired of the pale horseman as to whether he knew aught of the woman.

" I know her not," was the answer. " She is out of her wits, doubtless."

But by this time Nele had helped up Katheline from the ground. " If this woman is mad," she said, " at least, my Lord, I am not. And I am ready to die here and now of this snow that I am eating "—and here Nele took and ate of the snow with her fingers—" if this horseman has not had knowledge of my mother, and if he has not forced her to lend him money, nay, all the money that she had, and if it was not he that killed the dog which belonged to Claes, so that he might take from the wall of the well those seven hundred caroluses which belonged to the poor man that is dead."

" Hans, my pet," sobbed Katheline, " give me the kiss of peace. Time was when you killed your friend because you were jealous, by the dike. . . . You loved me well in those days."

" Who is that man she speaks of ? " demanded the bailiff.

" I know not," said the pale horseman. " The talk of this beggar-woman is no concern of ours. Let us move on."

But by now a crowd of people had collected, workpeople of the town, and they all began to take Katheline's part, crying : " Justice ! Justice, my Lord Bailiff ! Justice ! "

And the bailiff said to Nele : " Who is the one that was killed ? Speak the truth in God's name."

Then Nele said her say, pointing the while at the pale horseman :

" This is the man who came every Saturday to the *keet* to visit my mother, and to take her money from her. He killed one of his own friends, Hilbert by name, in the field of Servaes Van der Vichte ; and this he did not from any love of Katheline, as she in her innocent folly believes, but rather

267

that he might get hold of her seven hundred caroluses and keep them all for himself."

" You lie," said the pale horseman.

" Oh no ! " said Nele. " For it is you that caused the death of Soetkin ; you that reduced her orphan son to misery ; you—nobleman that you are—who came to us, common people, and the first time you came you brought money to my mother, so that ever afterwards you might take her money from her ! And you it is that introduced into our house that friend of yours to whom you would have given me in marriage ; but, as you know, I would have none of him. What did he do, your friend Hilbert, that time I tore his eyes with my finger-nails ? "

" Nele is naughty," said Katheline. " You must not pay any attention to her, Hans, my pet. She is angry because Hilbert tried to take her by force ; but Hilbert cannot do so any more. The worms have eaten him. And Hilbert was ugly, Hans, my pet. It is you alone that are beautiful, and Nele, she is naughty."

Now the bailiff ordered the women to go about their business, but Katheline would not budge from where she stood. They were obliged, therefore, to take her into the cottage by force. And all the people that were there assembled began to cry out :

" Justice, my Lord ! Justice ! "

At this moment the sergeants of the commune came upon the scene, attracted by the noise, and the bailiff, bidding them wait, addressed himself to the Lords and nobles in the following manner :

" My Lords and Gentlemen,—Notwithstanding all those privileges which protect the illustrious order of the nobility of Flanders, I find myself constrained to arrest Joos Damman on account of the accusations which have been brought against him. And I therefore order him to be confined to prison until such time as he can be brought to trial according

NELE ACCUSES HANS

to the laws and ordinances of the Empire. Hand me, then, your sword, Sir Joos!"

At this command Joos Damman was seen to hesitate, but all the people cried out as with one voice:

"Justice, my Lord! Justice! Let him deliver up his sword!"

And he was obliged to do so in spite of himself; and when he had dismounted from his horse he was conducted by the sergeants to the prison of the commune.

Nevertheless he was not confined in one of the dungeons, but was placed in a room with barred windows, where, for a payment of money, he was made not too uncomfortable. For he was provided with a fire, a good bed, and some good food, half of which, however, went to the gaoler.

XXX

On the morrow there came a soft wind blowing from Brabant. The snow began to melt and the meadows were all flooded.

And the bell that is called *Borgstorm* summoned the judges to the tribunal of the *Vierschare*. And they sat under the penthouse, because the grassy banks where they were accustomed to sit were too damp. And round about the tribunal stood the people of the town.

Joos Damman was brought before the judges. He was not in bonds, and he still wore the dress of a nobleman. Katheline was also brought there, but her hands were tied in front of her, and she wore a grey dress, the dress of a prisoner.

On being examined, Joos Damman pleaded guilty to the charge of having killed his friend Hilbert with a sword in single combat; and this he confessed willingly because, as he said, he was protected by the law of Flanders, which made a murderer safe from conviction after the space of ten years.

269

Then the bailiff asked him if he was a sorcerer.

" No," replied Damman.

" Prove it," said the bailiff.

" That I will do at the right time and in the proper place," said Joos Damman, " but not now."

Then the bailiff began to question Katheline. She, however, paid no attention to his questions, but kept her eyes fixed on Hans, saying :

" You are my green master. Beautiful you are as the Sun himself. Put out the fire, my pet ! "

Then Nele spoke on Katheline's behalf.

" She can tell you naught, my Lord, that you do not know already. She is not a sorceress. She is only out of her mind."

Then the bailiff said his say :

" A sorcerer, I would remind you, is one who knowingly employs a devilish art, or devilish arts, for the attainment of a certain object. Well, these two persons, the man and the woman, I find to be sorcerers both in intention and in fact ; the man because, as the evidence states, he gave to this woman the balm of the Witches' Sabbath, and made his visage like unto Lucifer so as to obtain money from her and the satisfaction of his wanton desires. And the woman also I find to be a sorceress because she submitted herself to the man, taking him for a devil and abandoning herself to his will. I ask, therefore, if the gentlemen of the tribunal are agreed that it is a case where the prisoners should both be sent to the torture ? "

The aldermen did not answer, but showed clearly enough that such was not their desire, so far at any rate as Katheline was concerned.

Then the bailiff spake again :

" Like you I am moved with pity and compassion for the woman, but mad as she undoubtedly is and obedient in all things to the devil, is it not probable that at the behest of her leman she might have committed the most horrible crimes and abominations, as do all those who resign themselves to the devil's will ? No. Since Joos Damman has refused to acknowledge any crime save that of murder, and since Katheline has not told us anything at all, it is clear that by the laws of the Empire we are bound to proceed in the manner I have indicated."

And the aldermen gave sentence to the effect that the two prisoners were to be committed to torture on the following Friday, which was the day but one following.

And Nele cried out for mercy upon Katheline, and the people joined with her in supplication, but all in vain. And the prisoners were taken back into the gaol.

There, by order of the tribunal, the keeper of the gaol was ordered to provide a couple of guards for each prisoner, and these guards were commanded to beat them whenever they looked like going off to sleep. Now the two guards that were allotted to Katheline suffered her to sleep during the night ; but they that were assigned to Joos Damman beat him unmercifully every time that he closed his eyes or even hung his head down. And neither of the prisoners was given anything to eat through all that Wednesday, and through all the night and day which followed. But on the Thursday evening they were given food and drink—meat, that is to say, which had been soaked in salt and saltpetre, and water which had been salted in a similar fashion. And this was the beginning of their torture. And in the morning, crying out with thirst, they were led by the sergeants into the chamber of doom.

There they were set opposite to one another, bound as they were, each to a separate bench which itself was covered with knotted cords that hurt them grievously. And they were both made to drink a glass of water saturated with salt and saltpetre.

Joos Damman began to fall off to sleep where he was,

but the sergeants soon beat him awake again. And Katheline said :

"Do not beat him, kind sirs. He has committed but a single crime, when he killed Hilbert—and that was done for love's sake. Oh, but I am thirsty! And you also are thirsty, Hans, my beloved! Pray give him something to drink first of all. Water! Water! My body is burning me up. But spare him. I will die for him. Water!"

Joos said to her :

"Ugly old witch that you are, go and die for all I care! Throw her into the fire, my Lords! Oh, but I am thirsty!"

Meanwhile the clerks of the court were busy writing down every word that was being said. And the bailiff asked him :

"Have you nothing to confess ? "

"I have nothing more to say," replied Damman. "You know all that there is to know."

"Forasmuch as he persists in his denials," said the bailiff, "let him remain where he is until he shall have made a complete avowal of his crimes. Let him neither eat nor drink nor go to sleep."

"So be it," said Joos Damman. "And I will amuse myself by watching the sufferings of this old witch here."

And Katheline answered him, saying :

"Cold arms, warm heart, Hans, my beloved! I am thirsty, my head is burning!"

The clerk of the court wrote down what she said, and the bailiff asked her :

"Woman, have you nothing to say in your own defence ?"

But Katheline only gazed at Joos Damman, and said very amorously :

"It is the hour of the sea-eagle, Hans, my pet. They say that you will give me back the seven hundred caroluses. Put out the fire! Put out the fire!" Then she began to cry out most horribly: "Water! Water! My head is burning! God and His angels are eating apples in heaven!"

272

And she lost consciousness.

Thereupon the bailiff ordered her to be released from the bench of torture ; which was done, and thereafter she was seen to stagger to and fro because of her feet, which were all swollen from the cords that had been bound too tight.

" Give her to drink," said the bailiff.

And they gave her some fresh water which she swallowed greedily, holding the goblet between her teeth as a dog holds a bone and refusing to let it go. Then they gave her more water, and this she would have carried over to Joos Damman had not the torturer wrested the goblet from her hand. And she fell down asleep, like a piece of lead.

But Joos Damman cried out in his fury :

" I also am thirsty and sleepy. Why do you give her to drink ? Why do you let her fall asleep ? "

" She is a woman," answered the bailiff. " And she is weak and out of her mind."

" Her madness is only pretence," said Joos Damman. " She is a witch. I want to drink, and I want to sleep."

And he closed his eyes, but his tormentors struck him in the face.

" Give me a knife," he cried, " that I may cut these varlets in pieces. I am a nobleman ; no one has ever struck me in the face before ! Water ! Let me sleep. I am innocent. It is not I that took the seven hundred caroluses, it was Hilbert. Water ! I have never committed any sorceries nor any incantations. I am innocent. Leave me alone and give me something to drink."

But the bailiff only asked him how he had passed the time after he left Katheline.

" I do not know Katheline at all," he said, " therefore I never left her. You have asked me an unfair question, and I am not bound to answer it. Give me something to drink. Let me go to sleep. I tell you it was Hilbert who was responsible for everything."

273

"Take him away," said the bailiff, "put him back into his prison. But see that he has nothing to drink, and that he does not fall asleep until he has admitted his sorceries and incantations."

And now Damman suffered the most cruel torture of all, and he cried out continually in his prison : "Water! Water!" And so loudly did he cry that the people outside could hear him, nevertheless they felt no pity for him. And when he began to fall off to sleep the guards struck him in the face, and he cried out again, like a tiger :

"I am a nobleman, and I will kill you, you varlets! I will go to the King our master. Water!"

But he would confess nothing at all, and they left him where he was.

XXXI

It was the month of May. The Tree of Justice was green again. Green also were those grassy banks where the judges were wont to seat themselves. Nele was summoned to give evidence, for it was the day on which the judgment was to be promulgated. And the people—men and women—of Damme, stood around the open space of the court, and the sun shone brightly.

Katheline and Joos Damman were now brought before the tribunal, and Damman appeared more pale than ever because of the torture he had suffered, the many nights he had passed without sleep or anything to drink. As for Katheline, she could scarcely support herself on her tottering legs, and she pointed to the sun continually, and cried out : "Put out the fire! My head is burning!" And she gazed at Joos Damman with tender love. And he looked back at her with hate and despite. And his friends, the Lords and gentlemen who had been summoned to Damme, were all present there before the tribunal as witnesses.

Then the bailiff spoke as follows :

"The girl Nele here, who is protecting her mother Kathe-

line with such great and brave affection, has found sewn into
the pocket of Katheline's Sunday dress a letter signed by
Joos Damman. And I myself, when I was inspecting the
dead body of Hilbert Ryvish, which was dug up in the field
near Katheline's cottage, found thereon a second letter,
addressed to him and signed by the said Joos Damman, the
accused now present before you. Is it your pleasure that
these letters be now read to you?"

"Read them, read them!" cried the crowd. "Nele is
a brave girl! Read the letters! Katheline is no witch!"

And the clerk of the court read out as follows:

"To Hilbert, son of William Ryvish, knight, Joos Dan.
man, knight, Greeting.

"Most excellent friend, let me advise you to lose no
more of your money in gambling, dicing, and other foolishness
of that kind. I will tell you a way of making money safe
and sound. My plan is that we should disguise ourselves as
devils, such as are beloved by women and girls, and then
choose out for ourselves all the pretty ones, leaving alone all
such as are ugly or poor; for we will make them pay for
their pleasure. Do you know that when I was in Germany
I acquired by this means as much as five thousand *rix-
daelders*, and all within the space of six months? For a
woman will give her last denier to the man she loves. When,
therefore, such an one is willing to receive you in the night,
the thing is to announce your coming by crying like a night-
bird, so it may seem that you are really and truly a devil;
and if you want to make your countenance appear devilish
you must rub it all over with phosphorus, for phosphorus
burns when it is damp, and the smell of it is horrible; and
the women mistake it for the odour of hell itself. And if anything gets in your way, be it man, woman, or beast, kill it.

"Before long we will go together to one Katheline, a
handsome woman I know. And she has a daughter—a child

275

of mine forsooth, if indeed Katheline has proved faithful to me. And she is a right comely lass, and I give her to you, for these bastards are nothing to me. And you must know that I have already had from the mother a sum of three and twenty caroluses. This money all belonged to her. But somewhere, unless I am a dunce, she keeps secreted the fortune of Claes, that heretic, you remember, who was burned alive at Damme—seven hundred caroluses in all, and liable to confiscation. But the good King Philip, who has burned so many of his subjects for the sake of their inheritance, cannot lay his claw upon this, and assuredly it will weigh heavier in my purse than ever it would in his. Katheline will tell me where it is hidden, and we will share it between us. Fortune favours the young, as His Sacred Majesty Charles V was never tired of saying, and he was a past master in all the arts of love and war."

Here the clerk of the court stopped reading and said :
" Such is the letter, and it is signed Joos Damman."
And the people cried out :
" To the death with the murderer ! To the death with the sorcerer ! "
But the bailiff ordered them to keep silence so that judgment might be passed on the prisoners with every form of freedom and legality. After that he addressed himself again to the aldermen.
" Now I will read to you the second letter, which is the letter Nele found sewn into the pocket of Katheline's Sunday gown. These are the terms of it :

" Sweet witch, here is the recipe of a mixture which was sent to me by the wife of Lucifer himself. By the aid of this mixture it is possible to be transported to the sun, the moon, and the stars, and you can hold converse with the elemental spirits who carry the prayers of men to God, and can traverse

the cities, towns, rivers, and fields of all the world. Mix
equal parts of the following : stramonium, solanum, somni-
ferum, henbane, opium, fresh ends of hemp, belladonna, and
thorn-apple. Then drink. If it is your wish we will go this
very night to the Sabbath of the Spirits. But you must
love me more, and not be cold to me like you were the other
night, refusing to give me even ten florins, and denying that
you had got them ! For I know very well you have a
treasure in your hiding but will not tell me where. Do you
not love me any more, my sweetheart ?—Your cold devil,

"HANSKE."

"To death with the sorcerer ! " cried the crowd.
The bailiff said :
"Let the two handwritings be compared."
When this had been done, and when it had been found
that they were in all respects similar, the bailiff said :
"After these proofs, Messire Joos Damman is found to be
a sorcérer, a murderer, a seducer of women, a robber of the
property of the King, and as such he must be accounted
guilty of high treason against God and man."
And the bailiff and the aldermen gave judgment on Joos
Damman, and he was condemned to be degraded from the
rank of a nobleman, and to be burned alive in the slower
fire till death supervened. And he underwent this punishment on the following day in front of the Town Hall. And
all the time he kept on crying : "Let the witch perish, it is
she and she alone who is guilty ! Cursed be God ! My
father will avenge me ! "
And the people said : "Behold how he curses and blas-
phemes. He is dying the death of a dog."
On the next day, the bailiff and the aldermen gave
sentence upon Katheline. She was condemned to undergo
the trial by water in the Bruges Canal. If she floated she
would be burned for a witch. If she sank and was drowned

she would be considered to have died the death of a Christian and would be buried in the churchyard.

So on the morrow Katheline was conducted to the canal-bank, holding a candle in her hand and walking barefoot in a shift of black linen. Along by the trees went the long procession. In front was the Dean of Notre Dame, chanting the prayers for the dead, and with him were his vicars, and the beadle carrying the cross. Behind came the bailiff of Damme, the aldermen, the clerks, the sergeants of the commune, the provost, the executioner and his two assistants. On the edge of the procession there followed a great crowd of women crying, and men mourning, in pity for Katheline, who herself walked like a lamb that allows itself to be led whither it knows not. And all the time she kept on crying:

" Put out the fire ! My head is burning ! Hans, where are you ? "

In the midst of the women was Nele, who kept crying also :

" Let them throw me in with her ! "

But the women did not suffer her to come near to Katheline.

A sharp wind came blowing in from the sea, and from the grey sky a fine hail fell dripping into the water of the canal. Now there was a boat moored by the side of the water, and this boat the executioner and his assistants commandeered in the name of His Royal Majesty. Then Katheline was ordered to step down into the boat. She obeyed at once, and the executioner was seen standing by her side and holding her securely. Then the provost raised the rod of justice, and the executioner threw Katheline into the canal. For a while she struggled, but soon sank, with one last cry: " Hans ! Hans ! Help ! "

And the people said : " This woman was no witch."

Thereafter certain men who were there jumped into the canal and dragged Katheline out again, senseless and rigid as one dead. And she was taken into a tavern near by, and

278

KATHELINE LED TO THE
TRIAL BY WATER

placed in front of a bright fire. Nele took off her garments wringing wet as they were, meaning to put dry ones on her. After a while she regained consciousness, and cried out, all trembling and with her teeth chattering: "Hans! Give me a cloak of wool!"

But Katheline could not be warmed. And on the third day she died. And she was buried in the garden of the church.

And Nele, the orphan, went away into Holland, and dwelt at the house of Rosa van Auweghem.

XXXII

In those days it was that the Beggarmen, among whom were Lamme and Ulenspiegel, took the city of Gorcum by storm. And they were led in this enterprise by one Captain Marin. This Marin had once been a workman on the dikes, but now he bore himself with great haughtiness and effrontery, and he signed an agreement with Gaspard Turc, the defender of Gorcum, by which it was agreed that the city should capitulate on condition that Turc himself, together with the monks, citizens, and soldiers who had been shut up in the citadel, should be allowed to pass out freely, their muskets on their shoulders and with anything that they could carry with them—save only what belonged to the churches, which was to remain in the hands of the victors. But in spite of this agreement, Captain Marin, acting under an order from Messire de Lumey, detained nineteen monks as his prisoners, while the rest of the citizens were allowed to go free as had been promised.

And Ulenspiegel said:

"Word of a soldier, word of gold. Why has the captain been false to his promise?"

An old Beggarman answered Ulenspiegel:

"The monks are the sons of Satan, the canker of our nation, the shame of our country. Dogs are chained up—

let the monks be also chained, for they are the bloodhounds of the Duke. Long live the Beggarmen!"

"But," answered Ulenspiegel, "we must remember that my Lord of Orange, the Prince of Liberty, has ordered us to respect the property and the free conscience of all such as give themselves up into our power."

Some of the older Beggarmen replied that the admiral could not do so in the case of the monks. "And he is master here," they added. "It was he that took La Brièle. To prison with the monks!"

"A soldier's word is a word of gold," said Ulenspiegel. "*Parole de soldat, parole d'or.* Why should we ever break our word?"

"No longer do the ashes beat upon your heart," they told him. "Hear you not the souls of the dead that cry for vengeance?"

"The ashes beat upon my heart," said Ulenspiegel. "*Parole de soldat, c'est parole d'or.*"

The next day a message arrived from Messire de Lumey to the effect that the nineteen monks were to be brought as prisoners from Gorcum to La Brièle where the admiral was then stationed.

"They will be hanged," said Captain Marin to Ulenspiegel.

"Not as long as I am alive," said Ulenspiegel.

"My son," said Lamme, "you must not speak in this way to Messire de Lumey. He is a stern man, and will have you hanged as well as the monks if you are not careful."

"I shall tell him the truth," answered Ulenspiegel. "*Parole de soldat, c'est parole d'or.*"

"If you think that you can save them," said Marin, "I will give you permission to go with them by ship to La Brièle. Take Rochus with you as pilot, and your friend Lamme if you please as well."

"I will," said Ulenspiegel.

280

By Ship to La Brièle

The ship was moored by the quay side, and the nineteen
monks were taken aboard. Rochus took charge of the helm,
while Ulenspiegel and Lamme placed themselves at the bow.
Certain vagabond soldiers who had joined the Beggarmen for
the sake of plunder were stationed by the monks, who now
began to wax hungry. Ulenspiegel gave them food and drink.
Then the sailors began to murmur one to another, saying:
"This man is a traitor." Meanwhile the nineteen monks were
seated sanctimoniously in the midst, and they were shivering
although the month was July and the sun was shining hot
and clear, and a gentle breeze filled the sails of the ship as it
glided, heavy and full-bellied, over the green waves.

Father Nicholas then began to speak, addressing himself
to the pilot:

"O Rochus," he said, "are they taking us to the gallows-
field?" Then, turning his face towards Gorcum: "O city of
Gorcum," he cried, stretching out his hands, "O city of
Gorcum, how many evils hast thou still to suffer! Verily
thou shalt be cursed among all the cities of the earth, for thou
hast nurtured within thy walls the seed of heresy! O city of
Gorcum! For now no longer shall the angel of the Lord
stand watch above thy gates, no longer shall he have any care
for the modesty of thy virgins, or the courage of thy men,
or for the fortunes of thy merchants! O city of Gorcum,
accursed thou art and doomed to misfortune!"

"Cursed and accursed indeed!" answered Ulenspiegel.
"As accursed as is the comb that has combed away the lice
of Spain, or accursed as the dog that has broken the chain
that held him captive, or as the proud charger that has
thrown from his back the cruel cavalier! Be cursed yourself,
silly preacher that you are, who think it an evil thing to
break the rod upon the back of a tyrant, even if it be a rod
of iron!"

The monk was silenced, and dropping his eyes he seemed
lost in a dream of hate and bigotry.

281

The next morning they arrived at La Brièle, and a messenger was sent to advise Messire de Lumey of their coming.

As soon as he had received the news he set out to go to them on horseback, half dressed as he was, and with him went a company of armed men, some on foot and some on horseback. And now once again was it given to Ulenspiegel to behold this fierce admiral dressed as he was like some noble, proud and opulent.

"Welcome," said he, "Sir Monks. And now hold up your hands and show me there the blood of my Lords of Egmont and Hoorn ! "

One of the monks, whose name was Leonard, made answer :

"Do what you like with us. We are monks. No one will make any objection."

"He has well spoken," said Ulenspiegel. "For having broken with the world—that is with father, mother, brother and sister, wife and sweetheart—a monk finds no one at the hour of God to claim anything on his behalf. Nevertheless, your Excellency, I will do so. For Captain Marin, when he signed the treaty for the capitulation of Gorcum, stipulated that these monks should be free like all the others that were taken in the citadel and were allowed to go out from it. But in spite of this, and for no adequate reason, these monks were kept prisoner, and now it is reported that they are to be hanged. My Lord, I address myself to you right humbly on their behalf, for I know that the word of a soldier is a word of gold—*parole de soldat, c'est parole d'or.*"

"And who are you ? " asked Messire de Lumey.

"My Lord," replied Ulenspiegel, "a Fleming I am from the lovely land of Flanders, working man, nobleman, all in one—and I go wandering through the world, praising things beautiful and good but boldly making fun of foolishness. And verily I will sing your praises if you will keep the

promise which was made to these men by the captain :
parole de soldat, c'est parole d'or."

But the good-for-nothing Beggarmen who were on the
ship cried out at this.

" My Lord," said they, " this man is a traitor. He has
promised them that he will save them, and he has been
loading them with bread and ham and sausages. But to us
he has given nothing at all."

Then Messire de Lumey said to Ulenspiegel :

" Wandering Fleming that you are, and protector of
monks, I tell you I will have you hanged with them."

" I am not afraid," replied Ulenspiegel. " *Parole de soldat,
c'est parole d'or.*"

The monks were led away to a barn, and Ulenspiegel with
them. There they tried to convert him with many theological arguments ; but these soon sent him to sleep.

In the meanwhile Messire de Lumey was feasting at a table
covered with meats and wines when a messenger arrived from
Gorcum from Captain Marin, bringing with him copies of
those letters of William the Silent, Prince of Orange, which
ordered " all governors of cities and other places to confer
the same privileges of safety and surety on ecclesiastics as
on the rest of the people."

The messenger asked to be brought into the presence of
de Lumey so that he might put into his own hands the copies
of these letters.

" Where are the originals ? " inquired de Lumey.

" My master has them," said the messenger.

" And the churl sends me the copy ! " said de Lumey.
" Where is your passport ? "

" Here, my Lord," said the messenger.

Then Messire de Lumey began to read it aloud :

" My Lord and Master Marin Brandt commands all
ministers, governors, and officers of the Republic that they
should allow to pass . . ." etc.

De Lumey struck the table with his fist, and tore the passport in two.

"*Sang de Dieu!*" he cried. "What is he doing meddling here, this Marin? This trumpery fellow who before the taking of La Brièle had not so much as the bone of a smoked herring to place between his teeth! He calls himself 'My Lord' forsooth, and 'Master,' and sends to me his 'orders'! He commands and orders! You may tell your master that since he is so much of a Captain and so much of a My Lord, ordering and commanding so excellently well, the monks shall be hanged forthwith, and you with them if you don't get out at once."

And he gave the man a great kick and had him removed from the room.

"Bring me to drink," he cried. "Have you ever seen anything to compare with the effrontery of this Marin? I could spit my food out, so angry I am. Let the monks be hanged immediately, and let the wandering Fleming be brought hither to me as soon as he has witnessed the execution. We will see if he still dares to tell me that I have done wrong. Blood of God! What are these pots and glasses doing here?"

And with a great noise he brake the bowls and dishes, and no one durst say anything to him. The servants would have cleared up the debris but he would not allow them, but went on drinking yet more; and growing more and more enraged he strode up and down the room, treading the broken pieces and stamping upon them furiously.

Ulenspiegel was brought before him.

"Well?" he said. "What news of your friends the monks?"

"They have been hanged," said Ulenspiegel. "And those cowards of executioners, whose game it is to kill for profit, have cut one of them open to sell the fat to an apothecary. And now the word of a soldier is gold no more. *Parole de soldat n'est plus parole d'or.*"

284

" SHAME ON YOU,"
CRIED ULENSPIEGEL

The Word of a Soldier

Then de Lumey stamped again upon the broken dishes.

" So you defy me, do you, you good-for-nothing beast !
But you also shall be hanged, not in my barn forsooth, but in
the open street, most ignominiously, where all can see you ! "

" Shame on you," cried Ulenspiegel. " Shame on us all !
Parole de soldat n'est plus parole d'or."

" Silence, Iron-pate ! " said Messire de Lumey.

" Shame on you again ! " cried Ulenspiegel. " *Parole de
soldat n'est plus parole d'or.* You ought rather to be punishing
those rascals that are merchants in human fat ! "

At this Messire de Lumey rushed at Ulenspiegel and raised
his hand to strike at him.

" Strike," said Ulenspiegel. " I am in your hands. But
I have no fear at all of you. *Parole de soldat n'est plus parole
d'or.*"

Messire de Lumey drew his sword, and would certainly
have killed Ulenspiegel had not Messire Très-Long taken him
by the arm, saying :

" Have mercy. He is a brave and valiant man and has
committed no crime."

Then de Lumey thought better of the matter.

" Let him ask my pardon then," he said.

But Ulenspiegel stood his ground.

" Never," he said.

" At least he must admit that I was not in the wrong,"
cried de Lumey, growing angry again.

Ulenspiegel answered :

" I will lick no man's boots. *Parole de soldat n'est plus
parole d'or.*"

" Tell them to put up the gallows," said de Lumey,
" and let this man be taken where he may hear the way a
halter speaks."

" Yes," said Ulenspiegel, " and I will cry out there in
front of all the people, *Parole de soldat n'est plus parole d'or.*"

The gallows was set up in the market square, and the news

285

spread swiftly through the city how Ulenspiegel, the brave
Beggarman, was going to be hanged. And the populace was
moved with pity and compassion, and a great crowd collected
in the market square. And Messire de Lumey came there
also, being desirous himself to give the signal for the execution.

He regarded Ulenspiegel without pity as he stood upon
the scaffold, dressed to meet his death in a single garment
with his arms bound to his sides, his hands clasped together,
the cord round his neck, and the executioner ready to do
the deed.

Très-Long said :

" My Lord, pardon him now ; he is no traitor, and no one
has ever heard of a man being hanged simply because he was
sincere and pitiful."

And the men and women in the crowd, hearing Très-Long
speak in this wise, cried out also : " Have pity, my Lord !
Mercy and pardon for Ulenspiegel ! "

" The Iron-pate has defied me," said de Lumey. " Let
him admit he was wrong and that I was in the right."

" Will you ? " said Très-Long to Ulenspiegel.

" *Parole de soldat n'est plus parole d'or,*" Ulenspiegel
answered.

" Draw the cord," said de Lumey.

The executioner was about to obey when a young maid,
dressed all in white and with a wreath of flowers round her
head, ran up the steps of the scaffold like one mad, and threw
herself on the neck of Ulenspiegel.

" This man is mine," she said. " I take him for my
husband."

And the people broke into applause, and the women cried
aloud :

" Long live the maid, long live the maid that has saved
the life of Ulenspiegel ! "

" What does this mean ? " demanded Messire de Lumey.

Très-Long answered :

" You must know that by the legal usages and customs of our city any young maid or unmarried girl has the right to save a man from hanging, provided that she be willing to take him for her husband at the foot of the gallows."

" God is on his side," said de Lumey. " Unloose his fetters."

Then riding up close to the scaffold he saw how the executioner was endeavouring to prevent the maid from severing the cords which bound Ulenspiegel, telling her at the same time that he didn't know who would pay the price of the cords if she cut them. But the damsel did not appear even to hear him. Seeing her so hasty in her love and so cunning withal, the heart of de Lumey was softened within him, and he asked the maid who she might be.

" I am Nele," she answered him, " the betrothed of Ulenspiegel, and I am come from Flanders to seek him."

" You have done well," said de Lumey in a disdainful tone. And he went away.

Then Très-Long approached the scaffold.

" Young Fleming," he said, " when once you are married, will you still serve as a soldier in our ships ? "

" Yes, sir," answered Ulenspiegel.

" But you, my girl, what will you do without your husband ? "

Nele answered :

" If you will allow me, sir, I am fain to become a piper in his ship."

" Very well," said Très-Long.

And he gave her two florins for the wedding feast. And Lamme cried for joy and laughed at the same time, and he gave her three other florins, saying : " We will eat them all. And I will pay. Let us to the sign of the Golden Comb. He is not dead, my friend. Long live the Beggarmen ! "

And the people shouted assent, and they repaired to the tavern of the Golden Comb, where a great feast was ordered, and from an upper window Lamme threw down pennies to the people in the street below.

And Ulenspiegel said to Nele :

" Sweetest and best beloved, here we are together once again ! Noel ! For she is here, flesh, heart, and soul of my sweet love. Oh, her soft eyes and her red and lovely lips that can speak naught but words of kindness ! She has saved my life, my tender lover ! And now it's you and only you that shall play upon our ship the fife of deliverance ! Do you remember . . . but no . . . This is our hour of joy, and all for me is now this face, sweet as June flowers. I am in Paradise. But why, tell me . . . You are crying ! "

" They have killed her," she said. And then Nele told him all the sad story of the death of Katheline. And gazing one at the other they wept for love and for sorrow.

But at the feast they ate and drank, and Lamme as he looked upon them grieved within himself, saying :

" Alas ! my wife, where are you ? "

And the priest came and married Nele and Ulenspiegel.

And the morning found them side by side in their bed of marriage.

And Nele's head was resting on the shoulder of Ulenspiegel. And when the sun had awakened her he said :

" Fresh face, soft heart, we two will be the avengers of the land of Flanders ! "

She kissed him on the mouth, saying :

" Wild head, strong arms, God bless my fife and your sword."

" I will make for you a soldier's habit," said Ulenspiegel.

" Now ? At once ? "

" At once," he told her. " But who was that man who said that strawberries were sweet in the early morning ? Your lips are far, far sweeter."

The End of King Philip

XXXIII

By sea, by river, in fair weather and foul, through snows of winter and summer's heat, the ships of the Beggarmen sailed before the breeze. Full-bellied was their canvas and white as the down of swans—white swans of Liberty.

But to the King of Blood came the news of their conquests, and death was already at work upon his vitals, and his body was full of worms. And he dragged himself along the corridors of his palace at Valladolid, and he never laughed —not even at daybreak, what time the Sun rose to irradiate all the lands of his empire as with the very smile of God.

But Ulenspiegel, Lamme, and Nele sang out like birds, living from day to day, having joy to hear of many a funeral pyre put out by the brave Beggarmen. And Tyl sang five songs, all to the glory of the land of Flanders and to the despite of her enemies.

And it came to pass that on a day, having taken the towns of Rammeken, Gertruydenberg, and Alckmaer, the Beggarmen returned to Flushing. And there in the harbour they beheld a little boat moored. And in the boat was a pretty-looking woman with golden-brown hair, brown eyes, fresh cheeks, rounded arms, and white hands. And all at once the woman cried out:

"Lamme! Lamme!" And then again: "Ah, but you must not approach me! I have taken a vow before God. . . . Yet I love you. Ah, my dear husband!"

Nele said: "It is Calleken Huysbrechts—the fair Calleken!"

"Even so," answered the woman. "But, alas! the hour of noon has already struck for my beauty." And she looked very sorrowful.

But now Lamme jumped down from the ship into a little skiff, which was straightway brought alongside of the boat wherein was his wife.

" What have you been doing ? " he asked her. " What has been happening to you ? Why did you leave me ? And why now do you make as though you would have none of me ? "

Then Calleken told him, in a voice that oftentimes trembled with tears, how that she had entrusted the care of her soul to a monk, one Brother Cornelis Adriaensen, and how he had warned her against her husband for that he was a heretic and a consorter with heretics. How also by his eloquence he had persuaded her that a life of celibacy was most pleasing unto God and his saints, albeit he oftentimes profaned the holy confessional with many a penance that was most distressful to her modesty. " Nevertheless," she ended, " I swear before God that I remained ever faithful to you, my husband, for I loved you."

But Lamme gazed upon her sadly and reproachfully, so that Nele said to him :

" If Calleken has been faithful as she says, it behoves her now to leave you in very deed, as a punishment for your unkindness."

" He knows not how I love him," said Calleken.

" Is this the truth ? " cried Lamme. And then seeing that it was so : " Then come, wife," he cried, " the winter is over ! "

Thereafter, having given and received from all the kiss of peace : " Come now," cried Lamme, " come, wife, with me. For now is the hour of lawful loves ! "

And together they sailed away in their little boat.

Meanwhile the soldiers, the sailors, and the ship's boys that stood around, all waved their caps in the air and shouted : " Adieu, brother ! Adieu, Lamme ! Adieu, brother —brother and friend ! "

And Nele removed with the tip of her sweet finger a tear that had settled in the corner of the eye of Ulenspiegel.

902

" You are sad, my love ? " she asked him.

" He was good," Tyl said.

Nele sighed.

" Ah ! This war—will it never end ? Must we live for ever thus, in the midst of blood and tears ? "

" Let us seek the Seven," said Ulenspiegel. " The hour of deliverance is at hand."

XXXIV

It was the season of harvest. The air was heavy, the wind warm. They that gathered the harvest were able now to reap at their ease, under a free sky and from a free soil, the corn they had sown.

Frise, Drenthe, Overyssel, Gueldre, Utrecht, Noord Barbant, Noord and Zuid Holland ; Walcheren, Noord and Zuid Beveland ; Duiveland and Schouwen which together make up Zeeland ; the sea-bordering lands to the north from Knokke to Helder ; the isles of Texel, Vlieland, Ameland, and Schiermonik Oog—all were being delivered from the Spanish yoke, from the Eastern Scheldt to the Oost Ems. And Maurice, the son of William the Silent, was continuing the war.

Ulenspiegel and Nele kept still their youthfulness, their strength and their beauty, for the Love and the Spirit of Flanders never grow old. And they lived happily at the Tower of Neere, waiting for that day when, after so many cruel trials, they would be able to breathe the breath of liberty upon their native land of Belgium.

Ulenspiegel had asked to be made governor and guardian of the Tower. For he had, so he said, the eyes of an eagle and the ears of a hare, and so he would be able to see at once if the Spaniard ever dared to show himself again in the lands that had been delivered from his yoke. Then quickly would he sound the *wacharm*, the alarm-bell as we call it in our tongue.

To this request the magistrate consented, and in virtue

of the good service he had rendered, Ulenspiegel was allowed
a florin every day, two pints of beer, a ration of beans, cheese,
biscuits, and three pounds of beef weekly.

And so did Ulenspiegel and Nele live on the Tower
together very happily, having joy to see in the distance the
free isles of Zeeland, and near at hand the woods and castles
and fortresses, and the armed ships of the Beggarmen that
guarded the coast.

At night they would often mount to the top of the Tower,
and there they would sit together on the flat roof, talking of
many a stern battle and telling many a tale of love, past and to
come. And from their Tower they could see the ocean, which,
when the weather was hot, furled and unfurled along the
shore its shining waves, and threw them upon the island-
coasts like wraiths of fire. And among the polders the
will-o'-the-wisps would come a-dancing. And Nele was
afraid of them, for she said they were the souls of the poor
dead. And true it was that all those places where they danced
had once been fields of battle. And the will-o'-the-wisps
would oftentimes spring forth from the polders, and run
along the dikes, and then return again to the polders, as
though unwilling to leave the bodies whence they had come.

One night Nele said to Ulenspiegel :

" Behold how many spirits there are in Dreiveland, and
how high they fly ! Over there by the Isle of Birds they seem
to crowd the thickest. Will you come with me there one
night, Tyl ? We would take with us the balm that can show
us things invisible to mortal eyes."

But Ulenspiegel answered :

" If you mean the balm we took when we went to the
great Sabbath of Spring, I have no more faith or confidence
in what we saw there than in any idle dream."

" It is wrong to deny the power of charms," said Nele.
" Come, Ulenspiegel ! "

" Very well," he said.

The Isle of Birds

The next day Ulenspiegel arranged with the magistrate that one of the soldiers who had clear sight and a faithful heart should take his place at the Tower for that one evening. And away he went with Nele towards the Isle of Birds.

They passed along by many a field and dike, till at last they saw the sea in front of them, and in it were set many little green islands with the waves coursing in between. And all about the grassy hills, which soon began to lose themselves in the sand-dunes, a great quantity of peewits were flying high and low, and sea-gulls and sea-swallows. Some of these birds would crowd together on the surface of the sea, and stay there quite still, so that they looked like little white islets ; and above them and about flew thousands of their fellows. The very soil itself was full of their nests, and Ulenspiegel stooped down to pick up one of their eggs which was lying on the road. No sooner had he done so than a sea-gull came flapping towards him, crying out the while most dolefully. And in answer to this summons there flew up a hundred other sea-gulls, crying out as if in anguish, hovering about the head of Ulenspiegel and over the neighbouring nests. But they did not dare to approach him.

" Ulenspiegel," said Nele, " these birds are asking you to have mercy on their eggs."

Then she began to tremble, and said :

" I am afraid. Behold, the sun is setting, the sky is pale, the stars are awakening, it is the hour of the spirits. And look at these ruddy exhalations which rise all about us and seem as it were to trail along the ground. Tyl, my beloved, what monster from hell may he be who thus in the mist begins to open his fiery mouth ? And look over there towards Philipsland. It was there that the murderer king had all those poor men done to death, not once but twice, and all for the sake of his cruel ambition ! And there this night the will-o'-the-wisps are dancing. For this is the night when the souls of poor men killed in battle leave their bodies all

293

cold in purgatory, and come to warm themselves once again in the tepid air of earth. This is the hour when you may ask anything you will of Christ, He who is Lord of all good wizards."

"The ashes beat upon my heart," said Ulenspiegel. "Would that He would show me those Seven whose ashes, they say, when thrown to the winds, would make Flanders happy again, and all the world!"

"O man without faith," said Nele. "By the power of the balm it may be you will see them."

"Maybe," said Ulenspiegel, "if some spirit, forsooth, would come down to visit us from that cold star." And he pointed with his finger to the star Sirius.

No sooner had he made this gesture than a will-o'-the-wisp that had been flying round them came and attached itself to his finger, and the more Ulenspiegel tried to shake it off the firmer the little wisp held on. Nele tried to free Ulenspiegel, but now she also had a little wisp firm on the tip of her finger, and neither would it let her go. Ulenspiegel began to flick at the wisp with his free hand, saying:

"Answer me now, are you the soul of a Beggarman or of a Spaniard? If you are a Beggarman's you may go to Paradise, but if a Spaniard's, return to the hell whence you came."

Nele said to him:

"Do not abuse the souls of the dead, even though they be the souls of murderers!"

Then, making the little will-o'-the-wisp to dance at the end of her finger:

"Wisp," she said, "gentle wisp, come tell me what news do you bring from the land of souls? What rule do they live by down there? Do they eat and drink, having no mouths? For you have none, my sweet! Or wait they, perhaps, till they come to blessed Paradise ere taking upon themselves a human form?"

294

The Giant Hand

" Why waste time in talking to a peevish little flame that has no ears to hear with, no mouth wherewith to answer ? " said Ulenspiegel.

But paying no attention to him, Nele went on :

" Wisp of mine, answer me now by dancing. For I am going to question you thrice. Once in the name of God, once in the name of Our Lady, and once in the name of the Elemental Spirits who are the messengers between God and men."

And this she did, and three times did the elf dance in answer.

Then Nele said to Ulenspiegel :

" Take off your clothes, and I will do the same. See, here is the silver box which holds the balm of vision."

" Be it as you wish," answered Ulenspiegel.

When they had undressed and anointed themselves with the balm of vision, they lay down naked as they were beside one another on the grass.

The sea-gulls screamed ; the thunder growled and rumbled, and in the darkness the lightning flashed. Between two clouds the moon scarcely showed her crescent's golden horns ; and the will-o'-the-wisps departed from Nele and Ulenspiegel to go off dancing with their comrades in the fields.

Suddenly a great giant hand took hold of Nele and her lover, and threw them high in air as though they had been a child's playthings. Then the giant caught them again, rolled them one on the other and kneaded them between his hands, and after that he threw them into a pool of water that lay between the hills, and last of all he dragged them out again full of water and water-weeds. And the giant began to sing in a voice so loud that all the sea-gulls of the islands awakened in terror :

With eyes that squint they would discern,
These silly, wandering insect-mortals,
The sacred symbols none may learn,
Safe guarded now within our portals

The Legend of Tyl Ulenspiegel

Read then, flea, the mystery high,
Read then, louse, the secret vast,
Which to earth and air and sky
By seven nails is anchored fast !

And now it was that Ulenspiegel and Nele discerned on
the grass and in the air and in the sky, seven tablets of bronze
all strangely luminous. And they were held there by seven
flaming nails. And on the tablets was written :

From the dung-heap flowers arise,
Seven are wicked, but seven are good.
Hid in coal the diamond lies,
Bad teacher oft makes pupil wise ;
Seven are bad, but seven are good.

And the giant walked on, followed by all the will-o'-the-
wisps, who were whispering together like grasshoppers, and
saying :

Look at him well—the Master of All,
Before him Cæsar himself must fall.
Pope of Popes, King of Kings,
Fashioned of wood he is Lord of All Things.

Suddenly the lines of the giant's face suffered a change.
He seemed thinner, sadder and greater than ever. And in
one hand he held a sceptre, and in the other a sword. And
his name was Pride.

And throwing Nele and Ulenspiegel to the ground, he
said :

" I am God."

Then by his side there appeared a ruddy-faced girl, and
she was seated on the back of a goat, and her bosom was
bare, her gown half open, and she had a wanton eye ; and
her name was Luxury. After her there came an old woman,

a Jewess, who was busy all the time, scraping up the egg-shells of the sea-gulls that lay about on the ground ; and her name was Avarice. Then a monk appeared, most greedy and gluttonous, eating chitterlings he was, and cramming himself with sausages and champing his jaws together without ceasing, like the sow whereon he rode ; and his name was Greed. Thereafter came Idleness, dragging one leg after the other ; wan she was and bloated, and she had a dull eye. And Anger came chasing after Idleness with a sharp needle with which she pricked her so that she cried aloud, and Idleness grieved and lamented with many tears, and kept falling down on to her knees so tired she was. Last of all came Envy, a thin figure with a head like a viper and teeth like the teeth of a pike. And she kept biting all the others with those crúel teeth of hers—Idleness because she had too much leisure, Anger because she was too lively, Greed because he was too well fed, Luxury because she was too ruddy, Avarice because of the treasure of shells she had amassed, Pride because of his robe of purple and his crown. And the wisps kept dancing all around, and they spake with many voices like the voices of men, women, and girls, and in the plaintive voices of children, and they groaned, saying :

"O Pride, father of Ambition, and you, O Anger, that are the source of cruelty, you slew us on many a battlefield, and caused our death in many a prison and many a torture-chamber, that you might keep your sceptres and your crowns ! And you, O Envy, that have destroyed so many useful thoughts while yet in the germ, we are the souls of the inventors whom you have persecuted. Avarice, you it is that have turned the blood of the poor into gold, and we are the souls of your victims. O Luxury, you are the friend and the sister of Murder ; Nero, Messalina, Philip King of Spain —such are your children, and you buy virtue and you bribe corruption, and we are the souls of your dead. And you, O Idleness, and you, Greed, you befoul the world, but the world must be cleansed of you; we are the souls of those who have perished at your hands."

And a voice was heard saying:

> *From the dung-heap flowers arise,*
> *Seven are wicked, but seven are good.*
> *Bad teacher oft makes pupil wise.*
> *Now longs the wandering louse comprise*
> *Both coal and cinder if he could!*

Then spake the wisps:

" Fire. We are Fire—the avenger of all old tears and all old pains which the people have suffered; the avenger of all the human game that has been hunted for pleasure by the Lords of this land; the avenger of all battles fought to no purpose, of all the blood that has been spilt in prison, of all the men burned at the stake and the women and girls buried alive; the avenger of all the past of blood and chains. The Fire—that is Us—we are the souls of the dead."

At these words the Seven were suddenly transformed into images of wood, though they still lost nothing of their former outline; and a voice was heard saying:

" Burn the wood, Ulenspiegel."

And Ulenspiegel turned towards the will-o'-the-wisps:

" You that are made of fire, do your office."

And the wisps thronged around the seven images, which straightway burst into flame and were reduced to ashes.

And from the ashes there flowed a river of blood.

But out of the ashes arose now seven other figures, and the first said:

" Once I was called Pride. But now my name is Nobility."

And the rest spake after the same fashion, and Nele and Ulenspiegel saw how Economy came forth from Avarice; Vivacity from Anger; Healthy Appetite from Gluttony; Emulation from Envy; and from Idleness the Dreams of poets and

298

wise men. And Luxury, on her goat, was now transformed into
the likeness of a beautiful woman, and her name was Love.

And all around them danced the will-o'-the-wisps most joyously. And thereafter did Ulenspiegel and Nele begin to hear
a thousand voices as of hidden men and women, that spake
with a sonorous, clicking sound, like that of castanets, and
thus sang they :

> *When over the earth and over the sea*
> *These Seven transformed shall reign,*
> *Mortals lift up your heads again,*
> *For happy the world shall be !*

And Ulenspiegel said : "These spirits are making mock
of us."

And a powerful hand seized Nele by the arm, and threw
her away into the void. And the Spirits sang :

> *When the North*
> *Shall kiss the West*
> *Then shall be the end of ruin.*
> *Find the Cincture.*

"Alas !" cried Ulenspiegel. "*North, West, Cincture !*
You speak in riddles, Sir Spirits !"

But they went on with their singing and chattering :

> *The North is the Netherland,*
> *Belgium is the West.*
> *Cincture is friendship,*
> *Cincture is Alliance.*

"Now you are talking sense, Sir Spirits," said Ulenspiegel.
And yet again they sang :

> *The Cincture, little man,*
> *'Twixt Holland and Belgium—*
> *Firm Alliance,*
> *And beautiful Friendship.*

> *Alliance of Counsel,*
> *Alliance of Action,*
> *By death*
> *By blood,*
> *Were it not*
> *For the Scheldt,*
> *Little man, for the Scheldt.*

" Alas ! " said Ulenspiegel, " such is our life ! Tears of man and laughter of destiny ! "

And again the Spirits repeated their rune, and their voices were like the clicking of castanets.

> *Alliance by blood*
> *And by death*
> *Were it not*
> *For the Scheldt.*

And a strong hand took hold of Ulenspiegel and threw him into the void.

XXXV

As she fell, Nele rubbed her eyes but she could see nothing save the sun that was rising, wreathed in a golden mist. And then the tips of the grass all golden too, in that radiance which was soon to tinge with gold the plumage of the sea-gulls who slept as yet, but were about to awaken.

Nele looked downwards at herself, and seeing that she was naked she put on her clothes with all haste. Then it was that she noticed the body of Ulenspiegel where it lay there, naked also, and him also she covered with his clothes. He seemed to be still asleep and she gave him a shake, but he remained quite motionless like one dead. Then was Nele seized with fear. " Have I killed him ? " she cried. " Have I killed my love with this balm of vision ? Would that I too might die ! Ah, Tyl, wake up ! But he is as cold as marble ! "

The Burial of Ulenspiegel

Ulenspiegel did not awake, and two nights passed and a day, and Nele still watched by his side in a fever of grief and fear.

It was at the dawn of the second day of her vigil that Nele heard the sound of a little bell in the distance, and saw presently a peasant approaching with a shovel in his hand. Behind him came a burgomaster with two aldermen carrying candles, and then the curé of Stavenisse with a beadle holding a parasol over his head. It appeared that they were going to administer the Holy Sacrament of Unction to one Jacobsen, a brave Beggarman, who had adopted the new religion by compulsion, but being about to die had returned to the bosom of the Holy Roman Church.

When they came opposite to Nele they found her still crying, and they saw the body of Ulenspiegel laid out on the grass in front of her, covered with clothes. Nele fell upon her knees in front of the little procession.

" My girl," said the burgomaster, " what are you doing by this corpse ? "

Without daring to raise her eyes, Nele made answer :

" I am praying for the soul of my beloved, he that has fallen dead as if struck by lightning. I am alone now, and I am fain to die."

But already the curé was puffing with pleasure.

" Ulenspiegel the Beggarman dead ! " he cried. " Praise be to God ! Be quick there, peasant, and dig a grave, and take his clothes off before you bury him."

" No," said Nele, getting up from the ground. " No, you shall not take his clothes, he would be cold there in the cold earth."

" Quick ! " cried the curé, addressing himself again to the peasant with the shovel.

" You may bury him," said Nele, all in tears. " I give you leave ; for this sand is full of lime, so that his body will keep for ever whole and beautiful, the body of my beloved."

And half mad with anguish as she was, Nele bent over the body of Ulenspiegel, kissing him through her tears.

Now the burgomaster, the aldermen, and even the peasant had compassion on the girl, but not so the curé, who ceased not to cry out most joyfully: "The great Beggarman is dead! God be praised!"

Then the peasant dug the grave, and Ulenspiegel was placed therein, and covered all over with sand.

And over the grave the curé said the prayers for the dead, and the others knelt all round. Suddenly there was a great commotion in the sand, and Ulenspiegel arose, sneezing and shaking the sand from his hair, and he seized the curé by the throat.

"Inquisitor!" he cried. "I was asleep, and you buried me alive! Where is Nele? Have you buried her also? Who are you?"

The curé began to cry out in terror:

"The great Beggarman returns to this world! Lord God have mercy on my soul!"

And away he fled like a stag before the hounds.

Nele came to Ulenspiegel: "Kiss me, dearest," she said.

Then Ulenspiegel looked about him once more. The two peasants had run off like the curé, and that they might run the faster they had thrown to the ground both shovel and parasol. As for the burgomaster and the aldermen, they lay groaning on the grass, stopping up their ears in their fright.

Ulenspiegel went to them and gave them a good shaking.

"Think you that they can be buried in the ground," he asked them, "Ulenspiegel and Nele? Nele that is the heart of our Mother Flanders, and Ulenspiegel that is her soul? She can sleep too, forsooth, but die—never! Come, Nele."

And they twain departed, Ulenspiegel singing his sixth song. But no man knoweth where he sang his last.

THE SIXTH SONG